WOLVES AT THE GATE

by
Bart Stark

Wolves at the Gate is a work of alternative history, offering a mixture of historical and fictional characters. Where historical figures appear, the situations, incidents, and dialogues concerning those persons are not intended to depict actual events, but rather are products of the author's imagination and entirely fictional.

Library and Archives Canada Cataloguing in Publication
Stark, Bart, author
Wolves at the Gate / Bart Stark

Issued in print and electronic formats.
ISBN: 978-1-998501-07-6 (paperback)
ISBN: 978-1-998501-08-3 (ebook)

Cover Image: Renato Dalmaso
Cover Design: James Leslie
Interior Design: Muhammad Tahir

Warpath Press
Toronto, Ontario, Canada
www.warpathpress.com

DRAMATIS PERSONAE

Walter Anderson: Admiral and commander of U.S. Navy Pacific Fleet ships surviving Japanese air raids on Pearl Harbor. Minor historic character.

Henry "Hap" Arnold: U.S. Army general and commander of the U.S. Army Air Corps. Minor historic character.

Helmut Arpke: Senior sergeant and paratrooper in the German Flieger Division. Lover then husband of Louisa Grafenberg. Major historic character, who is the German counterpart to Jim Fraser.

Kurt Asendorf: Pilot for Erwin Rommel. Minor fictional character.

Clement Attlee: Prime Minister of England following Churchill. Minor historic character.

Carlo Bergamini: Italian admiral and commander of Special Naval Force. Major historic character and Italian counterpart to PJ Tigert.

Valerio Borghese: Captain in the Decima MAS – the Italian Navy's underwater commando unit, commander of the Italian submarine *Scirè* and lesser aristocracy known to his men as the "Black Prince." Minor historic character.

Winston Churchill: Prime Minister of England. Minor historic character.

Ludwig Crüwell: Erwin Rommel's army chief of staff. Minor historic character.

Billy Deal: U.S. Army corporal and sniper in the American Hawaii Division. Major fictional character and American counterpart to Otozo Hayashi.

Sam Denard: FBI Agent investigating Katarina Kolotsiev. Minor fictional character.

Elizabeth II: Queen of England in exile. Minor historic character.

Wolf Fleischer: U.S. Army sergeant in the South Carolina National Guard and butcher in civilian life. Jim Fraser's platoon sergeant. Major fictional character.

"Big Dan" Fraser: Father of Jim Fraser and owner of Fraser & Sons Dredging. Minor fictional character.

Florrie Fraser: Wife of Jim and mother to twin daughters Donna and Lisa. Major fictional character and American counterpart to Louisa Grafenberg.

Jim Fraser: U.S. Army lieutenant in the South Carolina National Guard and Fraser & Sons Dredging project manager in civilian life. Husband of Florrie and father to twin daughters Donna and Lisa. Major fictional character and American counterpart to Helmut Arpke.

Mitsuo Fuchida: Commander of the Japanese Navy's First Air Fleet. Major historic character.

Minoru Genda: Planning officer of Japanese Navy. Minor historic character.

George IV: King of England. Minor historic character.

Herman Goering: Field Marshall of the German Air Force and friend of Adolf Hitler. Minor historic character.

Louisa Grafenberg: Lead soprano at the Linden Opera in Berlin. Lover then wife of Helmut Arpke. Major fictional character and German counterpart to Florrie Fraser.

Werner Grafenberg: Berlin physician and father of Louisa. Minor fictional character.

William "Bull" Halsey: U.S. Navy admiral and commander of *Enterprise* carrier task force. Major historic character.

Hikaru Hayashi: Colonel in the Japanese Army and father of Otozo. Minor fictional character.

Otozo Hayashi: Captain in the Japanese Army and son of Hikaru. Major fictional character and Japanese counterpart to Billy Deal.

Joji Higai: Commander of Japanese Navy's 701st Air Group. Minor historic character.

Michinomiya Hirohito: Emperor of Japan. Minor historic character.

Adolf Hitler: *Führer* of the Third Reich. Major historic character.

Masaharu Homma: General and commander of the Japanese Expeditionary Army Group. Minor historic character.

Harry Hopkins: Special advisor to the U.S. President. Minor historic character.

Cordell Hull: U.S. Secretary of State. Minor historic character.

Sally Jenkins: U.S. Army nurse who joins Billy Deal's sniper team. Minor fictional character.

Alfred Jodl: German Army Chief of Staff. Minor historic character.

Joe Kennedy: U.S. ambassador to England. Minor historic character.

Tyler Kent: Employee of the U.S. Embassy in London. Minor historic character.

Husband Kimmel: U.S. Navy admiral and commander of Pacific Fleet. Minor historic character.

Earnest King: U.S. Navy Chief of Staff after Betty Stark. Major historic character and American counterpart to Isoruku Yamamoto and Erich Raeder.

Katarina Kolotsiev: German spy. Daughter of Grand Duke Mikhail Kolotsiev. Major fictional character.

Mikhail Kolotsiev: Russian Grand Duke, military attaché to England and officer of Russian secret police. Father of Katarina Kolotsiev. Minor fictional character.

Max Krueger: Son of German immigrant, farmer and member of Klu Klux Klan. Minor fictional character.

Walter Krueger: U.S. Army general and commander of Third Army. Minor historic character.

Gunther Lutjens: Admiral and commander of German Atlantic Fleet. Minor historic character.

Brent Marcus: Captain and commander of *U.S.S. Leary*. Minor fictional character.

George Marshall: U.S. Army general and Chair of the American Joint Chiefs of Staff. Major historic character.

Gunichi Mikawa: Admiral and commander of Japanese surface fleet attacking Pearl Harbor. Minor historic character.

Joan Miller: Employee of English War Department and agent of MI-6 investigating English fascists. Minor historic character.

Mike Morgan: U.S. Army private in the American Hawaii Division. Sniper spotter for Bill Deal. Major fictional character.

Ernst Mueller aka "Yiannis Christidis:" Captain of the freighter *S.S. Aneos*. Minor fictional character.

Benito Mussolini: Dictator of Italy. Minor historic character.

Chuichi Nagumo: Admiral and commander of Japanese fleet attacking Pearl Harbor. Minor historic character.

Mike O'Malley: U.S. Army engineer sergeant. Minor fictional character.

Matt Moore: U.S. Army major and battalion commander of Jim Fraser. Minor fictional character.

George Patton: U.S. Army general and commander of the Second Armored Division. Husband of Bea. Major historic character and American counterpart to Erwin Rommel.

Luigi de la Penne: Frogman in the Decima MAS – the Italian Navy's underwater commando unit. Minor historic character.

Erich Pfeiffer: Intelligence officer for the German Navy. Minor historic Character.

Adolph Piening: German navy captain and commander of submarine U-155. Minor historic character.

Erich Raeder: Grand Admiral of the German Navy. Major historic character and German counterpart to Earnest King and Isoruku Yamamoto.

George Roberts: German Navy intelligence contact for Katarina Kolotsiev. Minor fictional character.

Erwin Rommel: General and commander of the German Seventh *Panzer* Division. Husband of Lu. Major historic character and German counterpart to George Patton.

Erich Schuster: Junior sergeant and paratrooper in the German Flieger Division. Helmut Arpke's subordinate and confidant. Minor historic character.

Walter Short: U.S. Army general and commander of the land forces in Hawaii. Minor historic character.

Harold "Betty" Stark: U.S. Navy Chief of Staff. Minor historic character.

Ben Stockton: Moonshine maker and cousin of Florrie Fraser. Minor fictional character.

Mae Stockton: Mother of Florrie Fraser. Minor fictional character.

Charles Summerall: Retired U.S. Army general and Chief of Staff. Commandant of the Citadel military academy. Minor historic character.

Isamu Tada: Lieutenant in the Japanese Army. Platoon leader under Otozo Hayashi. Minor fictional character.

PJ Tigert: U.S. Navy commander, military attaché to England and later commander of *U.S.S Forrest*. Major fictional character and American counterpart to Carlo Bergamini.

Hideki Tojo: General and commander of Japanese Army. Minor historic character.

John Wilcox: U.S. Navy admiral and commander of Task Force 39. Minor historic character.

Bonnie Sue Willis: Sister of Florrie Fraser, wife of Henry Willis and mother to Ricky. Minor fictional character.

Isoruku Yamamoto: Admiral and commander of Japanese Navy. Major historic character and Japanese counterpart to Erich Raeder and Earnest King.

GLOSSARY

Abwehr: German naval intelligence.

Ameko: Japanese slang for Americans.

Ami: German slang for Americans.

Banzai: Japanese battle cry.

CAG: Acronym for commander of the carrier air group.

CCA: Acronym for Combat Command A, an American brigade-size unit.

Chancorro: Japanese derogatory term for Chinese.

ENIGMA: German code system.

FBI: Acronym for The U.S. Federal Bureau of Investigation.

Flieger Division: German term for airborne or paratroop division.

Führer: German term for leader. The title Hitler granted himself.

HE: Acronym for high explosive.

Heil: German term for hail.

Hentai: Japanese term for its soldiers.

Jap: American slang for Japanese.

Kraut: American slang for Germans.

Kriegsmarine: German term for its navy.

Luftwaffe: German term for its air force.

MAGIC: U.S. Navy code breaking section.

NKVD: Acronym for Soviet secret police.

Okhrana: Russian term for the Tsarist secret police.

Panzer: German term for its tanks.

Prosit: A German term for cheers.

Regia Marina: Italian term for its navy.

Reich: German term for its state.

Samurai: Japanese term for noble warrior or knight.

-san: Japanese suffix meaning honorable.

U-boat: German term for submarine.

ULTRA: British code breaking system.

Volksdeutsche: German term for ethnic Germans.

Wehrmacht: German term for its military.

PROLOGUE

East Point, Georgia
17:08 Hours, 10 November 1918

The prisoner of war was becoming fond of his life in *Amerika*. After spending the day helping his host slaughter and butcher a hog, the German sailor reclined on the rough-hewn planks of the Georgia farmer's porch, salivating over the smell of slow roasting pork wafting out of the opened windows. The lady of the house was a superb cook, transforming the bounty of this rich land into delicious meals.

Things were not always so.

The thin young man with pale blue eyes never intended to become a sailor. He instead fancied himself a fine painter. Only a few short years ago, he spent his days drawing and dabbing watercolor post cards on the streets of Munich for sale to passersby, then evenings working on a portfolio of oil landscapes to someday convince a great art academy to accept him as a student.

Early in 1914, on a chill Saturday afternoon, the young man's life changed. With a bang on his door, the Munich police served him with papers deporting him into the Austro-Hungarian Army. Instead of reporting for this unwelcome foreign draft, he escaped into the Merchant Marine. He was German now and would never return the old country of his youth.

Germany went to war later that year, while the young man was at sea. His ship was the *S.S. Liebenfels*, a new freighter of the Hansa line carrying cargo from Bremen to *Amerika*. After England declared war on Germany, the captain immediately steamed the freighter into the nearby port of Charleston to keep the Royal Navy from capturing her as a war prize.

Before the war, old hands among the crew would regale the young man with stories of how the Kaiser dramatically expanded the merchant fleet and transported them to far parts of the globe he had only read about in books. Now, the damned *Englander* were denying the Fatherland its rightful place among the great sea faring nations of the world!

As the years passed, sanctuary turned into imprisonment. The *Englander* blocked the ship from going home and the *Amerikaner* would not allow the crew to come ashore. In 1917, when *Amerika* seemed ready to enter the war, the sailor joined his comrades in scuttling the *Liebenfels* to keep her from being used against Germany.

The *Amerikaner* first interned the sailor and his stranded crew mates at an Army fort in their state of Georgia. When a military officer offered parole to work at a local farm, the young man immediately volunteered. Anything to be free in the world again, even if it was in an enemy country.

The farmer to whom he was assigned offered a forbidding first impression - hulking and gruff. Once the young man proved himself a hard worker, though, Max Krueger generously accepted him into his family like a son.

The sailor was delighted to discover the farmer was the child of German immigrants. In fact, Krueger informed him millions in the United States were *volksdeutsche* and an important part of nearly every community.

The farmer was also a member of a strange paramilitary organization whose name the German struggled to pronounce – the Ku Klux Klan. Krueger complained the Jews controlling the banks made it difficult for Christian farmers like himself to get loans. The Klan was fixing that. Three years before, they hung the Jew bastard who murdered young Mary Phagan and the kikes left Georgia ever since.

Yesterday evening, the farmer donned a white uniform and asked if the sailor would like to see some Klan justice. His curiosity piqued, the sailor eagerly agreed. As the men rode from the farm on a horse drawn wagon, Kruger explained the Klan had arrested a nigger who laid hands on a white woman over in the next county. Only Klansmen were allowed at the trial, however, so the young man would have to stay out of sight.

From the woods at the edge of a field, the German stared in fascination at the "trial." Hooded Klansmen dragged a terrified black man under a tree in the middle of the clearing and walked him on top of a pile of logs. From there, they hoisted the black off the ground by his bound hands and gelded him with a knife like the farmer had done with one of his horses the winter before. Finally, the white uniformed men dismounted the log pile and lit it on fire. The sailor cackled at the memory of the shrieking black struggling to pull his blood-covered legs up and away from the rising flames. Eventually. blood loss and gravity won out as fire consumed the man. These *Amerikaner* knew how to deal with the inferior races.

Mrs. Krueger interrupted the young man's reminisces by calling him inside for dinner. After the family prayed over the evening meal, the farmer handed a plate of pork loin to the sailor.

"Son, you've been a hard worker and it's been a pleasure having ya in our home these past few months, but the Army's gonna to take ya back next week."

"Why?" asked the young man.

"Germany surrendered and..."

Shock washed over him like a cold wave, followed by the heat of disbelieving rage. Jumping up from the kitchen table, the sailor yelled at the farmer in a jumble of German and English. "*Der lugner*! Liar! The Fatherland could not lose the war."

Krueger's countenance hardened and he snapped back, "Enough of that, son. I'm telling you the truth. The armistice starts tomorrow."

The sailor shook his head and ran out of the house into the front yard. Hot tears streamed down his cheeks as he watched the last of the sun sink below the horizon. This evil thing must be true, he thought. Krueger was an honest man and would not lie to him.

The young man swore an oath to the sliver of a new moon brightening in the evening sky. When I return, Germany will rise again and its enemies will be humbled. I swear it!

"When I return?" the sailor muttered to himself.

A new and more hopeful thought came to the prisoner. If the war was over, the *Amerikaner* would have to return him to Germany.

Adolf Hitler was going home.

I. EURASIA

CHAPTER 1

Dover Cliffs, England
04:47 Hours, 16 August 1940

Senior Sergeant Helmut Arpke floated for a moment or two over the Dover Cliffs, like a hawk riding an Alpine thermal, before beginning a slow descent towards his prey.

Tightly packed in a DFS-230 assault glider, the German paratrooper and his eight-man squad flew over the darkened countryside, in the midst of dozens more of the silent birds. Brightly burning tracers leading streams of steel projectiles arced up from *Englander* anti-aircraft batteries, reaching out into the moon-less sky for the *Luftwaffe* aircraft. Here and there, a Tommy gunner would find a glider, shredding its thin canvas skin, along with the human cargos within.

Arpke pulled a rosary out of his battle smock, kissed the crucifix and prayed silently for a quick landing and the Mother Mary's protection on the way down.

The Tommies were providing a far hotter welcome than did the Belgians earlier in the summer. In their first action of the war, Arpke's company swooped down to capture the Veldwezelt Bridge over the Albert Canal, opening the door for the German Eighteenth Army to march into the heart of Belgium. Instead of landing by the east end of the bridge as planned, Arpke's misoriented pilot put their glider down in the middle of a Belgian trench complex.

Luck was with them, though. In the early morning darkness, the Belgian sentries did not respond to the near silent landing of the glider. The sergeant and his comrades poured out of the craft and descended into the trenches before the surprised enemy could get off a single shot. Throwing grenades and firing their machine pistols around every corner, the paratroopers rapidly worked their way through the fortifications. Thinking a far larger force was overrunning them, a sleepy, half-dressed Belgian officer surrendered over a hundred of his men to Helmut and his little band.

While Arpke attributed this unexpected success to a minor miracle of God, a very pleased battalion commander generously gave all the credit to the audacious young sergeant. In a ceremony back in Germany, Major Koch hung the coveted Knight's Cross medal around Helmut's neck and handed him the chevrons of a senior sergeant. None of this new tinsel and cloth would protect him here in England, though.

The plan was for the entire German *Flieger* Division to drop in on and capture the English port city of Dover during the largest airborne operation of the war. Most of the paratroopers parachuted directly onto the city. Meanwhile, the glider boys like Helmut landed on the fields behind the white chalk cliffs on both sides of Dover to knock out the coastal guns guarding the port. Once the door to the city was open, the Army could cross the English Channel and reinforce Dover before the Tommies could push the lightly armed paras into the sea.

Arpke's glider landed with two gentle bounces, then a short slide into a gully. After his men quickly dismounted and took up defensive positions around the bird, the sergeant took a knee and looked around. The moon set some hours before, leaving only the sparse sparkle of early morning starlight. Arpke could just make out the movements of his fellow paratroopers in their signature round nutshell helmets and baggy jump uniforms.

Apart from the gentle sea breeze ruffling the tall grass, the area around them was quiet.

Good. No Tommy patrols to deal with.

The platoon leader, Lieutenant Gustav Altmann, emerged from the darkness with two engineers in tow. The pair carried a pole on their shoulders with a large metal half-sphere hanging by a chain from the middle. As they practiced innumerable times during training, Arpke and his squad silently rose from the grass, spread out into a skirmish line and walked quickly toward the cliffs, with the engineers falling in behind.

Before his men could reach the cliffs, though, the sounds of battle brewed up behind them – first the crackle of rifle shots, followed by rhythmic bursts of machine gun fire. A Tommy patrol must have blundered into the rest of the platoon providing rear security.

So much for the element of surprise, Arpke fretted. They better get moving before any more Tommies crashed the party. The sergeant eased into a slow jog and his squad effortlessly matched the pace. The more heavily laden engineers struggled to keep up, their heavy metal cargo swaying on the carrying pole, pulling the men back and forth.

As the first tendrils of sunrise reached out into the dawn sky, their objective came into view. A newly constructed concrete bunker, not yet buried or camouflaged, hulked out of the grassy field. The sergeant could make out the gray steel barrels of the three large naval guns extending from the bunker towards the English Channel and the approaching German invasion fleet.

Suddenly, the ground around the rear of the bunker flashed with rifle fire. One of the engineers shrieked and tumbled over onto the grass grasping his belly. The metal half-sphere thudded onto the ground and rolled to rest on its side. The paratroopers automatically dove for the ground and returned fire without orders.

Waving his arm forward, the sergeant jumped up and sprinted around the left with half of his squad. The paras took a few steps and went back to ground before the enemy riflemen could get a bead on them, then repeated the process without any casualties until they made their way around to the side of the bunker.

Things did not go so smoothly after that.

Just short of reaching his destination, Arpke's boot caught on a rock and he crashed head first into the bunker wall. "Graceful as always," Helmut grumbled to himself as he regained his feet and pushed his helmet back into place. Glancing back over his shoulder to find three of his men grinning back at him, the sergeant ruefully shook his head. *I will never live this down.*

Arpke peeked around the corner of the bunker straight into trouble - a Tommy holding a pistol stood no more than a meter away! The enemy officer shot first, gouging the corner of the bunker and spraying bits of concrete into the paratrooper's face. Blinking furiously against the gravel, Helmut blindly squeezed off a short burst from his machine pistol, then fell back behind the wall to brush off his eyes. When he glanced around the corner again, Arpke found the Tommy lieutenant crumpled motionless on the ground, a look of complete surprise on his blood-spattered face.

Time to end this. The sergeant grabbed at his belt for a hand grenade, pulled the igniting cord at the bottom of the handle, then threw it end over end towards the trench. The "potato masher" fell short, but managed to bounce into the pit before detonating.

When the Tommy rifles fell silent, replaced by screams and curses, the paratroopers rose as one to charge the trench and finish off the survivors. The enemy were quicker, though. By the time Arpke and his men reached the trench, the last enemy soldier dragged a wounded comrade into the bunker and slammed a heavy metal door closed behind him.

The Tommies barricaded themselves behind the bunker's several tons of concrete and steel to await rescue – precisely where Arpke wanted them.

The surviving German engineer went to work, rolling the metal half sphere on top of the bunker roof with help of a handful of Arpke's squad. These devices were shaped-explosive charges, specially designed to knock out heavy fortifications where ordinary artillery and bombs failed.

Moments after everyone found cover, the thundering CRUMP of the detonation painfully battered the paratroopers' ears. They were the lucky ones. The directed explosion turned the cement and steel of the bunker ceiling into molten slag and hurled it into the unfortunate Tommies below.

The mission completed, Arpke stood by the cliff and looked out at the channel below. The sergeant could make out destroyers and gunboats skirmishing with one another, while the invasion fleet of tug boats and barges scattered in all directions, frantically attempting to evade the predators swimming amongst them. Splashing men in the water, abandoning sinking vessels, frantically searched for anything that would float.

My God! Helmut thought. Would the Army even make it ashore?

Führer Headquarters "Wolf's Gorge II," Fort Risban, Calais, France
08:22 Hours, 16 August 1940

Grand Admiral Erich Raeder felt nauseous.

Throughout the night, the speakers mounted on the walls of the *Führer* headquarters broadcast messages of panic and disaster. The civilian tugboats and barges pressed into service to transport the German Army across the English Channel broke radio silence, broadcasting distress calls begging for rescue. The German Navy destroyers and e-boats tasked with protecting the invasion fleet added reports of chasing, but never quite catching their Royal Navy counterparts in the pitch blackness of the moonless night.

Adolf Hitler stoically endured these reports, starring stone-faced at the map table, as if he could make the invasion succeed through the pure force of will. Occasionally, the *Führer* would look up and quietly ask a question following a radio report, but Raeder had no information to offer beyond the reports themselves.

The Army generals were huddled off to the side of the conference room, murmuring to one another. The *Wehrmacht* high command wanted no part of a catastrophe many of their officers opposed from the beginning.

How could things have gone so wrong after Raeder's grand strategy set the table so spectacularly?

Hitler first summoned him in the spring of 1936, with an invitation to dinner at the Berghof – the *Führer's* home in the Bavarian Alps. The admiral very much supported the Nazi goal of restoring Germany to its previous glory as a world power, but was unsure what that meant for the fleet. The Army dominated military politics in Germany, while the Navy was treated like the proverbial red-headed stepchild. Now, the *Luftwaffe* and its shiny new airplanes threatened to reduce the *Kriegsmarine's* status even further. Perhaps, this meal would provide Raeder with an opportunity to convince the *Führer* the fleet could serve a useful role in restoring German power.

Hitler was a charming host with a surprising breadth of knowledge for a politician. Over dinner, the men discussed subjects ranging from the nature of God to the economy necessary to support a modern navy. Hitler was so deft at putting Raeder at ease, the admiral needed several minutes to realize the *Führer* was actually taking his measure.

After dinner was finished, Hitler invited Raeder into a back room for tea. Before the admiral could launch into his prepared arguments on behalf of the *Kriegsmarine*, the *Führer* pre-empted him.

"Admiral, I have read your multiplicity theories. Would you please expand on them for me?" Hitler asked. Raeder was stunned and more than a little flattered. Hitler had actually read his papers!

"My *Führer*, Germany dominates the center of Europe. In order to contain the Fatherland, England has built the world's largest fleet and deployed it around Europe and into the Far East. I propose Germany execute military operations around the periphery of Europe to force the Royal Navy to disperse and allow our smaller *Kriegsmarine* to achieve local superiority in the North Sea between Germany and England."

"Excellent," Hitler murmured, placing his teacup on the table.

When the *Führer* rose, Raeder sprang to his feet in the position of attention. Hitler smiled and rested his hands on the naval officer's shoulders "Raeder, you are now my Grand Admiral of the *Kriegsmarine*. From this point on, the sole mission of the Navy will be to defeat England. By this time next year, you will provide me with plans to accomplish this goal."

His mind swimming with possibilities, Raeder could only sputter, "Yes, my *Führer*, it will be done."

Four years later, Raeder's plans ran like a fine watch.

In April, the *Kriegsmarine* invaded Norway, forcing the Royal Navy to defend the Atlantic corridor between England and Iceland.

By June, Germany overran France, compelling England to deploy even more of its fleet out into the Atlantic to protect merchant ships from Raeder's U-boats now based along the French coast.

Finally, July sprang Germany's final trap. Hitler convinced Spain to secretly join the Axis by giving it French Morocco. In return, the dictator Francisco Franco allowed the *Luftwaffe* and a German Army corps to cross Spain and capture the English naval base at Gibraltar in a surprise attack. The Royal Navy's largest fleet found itself bottled up in the Mediterranean.

With the Royal Navy successfully dispersed, the stage was now set for Operation Sea Lion – the German invasion of England. Over the past three weeks, the *Luftwaffe* bombed Royal Air Force bases across southern England, seizing air superiority over the invasion zone. All that remained was for the Army to cross the narrow English Channel to claim its prize.

Raeder's plan called for the *Kriegsmarine* to land three Army divisions along the arc of beaches between the English coastal towns of Folkstone and New Romney, while the *Luftwaffe* dropped all of its paratroopers onto the port of Dover.

The English land defenses were minimal. The cream of the British Army was dead or interned in prisoner of war camps after the *Führer* cut off their escape from France by overriding his generals and ordering the *panzers* to capture the port of Dunkirk.

Raeder's problem was the *Kriegsmarine* lacked amphibious landing craft to transport the Army. Before the war, the *Führer* directed the Reich's scarce steel to build a new generation of warships. Consequently, the Grand Admiral was reduced to pressing into service nearly every civilian tug and barge across occupied France and the Netherlands. Hardly an ideal option. Given the night's reverses, perhaps a disastrous one.

The gloom inside the *Führer* headquarters lifted a bit with the dawn. Daylight allowed the German warships to find and chase off the Royal Navy ships harrying the invasion fleet. Free to safely move again, the pig pile of tugs and barges moved straight to the nearest English beach to deliver their passengers, then scurried back to the safety of their homeports.

By mid-morning, the Army was safely ashore, but its units were hopelessly snarled along the coast. When the Tommies counterattacked, would the disorganized German soldiers be able to hold the beaches?

The rest of the morning crawled by without an answer to that nagging question. Communications with England were infuriatingly sporadic. What radio messages arrived made little sense because the transmitting units were lost, often kilometers from their intended landing zones.

Reports finally started to flow just before noon. German commanders on the beaches formed battle groups out of whatever units landed nearby and drove inland, brushing aside the local English militia defending the coastal towns. A century before, the English built the Royal Military Canal behind these towns to contain a Napoleonic invasion which never came. The Army's Seventeenth Infantry Division reported crossing the canal only an hour after landing.

With this favorable turn of events, the now jubilant Army generals returned to the map table to celebrate victory with the *Führer*. The Grand Admiral could only frown in disgust at the rank hypocrisy. What was it the *Italianer* said? Ah, yes… Victory has a thousand fathers, while defeat is an orphan.

The reality was the battle was far from won. The invasion of England was indeed a great achievement, the first since the Normans stormed the beaches to defeat the Saxons a millennium ago. However, the *Kriegsmarine* must still hold the Channel against an inevitable Royal Navy counterattack.

Charleston, South Carolina
07:58 Hours, 17 August 1940

The summer scent of the jasmine tree out front washed over him as Jim Fraser opened the kitchen windows to let in the sea breeze. It would be another hot one and the Boston Yankee was determined to grab as much relief as he could.

When Fraser & Sons Dredging tapped him to manage their first out-of-state project expanding the Charleston harbor, the youngest son had no idea he'd still be there almost six years later, taking on a family to boot.

Jim met Florrie Stockton working as a secretary at the port. She was plump and mousy, but he thought she was as cute as a kitten. The scarecrow tall Yankee invented pretexts to come down to her office and pepper the poor girl with bad jokes and requests for a date, but she kept politely putting him off.

After offering a real clunker one afternoon, the port director yelled out of his office, "Oh, for God's sake! Miss Stockton, will you please go out with him so he'll shut up and we can get some work done?"

Jim felt like dying on the spot, but Florrie giggled uncontrollably. He finally made her laugh.

Once the ice was broken, things moved along quickly. They married later that summer. Nine months after their honeymoon, Florrie delivered twin girls. The sudden couple was suddenly a family.

Daddy took his seat and a sip from his coffee mug at the head of dining room table between his freckled daughters. As soon as Mommy placed pancakes in front of the girls and turned back for the kitchen, Donna and Lisa went to work. The four-year olds recently learned how to use table knives and started a race to see who could cut up their pancake first.

Jim was grinning broadly when Florrie turned to see what the girls were giggling about. "Little ladies, y'all slow down right now before someone gets hurt!"

When Daddy started biting his fist, struggling not to laugh, Mommy shot him the stink eye. "A lotta help you are, mister," Florrie scolded, before giving into a grin herself.

As his wife went back into the kitchen a last time to fetch her own plate, Jim unrolled the morning paper and flinched at the screaming headline: GERMANY INVADES ENGLAND! He raced through the article with a professional eye. Mainly speculation and innuendo. Nothing solid apart from the fact the Germans successfully crossed the channel and landed on the beaches south of London.

Fraser brought a second profession with him from Massachusetts to South Carolina – that of an infantry officer in the Army National Guard. The first lieutenant currently served as the Bravo Company executive officer, responsible for planning training for the one weekend a month and two weeks each July the unit assembled for a "drill."

Over the past couple years, Jim's concern America would get dragged into another Great War increased with every new country Germany overran with its new blitzkrieg. If England fell next, there would be nothing between Hitler and the old US of A except for water.

The lieutenant wasn't sure about the rest of the Army, but Bravo Company sure as hell wasn't ready for a fight. The summer drill a month ago was a fricken joke. The company commander filed Fraser's rigorous training plan into the circular file cabinet next to his desk. Instead, the good old boys walked through a series of simulated attacks their daddies made against the Huns back during the Great War, then rewarded themselves with drunken barbecues in the evening.

"Gawd help us," Jim muttered under his breath.

"What's wrong, baby?" Florrie asked, wiping off Lisa's mouth before scooting her off to play.

He lifted up the paper to show her the headline.

"Shame. But, thankfully, it doesn't have nothin to do with us."

"I'm not so sure. The Great War didn't have much to do with us either."

"Now, you stop that," Florrie snapped. "Roosevelt promised to keep us out of this war and I believe him. Go finish your flapjacks so I can clean up."

Jim stabbed a couple pieces of pancake with his fork and silently finished the article. The lieutenant wasn't sure the president could keep that promise. Wasn't sure at all.

Battleship H.M.S. Nelson - 52 miles east of Dover, England
08:01 Hours, 18 August 1940

As another German *Stuka* dive bomber screamed overhead, Commander PJ Tigert, U.S. Navy, struggled to maintain the calm demeanor the British officers around him displayed so effortlessly. His Majesty's Battleship *Nelson* leaned into another hard starboard turn to evade the *Luftwaffe* war bird. The old lady's move seemed excruciatingly slow to the American, but her luck held one more time. The *Stuka's* bomb splashed harmlessly into the sea, barely a dozen yards wide of the bow.

As if discouraged by their inability to sink the big battlewagon, the *Luftwaffe* planes ended their runs and turned back for their bases in France.

Home Fleet Admiral Charles Forbes softly ordered the helm to return the *Nelson* to its original heading and the radio room to order the other captains of the task force to reform on the flagship. Turning to the American officer, the Englishman dryly quipped, "Mr. Tigert, I hope our little cruise has given you something to report back to the colonies."

"Perhaps an item or two, Admiral," the shorter American replied.

Tigert's official job was the American assistant naval attaché to England. When Ambassador Joe Kennedy made it quite clear the commander's prediction Hitler would invade England was not appreciated, he requested and received a posting as an observer with the British Home Fleet. The Royal Navy base at Scapa Flow in Scotland was about as far away from the London embassy a disfavored diplomatic officer could get without leaving the country altogether. It all worked out in the end, though. Not only was he correct about the invasion, Tigert would also be the first American officer to see combat during the new war.

The *Nelson* was leading a task force rallying every available capital ship to evict the German ships from the English Channel, stranding the invaders on the beaches. Despite the Royal Navy's other commitments around the world, Task Force 22 still outnumbered the anticipated *Kriegsmarine* force.

Admiral Forbes entered the Straights of Dover just after midnight, hoping to catch the enemy in a night battle. The Brits excelled at such engagements and the darkness would ground the *Luftwaffe*. Instead, the forward screen of the task force sailed right into one of the minefields the Germans spent the past two days laying on the flanks of their invasion corridor across the Channel. The destroyers *Bedouin* and *Ashanti* exploded and sank in only moments with most hands aboard. The admiral had no choice but to halt his task force, while the minesweepers cleared a route to the enemy.

The *Luftwaffe* arrived not long after dawn, but the airstrikes were piecemeal, arriving from every direction with no obvious coordination. The Germans probably departed at first light, Tigert concluded. Their arrival depended how far they had to fly to reach the task force.

While the *Luftwaffe* was disorganized, the Royal Air Force was nowhere to be seen. From frustrated conversations on the bridge as the mine sweepers slowly went about their work, Tigert gathered the Brit fighters were providing air cover over the German invasion corridor, while Task Force 22 lay stalled some thirty miles to the east. The English brass had not thought to provide a radio link between the *Nelson* and the Royal Air Force fighter command in case their meticulous plans went to hell.

With no way forward and retreat out of the question, Admiral Forbes ordered his ships to take evasive maneuvers. The tactic worked better than anyone had reason to expect. The *Luftwaffe* trained to drop bombs on fixed fortifications or slow-moving masses of men, not on ships frantically twisting and turning at sea. Only a small fraction of the enemy birds making runs at the task force actually landed a bomb on a ship. By the time they turned for home, the Germans only disabled two light cruisers and inflicted superficial damage on a handful of other ships. The *Nelson* emerged unscathed.

Just when Tigert thought the task force had weathered the storm, though, another far more deadly threat arrived on the horizon.

"Admiral, more Jerry aircraft are arriving off starboard," reported the ensign manning the intercom.

Tigert trained his binoculars through the bridge window and quickly found the new planes. These weren't the camouflaged *Luftwaffe* bombers which had chased them around the ocean for the past hour. The new bandits were dark gray birds, many of them carrying torpedoes.

Christ almighty! These are carrier planes, the American commander realized. The Germans didn't have carriers...did they?

The admiral again ordered the task force to perform evasive maneuvers. This time, the tactic didn't work so well. The pilots flying the grey warbirds knew their business at sea.

First, torpedo bombers arrived in pairs, ignoring the smaller ships to hunt the big battleships and heavy cruisers. The still scattered task force could not coordinate its anti-aircraft fire against the new threat. Many batteries failed to fire at all because they ran out of ammunition during the previous attacks. The unmolested bombers flying in low towards the *Nelson* were able to adjust to the ship's turn and close to a few hundred yards before releasing their deadly fish into the sea.

Tigert gripped the wall to brace himself for impact, but the two torpedo explosions hardly seemed to move the big battleship at all. One fish hit amidships and threw up a geyser of water towards the bridge, while the other one hit unseen behind the bridge. The damage reports from below decks weren't too bad. The ship was taking on water in one of the center compartments, but not enough to sink her. Then, the helmsman softly cursed under his breath as he struggled against the wheel.

"Mr. Whitaker, is there a problem?" asked the admiral.

"Aye sir. I've lost all ability to steer and we are stuck in starboard turn. I think the second torpedo hit our rudder." In other words, the *Nelson* could only move in circles.

The now familiar scream of a diving *Stuka* interrupted the admiral when he ordered an inspection of the rudder section. As Tigert turned to look for the bomber, the bridge window imploded, swatting him across the room like a bug.

When he regained consciousness, PJ found himself lying on the battleship's deck, surrounded by wounded sailors. Bandages swaddled the crown of his head and right eye, while a life preserver encased his upper torso. When he sat up, a white-hot pain shot out from his covered eye and clawed its way across his skull.

"Please lay back down, sir," a nearby medic asked. "Your head took a damned good bashing."

Ignoring the request, Tigert sat very still. When the pain subsided, he opened his good eye and immediately wished he had left it shut. A dozen smoldering ships in various stages of sinking littered the sea around him. Destroyers clustered alongside the stricken ships like seagulls, rescuing survivors. The *Nelson* herself lay dead in the water, her superstructure obscured by the smoke rising from fires around the deck.

"Excuse me, what happened to the bridge?" Tigert softly asked.

"A bomb took it out," the medic grimaced. "You were the only one who survived."

"And the rest of the task force?"

"After minesweepers finally broke through, the rest of the ships went into the Channel an hour ago." The Englishman paused for a moment and growled, "I hope they sink all the bastards."

After wiping something from his cheek, the medic walked over and put his hands behind PJ's head. "Really, sir, you need to lie back. A destroyer will be along shortly to evacuate us."

The American commander relented, allowing the medic to ease him back down onto the deck. Looked like PJ Tigert's war was over.

R.N. Littorio, 5 miles south of Dover, England
14:39 Hours, 18 August 1940

Instead of turning to fight, the Royal Navy relentlessly closed on the Special Naval Force. The line of Italian battleships and cruisers fired one unanswered volley after another, scoring multiple hits on the advancing *Inglese*. Still, the enemy advanced.

Admiral Carlo Bergamini, ignored the looks of his sub-officers around the bridge. The Force would not retreat. Not this time.

When the high command gave him the Force, Bergamini felt truly blessed. The admiral would command the first Italian fleet in the English Channel since the days of Caesar, and would do so from the bridge of one of Italy's sleek and powerful new super-battleships – the *Litorrio*.

In June, *il Duce* Benito Mussolini negotiated a bargain with the *Germano* leader, committing the Italian Navy – the *Regia Marina* – to support the imminent invasion of England in exchange for *Germano* recognition of Italy's sphere of control over the Balkans.

At the time, Inigo Campioni commanded First Squadron and Bergomini was his subordinate training the new ship crews entering the fleet. However, during Italy's first battle with the Royal Navy off of Punta Stila, Campioni disgraced himself by withdrawing in face of an outnumbered enemy. Unwilling to risk a second disgrace in what could be a pitched battle off of England, the *Supermarina* headquarters tapped Bergamini to lead the operation. A blessing indeed!

The *Germanos* were as good as their word, capturing the *Inglese* base at Gibraltar to open up the Atlantic, then providing the Force with tankers to fuel the movement to the Channel. Bergamini's fleet sailed mostly at night, bounding from port to port up the Spanish and French coasts to avoid British reconnaissance flights, until arriving at Le Havre on the night of the invasion.

Admiral Raeder's plan was to draw the Royal Navy into a counterattack against the *Germano* invasion corridor, delay the *Inglese* with minefields while the *Luftwaffe* worked them over, then defend the Channel with the combined fleets of *Regia Marina* and *Kriegsmarine*. Not a bad idea.

The Force alone should be a match for any Royal Navy group after the *Luftwaffe* worked it over. Bergamini commanded five battleships, ten cruisers and twenty-four destroyers, nearly half of which were modern ships built over the past decade.

The Italian admiral's reserve force and the pride of the *Regia Marina* were the fleet's two newest battleships, his flagship *Litorrio* and the *Vittorio Veneto*. Italy generally built fast, lightly armored ships, with longer-range guns than their rivals. The resulting fleet could engage the opponents at long distance, then use its superior speed keep its distance from more heavily armored enemies. The *Littorio* class of battleships added heavy armor and even heavier guns to this formula. While other navies were in the process of building such battleships, for the moment, the *Regia Marina's* duo remained without peer.

Yesterday, the *Kriegsmarine* radioed that the Royal Navy Home Fleet was sailing at full speed from Scotland and should enter the Channel during the night. The Force immediately sortied from Le Harve and took up its positions a few kilometers south of the *Inglese* coast ready for a fight.

As night gave way to dawn, scattered patrols of enemy fighters droned over the gleaming white chalk cliffs of Dover, but the sea remained empty. The morning hours and the midday meal then crept by without any sign of the Royal Navy. Had the *Germano* minefields and *Luftwaffe* turned the enemy back? The silent *Kriegsmarine* radio channels provided no clue.

At last, the destroyer *Aviere* reported a large flotilla of *Inglese* ships approaching rapidly from the east. The rotund admiral audibly exhaled. After nearly four decades of service, his first battle finally arrived.

Bergamini cleared his throat and ordered his battleship and cruiser divisions to converge on the *Inglese* task force, holding the *Litorrio* and *Vittorio Veneto* back until he could see how the engagement developed.

The Force opened fire when the Royal Navy ships came within the outer range of its main guns. Instead of forming a line to return fire, though, the columns of enemy ships increased speed!

Clasping his hands together in a steeple as if praying, Bergamini considered his next move. The more heavily armored *Inglese* undoubtably wanted to close and slug it out with the lighter Italian ships. Doctrine called for him to pull back, but Carlo had no intention of being accused of withdrawing in the face of the enemy like his predecessor. Let us see how much damage we can inflict on the *Inglese* before they arrive, the admiral concluded.

The Force unleashed two unanswered volleys of cannon fire, scoring hits against a half dozen enemy ships. Still, the enemy pressed forward. When the fleets closed to within about 14,000 meters of one another, the Royal Navy task force final swung into a line and opened fire.

According to the radio reports, a *Nelson* class battleship anchored the center of the enemy line. It was a big bastard, with nine heavy sixteen inch guns arrayed across three turrets on the front of the ship. A killer whale among dolphins!

The *Inglese* gunnery unfortunately proved its historic reputation for accuracy. By the second volley, the enemy found its range and a large caliber round ripped through the deck of the Italian battleship *Cavour*, subtracting it from the battle.

Knowing his renovated Great War battleships on the forward line could not long trade blows with the *Nelson*, Bergamini played his trump cards. Side-by-side, *Litorrio* and *Vittorio Veneto* leapt forward at top speed.

As *Veneto* closed, the enemy battleship snapped off a volley from extreme range. With the devil's help, the damned *Inglese* somehow placed a round into *Veneto*'s forward turret. The powder inside ignited like a crazy quilt of fireworks, while heavy black smoke enveloped the rest of the ship.

Bergamini carefully maneuvered *Littorio* so it closed on the Royal Navy battleship behind the smoke rising from *Veneto*. When she emerged, his flagship was ready to fire.

A battleship duel is a race between opposing crews to be the first to accurately gauge the distance to and lay fire on the enemy ship. While the Royal Navy's skills were well known, Bergamini had every confidence in his own men. The admiral spent the past several months personally supervising the calibration of the *Littorio's* big fifteen inch guns and training the fire control crews to quickly and accurately lay long-range fire.

Littorio's three main gun turrets fired one after the other, each set for slightly different ranges. The fire control crews then used telescopic rangefinders to observe the geysers of water rising around the *Inglese* battleship and methodically ordered the turret crews to revise their aim.

The enemy battleship lashed back with another hastily aimed volley, but without the same damnable luck they enjoyed against *Veneto*. The incoming rounds instead splashed harmlessly a few hundred meters starboard of *Littorio*.

The wasted *Inglese* volley provided all the time Bergamini needed to land the knockout blow. One of the enormous armor-piercing shells from *Littorio's* second volley crashed through the enemy's deck and into the ammunition magazine deep below. Several kilometers away, ensconced in a metal bridge, the Italian admiral could still hear the massive explosion ripping the proud *Inglese* ship in two.

With less than half of its original number still combat effective, the loss of the big battleship was more than the enemy could bear. Now heavily outgunned by the Force and facing the prospect of renewed *Luftwaffe* air strikes, the surviving *Inglese* ships deployed smoke screens and withdrew to the east.

Littorio's bridge erupted in cheers, but Bergamini merely looked up and said a silent prayer. God smiled on them today and, for that, he would be eternally thankful.

Temple Ewell, England
15:09 Hours, 18 August 1940

The enemy *panzer* slowly turned its turret towards Erwin Rommel and fired its main gun. The day was definitely not going the way the general anticipated.

Rommel arrived in England just before dawn aboard a freighter carrying the lead battalion of his *panzer* division. As soon as the unit offloaded onto the Dover docks, the commander led it to the front, leaving his staff behind to bring up the rest of the division.

The situation was desperate. Two days ago, the *Flieger* Division dropped on Dover, suffering heavy casualties wresting the port away from an enemy regiment. Yesterday, the Tommies threw their reserves against the greatly diminished paratroopers, reportedly pushing to within a couple kilometers of the docks. As he raced through the Dover streets ahead of his *panzers* looking for the *Flieger* headquarters, Rommel wondered if the remainder of the division would land in time.

Following the directions of a pair of bleary-eyed paras manning a checkpoint, Rommel found a colonel at an *Englander* pub turned field command post, smoking a cigarette and partaking of a pint of dark beer. A filthy captain with a heavy stubble beard was reporting the Tommies were concentrating to the north for another attack down the London Road.

The colonel turned to Rommel and smiled broadly. "General, you are a very welcome sight. Please tell me your *panzers* are in Dover."

"Where can I find General Putzier?"

"The division commander died when he landed in the middle of a Tommy company during the initial drop," the colonel replied. "My name is Sturm and I am in charge of the *Flieger* Division."

"I'm sorry to hear that," Rommel commiserated, as he removed his goggles and helmet. "As for my *panzers*, I only have the first of three battalions, which should be arriving shortly. Offloading the rest will probably take another day or two."

Disappointment shadowed Sturm's face as he motioned the *panzer* general over to the bar and pointed at a civilian road map lying there. "General, the Tommies attacked us here with nearly fifty tanks yesterday. My boys were only able to hold because we placed obstacles across the road and the enemy neglected to bring engineers along to breach them." Looking back up, Sturm shook his head. "Sir, I am sure their engineers will join today's festivities."

Rommel considered the map for a moment and turned to the paratrooper. "I agree, Colonel. This enemy rarely makes the same mistake twice, so I want you to let them down the London Road."

"Excuse me?"

"You heard me, Sturm. Let the Tommies through."

Two hours later, the enemy *panzers* drove slowly down the main London Road towards the docks, seemingly unconcerned about why the road obstacles suddenly disappeared. After all, the lightly armed German paras possessed no weapons capable of penetrating their armor.

Rommel impatiently watched this procession from behind the turret of one of his own *panzers* carefully hidden down a side alley. Soon… Soon… Wait for it.

The sharp cracks of a half dozen *panzer* main guns firing a few blocks to the south echoed up the city streets. Fifty meters away, a *Cruiser* light *panzer* trundling down main road suddenly ground to a halt to avoid ramming the braking vehicle to its front. The Tommy vehicles were stacked up on the road like a row of metal ducks on a fairground shooting gallery. The perfect ambush.

Rommel's *panzer* turned its turret slightly toward the target, then fired its main gun. The round was low, splintering the track of the enemy vehicle.

The Tommy commander standing out of the turret hatch of the *Cruiser* snapped his head around toward Rommel and started shouting into the vehicle. Erwin tensed as the tank's turret started to turn slowly towards him.

The German *panzer* fired a second time. Rommel could not make out where the round landed, but the enemy engine compartment started smoking.

Still, the *Englander* turret continued to turn until its main gun lined up perfectly with the *panzer* officer. Erwin stared down the enemy gunner watching him through a slit in the *Cruiser*. He wagered the man had never seen a German general before. Well, take your best shot, you bastard. My *panzer* will get the final shot.

As if shrinking from his gaze, the *Cruiser* gunner lowered the main gun slightly and fired. The armor-piercing round punched through the thin frontal armor of the *panzer* below his feet with a loud clang. The subsequent silence and smoke wafting out of the vehicle gave testament to the effectiveness of the enemy marksmanship.

The *Cruiser* did not die so quietly. Seconds later, the engine fire started by the last German round reached the gasoline tank of the Tommy *panzer*. The enemy vehicle shuddered, then fire erupted out of the turret hatch, turning its commander into a thrashing human torch.

Rommel could only gape at the hellish scene around him. As a young lieutenant in the Great War, he made his name routing *Italianer* soldiers in the Alps with attacks featuring surprise and few losses. As a general in the new war, casualties in the lightning campaign across France were merely numbers on a report. This was the first time he personally witnessed the industrial slaughter of a modern battle.

Erwin looked away and hopped off the back of his dead *panzer*. There would be time enough later to consider with what he witnessed. Today, the general had a battle to win.

24

CHAPTER 2

South Kensington, England
19:30 Hours, 25 August 1940

The tall woman dressed stylishly in a long black dress adorned with a string of pearls. It was not that she disliked the bright colors of summer normally worn in August, but rather black was the preferred color of fascists.

Katarina Kolotsiev took the seat offered by Nikolai Popov with a smile. Popov was the proprietor of the Russian Tea Rooms and a dear family friend. Since the passing of her father and his eldest child, Nikolai treated Katarina like his lost daughter.

The Tea Rooms offered the finest Russian food in London and was a particular favorite of Kolotsiev. Wartime food shortages were beginning to take their toll on the menu, but Mrs. Popov did her best to keep up appearances. The restaurant windows were gayly covered with holiday gift-wrapping paper in order to comply with the government blackout orders.

The tall woman barely noticed the short, frumpy man with slightly askew spectacles walking by, until he turned toward her and extended his hand. "Miss Kolotsiev, I am George Roberts. Thank you so much for agreeing to dine with me tonight."

Shaking his hand with a firm grip, Katarina replied, "How could I resist after your intriguing letter of introduction."

The two exchanged light conversation about the inconveniences of the German invasion as a waiter poured the water. Roberts gratefully accepted her recommendations concerning the cuisine offered by the Tea Rooms and they passed the time before dinner with a mutually agreeable Italian wine.

Gently swirling the white Pino Grigio around in his glass before taking a sip, Roberts got to the point. "As I mentioned in my letter, I represent a doctor on the continent who collects rare historical items."

"That must be interesting work, but I don't know how I can be of assistance," Kolotsiev responded. "I own some family heirlooms from the Motherland, but nothing I would care to sell."

"I wouldn't think of asking you to part with your keepsakes," the man chuckled. "A mutual friend informed my employer you were in possession of a collection of contemporary correspondence of great historical value. This is what I am interested in acquiring."

Her green eyes turning flinty, Kolotsiev stated evenly, "I am certain I do not know the correspondence to which you refer."

Roberts was definitely a spy, she concluded. But for whom? Although it would surprise her friends and acquaintances in British society, who only knew her as the flamboyant daughter of a wealthy Russian émigré, the elegant woman was actually quite well-versed in the dark arts of espionage.

Katarina was the only child of an admiral of the Imperial Russian Navy – Grand Duke Mikhail Kolotsiev. Before the Great War, Papa served as the Tsar's naval attaché to England and stayed on to marry the Lady Cecelia Crawford. Mama died in childbirth, leaving the Russian aristocrat with an infant daughter and a lucrative family trading business.

The admiral unsparingly raised his beloved girl as he would any son. Naming her after the Russian Empress Catherine, Papa provided her with stern lessons taken from his old life of palace intrigue and defending a Motherland surrounded by enemies. After the Bolsheviks murdered the Tsar and his family, hatred of Jewish communists was added to the paternal lesson plan.

Tutors followed by university added a classical education and mastery of multiple languages. With a generous contribution, the admiral ensured his daughter was one of a select handful of women educated at Oxford. The young woman proved a brilliant student, graduating with first class honors.

Katarina returned from university tall like her father, with an intimidating intellect and a personality matching her flaming red hair. The admiral decided it was time to put her education to practical use.

Papa revealed his secret double life to his daughter. In addition to his diplomatic service, the admiral coordinated the London branch of the Tsar's secret police – the *Okhrana*. Their mission was to gather intelligence on Russian communists and send the information back to St. Petersburg. After the 1917 revolution, the flow of information reversed. The surviving *Okhrana* infiltrated the new Bolshevik government, sending intelligence back to London for dissemination to tsarist organizations around Europe.

Receiving a post-graduate education in espionage, Katarina ran an increasing number of the admiral's agents and learned how to distill the information they provided into useful intelligence.

A decade ago, her Papa provided one last brutal lesson. While on a trip to meet his contacts in Paris, the admiral ceased sending telegrams back to London. Katarina quickly ran down his trail, where she found a French waiter who witnessed men club her father over the head and throw him into the back of a car. As her agents in Russia went silent over the following months, she was forced to conclude the worst. The Bolshevik

NKVD must have kidnapped Papa and tortured him in their Lubyanka dungeon until he gave up his comrades.

Katarina's profound grief crystalized into calculation. If the red bastards could take down such an accomplished man, they could surely reach her if she was not extraordinarily careful.

Tea Room waiters brought cups of sour Shchi soup, which Kolotsiev and Roberts ate in silence. After wiping his mouth with a napkin, the man reached into his suit jacket and retrieved an envelope. "Perhaps this will refresh your memory concerning the correspondence I am seeking."

Kolotsiev opened envelope on her lap and partly pulled out the photographs within. These were the copies of the correspondence between Roosevelt and Churchill she obtained from the American embassy!

"Interesting documents. May I ask how you come to possess them?"

"My client has friends across the continent. These items were provided by an Italian duke, who used to reside here in London before the war compelled him to return home."

The tall woman picked up her wine glass and took a slow swallow as she considered the man sitting across from her.

In the years since the Bolsheviks took her father, Kolotsiev admired how Adolf Hitler cleansed Germany of the communists and Jews, returning prosperity to his *Reich*. England could use a similar cleaning, in her opinion. When it became obvious Germany and England would go to war, the admiral's daughter decided to put her skills to work to ensure the *Reich* prevailed.

During the last New Year's celebrations at the Tea Rooms, Kolotsiev stumbled upon an opportunity. A drunken American was making a scene at the bar, alternatively bragging about his classified work at the embassy and deriding the treason of his president. Her curiosity piqued, she chatted up the bloke.

After drinks at his flat that evening, Tyler Kent revealed he worked in the code room of the American embassy. Pulling a box out of the closet, the clerk showed her a series of telegrams between his president and the British Lord of the Admiralty. Roosevelt and Churchill were actually plotting to bring the United States into the war against Germany!

Driving home, Kolotsiev considered the implications of the telegrams. The United States was a famously isolationist nation entering an election year in which their president was promising to keep the Yanks out of the war. If she could expose Roosevelt's double-dealing with Churchill, his isolationist opponent could win election, leaving England and France to face Germany alone. Excellent.

Kolotsiev became Kent's lover, inviting him over to her far more spacious home for meals, unsatisfying sex and classified document reading. She quickly convinced him to leave the papers with her for safe keeping. Men were so easily manipulated.

The far more difficult problem was dispatching the documents to Germany for publication. With the onset of hostilities, England no longer enjoyed direct contact with the *Reich*. A solution presented itself in the person of Duke del Monte, an acquaintance at the Italian diplomatic delegation. Katarina entrusted photographs of three of the more damning telegrams to the Duke, with his assurance they would travel by diplomatic pouch to the authorities best able to exploit them.

Germany's response was George Roberts.

"Your bona fides are impeccable, sir," Katarina observed as she handed the envelope the envelope back to the spy. "I believe I now recall the correspondence you are seeking."

"Wonderful, Miss Kolotsiev."

"All my friends call me Kat and I think we shall be very good friends."

White House, Washington D.C.
11:11 Hours, 16 September 1940

Chief of Staff General George C. Marshall glanced over to the Boss in disbelief. Was the President seriously considering Harry's suggestion?

Last week, President Roosevelt dispatched Harry Hopkins to gauge the situation in England after the German invasion. A member of the original New Deal "brain trust" turned diplomat, this advisor enjoyed the Boss's complete trust. Hopkins returned last night after a twenty-hour flight on a Pan American airboat with a letter from Prime Minister Churchill. The fact Marshall was summoned to the White House the next morning for a rare Sunday meeting suggested the letter did not convey good news.

The Chief of Staff found the Oval Office quiet, with none of the usual pre-meeting banter. Sitting behind a desk covered with mementoes and knick-knacks, the normally jovial Roosevelt appeared pained. The president started the meeting by reading aloud from Churchill's letter.

The darkness which covered the continent during the Spring has now reached our nation. Hitler's forces are gathering in marked preponderance along our southern shores and we expect him to attack towards London in short order.

Mr. President, we can no longer carry on the war against the enemy alone. What we lack above all are trained soldiers to hold the line against the Nazi to allow our Army and Air Force a chance to rebuild.

Our two nations are the only remaining bastions of civilization left in the world. I most earnestly ask you to lead the United States into the fight. If Great Britain falls, then America stands alone.

Roosevelt laid the letter back on his desk and took a couple puffs from his cigarette before speaking again. "I don't want to leave England in the lurch. Confound the timing, though, with the election only weeks away."

The president pulled his half-smoked cigarette out the holder and mashed it out in an overfull ashtray. "I've spent the summer promising the voters that I wouldn't send their boys into any foreign wars, only to have some son of a bitch provide my private correspondence with Mr. Churchill to Germany. Now the traitors at the Republican papers are using what the Nazis gave them to call me a liar."

Marshall shifted uncomfortably as Roosevelt leaned forward. "Harry, you just came from England. What do you think?"

The tired and rumpled Hopkins rose from the sofa. "The Brits are amazing, from Churchill on down. If courage alone could win the war, England would more than hold their own. However, the reality is they don't have the men or weapons to survive the upcoming Nazi blitz."

"OK, what do you recommend?"

"Franklin, I know the politics are tough, but I recommend we go to war."

Marshall looked down to the carpet and shook his head slightly. Harry was a friend and the man who convinced the President to appoint him as chief of staff, but he was just flat out wrong.

"You don't agree George?" Roosevelt asked.

The Chief of Staff looked up and strode to the middle of the room. "I'm sorry, Mr. President, but we just don't have the ability to go to war now."

"Why not?"

"Sir, the Army only has five infantry divisions remotely combat ready and they're all substantially understrength with Great War weapons. Moreover, we only have enough ammunition for maybe a month of combat operations. This is all we have to defend the nation until we mobilize the National Guard and build our own armored divisions."

Marshall looked over to the Navy Chief of Staff. "Admiral Stark, if the President were to order these divisions and their supplies to Britain, how long would it take the Navy to get them there?"

"Not for several weeks…probably months," Harold "Betty" Stark responded, scratching his chin. "The Merchant Marine is scattered all over the globe and would take some time to reassemble."

Turning back to the President, Marshall summed up, "Sir, Germany will defeat England before we could arrive. Even if the British held out, I am sorry to say that our men do not have the weapons or training to stand up very long to German tanks and aircraft."

"And whose fault is that, General?" Hopkins demanded.

"The government of the United States has seen fit to fund an army smaller than Belgium," Marshall replied evenly. "I would remind you the Germans overran Belgium in days."

Leaning back in his wheel chair, Roosevelt tossed up his hands and exclaimed, "There's no good choice here! If I go to war, Harry, I confirm everything the Nazis are saying about me and the Republicans will probably win the election. Even if I hang on and win, I can't very well strip the country of its defenses, only to lose them on an English battlefield."

The President paused and looked over to his Chief of Staff. "On the other hand, our brave English cousins deserve all the help we can reasonably provide."

Oh no, the Boss is going to cut the baby in half.

"OK, here's what we'll do. George, divert all current production of weapons and supplies to England. Betty, find a way to get it there as soon as humanly possible."

The Chief of Staff opened his mouth, but Roosevelt cut him off.

"I've made up my mind, George. I know this will delay modernizing the Army, but I will not completely abandon the English people in their hour of need."

Marshall swallowed his objection and responded with a crisp, "Yes sir."

"Now if you will excuse me, gentlemen," the President concluded, "I have the unhappy task of writing Mr. Churchill to let him know the U.S. cavalry will not be coming to the rescue."

Charleston, South Carolina
07:39 Hours, 17 September 1941

The lieutenant felt all alone in the crowded rail station. Families jammed the platform, saying goodbye to their soldiers departing for Fort Jackson, but his own were nowhere to be seen.

Jim Fraser hardly lacked for family. In addition to his own fledgling tribe, he was the part of a sprawling Boston clan, the youngest of his mother's five children.

Although he was the baby of the clan, the collapse of a crane killing his only brother made fourteen year old Jim the heir apparent of Fraser & Sons Dredging. "Big Dan" Fraser thereafter dedicated his son's life and education to taking over the family business. When he was not attending high school and then college, Jim was at a worksite learning the ropes of developing Boston harbor.

The dutiful son's first stab at independence was joining Boston College ROTC to gain a commission in the Massachusetts National Guard. Since he was old enough to read, Jim thrilled to stories of America's wars. The boy wasn't dumb enough to believe combat was fun and games. His Uncle Dougie lost a leg in France during the Great War and then died a couple weeks later from infection. Still, Jim saw serving his country to free people as something truly noble.

Becoming an Army officer would allow him to live out his fantasy, even if only part time.

Jim never told anyone about his dream. Big Dan would have laughed in his face, then chewed him out. In his father's opinion, only losers and criminals joined the Army. The son sold his old man on ROTC as a way to save the family the cost of a college tuition. Even then, Big Dan warned him summer drills would constitute his only vacation from the company.

Florrie dismissed his National Guard drills as a hobby, which brought a little more money into the family budget and gave her an opportunity to bring the kids to visit family around Charleston without her Yankee husband tagging along and becoming a topic of conversation.

Then, the lieutenant's orders to report for active duty arrived.

After several attempts, Jim got through by telephone to Boston late in the afternoon. After answering Big Dan's questions about the status of the Charleston harbor work, Jim got to the point of the call. "Dad, I received orders from the Army today. The South Carolina National Guard is being called up next week."

"Have you put in the paperwork for a deferment?"

Well hell, the old man did know about the new deferral programs, allowing soldiers to leave the Guard if they had a wife and children or worked in a defense related job like his dredging Charleston harbor.

"No Dad, I plan on activating with my unit."

"What the hell for?" Big Dan exploded over the telephone.

"I've prepped the local manager, Dave Rogers, to take over," Jim deflected. "He's perfectly capable of subbing in for me until this activation is over."

"Prepped? Just how long have you known about this?"

The son struggled to keep the rising anger out of his voice, but was certain he was failing. "A couple weeks after Congress called up the Guard. I assumed you read the papers."

"Don't get flip with me, boyo! Get your ass in gear and put in your deferment papers. I've invested too much in you to have you walk away from the business for this horse crap."

"Listen, I have a job to do. The business can wait until I finish up my hitch."

"Damn it, Jim, you listen…"

"Dad, I have to go home to tell Florrie and the girls. We can talk…

The line clicked dead.

Well, that could have gone better, the son thought, slapping the telephone handset back down on the cradle.

Driving back to the more understanding confines of home, Jim decided to cool his temper over a nice dinner and then tell Florrie about the orders later that evening. After he put the girls to bed and Florrie finished up the dishes, Jim handed his wife a beer and told her he had some news. Her pretty smile disappeared when he reported the Army was activating the South Carolina Guard and sending him to Fort Jackson for the foreseeable future.

"When I told my Dad this afternoon," Jim sighed, "he acted like I was a traitor to the family for not taking a deferment to stay on the job."

"Wait a minute, Jimmy," Florrie demanded. "The Army will let ya stay home and you're going anyways?"

"Honey, I have to go. It wouldn't be fair to…"

"Fair! How is it fair to me and the kids if you leave us alone to go off and play soldier?"

Jim was completely taken aback. He'd never seen Florrie act this way and didn't know what to say. His wife wasn't at a loss for words, though.

"Jimmy Fraser, you have responsibilities here. I can't do this alone."

When he didn't reply immediately, she broke down, tears streaming down her cheeks. "Oh, you…you just don't love me anymore!"

"After all I've done for this family, how can you frickin' say that?" Jim barked back, louder than he intended.

Florrie fled sobbing to the bedroom and slammed the door.

His pride kicking in, Jim was not about to run after his wife and beg her forgiveness for doing the job they both knew he volunteered for. She wouldn't even give him a chance to explain!

After peeking in to make sure the kids slept through the fight, he walked to a nearby bar and simmered over a couple beers. First Dad and now Florrie. Deciding he didn't want to deal with his wife again until things cooled down, Jim went to the office and slept on the couch.

After work the next day, he came home ready to make up with flowers and a bottle of wine, only to find Florrie and the girls had packed and gone. The letter his wife left behind was blunt – she would come home if he obtained a deferral, but planned to live with her sister in Summerville if he deployed.

Jim telephoned the sister, but Bonnie Sue said Florrie didn't want to come to the phone. She put all she had to say in the letter. Then, the sister added something about no good Yankees before hanging up.

Well, that tore it.

Lieutenant Fraser put on his uniform and reported for duty early. This was definitely not how he pictured the starting his hitch in the regular Army.

Bristol, England
12:18 Hours, 19 September 1940

Katarina Kolotsiev's preparations to leave England were almost complete. She offered the crew of her yacht triple wages to provision and man the *Empress Catherine* for a cross-Atlantic trip. Three of the four accepted and the ship was finally ready to depart. All that remained was waiting for her love to arrive for a slow voyage to Cuba together.

When the police started arresting anyone in London they suspected of being a German sympathizer, Kolotsiev drove immediately to west coast without stopping at home for any of her possessions. She was unsure if British intelligence knew of her work, but was not about to wait around to find out.

Mama was the sole heiress to the Crawford Trading Consortium and a family estate in Bristol. When she passed, Papa left the Bristol properties in the Crawford family name to hide their existence from the Bolsheviks. Katarina was confident her relationship to properties was also unknown to the British authorities and would provide her with temporary sanctuary.

A week later, a short article tucked away in the Evening Post reported American embassy officer, Tyler Kent, was detained and then deported for undisclosed reasons. Kolotsiev rewarded herself with a self-satisfied smile. Before she convinced him to allow her to secure the Roosevelt and Churchill correspondence, the idiot had actually kept the documents in a closet of his flat. The only reason the police would have released Kent is if he kept his mouth shut and a search of his home found nothing.

Her current concerns lay elsewhere. Last year, Kolotsiev used her friendship with the Popovs as an entree to join the Right Club, a secret society of British fascists who met at the Russian Tea Rooms. For her purposes, the organization proved to be a singular waste of time. Members gave long-winded speeches condemning Jewish control of England and competed with the local communists in defacing London with propaganda stickers.

Joan Miller was the only reason she stayed on. A vivacious brunette with smoldering eyes, Miller enjoyed a natural beauty which attracted the attention of a parade of suitors at the Right Club, all of whom she laughingly turned away.

Kolotsiev's interest was initially professional. Miller worked at the War Department, with access to a potentially rich trove of information. However, upon discovering they shared a lively intelligence and a fascination with fascism, the women became quick chums and constant dinner companions.

This is when Kat decided to take a rare risk. Over drinks one night, Joan chatted about her boss bringing her to a diplomatic dinner, where she met a very charming Italian duke telling stories about Venice. Seeing a possible means of delivering the correspondence to the Germans, Kat asked if her friend could provide an introduction to the diplomat. When asked why, she mischievously replied she would provide Italy something that would change history.

Following the introduction, Kolotsiev twice met with del Monte alone, passing him photographs of the correspondence enclosed within a newspaper at a city park. Giddy from the successful operation, Kat drove back to Joan's flat to celebrate. While declining to reveal the nature of the documents, she provided her friend with a detailed description of the handoff, slightly embellishing it for dramatic effect.

Kat hugged Joan and exclaimed: "Darling, we did it!" When the embrace loosened, they looked curiously at one another for a moment. Then, Kat impulsively kissed the beautiful woman in her arms. This was the kiss of a lover, rather than a friend. And the kiss was returned.

Warmed by the memory, Kat rung Joan's number for the umpteenth time. The military had taken over the London telephone exchanges for its own use and personal calls were a hit and miss proposition. It was well after midnight before her call went through.

The sleep in Joan's voice vanished when she recognized the voice in the phone. "Where have you been? The police arrested everyone in the Right Club and the Popovs told me there's a detail posted outside of your house."

"I'm safe," reassured Kat. "What about you? Why didn't they arrest you?"

"Uh…I'm not sure actually. Maybe they didn't know I was a member."

"Joan, listen to me. England isn't safe for us any longer. I'll be leaving tomorrow and I need you to come with me."

"What? Where would we go?"

"My family has property in the Caribbean. Once there, we can go anywhere in the world we like."

"Kat, you need to leave now, while you still can," plead Joan. "I can't leave England. This is my home."

"Darling, I love you and can't leave you behind. Please come with me."

The phone went silent for a moment.

"All right, tell me where you are and I'll leave London as soon as I can."

The next day around noon, Kat flew down the stairs to answer a knock on the door. Instead of Joan, though, two large men in overcoats stood on the porch in the rain.

"Katarina Kolotsiev?" demanded the taller of the two.

"Please come inside out of this dreadful weather, won't you?"

The men cautiously entered. Looking around at the sheet-covered furniture, the shorter one quipped, "Planning on going somewhere?"

"I am Katarina Kolotsiev. How may I help you gentlemen?"

The taller man pulled an identity card out of his pocket and intoned, "Miss Kolotsiev, I am Agent Rogers and this is

Agent Wilson. We are from Special Branch. You are under arrest for violating the Defense Regulation Order."

"The Defense Regulation Order? I am quite sure I don't know what you mean," she demurred.

"There's no use pretending you do not know why we are here," lectured Rogers. "Your entire ring is in custody." The agent then proceeded to rattle off the names of a handful of friends and acquaintances.

Did these bastards have Joan?

"I know nothing of a 'ring,' but you appear to have arrested some of my social circle, except for maybe Vera Popov and Joan Miller."

"You stupid dyke," Agent Wilson sneered. "Miller is one of ours. Who do you think sent us?"

Don't respond. Ignore him. Deal with the problem at hand.

"Since it appears I will be going with you gentlemen," Kolotsiev conceded, "may I put on my mack hanging there?"

Rogers took the raincoat off the rack by the front door and held it out for her. She shrugged into and buttoned the coat, then asked for her hat. When the agent turned, she eased her hand into the coat pocket and retrieved the pistol there.

Kat first shot the loathsome Wilson through the eye, then snapped off two more rounds at the other agent. Rogers yelled as a bullet slammed into his shoulder, but managed to swat the revolver out of her hand with his remaining good arm.

Kolotsiev started after the pistol skittering across the floor, but the surviving agent lunged and grabbed her ankle, toppling her to the ground. She repeatedly kicked at the man's face, but he simply would not release her.

In frustration, she started to scream and thrash about, knocking over the entryway table. The green marble tabletop broke in two by her head, scattering nick knacks around the foyer. Kolotsiev grabbed a chunk of the stone and swung it down on the stubborn man. Rogers let go of her ankle and raised his good arm to shield himself, but it was no use. She had lost all control.

"Who…is…a…stupid…dyke?" Katarina shrieked as she struck him again and again, breaking his arm and then his face. Her fury finally spent, she rose to drop the marble on the smashed body and collapsed on the couch.

Oh Joan, how could you?

The dutiful daughter immediately pushed the lover's thought away. Papa was correct. Self-pity was something she couldn't afford if she wanted to survive in this world.

After telephoning her first mate to inform him they would be departing within the hour, Kat wearily walked to the bath to wash off the blood.

Summerville, South Carolina
16:03 Hours, 6 October 1940

When Jimmy's letter arrived with the Saturday mail, Florrie skedaddled off to her bedroom to read it. Instead of the corny love letters her hubby used to send whenever he was out of town, this one was cold and short. He gave a brief description of his job at Fort Jackson, asked how the kids were doing, then noted his new military address.

I'm losing him.

Florrie started to cry softly. As a tear fell on the letter, dragging the ink down the paper, there was a gentle knock at the door and her mother peeked in.

"Is everything all right?"

"No Mama, nothin is right no more."

When her mother sat on the bed next to her, the story of the Army calling up Jimmy and their fight came pouring out.

"Baby doll, you're hardly the first woman whose husband was called into the Army."

"But he had the chance to stay with me and the girls, and went anyways."

"We were all surprised when you decided to marry a Yankee, but your Jim is a good man. I'm sure he's doing what he thinks is right." Then, Mama gave her one of those mother looks. "What's really wrong, child?"

The tears started flowing again. "This is what happened to Daddy all over again. The Army took him away to the Great War and he got killed over in France. I can't stand the thought of losing Jimmy that way. It's the awfullest feeling I've ever had."

Now it was Mama's turn to tear up. "Even after all these years, there aren't many days I don't think about your Daddy. God has a plan for each of us and we were only meant to be together for a short time. God willing, you and Jim will have much longer."

Mama wiped the tears off her cheeks and then her daughter's. "Enough of that. Let's go to supper."

The women hugged and walked into the living room. Bonnie Sue stuck her head out of the kitchen, holding her hand over the mouthpiece of the telephone. "Your husband's on the line. Do you wanna to talk with him?"

Florrie ran over and grabbed the phone. "Jimmy, is that you?"

"Hi sweetie, can we talk?"

"Oh yes, darling."

"I'm so sorry for the way I left you and the girls. I miss you all so much. I dunno…I'm such a chowdahead."

"No, it's all my fault. I was afraid of you going off to war."

The line went silent for a moment.

"Hon, there's no war. Really," Jim reassured. "The Army is calling up the Guard as a precaution. I'll be fine."

"OK, I guess. Would you like to speak with the girls?"

"Would I ever!"

Donna squealed when Florrie handed her the telephone, leaving Lisa jumping up and down, impatiently waiting her turn. They were Daddy's girls.

Florrie looked over to Mama and they exchanged smiles. Everything was good again.

Fort Benning, Georgia
10:37 Hours, 19 November 1940

Brigadier General George S. Patton donned his well-practiced war scowl as Second Armored Division performed a crossing of the Chattahoochee River for the visiting Secretary of War. Inside, George was smiling broadly. He had Henry Stimson exactly where he wanted him.

The show opened with reconnaissance companies roaring up and securing the intended crossing sites. Then, dive bombers and the artillery launched a real-life bombardment of the opposite bank, while the engineers laid bridges across the river.

Patton ensured the Secretary of War had a catbird seat near the crossing, so he could feel the concussions of the explosions. Civilians always loved fireworks.

Finally, tanks and trucks of infantry sprinted across the bridges, followed closely by the artillery which provided the opening bombardment. The entire operation took less than a half hour.

While Patton thought his men had a long way to go before they were ready for a shooting war, the Secretary gushed about the demonstration. "General Patton, allow me to congratulate you on a superb exercise. How did you manage it?"

"Training and more training. I rewrote the Second Armored rulebook to include all the lessons the Krauts taught the world about combined arms and added a few tricks of my own."

"Well, I think it is safe to say you have produced the first American *panzer* division."

Now for some lobbying. "Mr. Secretary, is the scuttlebutt true that the Army will be creating its first armored corps?" Patton inquired.

"It's true. The new corps will be our next step in playing catch up with the Germans."

"Sir, I would very much appreciate if you kept my name in mind when you consider staffing the new corps."

"I heard you were ambitious," Stimson laughed. "Don't worry, General, I'll remember what I saw here today."

"Thank you, Mr. Secretary," Patton saluted with his swagger stick.

Everything was coming together. After the Great Depression's years of bare bones budgets and promotion freezes, Patton finally earned his first star last month and then command of Second Armored Division. The newly minted general was determined this star would only be his first. There was a war coming and George was damned if he would not play a leading role.

Patton's complete focus on his new command nearly destroyed his marriage, though. Feeling abandoned, Bea returned to her family home in Boston over the summer. The general's warrior facade immediately crumbled. In a rapid-fire series of letters, George apologized profusely for ignoring Bea and begged her to forgive him, until she relented and returned in the fall. While he would be the first to admit the military was the focus of his life, confound it, he truly loved his wife.

With both his career and his marriage back on track again, life was damned near perfect.

Balmoral Castle, Scotland
06:43 Hours, 18 December 1940

Platoon sergeant Helmut Arpke stared out the glider window into the swirling white and wondered where the hell they were going.

Their mission plan was straight forward. The glider battalion would land on the lawns of Balmoral Castle, dispatch any Tommy soldiers who might be on guard, then capture the *Englander* royal family. However, none of the staff officers who came up with this fine plan anticipated a descent into a morass of Scottish fog and snow.

The fog cleared a bit, revealing a snow-blanketed field hurtling towards them. The pilot jerked up on his stick to slow down, but the glider bounced hard off the frozen ground, snapping off the left wing; then spun to a halt, throwing a sheet of snow into the air.

Helmut rolled out of the broken bird and looked around. No building or other landmarks in sight. No sound of the other gliders or exchanges of small arms fire with the Tommies. Nothing but whispering white. How far away from the castle did they land?

Sergeant Erich Schuster trotted up with a slight limp, took a knee and quietly reported, "None of the men are seriously injured and the platoon is ready to move out."

Before the war, Schuster joined the *Luftwaffe's* new paratroopers a year after Arpke. The easy-going Rhinelander and the serious Prussian soon became fast friends and easy rivals. The Fatherland decorated each man for heroism in Belgium. When Lieutenant Altmann was killed during the September attack on London, the company commander promoted both men, giving second platoon to Helmut and Arpke's old squad to Erich.

In the heavy fighting up the English coast, the platoon gained a reputation for good fortune – taking even the most stubborn objectives with few casualties. Schuster nicknamed his friend "Lucky Helmut" and the name stuck with the men.

They needed a bit of that luck to find their current location and fast.

After working their way north for a short while, the paras came across a narrow road, then followed it for about a kilometer until a stately stone building came into view. Arpke recognized the place from the pre-mission briefing as the Craigowan Lodge – the castle's guesthouse and one of the battalion objectives. Because no one else was around, they might as well do the honors of conducting the search.

The home was dark and quiet, with no sign of enemy troops, so Arpke decided to introduce himself properly to the residents. He walked right up and banged on the large oak front door. A moment later, a maid answered and stared dumbfounded at the German paratrooper. He caught the door before the woman could slam it in his face and the poor creature ran screaming into the house.

The platoon sergeant started directing his men down the hallways of the ground floor. When he looked up the stairs, Helmut found himself looking down the barrel of a shotgun held by an old man on the second floor. The man was dressed like a simple gardener, but his aim appeared to be true enough. Maybe his luck had finally run its course.

Schuster fired a quick burst from his machine pistol, hurling the gardener against a bloodied wall. Screams and crying started issuing out of the recesses of the upper floor.

A second man walked into view at the top of the stairs, holding his hands up in the air. "Puh...please do not harm muh..my ser... servants," he begged.

Arpke studied him for a moment. Was this thin, stuttering man… Reaching into his smock, he pulled out the photo issued at yesterday's briefing and a chill washed across him.

"Everyone lower your weapons," the platoon leader quickly ordered.

Arpke looked up at the man on the stairs, struggling to find the correct English words he picked up over the past few months. "Come down stairs, please. You are *mein* prisoner."

In as much dignity he could manage with tears in his eyes, King George VI walked down the stairs into captivity.

Summerville, South Carolina
16:18 Hours, 24 December 1940

Like Santa Claus making his first stop on Christmas Eve, Jim Fraser trotted onto the stoop of Bonnie Sue's house with a bag of gifts thrown over his shoulder and rang the bell. The lieutenant was able to finagle a last-minute Christmas leave and decided to surprise his wife and daughters.

Florrie's mom opened the door and the sounds of a big family celebration flowed out with her. "Why Jim, this is a pleasant surprise. We have some ladies here who'll be thrilled to see you."

Jim followed Mae down the hallway and stopped in the entrance to the living room. His twin girls – Donna and Lisa - looked over from playing by the Christmas tree and screamed "Daadee" in perfect unison. Daddy put the bag of gifts on the floor and scooped his daughters up, giving them both sloppy kisses on the forehead.

Florrie ran out of the kitchen wearing an apron and planted her flour-covered hands on her hips in mock outrage. "Jimmy Fraser, why didn't you call to let us know you were coming?"

"Sorry Hon, but I caught a ride on Santa's sleigh and he didn't have a telephone."

"Well, I guess ya are forgiven. Come over here and gimme some sugar."

Jim put the girls down and gave his wife a long and long overdue kiss.

Tugging at his uniform pants, Donna asked, "Daddy, did you really ride with Santa Claus?"

"Ayuh, I sure did, pumpkin." Daddy grinned, pointing at the bag on the floor. "These are the presents Santa asked me to drop off for my girls."

When the family sat around the dining room table for supper, they squeezed him in at a corner next to his wife. When he married Florrie, the Stocktons were coolly polite to their new Boston Yankee in-law. After the fight and separation, Jim wasn't sure if he was still welcome at all.

Florrie's Uncle Lee led the family holding hands and saying grace. "Lord, as we prepare to celebrate your Son's birth, we would like to thank You for bringing our family together and for all the blessings You've given us. We would like to especially thank You for bringing Jim back to us. Bless this food to our bodies. In Jesus name we pray, Amen."

Jim glanced up in surprise and Florrie squeezed his hand with a grin.

After supper, the men retired to the living room and Lee handed Jim a glass with a finger of bourbon. The older man sipped his drink and began to speak.

"Did ya know the Thirtieth Division is where all the Carolina Guard units serve during wartime?"

"Ayuh, I've been catching up on our unit history."

"Anyhow, what you may not know is my brother Fred and I were activated like you and served with the Thirtieth back during the Great War." Lee took a bigger swallow and continued. "In the last days of the Somme offensive back in '18, not long before the end, the Huns killed Fred and I caught some shrapnel in my hand."

"That's tough," Jim sympathized, not knowing what else to say.

"Something else. Fred is Florrie's real dad, not Mae's husband Don. Just thought you'd wanna to know that."

Jim's nodded slowly as the pieces fell into place.

After the festivities wound down and visiting family left for home, Florrie led Jimmy by the hand to their bedroom. During their time at her sister's home, the girls slept with their mother in the spare bedroom. However, not long after dinner, Florrie put the girls to bed in sleeping bags on the laundry room floor. The only one she wanted to share her bed with tonight was her man.

Locking the bedroom door, the couple shed their clothes in record time and hopped into bed. After a couple minutes of heated necking, Jim was getting on top of Florrie, when the doorknob turned back and forth.

"Momeee! Let me in," Donna cried.

"Sweet pea, go back to bed. Santa won't come if you're awake," Florrie replied, winking up at her husband.

"Mommy, please!"

That didn't sound good.

"OK, wait a minute."

Daddy slipped into his skivvies and Mommy into her nightgown before opening the door. Jumping up into his arms, Donna cried into her father's shoulder.

"There, there, pumpkin. Why are you crying on Christmas Eve?"

"Daddy, I had a really scary dream. I was lost with Lisa and Mommy. We were running away from something really bad. And you were looking for us, but you couldn't find us."

"Donna, I'm right here. I don't live too far away, so I'll always be able to find you."

Running her fingers over her daughter's blonde hair, Florrie added, "It's only a dream, baby doll."

"Mommy, it was so real. Can I please sleep with you and Daddy?"

When Florrie glanced over at him, Jim shrugged back in resignation.

"Me too, Mommy," said Lisa from the doorway.

"All right, hop in," Jim allowed. "But only if you go right to sleep."

When everyone settled into the overcrowded bed, the girls curled up between their parents, Daddy kissed his little angels goodnight, then leaned over to plant a kiss on his big angel.

"I want a rain check tomorrow," Jim whispered.

"It's a date, mister," Florrie giggled. "Mrs. Claus has a special present for Santa."

Tail of the Bank, Scotland
01:33 Hours, 25 December 1940

The clouded southern horizon irregularly brightened and rumbled with the explosions of German artillery. The rumor was the enemy *panzers* would overrun the port sometime on Christmas morning and tonight was their only window for escape.

Officially, the United States was a neutral country in this war and Commander PJ Tigert was a military attaché with diplomatic immunity. However, the U.S. Navy officer was not about to test those legal niceties and end up a German prisoner of war.

Dry swallowing three more bitter aspirin to dull the pain emanating from his destroyed right eye, PJ mulled over the unrelentingly bad war news.

Two days ago, Prime Minister Winston Churchill was killed when his motorcade had the misfortune to run into a *panzer* reconnaissance company. The old lion reportedly went down with a cigar in his mouth and pistol in his hand.

After German paratroopers captured the King of England in a daring snowstorm raid, his sixteen-year old daughter Elizabeth was crowned a few days ago during a somber ceremony at the Glasgow Cathedral. Both the new Queen and her Parliament were evacuating tonight on board a rag tag fleet of surviving Royal Navy ships to form a government-in-exile in Canada.

The U.S. Navy sent a smaller flotilla of destroyers escorting two passenger liners to pull out all remaining American nationals who made it to Scotland. Among those waiting by the piers to board in the freezing drizzle was Tigert's diplomatic group.

Ambassador Joe Kennedy was in a particularly foul mood. Missing an earlier opportunity to flee England because the civilian passenger ship upon which he booked passage declined to enter an increasingly hot war zone, "Yellow Joe" took every opportunity to prove his reputation for cowardice and bitched for days about the delays in his evacuation.

"Look at this complete mess," Kennedy moaned, as he watched groups of ships anchored outside of the port slowly rotate vessels in one at a time to load passengers. "I tell you that if this were an American operation, we would already be underway and halfway home to Boston."

Looking around to ensure none of the English on the docks could overhear, the ambassador added: "These Limeys couldn't organize a God damned square dance! No wonder the Germans are kicking their asses out of their own country."

"Yellow Joe" missed a Brit. In a flash, their English liaison officer stormed around the corner of the building, grabbed Kennedy by his coat and slammed him up against the brick wall, sending the ambassador's round glasses clattering onto the wooden planks of the pier.

"You are one incredible bastard!" spat Captain Walter Mint. "And your nation is an even worse friend. You Yanks abandoned us and now you have the unmitigated gall to complain about our misfortune!"

"Unhand me, sir," whined Kennedy. "I am the ambassador of the United States of America."

Mint's face contorted as if he just swallowed his own excrement. Giving the ugly American one final shove before releasing him, the Englishman stepped back and glared his cousin American officers with tears in his eyes. "My family is dead and buried in the rubble of Plymouth. If you think your families are safe in the States, you're sadly mistaken. Adolf won't stop with England. That damned maniac wants the entire world."

"The English Channel is not the Atlantic Ocean," Kennedy retorted, straightening out his coat. "Hitler will never get to America."

His anger dissipated, the Englishman looked immeasurably sad and weary. The officer simply shook his head and walked away into the dark.

Vividly recalling the gray German warbirds which took the *Nelson* and his eye, Tigert wondered if Mint was correct.

CHAPTER 3

The Berghof, Berchtesgaden, Germany
09:00 Hours, 1 January 1941

The entire *Wehrmacht* high command was seated around the conference table of the great hall, awaiting the arrival of Adolf Hitler. With the fall of England, the *Reich* was now the master of Western Europe and everyone present wondered what news the *Führer* would bring concerning the new year.

Two ceremonial guards opened the doors to the hall and Hitler strode in with an inscrutable look on his face. Raeder smiled inwardly. The man always liked to make a theatrical entrance.

Ever the toady, *Luftwaffe* Field Marshal Herman Goering immediately rose, waited a moment for the rest to join him, then led the assembled brass in giving the Nazi salute and a hearty "*Heil* Hitler!" "My *Führer*, may I be the first to congratulate you on your victory over England," the Air Force commander proclaimed.

Hitler did not reply, instead motioning everyone to retake their seats. Slowly surveying his assembled officers to ensure he commanded their total attention, the *Führer* began to speak. "Providence has restored the Fatherland and raised it to even greater heights. I am an instrument of that Providence. And Providence wills that I bring all of the people under the protection of a new *Reich*. This task remains incomplete."

What does he mean, Raeder wondered? What Germans remain outside of our control?

After a pregnant pause for effect, Hitler answered his unspoken questions. "Gentlemen, our next project is the conquest of *Amerika*."

The Grand Admiral's mind reeled. The United States! Why? More importantly, how?

Hitler smiled at the success of his stagecraft and his pale blue eyes took on an unearthly gleam. "Do not look so shocked, gentlemen. This is the *Reich's* next logical progression." Raising his thumb, the *Führer* counted down his list of reasons. "*Amerika* offers nine and a half million square kilometers of living space for Germans to realize their full potential. This nation is already home to nearly twenty million *volksdeutsche* - the descendants of generations of migrants from the Fatherland. The *Reich* is incomplete without *Amerika*."

Hitler paused his monologue to invite his commanders' reactions.

The Army Commander-in-Chief, Walther von Brauchitsch, led the military's previous opposition against what he privately called "Hitler's adventures" and reluctantly rose to do so again. "My *Führer*, you have offered us a grand vision of the future. My concern is Germany lacks the fuel to conduct this new operation. The war has already run our oil reserves down to dangerous levels. An operation against *Amerika* would easily require twice that amount."

Clearly anticipating this objection, Hitler pounced. "Has the *Wehrmacht* completed plans for Operation Orient, Field Marshal?"

"Uh… yes, the briefing books were delivered to the Chancellery last week for your review," replied von Brauchitsch. "Now that England has fallen, we estimate that it will take a *panzer* army two months to overrun Egypt, Iraq and Persia."

"There is your oil," Hitler noted triumphantly. "I am ordering Orient to commence in March." After the staff officer returned to his seat, the *Führer* looked around the table and challenged the others, "Are there any other concerns?"

Raeder bristled at the man's incredible arrogance. True, Hitler won his previous gambles, but no nation in history had accomplished a trans-oceanic invasion of another major power. Even the British Empire could not hold onto its *Amerikaner* colonies when it enjoyed undisputed command of the Atlantic. This proposal was madness!

Overcoming his customary reserve, the admiral stood and faced Hitler. "I have complete faith in the abilities of my men and their ships, my *Führer*, but even after removing the Royal Navy from the equation, the *Amerikaner* fleet still heavily outnumbers our own. I am unsure how the *Kriegsmarine* can carry out your wishes."

"Is the *Kriegsmarine* still on schedule to start sea trials of the next generation of ships in October?" queried Hitler.

"Yes, my *Führer*. Construction is actually ahead of schedule because of the additional workers you ordered to the yards."

"And once your new ships finish their sea trials, is it not correct that the combined Axis fleets will be twice as large as the *Amerikaner* navy?"

Raeder blinked. "Will Japan and Italy be joining this operation?"

Hitler turned to the rest of the table. "Gentlemen, Mussolini has committed the *Regia Marina* to this project and Foreign Minister Ribbentrop is arriving in Japan as we speak to secure their participation."

Turning back to Raeder, the *Führer* pressed, "Does this address your concerns?"

"There is also a long term issue to consider. The United States is currently engaged in a large-scale ship-building program of its own and will add several dozen modern ships to their fleet by 1943. Germany possesses far fewer ship yards and will not be able to keep pace."

Hitler put on a beneficent smile. "My Grand Admiral, the shipyards of England and France are now at your complete disposal. You may now complete the Plan Z fleet expansion two years early. By 1943, you will command the largest and most modern fleet in the world."

"I could not ask for more, my *Führer*," Raeder sputtered.

"Very good. This operation is code named Case Black and will commence no later than one year from today."

Berlin, Germany
16:32 Hours, 4 January 1941

Arpke felt like he was riding a runaway horse.

No sooner had the *Flieger* Division returned to Germany for rest and refitting, when the battalion commander called Helmut into his office. After returning Arpke's salute, Major Koch fixed the platoon sergeant with a stern face and gravely intoned: "Sergeant, you have been ordered to take the next flight to Berlin and report to the *Führer*."

"Major?"

"The higher authorities have not informed me what the *Führer* has in store for you, but I suspect it has something to do with your making the *Englander* king a guest of the *Reich*." Koch broke into a broad smile and vigorously shook Arpke's hand. "Do us all proud, Helmut."

Then it was off to the races in the company of a dour man from the propaganda ministry. To the airfield for an overnight flight to Berlin. To a tailor to be measured for a dress uniform. To a barber for a haircut and a shave. Then, back again to the tailor to be fitted with the uniform.

The tailor was a tall, distinguished gentleman, who proudly presented Arpke with a dazzling dress white uniform, adorned with all the proper insignia and awards. Helmut stared in shock at the garment on the hanger. This was the uniform of generals!

"Sir, there must be some mistake," he urged the tailor. "I cannot possibly afford this uniform on my pay."

"You need not concern yourself with such things," interjected the man from the propaganda ministry. "Just get into the uniform. We have a schedule to keep."

Standing on a small box as the tailor checked the fitting of the uniform, Arpke considered himself in the dressing mirror. The uniform fit his six foot frame like a glove. A year of combat had melted away the peacetime roundness of his face and sharply chiseled his features. With his straight blond hair combed back on top and barbered to a severe taper on the sides, the sergeant thought he looked like a damned recruiting poster.

Once he appeared the part of the heroic Germanic warrior, Helmut was whisked away to the center of the Nazi state - the Reich Chancellery. Entering through two towering metal doors, the paratrooper was led through a series of cavernous corridors with treacherously slippery polished floors, each larger and longer than the last. The journey ended at the *Führer's* personal study, a room larger than most apartments in Berlin, with walls of blood red marble adorned with a golden eagle holding the Nazi swastika in its talons.

Suddenly, the study doors opened and the *Führer* entered with *Luftwaffe* Field Marshal Hermann Goering in tow. Arpke snapped to attention and clicked his heels in the middle of the room as the man from the propaganda ministry retreated.

The grossly obese Goering waddled up in a dress white uniform like the one made for Arpke, but ornamented with unearned decorations. Although paratroopers were infantry who fought alongside the Army, Goering convinced Hitler to make them a subordinate branch of the *Luftwaffe*. The paratroopers did not return the affection, though, considering their nominal leader a largely useless braggart, derisively nicknaming him "Fat Herman."

"Ah, the hunter from the sky who fetched the King of England for me," nodded Hitler. "Field Marshal, how should the *Reich* recognize such initiative and daring?"

"It is time for the senior sergeant to join the brotherhood of officers, my *Führer*," Goering replied with a toothy grin.

Two *Luftwaffe* officers appeared on each side of Arpke and attached the shoulder boards of a lieutenant to the dazzling white uniform. Helmut shifted uneasily from one foot to the other. Prussian aristocrats are officers, not a barge sailor's son.

Hitler studied him intently for a moment, then spoke. "Lieutenant, the uniform makes all men equal. There are no classes in my new Reich. You can advance as far as your talents and audacity take you."

Arpke stood dumbfounded. How could the *Führer* have known what he was thinking?

"Look at me," Hitler motioned to himself. "I was a common man, a worker, and now I am the *Führer* of all the German people!"

The Führer clasped Arpke's right hand with both of his and stared into his eyes. "Will you serve as an officer of my paratroopers? Will you serve me?"

"Yes, my *Führer!*"

When Hitler released his grip, the newly brevetted lieutenant thrust his right arm forward in the Nazi salute and shouted, "*Heil* Hitler!"

The *Führer* stood with his hands clasped in front of him, beaming at Arpke like a beneficent god well pleased with his servant.

Tokyo Imperial Palace, Japan
11:01 Hours, 8 January 1941

Ignorance. Sheer ignorance! The Imperial Army pressed the Emperor for an alliance with an untrustworthy partner to wage war against a nation about which its generals knew nothing.

Admiral Isoruku Yamamoto bided his time, however, as General and current Minister of War, Hideki Tojo, attempted to sell the new German offer of alliance to carve up the Asian subcontinent, followed by a war on America.

"Your Majesty, war with the *Ameko* is inevitable," Tojo asserted. "The enemy moved their fleet to the Hawaiian Islands, within striking distance of Japan, and are now building a new generation of ships to execute that attack." The general pointed at a large globe his aides placed before the Emperor. "England has fallen, leaving America standing alone. In alliance with Germany and Italy, we have the opportunity to destroy the enemy navy while it is still weak."

Emperor Hirohito nodded toward his Commander of the Combined Fleet. "What is the Navy's view of this offer?"

Yamamoto distrusted Germany and suspected Hitler's proposal of alliance was meant to advance his goals – not those of Japan. In his strange autobiography, *Mein Kampf,* the German leader damned the Japanese with faint praise. Hitler viewed his allies as a second-class race falling between his mythical Aryan countrymen and the Jews and Africans. We Japanese were clever warriors, but reliant upon Germany for scientific advances.

Hitler's foreign policy also sacrificed Japan's interests for those of Germany. Although he repeatedly denigrated the Slavs and communists, Germany enthusiastically entered into a non-aggression pact with Japan's long-time enemy, Russia, in order to divide Poland between them.

Even so, Japan may need the Europeans in the future if the American threat becomes a reality. The *Kriegsmarine* and *Regia Marina* were very useful counterweights to the United States Navy. It would be unwise to foreclose a future alliance.

As he rose and bowed deeply towards his Emperor, Yamamoto decided on an alternate tack. "Your Majesty, I lived for years in the United States and have witnessed their strengths and weaknesses. When they are at peace, the *Ameko* are self-absorbed and neglect their military. However, when at war, they turn their considerable industrial might to the fight and can create large armies and navies in short order."

Walking over to Tojo's globe, the admiral illustrated the difficulty of the Army's proposed conquest of the United States. "Here is Japan. And here, on the other side of the world, is the United States. To conquer this enemy, our Navy must fight across the Pacific Ocean and then our Army must fight across an entire continent to reach the American capital city."

"Better to use diplomatic lullabies to keep this giant asleep," Yamamoto concluded.

The Emperor sat upright, contemplating what he had heard. While his was nominally the final word in all matters of state, the young sovereign understood the military governed Japan. His practice was to proceed cautiously concerning subjects of dispute between the Army and Navy, offering compromise whenever possible. His Majesty once again acted according to form.

"Thank you all for your wise counsel. We do not choose to go to war today, but recognize war may be unavoidable in the future."

Turning to his Minister of Foreign Affairs, Yosuke Matuoka, the Emperor instructed: "You will thank the German envoy for his nation's generous offer and inform him we are considering all options carefully. Meanwhile, continue talks with the *Ameko*, seeking to continue peaceful trade and to dissuade them from military expansion."

In a nod towards Tojo and Yamamoto, Hirohito concluded: "However, the military will commence planning for the war our European allies propose. If negotiations with the United States fail, we must be able to go to war very quickly before the *Ameko* can attack.

The men around the conference table all rose in unison and bowed to their Emperor.

Berlin, Germany
17:05 Hours, 11 January 1941

Helmut was a miserable movie star. The new lieutenant spent the past week as the featured actor in a ridiculous propaganda film, where he played a super soldier capturing an absurd caricature of the *Englander* king. God knows he could not act and the party member in charge sure as hell could not direct. After the twentieth take of the capture scene, Arpke was seriously considering shooting the Nazi, when the *Führer* summoned him to the Chancellery again.

After passing an unhappy trio of Asians in pin striped suits leaving the *Führer* study, the paratrooper found Hitler seated behind the large oak desk, intently studying some papers through a plain set of reading glasses. He looked like a careworn clerk, rather than the heroic *Führer* presented to the world.

Arpke saluted and waited a few moments at the position of attention for some acknowledgment. Looking up from his work, Hitler finally spoke. "Ah, it's you Arpke. Have you ever attended the opera?"

"No, my *Führer*."

"I thought not. You and Field Marshall Goering will attend the opera tonight as my guests." Shaking his finger at Helmut, Hitler lectured, "Before you can truly understand the

German people and my new Reich, you must first understand the operas of Richard Wagner."

Two hours later, Arpke found himself sitting in the *Führer's* box above the stage of the Linden Opera. According to the program, the opera told the story of the doomed love of the medieval knight Tristan and the lady Isolde. How thrilling, Helmut grumbled to himself.

During the slow orchestral prelude, the soldier struggled to stifle yawns. Then, the woman playing Isolde took the stage. A blur of raven hair and fury, her pure soprano voice seemed to reach up to the heavens. Helmut's boredom vanished and he remained entranced through the final act.

During the following reception, the orchestral director, Herbert von Karajan, approached Hitler and bowed. "May I introduce our Isolde, Louisa Grafenberg."

While Hitler lavished praise on Grafenberg's performance, all Helmut could do is stare. The woman was beautiful, with eyes of stunning violet. When the introductions reached him, the soldier could not think of a thing to say, so he impulsively bowed and kissed the singer's hand.

Goering snorted and quipped, "Our brave knight is smitten with the lady Isolde."

Arpke felt his face flush as Grafenberg uncomfortably withdrew her hand.

Hitler quickly came to his rescue with a generous introduction. "Lieutenant Arpke is one of my paratroopers. He recently returned from Scotland, where he captured the King of England and ended the war."

The singer looked at soldier with renewed interest and exclaimed, "How romantic! Your adventure could be an opera."

As they politely listened to the *Führer* opine on the finer points of Wagnerian opera, the soldier and the singer exchanged glances. Director Karajan excused himself when the monologue paused and led Grafenberg away to meet the other guests. The singer looked back briefly and smiled at the soldier.

Hitler gave Arpke a knowing look and suggested, "I think it is time you were off as well."

"Yes, my *Führer*," the soldier eagerly agreed.

Helmut quickly found the bar. Working steadily on a tall beer, he considered how to approach an opera star and wondered whether she would even deign to speak with him.

"I see you have also managed to escape your duties, Lieutenant."

The soldier turned to find the singer standing with a glass of champagne and without her director. Helmut grinned and rediscovered his power of speech.

"Miss Grafenberg, I hope you did not think I was too forward before. Uh… Well… I have never met an opera singer before. After watching you play a royal lady for hours, it just seemed to be the right thing to do."

Grafenberg laughed. After spending the past hour entertaining the staid patrons of the Linden, this awkward young officer was a joy and a relief. The wealthy and powerful men who attended her performances considered Louisa little more than an ornamental songbird to show off to their aristocratic peers. This soldier seemed to be genuinely interested in her.

"I am a doctor's daughter and hardly royalty. Formalities are so tiresome. Would you please call me Louisa?"

"As you wish, Miss Grafenberg…I mean Louisa," Arpke corrected. "Ah, I am sorry. I have been in the military for so long that formality is second nature. My name is Helmut."

"You are forgiven," Louisa laughed. "Now, I am dying of curiosity, Helmut. Tell me how on Earth you came to be at the Linden Opera in the company of our *Führer*."

Generally, the soldier did not like talking about himself. With the singer, however, the words came far easier than expected. He told her about Belgium and England, while minimizing his own role. Helmut did not want to repel this lovely woman by bragging.

"I envy you. You have enjoyed more adventure over the past year than I have in my entire life," sighed Louisa. "I dearly love singing, but I have spent nearly all of my years in practice or at performances. I have never been more than 100 kilometers from Berlin."

The soldier considered his response over another swallow of beer. "I do not know how to say this. I am good at what I do, but only a sadist enjoys the killing."

"The killing…" Helmut muttered as his expression darkened. "The cost of war's 'adventure' is high. I have lost so many friends, men I have known for years." Looking down at his beer, the soldier softly admitted, "I hope the war is over."

"I hope so as well." Taking one of his hands in hers, the singer asked, "What will you do now?"

"My work in Berlin ends tomorrow, then I will rejoin my unit in Stendhal."

One of the ushers approached and politely interrupted, "I'm sorry, Miss Grafenberg, but we are closing now."

"Thank you, Erwin. The lieutenant will be leaving shortly."

After paying his bar tab, Helmut turned back to Louisa. "I've really enjoyed our time together. Uh… If you do not mind, I would very much like to write you."

"What a wonderful idea!" Louisa agreed, writing her address on the back of an opera program and handing it to him.

"You know, Helmut, Stendhal is not that far away," the singer winked. "You could visit Berlin again."

The soldier half bowed his head and replied, "I would like that even more."

Louisa bounced on her tiptoes and sent him on his way with quick kiss. Flushing in surprise, Helmut could only nod and smile.

The soldier left the singer feeling like an idiot, but his walk down the streets of Berlin was a stroll on the clouds.

Fort Jackson, South Carolina
09:03 Hours, 20 February 1941

Jim Fraser was royally tired of being treated like an interloper by the unit good old boys. When the lieutenant transferred from the Massachusetts to the South Carolina Guard, the battalion commander tucked him away as the Bravo Company executive officer and his fellow officers largely ignored the Boston Yankee.

Things got worse after Congress activated the state Guard units and placed them under regular Army command. After a few months of evaluation, the Army removed old and incompetent guardsmen and replaced them with regular Army men from other states. Captain Michael O'Hara of New York became the new Bravo commander and chose Fraser to serve as his third platoon leader.

The lieutenant heard the grumbles about Yankees taking over a South Carolina unit, but ignored them, believing fair leadership and tough training would bond the men over time.

Fraser began his new command by meeting with his platoon sergeant. A short and powerfully built man, Wolf Fleischer was a Charleston butcher by trade. Because the prior lieutenant considered the Guard to be a social club, the sergeant served as the *de facto* platoon leader for years.

As Fraser laid out how he intended to train the men, Fleischer's non-committal silence was only interrupted by the occasional "yes sir." The lieutenant paused for a moment and turned the tables on his senior sergeant by asking for his evaluation of the platoon. Fleischer was plainly surprised an officer wanted his opinion, but didn't hesitate to give it, methodically breaking down the strengths and weaknesses of each of his men.

Fraser was impressed. The man knew his business. Now, for the more delicate business of setting out their respective roles. "Sergeant, I've done my homework and know how important you've been to the men. But, from now on, I command the platoon, while you and the other sergeants run it. Will that be a problem?"

"No sir, but can I ask ya a question, LT?"

"Shoot."

"Do you work for Fraser & Sons Dredging?"

"I used to manage their operations in Charleston. It's a family business."

"Do you know Tommy Douglas from Hotel Company?"

"Ayuh, he worked on one of my crews."

"Tommy got a deferment to keep working on that dredging crew."

"I heard that. What's this all about?"

"Well, if ya don't mind, sir, why didn't *you* take a deferment?"

Jim leaned back in his desk chair and decided to confide in his platoon sergeant. "I didn't think it was fair for me to dodge service when everyone else had to leave their regular lives and families. Besides, I think this job is important. Don't you?"

"Yes sir," Fleischer nodded without expression.

Over the next week, the men hammered out a training schedule and started to work their troops hard. But the grumbling persisted. While walking by the barracks before breakfast, Fraser's ears perked up when he heard the word Yankees used in a less than a complimentary fashion. Then, he recognized Private Jack Morris adding he would be damned if he'd follow any orders from the new lieutenant. We'll see about that.

During maneuvers later that morning, the Fraser chose Morris's squad to lead a mock attack on a hill. In the middle of the squad's advance, Fraser halted the exercise, declared three men wounded and ordered them to lay down. Then, he looked Morris in the eye and ordered him to pick up the heavy BAR automatic rifle carried by one of the 'wounded' men. The private dropped his gaze and started to walk up the hill.

"Morris, get over here on the double!" Fraser hollered.

The platoon leader felt a hand on his shoulder and looked back to see Fleischer. "Sir, this is sergeant's business. Lemme handle it."

The platoon sergeant emphatically pointed at Morris and then at the ground in front of him. The soldier trotted over with a grin on his face.

"Private, your lieutenant gave you an order. Pick up that weapon and git back in line."

"Awww Wolf, we can't let these Yankees boss us around."

Fleischer plowed through Morris like a bowling ball picking up a spare, knocking him hard to the ground. "Get your ass up and at the position of attention!"

The platoon sergeant looked around at his gawking men and growled, "Listen up and listen up good. You're in the regular Army now, not the Guard. No more weekend warrior grab-assing."

Fleischer pointed at Fraser. "This is your platoon leader," Y'all will address him as 'Sir' and finish whatever he tells you to do before he finishes telling you to do it."

Fleischer jabbed a thumb into his own chest. "I'm Sergeant Fleischer, not your neighbor, Wolf. Got it!"

"Yes, Sergeant!" the shocked troopers chorused.

"One more thing y'all need to get through your thick rebel sculls. This is not the Confederate Army or the Union Army. This is the United States Army," Fleischer instructed. "Your daddies served with men from all over the country during the Great War and you will too. Is that clear?"

"Yes, Sergeant!"

The platoon sergeant pivoted to his platoon leader. "What are your orders, sir?"

"What do you say we finish taking this hill?"

A couple of the men winked at their lieutenant, then they all gave him a hearty rebel yell as they turned back towards the hill. This may be the U.S. Army under a Yankee officer, but they were still Carolina rebels. Jim could live with that.

Suez Canal, Egypt
16:23 Hours, 23 March 1941

Lieutenant General Erwin Rommel floated above the desert like a war god looking down from the heavens as his plans played out on Earth. From the vantage point of his *Storch* reconnaissance plane, the *panzer* general could see for kilometers all around. On one side of the cockpit, Royal Navy ships were slowly moving down the Suez Canal as if on parade. On the other side, the *panzers* of his Fifteenth Light Division were closing in to cut off the enemy escape.

Panzer Army Kleist's initial objective during Operation Orient was to capture the Egyptian port of Alexandria and bag the Royal Navy's Mediterranean Fleet. Rommel's XIV *Panzer* Corps spearheaded the advance along the Mediterranean coast from Libya into Egypt.

The *Englander* and colonial troops in North Africa stubbornly refused to surrender along with the mother country, but they also declined to stand and fight. Instead, the Tommies would hold a coastal town just long enough to slow the German advance, then pull out to the next collection of adobe buildings.

Rommel quickly tired of the enemy delaying tactics and swung his entire corps south into the desert to get behind the Tommies and trap them against the northern coast. The enemy took flight and it was a sprint to see who would reach Alexandria first.

The Tommies narrowly won the race. The *panzer* general's men reached Alexandria just hours after the enemy passed through and found the port abandoned. The Royal Navy used the time purchased by their troops to evacuate. ·

Rommel was left to his own devices to figure out where the enemy fleet went. The *panzer* corps advanced so quickly, they outran the *Luftwaffe* air cover. Unlike his *Storch*, which could land and refuel in the open desert, the rest of the German reconnaissance planes were still tied down to their airfields back in Libya.

Pouring over the maps with his staff, Rommel quickly concluded there was no Mediterranean port outside of German control capable of supporting a fleet of that size. The Royal Navy must be using the Suez Canal to escape to their India colony. There was still a chance to take them! The general ordered his divisions to drive straight away to a stretch of the canal south of the town of el Qattara, with instructions to sink as many ships as possible and plug up the enemy escape route.

Rommel did not know much about naval ships, but enjoyed supreme confidence in the power of his *panzers*. Today, that assurance was misplaced.

A quick order over the intercom to his pilot brought the general back down to Earth for a closer look at the battle erupting along the canal. The division's lead *panzers* halted in a ragged line a half a kilometer from the canal. From this close range, the gunners could hardly miss the two large freighters lumbering down the waterway in front of them. However, the small fifty millimeter main guns of the Mark III *panzers* were only pockmarking the sides of the ships. The comparatively puny vehicles had no hope of sinking or even slowing these big ships.

After the freighters sailed past, a Royal Navy battleship and heavy cruiser took their places opposite the *panzers* and unleashed hell. Naval gun rounds up to the size of small cars hurled the desert and nearby vehicles up into the air like a child tossing his toys around a sandbox. Rapid-fire anti-aircraft guns shredded steel as if it were cardboard. His suddenly vulnerable *panzers* would not long survive this onslaught.

Snatching the microphone off the aircraft cockpit wall, the corps commander persistently radioed the division headquarters until someone finally answered. Rommel took over as the forward spotter for the entire division artillery group. This *ad hoc* arrangement seemingly took forever to implement. The general's fire orders bounced from the division headquarters to the individual artillery battalions, before the howitzers could adjust and fire. Precious minutes passed before he could fire for effect on the desired targets.

The two Tommy freighters enjoyed no room to maneuver in the canal and sailed right into the artillery barrage. Unlike the small caliber tank guns, the high explosive howitzer shells immediately started taking a toll on the ships, tearing up their decks and setting them ablaze. Still, the ships doggedly sailed forward, hoping to hang on long enough to move past the pounding artillery as they did with the *panzers*. Just as it appeared they might escape, a lucky round obliterated the bridge of the trailing freighter. The decapitated ship plowed into the canal bank, then gradually turned sideways, blocking the entire passage.

The Royal Navy was not about to allow this turn of events to stand, however. The heavy cruiser broke contact with the *panzers* and accelerated towards the freighter. As it approached, the warship slowed slightly, then rammed the aft of the stricken ship. Furiously churning the water, it slowly began to push the burning hulk out of the main channel.

As Rommel's *Storch* flew over the ships to get a closer look, the world suddenly filled with a blinding light, followed by a breathtaking boom. The aircraft hurled up into the sky like a leaf in a gust of wind, floated for a moment and then fell again in an uncontrolled spin. The pilot struggled mightily for a long minute with both hands wrapped around the stick before regaining control of his bird. Only after the *Storch* leveled off, did the *panzer* general start breathing again and released the death grip he had on the pilot's seat in front of him.

The scene below was a horror show. The stricken freighter was apparently an oil tanker. When deck fires reached the cargo below, the vessel transformed into gigantic firebomb. The resulting detonation tore apart and immediately sank both the freighter and adjacent cruiser. Only the superstructures of the dead ships remained above the burning water.

The mission of blocking the canal accomplished, a handful of surviving *panzers* withdrew to the west, leaving behind nearly a hundred smoking or burning vehicles.

The desert and the canal merged into one large funeral pyre.

CHAPTER 4

Charleston Bay, South Carolina
16:07 Hours, 21 April 1941

As the sun slipped under the city skyline, Katarina Kolotsiev tacked the *Empress Catherine* back across the bay and towards the marina. Charleston offered a magnificent port and the sum total of the U.S. Navy's presence were the four ships under construction at the naval yard. The location would be ideal.

Her mission complete, Kat released herself to the pure joy of sailing on a beautiful day. Papa's one true love was sailing. Under the admiral's tutelage back in England, Katarina became a proficient yacht captain and the first woman admitted to the Bristol Channel Yacht Club. On her twenty-first birthday, Papa presented her with the beautiful J-Class boat she commanded today.

The *Empress Catherine* provided her with the means to escape England and arrest by MI-5. The voyage from Bristol was initially nerve wracking, as the yacht passed numerous Royal Navy vessels steaming towards the English Channel in a futile effort to turn back the German invasion. Thankfully, none of the warships were concerned with the civilian yacht flying British colors headed in the opposite direction.

Cuba offered sanctuary and luxury. Mama's Crawford Trading Consortium enjoyed extensive tobacco holdings on the island. As an exile from Soviet Russia, Papa also had the foresight to disperse the family money into a variety of foreign banks and purchase a hacienda in Cuba in case another involuntary move became necessary.

Although her new home was beautiful and the money plentiful, Kolotsiev quickly succumbed to boredom. In England, she had a purpose. What would she do with her life now?

Kat mulled the question over a daiquiri and a fine cigar at the La Floradita, when the answer walked through the door. While he exchanged his rumpled tweed for a wrinkled white linen suit and a pasty English complexion for a tropical sunburn, George Roberts was the same unremarkable man who could pass transparently through life. The perfect spy.

"I'm so happy to see you well," Roberts said, sitting next to her. "Bristol was a nasty business."

The tall woman drew on her cigar and launched a plume of rich smoke to the ceiling. "Occasionally, life only offers bad choices."

"Yes, but how one deals with them says a great deal about her." Pulling out a linen handkerchief, Roberts patted his brow and took a swallow from a glass of water brought by a waiter. "In any case, I have a proposition you may find interesting. Is there a place we could speak in privacy?"

Kolotsiev finished her daiquiri and invited Roberts to come to her hacienda for dinner at seven. When she started to provide directions, the spy smiled and said he knew where she lived.

After a pleasant dinner of carnitas and plantains, the pair retired to the porch and watched the stars come out. Roberts broke the silence. "Miss Kolotsiev, the doctor whom I represent would like to commission you and your yacht to survey the ports along the eastern seaboard of the United States. Because of the currently strained relations between Europe and America, my client cannot perform this survey himself. As an English refugee, you could do so fairly easily."

Kat pondered the proposal. Survey the east coast of the States? Good heavens, the *Führer* must be considering an invasion. To be part of such audacity!

"Assuming I was willing to undertake such a venture, the Americans will need a reason to issue me a visa."

"I understand the Marblehead, Massachusetts to Halifax, Nova Scotia yacht race is still being held this summer. An accomplished captain such as yourself might like to compete in the contest. Of course, from Cuba, you would need to sail up the east coast to do so."

"*Herr Doktor*" had done his homework.

"There's one additional problem," she noted. "My English crew left for the States and Canada shortly after we arrived. Have you and your client considered where I might obtain another?"

"My client is nothing if not efficient. I can provide you with a crew of three experienced yachtsman. They're from the continent, but all speak impeccable English."

No doubt German *Kriegsmarine*, Kolotsiev guessed.

"Your proposal is very intriguing. However, I have two conditions before accepting."

"And those would be?"

"First, I must be satisfied your crew can expertly handle the *Empress Catherine*. Perhaps, a shakedown cruise around Cuba?"

"Of course. You will not be disappointed."

"Second, and this condition is non-negotiable, I command both my yacht and the mission. Your men will follow my orders."

For the first time since she met him, Roberts was at a loss for words.

"George, I will not go on this mission as window dressing. You know I can handle myself."

"I don't know how this will be received."

"You are a persuasive man," Kat winked. "I have faith you can convince '*Herr Doktor*' this arrangement gives his mission the best chance for success."

Nearly two weeks passed before Roberts returned to the hacienda with the promised sailors. Her conditions were acceptable.

Kolotsiev steered the *Empress Catherine* around the Charleston peninsula into its final approach to the docks. After they enjoyed a well-earned dinner at the yacht club, she would draft her report and hand it off to "Harry" for transmission over the shortwave hidden in the galley. "*Herr Doktor*" should be very interested in this one.

Fort Knox, Kentucky
20:18 Hours, 27 June 1941

George Patton was very pleased with how the evening was going. Right up to the point where he was asked to open his mouth.

Chief of Staff George Marshall traveled to Fort Knox to inspect the new tank command and surprised the hell out of the Second Armored Division commander by accepting his invitation to dinner with his wife Bea.

Patton was sure Marshall didn't like him. During social occasions over the years, when George laced some comment with a profanity, the higher ranked George would respond with a pointed comment concerning the proper decorum expected from officers. More recently, Patton spent months in division command before the Chief of Staff awarded him the second star standard for the position. Still, Marshall was his boss and the man who would decide if Patton would ever ascend to higher command. Consequently, every meeting between them was a job interview.

Bea made a wonderful meal of pot roast and red potatoes, with which George paired an excellent French red wine. A wine cellar was one of the perks of being the wealthiest officer in the Army with excellent taste.

After Marshall thanked Bea for the dinner, the men retired to Patton's study for brandy and cigars. Taking a sip of the wine, the chief of staff's eyes wandered over to the desk covered with books and papers.

"What are you working on, George?"

"General, I'm writing an analysis of the recent German campaign in the Middle East."

"In this job, I'm always busy and never able to keep up with my reading," Marshall complained. "Can you summarize Operation Orient for me."

Another test. The chief was fully briefed every time Hitler took a dump.

Patton succinctly broke down the entire campaign in less than five minutes, from the push to the Suez Canal, cutting off the British Mediterranean Fleet, to the subsequent offensive through Iraq and then Persia. The Germans now possessed enough oil to do just about anything they damned well pleased.

"And what lessons do you draw from Hitler's latest move?"

Patton puffed on his cigar. George doubted the Chief of Staff would like what he had to say, but what the hell. No guts, no glory.

"The Axis powers will go to war with the United States within the next year."

The normally unflappable Marshall's cigar almost fell from his opened mouth. "George, that statement is outrageous, even by your standards. Would you care to elaborate?"

"Of course, sir. All of the Axis powers have demonstrated an ability to project power overseas. Germany and Italy against England and now the Middle East. Japan against the entire East Asian coast."

"Go on."

"The fascist leaders' hunger for conquest is stunning, even by the measure of Alexander the Great and Genghis Khan," George continued. "After the Bolsheviks ruined Russia, the United States is the only power left in the world which can stop the Axis once we rebuild our military. Hitler and Tojo will not give us that time."

Patton could see the wheels turning behind the Chief's eyes, looking for weaknesses in his reasoning.

"Projecting force across the Pacific and Atlantic Oceans is an order of magnitude more difficult than anything these nations have accomplished to date," Marshall prodded.

"True, sir. I'm an old horse cavalry officer and don't claim to be an expert in naval warfare. But I can count ships and the balance of power decidedly tipped against us since England fell."

Marshall stared back at Patton in silence for what seemed like an eternity, before finishing his brandy and stubbing out his cigar. "Well, George, thank you for a very interesting evening. Would you please thank Bea again for that delicious dinner?"

"Of course, sir. Let me walk you to your car."

Well George, you probably kissed your career goodbye with that stunt.

Reich Chancellery, Berlin, Germany
10:03 Hours, 12 June 1941

Adolf Hitler leaned over the map of the United States laid across the conference table like a diner contemplating the first course from a buffet.

"My *Führer*, the decision of where to land the invasion is a tradeoff," began Admiral Raeder. "The *Amerikaner* fleet is based primarily between their states of Virginia and Massachusetts, positioned to defend the northern political and industrial centers. Thus, our most promising landing zones are also the furthest away from our ultimate objectives."

Hitler continued looking at the map in silence. The admiral was not even sure if the *Führer* was listening, but he plowed ahead with the briefing anyway. "From south to north, the suitable ports are Charleston in their state of South Carolina…"

"Wait," Hitler interrupted. "Tell me about Charleston."

"Charleston is an intriguing option. The port can receive our Army, the ship yards can service our Navy and, amazingly, there are no naval or ground forces defending the city. So far as we can tell, the nearest *Amerikaner* Army units are located 190 kilometers away at a base called Fort Jackson. It is the safest landing zone, but also the furthest from our objectives."

"How do you know these things?" Hitler queried.

"Our *Abwehr* intelligence service infiltrated a team sailing a yacht along their east coast and identified several ports capable of supporting the landing army."

"And are these reports reliable?"

"Extremely. The team was able to enter most of the ports and report their firsthand observations."

The *Führer* started speaking distantly, perhaps only to himself. "Incredible. Providence itself must be taking a hand in this."

Hitler straightened up and bid Raeder take a seat by one of towering windows of the study. The *Führer* sat across from the admiral and looked out the window into the courtyard for a long while before speaking.

"I once had a good friend who served in the Merchant Marine during the Great War. He spent the first years of the war trapped in the port of Charleston on board the *S.S. Liebenfels*. Then, *Amerika* entered the war and interned him in their state of Georgia until the armistice."

Impatiently waiting out another of the *Führer's* interminable monologues, Raeder suddenly enjoyed an epiphany. Hitler was recounting his own experience! The rumors were true. Hitler did not serve on the Western Front as trumpeted in the propaganda, but instead served as a common sailor. This was why he was so supportive of the *Kriegsmarine*.

Hitler looked up at the ceiling, as if recalling a distant memory, then continued. "My friend learned…and this is what I found fascinating…he learned *Amerika* is not only populated by millions of *volksdeutsche*, but the *Amerikaner* in their south share our understanding of the Jewish menace and the necessity of racial purity."

The *Führer* leaned forward in his chair and fixed Raeder's eyes with that intense stare he used to make an important point. "Do not concern yourself with the distance to our objectives," Hitler reassured. "When we land, both the *volksdeutche* and southern *Amerikaner* will greet us as liberators."

With an air of compete certainty, the *Führer* commanded: "My Grand Admiral, the *Kriegsmarine* will land my troops at Charleston."

Hyde Park, New York
16:29 Hours, 3 July 1941

MAGIC once again turned General George C. Marshall's carefully constructed world upside down.

MAGIC was the War Department code name for Bill Friedman's team of cryptologists tucked away in the Washington Munitions Building. Friedman broke the Japanese diplomatic code back in '39 and his latest intercepts were pure dynamite.

MAGIC was also one of the most closely held secrets in the United States military and its intercepts were never discussed over telegraph or telephone. Marshall and his Navy counterpart Admiral "Betty" Stark drove up to Roosevelt's Hyde Park home and "summer White House" to personally deliver the news to the Boss and the Secretary of State.

Mrs. Roosevelt was a delightful hostess. After leading the men back to her husband's office, Eleanor handed them tall glasses of lemonade. The cool drink was just the ticket after a long trip. The President's wife smiled shyly at Marshall's thanks and quietly closed the door behind her.

After bidding the officers to take seats around his cherry wood desk, Roosevelt asked, "Well gentlemen, what news do you have for me today?"

Marshall rose and walked over to the large globe by the President's desk. Turning the globe to the Middle East, the general began his report.

"Mr. President, back in March, the Germans launched an offensive they code named Orient against the remaining British forces in Egypt and cut off most of the Royal Navy's Mediterranean Fleet at the Suez Canal. A handful of ships made it to safety in India, while most ended up scuttling off of Palestine to keep their ships from falling into enemy hands."

Sweeping his hand across the globe, Marshall continued, "Over the past three months, the German spearheads have captured Arabia, Iraq, and now Persia. The Nazis now control all the oil in the Middle East."

"None of these ill tidings are new, George," Roosevelt shrugged. "I read the reports you send me."

"I'm just setting the table, Mr. President. What's new is that Japan may join Operation Orient."

The President closed his eyes and rubbed his forehead, then looked back up at his Chief of Staff. "Where is this coming from?"

"Mr. President, MAGIC has intercepted a series of dispatches from the Japanese ambassador in Berlin, General Hiroshi Oshima, back to Tokyo. Oshima has always been an enthusiastic advocate for a closer alliance between Germany and Japan. However, over the past week, Oshima has suggested that

Germany would welcome a Japanese advance from Indochina into India."

Secretary of State Cordell Hull jumped in, asking, "And what was Japan's response?"

"Tokyo was noncommittal, Mr. Secretary."

The dignified sixty nine-year old ambassador slowly rose from his purple cushioned chair. Reaching back into his Tennessee mountain vernacular, Hull addressed the President, "Dammit, it is time to fish or cut bait. If we do not act firmly here, these fascists will divide up the world between them."

"What do you suggest?" asked Roosevelt.

"It is time to take Japan off the American tit. Issue an executive order seizing all Japanese assets in the United States and impose a complete oil embargo until Japan agrees to withdraw from mainland Asia. Without money or oil, the Japs will have to capitulate."

"Mr. President, I'm afraid Japan's reaction to an embargo will be far more pointed," Admiral Stark responded. "The Japanese do have alternative sources of oil to their south in the Dutch East Indies. With the Royal Navy effectively out of the war, the only force in their way is our Pacific Fleet."

"If we do nothing, war will be equally inevitable." Hull insisted. "We need to use the economic leverage we have now."

Marshall reinforced his Navy colleague. "Sir, as you know, we are not prepared for war at this time. The National Guard divisions will not be fully trained and supplied until next year and the Navy's new ships will not come on line for nearly two years."

"If war is inevitable, let it be at a time of our choosing," the general pled.

"George, I would normally agree with you and Betty, but time is something we no longer appear to have," Roosevelt frowned. "Tell me, does the Japanese Army have the capability to take Indochina and India?"

"With Great Britain out of the war, I would say they do," Marshall admitted.

"Do you believe Japan will accept Hitler's invitation to join Operation Orient?"

The Chief of Staff felt trapped. The Japanese exploited France's defeat to take Indochina. Now that Britain was lost, he saw no reason why Japan would not press its advantage against Singapore and India as well.

"Yes sir, I believe Japan will likely join Orient."

"Unfortunately, that is my belief as well," the President nodded. "Cordell, draft an executive order for a complete economic embargo against the Japanese Empire for my signature as quickly as possible."

Tokyo Imperial Palace, Japan
18:22 Hours, 16 July 1941

The Commander of the Combined Fleet knew a summons to the Imperial Palace during the evening generally meant bad tidings. What he did not yet realize was the opportunity these tidings would offer.

The Emperor entered the palace conference room to the bows of all present and motioned toward Yosuke Matsuoka. "What news do you have for us, Minister-san?"

"Both bad and good, your Majesty. Excuse me, but allow me to start with the bad."

Matasouka proceeded to describe the new United States cessation of all trade with the Empire, most importantly trade in oil and iron. This embargo would remain until Japan withdrew all of its forces from mainland Asia.

"What happened to cause the *Ameko* to attack us in this way?" the normally quiet Emperor exploded in uncharacteristic public anger.

"This was not part of their public pronouncement, but their Secretary of State informed to our ambassador the United States was aware Japan intends to invade the Asian subcontinent and meet the Germans in India."

"Did the ambassador tell the secretary this is a lie?"

"So sorry, yes he did, your Majesty, but there was no reasoning with him."

Matasouka visibly shook as the Emperor slammed his opened hand on the conference table. "May I complete my report, your Majesty?"

Hirohito swung his hand toward the minister in disgust.

"Your Majesty, the German ambassador presented a further offer to enter into their proposed alliance. The Germans now control all oil production across the Middle East and are willing to ship whatever oil Japan needs, so long as we provide sufficient naval escort."

Admiral Isoruku Yamamoto snapped his head over to ensure he heard the diplomat correctly, then rose and bowed. "Your Majesty, pardon me for speaking out of turn. Minister-san, when did the Germans say they are prepared to start oil shipments?"

"By the end of the summer, Admiral-san. German tanks managed to overrun the oil production facilities with little or no damage."

Yamamoto remained standing in silence as all eyes fell upon him. This offer changes the entire strategic calculus in the Pacific. A plan the admiral developed and rejected during the Spring was now possible...even desirable.

"Admiral Yamamoto, do you have something to add to this discussion?" the Emperor inquired.

"Yes, your Majesty. Please pardon my rudeness and be patient with me as I think out loud." The Admiral quickly ordered his thoughts and continued. "The *Ameko* supply of our oil was always an implied threat against our economy and our fleet. By acting on that threat, the United States has demonstrated it desires war with Japan."

"General Tojo, may I use your map?" Yamamoto asked.

"Of course, Admiral-san"

"All of our contingency planning to meet this threat, required much of the Navy and Army to move to the south and east to secure alternative supplies," the Admiral noted. "If Japan obtains these supplies from Germany, then our forces are freed from these diversions to meet the true threat – the United States."

Beginning with the Emperor, the men around the conference table stared back at him in various states of shock. Over the past years, Yamamoto was the most persuasive advocate for diplomacy and peace with the United States. However, even the admiral's patience with the Americans reached an end.

"When we last met in this room, Admiral-san, you eloquently stated the difficulties in winning a war with the United States," the Emperor observed. "What changed your position?"

"The *Ameko* moved their fleet to Pearl Harbor in order to project power against Japan and into the rest of the Pacific Ocean, your Majesty," Yamamoto explained, pointing at the Hawaiian Islands on the map. "Now that our military is freed from securing alternative oil supplies, I propose to attack and invade the Hawaiian Islands with the full force of our Navy and with the Army units previously dedicated to other operations.

"Once our combined forces take Pearl Harbor," the Admiral concluded, "Japan controls the Pacific and the United States no longer poses a threat to the homeland."

"What about the *Ameko* Army in the Philippines?"

"Once the enemy navy is driven from the Hawaiian Islands, the Philippines will be little more than a self-sustaining prisoner of war camp."

Delighted with the navy's unexpected support for a military solution, Minister of War Tojo immediately rose in agreement with Yamamoto's plan.

"Is this the opinion of all of Our ministers and commanders?" the Emperor asked.

All nodded in assent.

"Then it shall be so," the Emperor commanded. "Minister Matasouka, please make the necessary arrangements to conclude this alliance with the nations of Germany and Italy. Minister Tojo, please execute everything necessary to bring Admiral Yamamoto's plan to fruition."

Reich Chancellery, Berlin, Germany
14:22 Hours, 19 July 1941

I will never get used to this place, Erich Raeder thought, as his footsteps echoed off the blood red stone of the Chancellery hallway. The Grand Admiral entered the anteroom to the *Führer's* study to find his Army and Air Force counterparts softly conversing in a corner. None of the commanders had a clue as to why they were there.

What game was Hitler playing?

A ceremonial guard opened the study door and bade the officers to enter. Hitler stood behind his desk with his hands clasped in front of him. The *Führer's* serious expression was belied, however, by a twinkle in his eyes.

After his officers took seats around the desk, Hitler nonchalantly began, "Gentlemen, it is time to move onto the second phase of our invasion planning – coordination with Japan."

Raeder sat back in his chair and gaped at the *Führer*.

Over the months since Hitler announced Case Black on New Year's Day, the preparations for the Atlantic crossing proceeded smoothly. Thrilled with their large role in the operation, the *Regia Marina* had no objection to Raeder drafting the crossing plans without the usual diplomatic wrangling. To spearhead the crossing, the German fleet was now weeks away from putting its new generation of carriers and battleships to sea for mechanical shakedowns and combat training.

However, even the combined *Kriegsmarine* and *Regia Marina* fleets could not execute the invasion alone against the United States Navy. This would only be possible in coordination with the Japanese fleet and its massed carriers. In a secret report for the Raeder's eyes only, the fleet's intelligence arm, the *Abwehr*, reported Japan declined Hitler's offer of alliance some months ago and were unlikely to change their minds. Thus, the admiral long ago concluded all of his meticulous planning was for nothing.

Hitler grinned and rubbed his hands together in self-satisfaction like a child who delighted in proving his parents wrong. Somehow, the man changed Japan's position without the military's knowledge.

"My *Führer*, what did Japan agree to do?" the Army chief of staff inquired.

"Our oriental allies have pledged to attack and destroy the *Amerikaner* Pacific Fleet, then invade the Hawaiian Islands before the end of the year."

Raeder reached up and rubbed his chin. This pledge was far more than he anticipated from the sons of the rising sun and fundamentally altered his own calculations. "If Japan takes the enemy Pacific Fleet out of the equation," the admiral noted, "*Amerikaner* resistance to our Atlantic crossing could be less than anticipated."

The *Führer* nodded with a knowing smile and allowed his admiral to continue.

"I suggest we give Japan sufficient time to complete their operation, my *Führer*, and postpone our crossing until the Spring of 1942."

"Exactly so," Hitler agreed, "but no later than March. The Army must have the summer to complete the ground campaign."

"Yes, March would work well," Raeder agreed. "Very well, indeed."

CHAPTER 5

Camp Perry, Ohio
14:12 Hours, 23 July 1941

Army Private First Class Billy Deal was only concerned with two results – his and those of marine Mark Billing. None of the other competitors were close to the pair.

When the scores for the 300-yard event were announced over the firing range loud speakers, the soldier notched a very respectable nine hits out of ten rifle shots, but the marine was perfect. Damn!

Billing looked over at Deal and winked. The two men were tied again for the overall individual lead in the National Trophy Team Match, with one more event to go.

The twenty-year old soldier could barely recall a time when he was without a rifle. Deal's pop was a gunsmith in the mining town of Cripple Creek, Colorado. When other boys went to work pulling gold out of the ground, Billy was either working as an apprentice under Bill Senior, learning how to build and repair firearms, or off hunting deer and elk in the hills to sell to the local taverns.

Deal soon concluded he preferred shooting rifles to working on them, but hunting was not much of a living in Depression-era Colorado, so he enlisted in the Army on his eighteenth birthday.

The cocky recruit could do nothing right in the eyes of his drill sergeants until he reached the firing range. Deal only missed one shot during basic training and that was due to a malfunctioning cartridge. Suddenly, the drills took Billy off KP duty and ordered him to tutor his fellow recruits on the finer points of marksmanship. When his platoon earned the highest score in the battalion during the final range training, the new private could do no wrong.

Getting up to speed with the Hawaii Division on Oahu was a bigger challenge. During field exercises on the hot and steamy island, sweat which normally evaporated in the arid Colorado mountains, now ran into his eyes and soaked his uniform. Billy's white skin turned red, then a dark brown, as any excess fat he carried from stateside melted away.

What remained unchanged, though, was Deal's ability with a rifle. After firing perfect scores during the annual range qualifications, then only missing one shot at the division marksmanship competition, he earned a promotion to private first class and a trip to the National Trophy Match at Camp Perry, Ohio. The competition was Billy's chance to prove he was the best damned shot in the military.

Deal felt the familiar calm return as he aimed *Springfield* rifle down range at the 600-yard target during the last event. The metal rifle sight nearly covered the distant sheet of paper at this range.

Billy ceased his shallow breathing for a moment, then pulled gently and steadily on the trigger. At this extreme long distance, the slightest movement would result in a miss. The eventual discharge of the round kicking the rifle stock back into his shoulder almost came as a surprise. The soldier methodically repeated this process ten times in a perfect expression of faith, knowing if he did everything correctly, the bullets would hit a target he could barely see.

Deal's faith was rewarded with a perfect score. During the entire existence of the National Match, no other shooter had come close to hitting all ten shots at this range. Billing came in second by tying the previous range record of seven hits.

The marine was the first to shake the soldier's hand and slap his back, promising him things would be different at next year's match. Neither marksman knew this would be the last National Trophy Match either of them would attend.

Ariake Bay, Japan
08:13 Hours, 5 September 1941

Commander Mitsuo Fuchida's competitive juices were flowing as his *Nakajima* B5N bomber rapidly closed on the *Ameko* freighter anchored out in the bay. The aircraft popped up after he released the nearly one ton torpedo into the ocean. As his pilot pulled the bomber away, Fuchida looked back at the ship to see if their aim was true.

Today, the flight instructor and his carrier pilots were enjoying the rare privilege of using live torpedoes against three old freighters consigned to scrap. Even better, they would do so in an even rarer competition against their land-based brethren from the 701st Air Group, led by Lieutenant Commander Joji Higai.

So far as Fuchida was concerned, the sea was the sole province of carrier aviation. He could see no sense in tying down precious torpedo bombers to land bases, when carriers could project air power across the Pacific. However, the Navy possessed more pilots and aircraft than they did carriers.

Ah well, Fuchida and his carrier pilots had little to fear in this competition. His pilots trained constantly and the instructor himself compiled nearly 3,000 hours in the air.

This morning's news made the subsequent competition all the sweeter. Not long after dawn started filling his modest office, Fuchida looked up from the day's training plan to find his long-time friend, Minoru Genda, standing in the doorway grinning at him.

"Fuchi, you are still as ugly as ever."

"You're just jealous you cannot grow such a fine specimen of male facial hair," Fuchida shot back, while stroking his short stylish mustache with a forefinger.

Both men broke into laughter and hugged one another.

Fuchida and Genda graduated together near the top of their classes at the naval academy, then the naval staff college a decade later. Fellow pilots saw the pair as visionaries, while the hidebound establishment considered them insane for their outspoken opinions that battleships were dinosaurs and the Navy of the future would feature fast carriers and their far-reaching aircraft. All recognized the officers' brilliance, however. Both men advanced quickly up through the ranks – Fuchida in command and Genda in planning.

"What on Earth are you doing here, Genda? I thought the brass had you chained to a desk at headquarters planning the ultimate triumph of the Imperial Japanese Navy."

"So they have…and those plans are almost ready for execution."

Closing the office door, Genda took a seat and motioned Fuchida to do the same. In a low and serious voice, his friend confirmed many of the rumors running wild through First Air Fleet. "Last Spring, Admiral Yamamoto tasked me with developing a contingency plan for a mass carrier air attack on Pearl Harbor to destroy the *Ameko* fleet."

Fuchida looked back in disbelief. The admiral was not generally considered a carrier advocate.

"Wait, it gets better," his friend continued. "In July, Yamamoto not only ordered my plan executed before the year's end, but assigned me to begin joint planning with the Army for an invasion of Oahu."

"Long past time," Fuchida grunted. "I advocated this option years ago."

"And you have a role to play as well, my friend," Genda winked. "When I recommended you to command the air attack, the admiral agreed."

The flight instructor leaned back in his desk chair, his mind reeling. He had dreamed of this moment since joining the Navy almost twenty years ago. To finally realize such an honor…

"Why, thank you for the recommendation, Genda," his friend pantomimed. "You are quite welcome, Fuchi. It was my honor."

Fuchida quickly refocused. "I'm sorry, Genda-san. You have done me a great honor and I cannot adequately express how grateful I am. I always expected this moment, but was overwhelmed when it finally arrived."

His friend rose and shook his hand. "All is forgiven, Fuchi. Congratulations on your promotion. With my plan and your skill, how can we lose?"

How indeed? Fuchida thought, as he watched his torpedo run straight and true into the middle freighter. The instructor then circled above and watched his carrier pilots each score a hit on one of the freighters. Perfection.

By the time the 701st launched their runs, the target ships were sinking fast. Fuchida was pleasantly surprised at the prowess of his competition. Only three of their torpedoes missed and one of those misses was because the ship sank before the fish could arrive.

Back at the naval airfield, the pilots bowed to one another in mutual respect. On reflection, Fuchida acknowledged these land-based pilots would be a worthy supplement to the Navy's First Air Fleet. Because there were no airfields within range of the upcoming battle for Oahu, though, he could not envision such an eventuality.

Defeating the arrogant *Ameko* fleet would be the sole honor of carrier aviation and he would lead the attack.

U.S.S. Maury, 48 miles west of Oahu, Hawaii
15:13 Hours, 27 August 1941

Boarding the destroyer was like coming home. "Bull" Halsey spent much of his career as a tin can skipper and may well have retired there if carriers weren't the ticket to an admiral's stars.

Halsey's excuse for taking a vacation from his flattop for a cruise on the *U.S.S. Maury* was to shake down the destroyer's new SG radar system. These new electronic gizmos could change everything.

The carrier *Enterprise* and her escort ships left Pearl Harbor yesterday and were on maneuvers west of the port. The Admiral gave the Maury's captain a big sector to conduct a radar search and the destroyer took off after the task force this morning.

Halsey didn't want to crowd the petty officer operating the radar system. One thing that always ticked him off was some senior officer looking over his shoulder when he was at work. Officers didn't get much more senior than a visiting admiral.

Instead of being intimidated, though, radarman George Jones was thrilled to show off his new toy to the big boss and proceeded to give the old man a crash course in radar theory and operation. The kid had a gift for gab and Halsey soon felt like a boy listening to an episode of Flash Gordon on the radio.

Shortly after Jones ran out of things to say, the new radar got its first hit. "Captain, I have a signal at about 14.5 miles, bearing 351 degrees," reported the petty officer.

The signal did not look like much to Halsey. Just a white blip on a black screen. "Mr. Jones, can you tell anything else from that signal?"

"Well, sir, the signal is not on a normal commercial traffic route, so most likely we are not looking at a merchantman. If the signal is coming from the task force, we're probably looking at Enterprise because it's the largest vessel."

Fascinating.

"In the next few minutes, we should close near enough for the system to start picking up signals from the smaller escort ships," Jones concluded. "Then we'll know for certain." Sure enough, additional blips started appearing around the original signal. Maury found the task force.

"Captain, can you slow and match the heading of the task force on the radar?"

"Yes, Admiral," the captain confirmed, before relaying the necessary orders around the bridge.

"Now, have your wireless contact *Enterprise* with the code word "Nashville." Bring me the report when it comes in."

As he had hoped, Enterprise confirmed Maury found the larger ships in the task force, while the carrier's radar never spotted the smaller destroyer. Outstanding!

At fifty-nine, Bull might be one of the older admirals in the Navy, but his child-like thrill with gee whiz technology never aged. His mind raced with the possibilities offered by this new gadget. Over the past year, the Navy equipped the big battleships and carriers with search radars, each with a range of about fifteen miles or about twice the range of a set of binocular-assisted eyeballs. Now that radar was reaching smaller ships like the *Maury*, Halsey could send his destroyers several miles out from the battle formation and exponentially extend a task force's radar coverage. While radar wouldn't replace long-range scout planes, it could see through the crappy weather which blinded pilots.

Halsey clapped Petty Officer Jones on the shoulder and handed him a cigar. "Good work, son. Damned good work."

Formosa Island, China
22:37 Hours, 6 September 1941

Captain Otozo Hayashi cast a displeased glare at his infantry company slogging down the jungle trail. His seasoned China veterans ground stoically ahead, but the new draftees were plainly struggling. The recent arrivals were tough men from the coal mines of the Owari Province, but the Imperial Japanese Army was an entirely different taskmaster and the company commander was one of its sternest teachers.

No one slept during the past three days of maneuvers, a blur of jungle navigation, water crossings and night bayonet attacks.

Hayashi concluded the exercise with a thirty-kilometer speed march back to camp. A tropical downpour drenched the final leg of the march. Feet sloshed in waterlogged boots, softening and tearing skin into blisters and then open wounds. The captain could not have planned better weather.

As the camp and the end of the march came into sight, the men's pace quickened slightly at the prospect of an end to their misery. Time for one last lesson.

The company commander bellowed out an order, the sergeants echoed down the column, for the company to double their pace. While his much-abused legs and feet screamed with pain, Hayashi ran to the front of the column to lead his company around the camp.

Before the column made it halfway around the fence line, the new men started to fall out of the ranks, gasping and stumbling in utter exhaustion and agony. The sergeants fell on the stragglers like cats, beating and kicking their charges back into the formation. No one else dared leave his place again.

When the column finally rounded the camp and returned to the entrance, the captain gave the order to resume quick march. The sergeants again descended on their men, screaming at them to return to a precise formation.

The company halted on the parade ground and executed a painful left face toward a wooden platform. Hayashi slowly marched up the platform stairs, concentrating on maintaining his officer's demeanor and not betraying any sign of weakness. Once atop, the captain surveyed his command for a long moment before speaking.

"Men, you are *kogun* - soldiers of the Emperor. You are members of a pure race imbued with warrior spirit. No physical obstacle can stop you." The captain paused and pointed at his head. "But do not let your mind defeat you. Never relent until you achieve victory and, even then, only when your commanders order you to stop and rest."

"Yes sir!" his company roared in one voice.

"My *kogun*, we will soon be at war with America. These *Ameko* are soft mongrel dogs. Barely human beings at all. You will drive through them like a bayonet on your way to victory!"

Following the lead of their sergeants, the men repeatedly thrust their rifles into the air in response, bellowing over and over: "*Banzai! Banzai! Banzai!*"

The captain nodded back in satisfaction. His company distinguished itself in China and would soon do so again.

Honolulu, Oahu, Hawaii
23:08 Hours, 6 September 1941

Billy Deal and Mike Morgan knocked back their third whiskies of the night, then chased them down with healthy swallows of beer. Returning his glass to the mahogany bar top, Billy absent-mindedly picked at the healing blister on his hand as a boozy warmth spread across his body.

"That ain't nothing. No siree," Mike bragged, holding up his own hands for inspection. "Now, these are blisters!"

"I thought you coal miners from Hillbilly Holler would be used to digging," Bill ragged, before taking another swallow of beer.

"Screw you. What would you know about real work? Army life has gone and made me soft."

The regiment just finished another week practicing deployment to Oahu's northern coast to repel a hypothetical Jap invasion, which seemed to exist only in the imagination of the new general. The routine was always the same. Hurry to the Schofield Barracks motor pool after breakfast, then wait an hour or so for the trucks to take them up to the beaches. Everyone would find the old hole they dug and refilled in a couple weeks before, then get to work again shoveling out the same old sand.

Hotel Company lucked out by being assigned to defend the division rifle range at the Haleiwa Air Field. If the general's war ever arrived, the wide packed sand surface was the perfect kill zone. Any Japs who surfed in on those blue and white waves breaking on the northern end of the field would sub in for the usual paper targets.

Better yet, the Army Air Corps would not tolerate a bunch of ground pounders digging up their landing strip in the name of training, so the men were limited to digging a single foxhole at the edge of the field, rather than the trenches Dog Company were digging. Break my heart, Billy thought.

"Ol buddy, I'm pretty sure the boys have the art of digging holes pretty much down. What did the First Sergeant say when you asked him about jungle training?"

"Top made his opinion of humping in the boonies very clear," Billy scowled. "I believe his exact words were: 'Shut the hell up and get back to your hole before I make you dig a second one.'"

"Too bad. We might have been able to scout out some new places to hunt."

Deal and Morgan arrived at Schofield Barracks with the same group of replacements. Mike came in second on the rifle range, but he was the undisputed champion at talking trash. When the West Virginian regaled the squad with a story about bagging a ten-point buck from four hundred feet, Billy discovered a hunting buddy.

Whenever they could finagle a weekend pass off base, the men would spend the days hunting the jungle around the twin mountain ranges dominating the east and west of Oahu, and the nights getting drunk down at Hotel Street in Honolulu's Chinatown.

After his triumphant return from the National Match, the company commander gave Deal the second stripe of a corporal and a section of three men to run – one of whom was Morgan. The friends were now inseparable on and off base.

"Billy, do ya think the Japs would actually invade Hawaii?"

"I've got no idea," Deal shrugged.

"I don't believe it. What would give the slant-eyed midgets the idea they could screw with Americans?"

Billy let the question pass unanswered. The Japs didn't appear much size-wise to the six foot Deal, but they worked like mules on the sugar and pineapple plantations surrounding the base. The corporal suspected soldiers like Mike were misreading them.

Morgan looked over at the shrinking line of GIs and sailors waiting for their turn at the hookers, then polished off his beer. "Well, ol buddy, duty calls. You coming?"

Billy was revolted at the thought of getting a quickie and maybe a much longer lasting case of the clap from some nasty whore after God knows how many other guys had a go at her.

"Nah, I'll be at the bar until you're done."

After Mike gave him a drunken salute and staggered off, Billy ordered another whisky and beer to keep him company.

CHAPTER 6

Highway 52 northwest of Cheraw, South Carolina
14:38 Hours, 16 November 1941

Major General George Patton was exactly where he was meant to be – leading men into battle. Well, maybe not a real battle. That would come soon enough with the upcoming war. Rather, the closest thing the military could devise during peacetime – a sprawling war game across the Carolinas between Army units with real tanks and guns.

In this exercise, a mostly mechanized "Red Army," including Patton's Second Armored Division, faced off against an infantry "Blue Army" twice its size. The exercise planners further handicapped the Reds by making his tanks advance over forty miles before reaching the Blues.

George wasn't about to allow official cheating deny his boys the victory they deserved. The night before, he staged a column of tanks followed by infantry on trucks along every road in the division sector. As soon as the referees gave the go ahead, his units charged at full speed due east towards the Blues.

The tank general knew this pell-mell advance would string his tanks out for miles along these country roads and reduce the punch of the lead units when they hit the Blues. But he also knew a surprise sucker punch could take down the biggest of men.

Patton threw out the manual during a similar exercise in Louisiana a couple months ago, when his boss ordered Second Armored to advance 350 miles to execute a frontal attack on the city of Shreveport. He never saw any sense in charging straight into the guns of an enemy who was lying in wait like the dumb ass British did during the charge of the light brigade. Instead, the general swung his tanks west into Texas in a wide loop to attack the city from the rear, paying cash out of his own pocket to refuel the vehicles at local service stations when they ran low on gas.

The surprise attack ended the Louisiana exercise days early and earned him glowing newspaper headlines across the country. Patton had every intention of reproducing those headlines here in South Carolina. Then, Marshall would have no choice but to give him command of the new armored corps.

Believing a general should always command from the front, Patton placed his armored car with the lead battalion of tanks. Well aware their perfectionist boss was watching their every move, the battalion executed a nearly perfect advance to contact.

Soon after the battalion turned south on Highway 52, their radios came alive with reports of Blues dead ahead. The tanks smartly deployed into a line and accelerated when they saw the "enemy" infantry marching up the highway. When the command to "Charge!" crackled over the radio, Patton ordered his driver to stay hard on his tankers' asses.

Hot damn, this should be fun!

Highway 52 northwest of Cheraw, South Carolina
14:39 Hours, 16 November 1941

Lieutenant Fraser was convinced his troops were ready for anything. Third platoon transformed into a regular Army unit faster than any of their National Guard peers. In his admittedly biased opinion, his men were now the best platoon in the battalion.

Jim brought his experience managing Fraser & Son Dredging to the job of platoon leader, methodically training his soldiers, like he did his old dredging crews, with a plan covering all the skills necessary to perform each job. After watching the platoon in action during the summer battalion exercises, Captain O'Hara ordered the rest of Bravo Company to adopt Fraser's training plan and placed third platoon in the lead during maneuvers.

In the lead is where the platoon found itself when the massive Carolinas wargame kicked off. Before dawn, Fraser's men crossed the Pee Dee River as part of a six division "Blue Army" and were the first to reach the Highway 52 objective a few miles to the west.

Bravo was then ordered to move up the highway to gain contact with the neighboring Forty-Fourth Division to the north. The march was relaxed. The "enemy" Reds weren't supposed to arrive until the next morning. The platoon leader was more concerned about avoiding friendly fire when his men came into contact with the other Blues.

About an hour into the movement, the Jim's ears perked up at the growing sound of heavy engines ahead of them. The Forty-Fourth was an infantry division with only a handful of trucks. That racket didn't sound like trucks.

The lieutenant trotted up the middle of the highway to get a better look. As he reached the lead squad, a line of tanks poured over the rise a couple hundred yards away and made a bee line straight for them!

Fraser stood transfixed. This was the first time he'd ever seen a tank in person. The fourteen ton armored vehicles were nearly twice the height of a soldier. Although they rode on tracks like a bulldozer, the tanks closed on Jim and his men with the speed of a car. Snorting diesel smoke and kicking up clouds of dust, the damned things looked like metal monsters out of a science fiction story. Jumping Jesus!

Struggling to suppress his own fear, the lieutenant screamed, "Everyone follow me to the woods now!"

After setting what he was sure was a new land speed record in boots, Fraser dove behind the nearest tree and turned back around. Only the lead squad crashed into the woods around him. The rest of the platoon was running for their lives in all directions.

Everyone but one. Peters from first squad stood in the middle of the highway, rooted in place by terror. Someone down the tree line yelled, "Joe, get your ass off the road!" Instead, the corporal just plopped on his ass in the middle of the tarmac and hugged his knees.

Jim watched in horror as the tanks roared past, not one of them taking the time to swerve. Damn them all to hell! Didn't they know this was just an exercise?

After the last of the Reds drove out of sight to the south, Fraser sprinted back towards the highway, yelling for Peters to sound off. But there was no response from the dust cloud billowing around the road.

When the breeze finally dispersed the haze, the lieutenant found his lost trooper still sitting on the tarmac, staring down the highway with a distant expression, stinking from the piss and crap in his trousers.

Watching the medic giving Peters the once over, Jim took off his helmet and scratched his curly brown hair. What a fricken circus! If this were the real thing, most of his platoon would be dead right now and it would all be his fault.

No way will the bastards catch us by surprise again. No way in hell.

Berlin, Germany
06:07 Hours, 17 November 1941

Helmut quietly slipped out from under the covers and put on his trunks. Louisa lay asleep like an angel, with her long raven hair splayed out over the white pillow.

The first light of day was sneaking in past the closed curtains of the bedroom. While his singer was used to sleeping through the morning after nightly opera performances, the soldier was trained to rise before dawn. It was a hard habit to break, even after only a couple hours of sleep.

Helmut strolled into the kitchen to see what Louisa kept for breakfast. Thankfully, her pantry was fully stocked. After putting some coffee on the stove to brew, he started slicing bread and let his mind wander.

The soldier and singer exchanged letters for months before Arpke was finally granted leave to visit. After greeting him at the train station with a smile and kiss, Louisa whisked Helmut away on a whirlwind tour of her beloved Berlin. Bypassing the landmarks, she showed him the cafes, parks and shops she frequented, cheerfully chatting about the memories which made each place special.

In turn, the singer took every opportunity to ask about her soldier. Touring the imperial capital with a famous artist made Helmut feel provincial and unworthy. He was a commoner from a small Prussian port town. Of what interest could his life be to her? However, when she took his hand and looked at him with those lovely eyes, the story of his life flowed out.

At the end of the first two evenings, the singer dropped her soldier off at the visiting officer quarters. Last night, she asked him up to her flat. They snuck hand-in-hand past the ground floor flat of the apartment manager giggling like a pair of teenagers coming back home after a curfew set by the girl's father. The famous and famously unmarried lead singer of the Linden Opera could not be seen bringing a man up to her bedroom after midnight.

Helmut 's first time with Louisa was hardly the slow and romantic affair he imagined back at the base. After an increasingly urgent kiss by the front door, she led him by the hand into her bedroom. The singer suddenly turned and pushed the soldier back onto the bed, pulled down his trousers and mounted him. The veteran of many far less pleasant battles succumbed to the onslaught of her love in only a few brief moments. After catching their breath, the couple undressed and took their time properly exploring each other, inside and out, until falling asleep hours later.

Smiling at the memory, Helmut returned to the bedroom with a tray of breakfast and softly kissed Louisa awake. As she sat up yawning, he handed her a steaming cup of coffee.

"You are a doll," Louisa smiled. "I was wondering where you went off to."

The soldier spread butter and jam over a slice of bread and handed it to his singer. "I had to gather provisions to keep up my strength. You wore me out last night."

"Oh really? Well, I am not through with you yet, Lieutenant!"

Louisa's lips tasted sweet and sticky as they rolled together again on the twisted sheets. When they joined this time, their bodies moved together as if they had known one other for years. Helmut took his time until Louisa arched her back with a soft moan and pulled him closer. He eagerly followed her lead.

Afterward, Helmut lay back with his eyes closed while Louisa gently ran her finger around his ear. "What are you thinking, darling?"

He turned toward her, kissed the tip of her nose and looked into those violet eyes. "I am thinking that I love you very much."

She ran her fingers down his arm and gently replied, "I love you too."

Helmut felt a warm glow spread as he marveled. This beautiful and accomplished woman loves me! He felt like a little boy on Christmas morning opening the gift he wished for all year long, but never expected to receive.

As he pulled the singer close and smelled the musky perfume of her hair, the soldier considered what to do next. Two months ago, Major Koch called the regiment's officers into the briefing room and ordered them to rotate out on leave to see their families. The official reason was the unit was to deploy on an extended training exercise after the New Year's holiday. The veterans looked at one another knowingly. The paratroopers were going back to war.

Helmut wanted to spend his life with Louisa, but did not have time for a proper courtship. The soldier was terrified that some wealthy aristocrat would steal his upper class love away while he was away at war slogging through some foreign hellhole. On the other hand, if he moved things along too fast, she might break things off.

Oh hell.

"Honey, let's get dressed and go for a walk."

Clouds were gathering on the horizon and threatened rain as the couple walked into the park. Helmut sat with Louisa on a nearby bench, took her hands and screwed up his courage to speak.

"I know everything between us has happened so fast, but I am sure about how I feel about you. I never want this feeling to end." She squeezed his hands tighter. "Louisa, will you marry me?"

Those violet eyes started to tear up and she looked down at their hands. Oh no, I have ruined everything!

"I'm sorry. Don't cry," Helmut pled. "I know you deserve someone better than me, but I swear I will be good to you."

Louisa looked up and put her fingers on Helmut's mouth. "Hush darling. You are the best man I have ever met. Of course, I will marry you."

As the soldier joyfully kissed his singer, the first thunder rumbled in the distance.

Highway 52 northwest of Cheraw, South Carolina
10:07 Hours, 17 November 1941

Watching four of the big *Lee* tanks carefully making their way down the dirt path through the woods, the lieutenant grinned to himself. Payback is a bitch.

The night before, Captain O'Hara gave third platoon a football field size section of forest to defend, but no way of stopping the Red tanks. The brass sent the division anti-tank guns elsewhere, leaving his men to fend for themselves.

Jim Fraser and Wolf Fleischer spent the night brainstorming what to do the next morning. The lieutenant half-jokingly suggested the platoon steal a section of the guns. His sergeant chuckled and shook his head. Stealing the guns from the sleeping artillery chuckleheads was doable, but the refs wouldn't let a bunch of infantry dogfaces use them during the maneuvers.

Jim looked through the trees at the stars for divine inspiration and unexpectedly received some. As the sergeant handed him a steaming tin of coffee, the lieutenant pitched his idea. Wolf laughed his ass off, drawing looks from a couple troopers huddled around a fire. The sergeant pointed at the curious troopers and sent them to the company first sergeant to fetch the tools to carry off his boss's plan.

As the lead tank trundled past, Jim ducked a little lower in his foxhole. There were two or three Red soldiers trudging behind each of the vehicles. Clearly unhappy to be eating dust and diesel smoke, the Reds were neglecting to check out the woods around them. They'll pay for that carelessness in about five seconds.

The crack and crash of the big pines dropping across the road to the front and back of the column of tanks was louder than Jim expected. The Red troopers nearly jumped out of their boots, staring wildly all around for more trees falling their way.

The woods came alive with the snap and pop of the blank rounds Fraser's squad fired from well-hidden positions along the south side of the path. A few seconds later, Fleischer and three other hand-picked men applied the *coup de grâce* to the Reds by scrambling up the sides of their tanks, yanking open the unlocked turret hatches and chucking dummy hand grenades inside.

A major wearing a white arm band quickly walked out of the woods, waving his arms above his head and yelling: "Cease fire! Cease fire!"

Early this morning, Fraser convinced a maneuvers referee at battalion headquarters to come out to his position for the day, promising the major something special. Jim was confident he delivered.

A red-faced captain jumped off the lead tank and stormed up to the referee. "Dammit sir, the Blues cheated by chopping down those trees. That's illegal!"

Not about to allow the Red officer to get in the final word, Fraser hopped out of his foxhole and presented his defense. "Major, these trees are anti-tank obstacles straight out of the manual. Nothing in the rule book says my men can't use what nature provides."

Jim's men added some rebel yells to punctuate the point, until hushed by their sergeants.

Struggling to keep a straight face, the referee pulled a copy of the maneuver rules out of his satchel and flipped through the pages before giving his verdict. "Lieutenant Fraser is correct. There's nothing in the rules which prohibits using trees as obstacles."

Before the Red officer could argue the point, the referee cut him off. "Captain, next time, put your infantry out front so they can sniff out ambushes before they happen. I rule your tanks are disabled and you've suffered 50% casualties."

Fraser decided to press his luck. "Sir, can I capture these tanks and drive them up to our front lines to assist in the defense."

"No sir!" yelled the horrified tank officer, his face turning another shade redder. "I'm sure as hell not allowing the infantry to destroy my tanks." When it appeared as if the referee was seriously considering the proposal, the captain concluded with a whine, "Please Major, I'm signed for these vehicles."

"Interesting idea, Lieutenant," the referee observed, "but you can't take the tanks. What I want you to do is move these trees so the Captain can use his vehicles to practice evacuation of the wounded back to the field hospital."

When the trees were moved and the Reds withdrawn, Fraser gathered his boys together for a quick after action pow wow. After making couple minor corrections concerning the execution of the ambush, Jim congratulated his happy troopers.

"See boys, there's nothing to be scared about. Hunting tanks is easy and fun!"

Cheraw, South Carolina
15:21 Hours, 17 November 1941

I'll be damned if I let the sons of bitches stop me, General Patton seethed. Haven't these dummies watched the Huns as they rolled over Europe and the Middle East? Antitank guns can't stop tanks!

The Carolina war game referees disagreed this morning, ruling the Blue guns around the city of Cheraw destroyed or disabled half of Second Armored Division's tanks attacking from the northwest.

Well, Patton wasn't about to allow this World War I thinking stand in his way. Time to grab the Blues by the nose and kick 'em in the ass.

The general succinctly gave orders to his brigade commanders gathered around his armored car. Division scouts reported a gap in the Blue defenses to the southwest of Cheraw. Combat Command A would attack again from the northwest as the enemy expected, while he would personally lead Combat Command B in an attack through the gap and into the city. Patton then made it abundantly clear to the CCB commander that his people would stay on their division commander's tail and not stop for anything unless he stopped first.

Taking back roads, sometimes little more than rutted dirt tracks, the general skirted outside of the Blue defenses for several miles before hooking a left onto Market Street leading into Cheraw. The gap reported by the scouts was not quite open, however. Three thirty-five millimeter antitank guns occupied sandbagged positions on the left, protected by a handful of infantry. As expected, a referee stepped out into the street and waved his hands overhead for the column of armored vehicles to stop.

Oh, hell no! When the armored car started to slow, Patton whacked his driver's helmet and pointed to a street on the right with his swagger stick, hollering, "Step on it!" One after another, CCB vehicles careened through the side streets following their seemingly possessed division commander, until he made his way back to Market Street in the center of Cheraw.

Once safely past the Blue guns, Patton instructed his driver to slow down and started to look for the enemy command post he suspected was located somewhere in the center of town. Even going fifteen miles per hour, an armored column trundling down the main street of a small city is a truly impressive sight for the uninitiated. Pedestrians on the sidewalk mostly smiled and waved, delivering a cheer here and there. One wide-eyed woman drove her Ford sedan onto the sidewalk. George thanked her for making way with a tip of his helmet.

Finally, Patton spotted the Blue headquarters in a city park and ordered his driver to go straight across the grass to the cluster of green Army tents. A company of a dozen tanks completely surrounded the command post, while the rest of the column halted on Market Street.

The Thirtieth Infantry Division commander, Major General Henry Russell, walked out of the largest tent to see what the racket was all about and found Patton glowering down from his armored car.

"Henry, you are my prisoner."

"The hell you say, George."

As the division commanders amicably bickered over who captured whom, a staff car drove up and a flustered lieutenant colonel wearing a referee's armband emerged to salute the generals.

"General Patton, I signaled your unit to stop two miles back there."

"Sorry Colonel, in all that maneuvering, I must have missed you."

"Sir, you can't just drive past a defensive position."

"And yet, here we are."

The referee glared back at Patton, but held his temper. Getting into arguments with general officers tended to be a very poor career move. "Very well, sir, I rule that eighty percent of your vehicles were destroyed or disabled back at that defensive point."

"That was damned good shooting for three pop guns parked at the side of the road," growled Patton. "OK, Colonel, that means twenty percent of my vehicles broke through to this division headquarters. Say this company of tanks right here in the park?"

Happy the general accepted the plainly absurd ruling without chewing his ass, the referee conceded the point. "Yes sir, that's a reasonable assumption."

Turning to his CCB commander, Patton ordered the vehicles in the street to return to the Second Armored motor pool for maintenance before the next day's maneuvers. Then, George put on his finest shit-eating grin for the referee and Blue division commander.

"Now gentlemen, shall we discuss the terms for the surrender of the Thirtieth Infantry Division?"

Cheraw, South Carolina
15:54 Hours, 17 November 1941

Watching the countryside fly by from the passenger seat of a truck, Lieutenant Fraser wondered what the frick was going on?

Less than an hour ago, Bravo Company received orders to pull off the line and move out to an undisclosed destination. Instead of marching, though, a couple dozen trucks arrived and loaded up the men. Captain O'Hara told the platoon leaders he would brief them when the company arrived, but everyone needed to be ready to fight.

The convoy booked all the way across Cheraw city and deposited their passengers on the far side of town. Why here? Had the Reds broken through to attack them from the rear?

The trucks squealed to a halt and O'Hara came jogging up to Fraser. "Jim, third platoon will defend this city block."

"Do you know the 'enemy' situation, sir? What should my men expect?"

"I haven't been briefed," the company commander shrugged. "Just be ready for anything, I guess."

Typical Army.

"Captain, this block is made up of stores," Fraser observed, sweeping his arm down the buildings. "Do I have the authority to enter them to set up defenses?"

"No, you can't go shopping" O'Hara chuckled. "Just position your men in a vaguely military manner around the buildings and wait for further orders."

So, third platoon did what soldiers do best - hurry up and wait. After the sergeants spread them down the block, the men awkwardly stood around the shops with their rifles slung over their shoulders, trying to stay out of the way of the townies making their way down the sidewalk. The novelty of the Army war game had long since worn off for the civilians, who mostly ignored the loitering soldiers.

After a monotonous hour, the Reds finally arrived from an unexpected direction. The groan of heavy engines joined by the clattering of tracks on the tarmac grew behind them. The Red tanks somehow made their way into the center of town. The infantry officer had to hand it to the armor boys. The fast tanks kept showing up in the most unexpected places.

Glancing up and down the street, Fraser decided nothing was likely to happen there. Let's have some fun and give the tankers another surprise. The lieutenant assembled two of his three squads and left the other one to hold their assigned "defensive line." The squads jogged down opposite sides of Market Street, halting at the end of every block to look both ways for tanks. They finally found the metal beasts idling in the city park.

Jim incredulously scoped out the enemy position. About a dozen tanks were facing the division headquarters tents erected in the center of the park, leaving their asses facing third platoon. No one was providing rear security.

Normally, the lieutenant would have crept up on the tanks using whatever cover was available. This time, he took a more direct approach. Figuring the tank engines would drown out the sound of running boots, Jim ordered his men to charge the chowdaheads.

As the line of soldiers trotted up on the unsuspecting tankers, Jim spotted an armored car sporting two giant silver stars of a division commander and changed course. This was the son of a whore who led the tanks which almost ran down Peters on the first day of maneuvers. *The brass hat is mine!*

Fraser hopped onto the rear of the vehicle, then tapped the leather jacketed general on his shoulder with the barrel of his rifle. When the startled officer turned his balding head around, the lieutenant politely informed him he was a prisoner of war. The rest of his men swarmed over the remaining vehicles with whoops and hollers.

"Lieutenant, unhand the General and get off that vehicle!" screamed a lieutenant colonel with a referee's armband. "All of you, off the tanks and be quiet."

Uh oh. Fraser hopped off the armored car, saluted the referee and identified himself.

"Lieutenant Fraser, didn't you hear me order a cease fire after the capture of the headquarters here?" demanded the referee.

"No sir, my platoon was not part of the headquarters defense."

"Well, now you know. Gather your men and get back to where you came from before I put you on report."

"Yes sir!" Fraser said. "Everyone on me. Let's move out."

As he turned to depart, the lieutenant found himself face to face with a glowering General George S. Patton. "Fraser, have your squad leaders return with the men. I would like a word with you."

Jim felt his stomach churn. *Out of the frying pan and into the fire.*

"Son, you said your boys weren't part of the headquarters defense. Where the hell did you come from?" Patton demanded.

"General, my platoon was stationed along Market Street about a half mile down the road," Fraser replied, pointing to the east.

The general's scowl turned into a look of befuddlement. "And why on Earth did you decide to join this party?"

"We've been tangling with your boys for the past two days, sir. I just marched to the sound of your tanks."

Patton stared at him for a moment, then launched into a belly laugh. "Lieutenant, ignore the referee. You and your men showed true initiative just now and caught me with my pants down."

Braced for an ass chewing and maybe being put up on charges for leaving his assigned post, Jim was at a loss for words.

"I wish I had a few more like you," the general sighed, looking over at his ambushed tankers. "Hey, wait a minute! How would you like to join Second Armored Division?"

"Thank you for the kind words and the offer, sir, but I don't want to leave my boys now that they're beginning to shape up."

"Damn straight!" Patton exclaimed, clapping Jim's shoulder. "Well then, you better rejoin your troops."

Fraser saluted and strode back down Market Street, feeling ten feet tall.

Berlin, Germany
20:48 Hours, 18 November 1941

"Helmut is not making this easy," Louisa muttered as she made her way down the hall to Papa's library. Her fiancé insisted on following tradition and asking for her father's blessing to marry. She was worried Papa would say no.

Dr. Werner Grafenberg was a well-respected physician, who treated many of the capitol's most prominent families. While her parents steadily pressed Louisa to marry over the past ten of her twenty-eight years, they were unwilling to settle for just any husband. Papa was determined his accomplished daughter would marry up in Berlin society.

Louisa was certain her fiancé was not the kind of match Papa had in mind. Her soldier was an orphan from the Prussian town of Gradenz. His mother died a day after delivering him. A few years later, his father was killed when the river barge on which he served crushed him against a dock. His Aunt Teresa raised Helmut until he came of age and joined the *Luftwaffe*.

Dr. Grafenberg was seated by the fireplace, reading a journal by its flickering light.

"Papa, can we talk?"

"Of course, sugar plum. What is on your mind?"

The doctor removed his reading glasses and motioned his daughter to take the opposite seat.

Louisa wrestled with how to begin and decided the direct approach was best. "Papa, a young man asked me to marry him and I have accepted."

Sitting up in his chair, a now stern father raised his voice slightly: "You have, have you? And do I know this young man?"

"No… Well, you may know of him from the papers or newsreels. My fiancé is Lieutenant Helmut Arpke, the paratrooper who captured the *Englander* king."

Dr. Grafenberg gawked at her in disbelief, then rose to pace the room.

Louisa described how Hitler introduced her to the soldier, then exaggerated their very short courtship, describing how they corresponded constantly and met occasionally over the past months before he proposed on Saturday.

"Oh Papa, I wanted to properly introduce Helmut to the family, but he could only leave his base in Stendahl with almost no notice for a day or two at a time. I was not expecting him to propose so soon."

"Tell me about the young man and his family."

As she rehearsed in her mind over the past two days, Louisa embellished Peer Arpke as an officer of a ship, but truthfully offered his son Helmut as a self-made military officer.

"Daughter, you are too old to be engaging in hero worship."

"You know better than that!" Louisa snapped back.

The doctor sighed and rubbed the back of his neck. "A junior military officer? I wanted so much more for you."

Louisa got up from the chair and took her father's hand. "Listen Papa, Helmut is a good man and I have grown to love him more than any other I have ever met. He is on leave in Berlin for two more weeks and wants to meet the family to ask you for my hand."

"Please say yes, Papa," Louisa pled. "If you love me, say yes."

The doctor's expression softened and he forced a smile. "You know I could never deny you anything, sweetheart. I will be fair with your young man. If he is everything you say, I will not stand in your way."

To her very happy surprise, Helmut and her parents got along splendidly. During a wine toast after dinner, Papa gave the soldier a warm blessing to marry his daughter.

Louisa was also pleased to discover the church readily accommodated quick wartime marriages between soldiers and their sweethearts. Mama and her sisters dove into the wedding preparations and somehow it was all done on time.

Only a week later, Louisa was walking down the aisle in a beautiful flowing gown, with Papa holding her arm. Helmut waited for her at the altar in his resplendent white dress uniform. They made a beautiful couple.

The bride's one regret was the inability of her friends and family outside of the city to attend the wedding on such short notice. Things were worse for poor Helmut. Only his Aunt Teresa and her two children were able come in by train from Prussia to sit on the groom's side of the church.

Helmut smiled without a care when he took Louisa's hands by the altar. She felt happy and worried at the same time. The singer loved her soldier very much, but how would they make the marriage work? Helmut appeared to be happy in the *Luftwaffe*, while her career was in Berlin. How could they do both and still be together?

After they exchanged vows, Helmut kissed her softly and Louisa put her worries away for the moment. Let us enjoy this moment and we will work out the rest later.

II. THE PACIFIC

CHAPTER 7

U.S.S. Enterprise, 99 miles west of Oahu, Hawaii
09:46 Hours, 7 December 1941

Nine days ago, Admiral Bull Halsey charged into the Pacific looking for a war, only to have it arrive back home while he was at sea.

Back on 27 November, Washington sent an opaque cable to the Pacific Fleet, warning of possible Japanese naval attacks on the Philippines, Malaya and Borneo, then concluding: "This dispatch may be considered a war warning."

Fleet commander, Admiral Husband Kimmel, immediately ordered his two carriers, *Enterprise* and *Lexington* to deliver Marine air squadrons to Wake and Midway Islands, with instructions to probe for any Jap activity to the west. The rest of the fleet would remain docked safely at Pearl Harbor.

Leaving the staff meeting to prepare his task force, Halsey asked his boss, "How far do you want me to go?"

Kimmel snapped back at his old friend, "Goddamit, use your common sense."

Bull treated the answer as a grant of total discretion. After returning to the *Enterprise*, he issued "Battle Order Number One" to the men, declaring the carrier task force was now operating under war conditions and to be prepared for action at any time, day or night.

Within minutes, his operations officer, Bill Buracker, ran onto the bridge, shaking a copy of the order. "Admiral, did you authorize this thing?"

When Halsey grunted in the affirmative, the ops officer exclaimed, "Admiral, you can't start a private war on your own! Who's going to take the responsibility?"

Arching his beetle brows, Bull fixed Buracker with one of his famous scowls. "I'll take it. If anything gets in my way. We'll shoot first and argue afterwards."

The *Enterprise's* cruise to and from Wake Island was uneventful, though. Task Force 8 did not sight so much as a Jap fishing trawler.

As they approached home early on the morning of the seventh, Halsey was not about to lower his guard, dispatching the eighteen bombers of Scouting Squadron Six to Pearl Harbor to ensure the carrier's final leg home was clear of Jap ships.

When the first report of a Japanese air raid came in over the wireless, Bull's initial concern was the base anti-aircraft gunners mistook Scouting Six for the Japs and opened fire on his planes. The reality was far worse. The Japs launched a pair of massive air raids, bombing and torpedoing the big battlewagons of the Pacific Fleet while they were docked within a supposedly invulnerable base. The damage assessments were confused, but it was plain the Japs landed a haymaker.

Within the hour, Admiral Kimmel shot off a directive placing Halsey in command of the three task forces currently at sea, with orders to hunt down the marauding Jap carriers.

Intelligence provided by the boys ashore at Pearl made no sense. Eyewitnesses observed the Jap planes fly in from the north before bombing the fleet. However, radio direction finding claimed the Jap fleet was located to the southwest. The best way Bull knew to find a carrier was to follow its planes back to the ship, but Kimmel was certain the enemy was shagging ass to the southwest back to their Marshall Islands base and ordered all the ships at sea to pursue.

Halsey followed the letter of the order by sending a screen of destroyers to the southwest on the boss's wild goose chase, but held his *Enterprise* in reserve and sent all the remaining dive bombers out as scouts in every other direction. Less than an hour later, the scout moving east below Pearl Harbor reported sighting a carrier and an unreported number of other ships, sailing southwest at full steam.

Below Pearl? The location didn't match either of the intelligence reports. Maybe the Japs displaced in an unexpected direction to avoid detection? Anyhow, Bull would figure out the whys and wherefores later. A sighting was a sighting.

Within fifteen minutes, Torpedo Squadron Six was airborne and hauling ass to intercept. Halsey impatiently walked the bridge, puffing on a stogie, until the radio woke up again with the chatter of the torpedo bombers.

"Raven Three to Raven Leader, I see multiple ships at two o'clock. No sign of any flat tops."

"Raven Leader to flock, follow me in low. Hopefully, we can dodge the Jap fighter cover."

"Raven Six to Raven Leader, I'm getting anti-aircraft fire from the cruiser at one o'clock. Can I punch a torpedo into her?"

"Negative, negative, Raven Six. Save all the fish for the flattops. Wait... Oh my sweet Jesus. Abort! Abort! They're our ships!"

A moment later, *Enterprise's* captain tapped Halsey on the shoulder and handed him a message from Admiral Draemel, commanding Task Force Two: "Draemel to Halsey: Anti-aircraft drove off Jap torpedo bomber attack. Request to join task forces to share *Enterprise* fighter cover. Immediate response requested."

Oh, for Christ's sake! The scout pilot must have spotted Task Force Two, not the Japs. Bull sent Torpedo Squadron Six after his own ships.

Could this day possibly get any worse?

Carrier Akagi, 111 miles north of Oahu, Hawaii
12:41 Hours, 7 December 1941

An ebullient Mitsuo Fuchida hopped out of his *Nakajima* B5N onto the wooden deck of the *Akagi*. His pilots ran up to their commander, pumping his hand and clapping his back in congratulations.

The air strikes on Pearl Harbor were far more successful than anyone had reason to expect. Amazingly, the *Ameko* had no aircraft in the air on combat air patrol. The unimpeded Japanese torpedo bombers easily executed the long practiced shallow torpedo attacks on the battleships lined neatly along the docks, followed by high explosive hammer blows delivered from above by the dive bombers.

In the carrier briefing room, a quick after-action review among the pilots confirmed the extensive damage they inflicted on the enemy fleet, and also the far sadder news of the loss of thirty comrades across the six carrier air groups. Naval aviation was a small, close-knit community. The senior flight commander personally trained many of the lost pilots and counted more than a few as friends. Every victory came with a cost. Thankfully, the human price of this one was not too dear.

His command responsibilities completed for the moment, Fuchida trotted up the several sets of stairs out of the bowels of the carrier up to the bridge to ask for his next assignment. The invasion fleet commander, Vice Admiral Chuichi Nagumo, and his operations officer, Lieutenant Commander Genda, were watching the aircraft rearm on the deck when their flight commander arrived.

"Ah, it's you Fuchida," Nagumo grunted. "Please, make your report."

The pilot suppressed his excitement and provided the sober summary of the situation upon which his admiral insisted.

"Did you see any sign of the *Ameko* carriers?" Genda asked.

"No. The report our agents on Oahu sent two days ago appears to be accurate. The enemy carriers left port and are at sea somewhere outside of our flight paths."

Turning back to Nagumo, Fuchida made his request. "Admiral-san, half of the day remains. May I have your permission to launch a final strike against the enemy fleet and destroy their remaining ships."

Genda shot him an alarmed glance. "With all respect to the honorable flight commander, I strongly advise against this course of action. The enemy carriers surely know of our attack by now and will return at full speed to defend the rest of the *Ameko* fleet and their homeport. We must keep our aircraft in reserve to sink them."

The flare of anger Fuchida felt at his old friend's unexpected opposition subsided almost immediately. Of course, Genda was correct. The enemy carriers were all important. He was allowing his desire for further glory to cloud his better judgment.

Admiral Nagumo quickly reached the same conclusion. "Send out another wave of scout planes, Fuchida, then ensure your pilots and planes are prepared to launch as soon as we find the enemy carriers."

"Yes sir," the flight commander bowed.

"Do not be concerned about the remainder of the *Ameko* fleet. Admiral Mikawa will deal with them tonight."

U.S.S. Maryland, 15 miles south of Oahu, Hawaii
19:20 Hours, 7 December 1941

Reading the message which was just handed to him, Rear Admiral Walter Anderson broke into his first smile since this hot mess began. Bull Halsey's ships were arriving. Now the Pacific Fleet would be consolidated to land a counterpunch on the Japs tomorrow. At least, what was left of the fleet.

Within an hour after the Jap air strikes on Pearl Harbor that morning, the admiral took the damaged *U.S.S. Maryland* and every other ship able to get underway out to sea, where they could join with the other task forces. He vividly recalled sailing slowly though Pearl past the wreckage of the Pacific Fleet. *Arizona* convulsed with fire and explosions as it foundered at dock. *Oklahoma* lay on its side, nearly completely submerged. Other ships ran aground around the bay attempting to escape the rain of Jap bombs and torpedoes. In total, the fleet lost eighteen of its finest ships and God knew how many sailors.

Task Force One spent the rest of the day maneuvering south of Oahu, searching the skies for another Jap airstrike, which thankfully never arrived. Now that *Enterprise* and *Lexington* were returning to the fold, the fleet would regain its airpower and even up the odds against the Japs.

Maryland's damaged radar array started picking up intermittent signals of Halsey's approaching force about a half hour before. The lack of radio communications was odd, though. While sailing under radio silence in a combat zone was standard procedure, the two task forces needed to coordinate their consolidation, especially considering how trigger-happy everyone was after the Jap sneak attack.

"Captain, I need you to do two things for me," Anderson requested. "First, radio a flash warning to the fleet that friendly forces are arriving from the west and not to open fire."

"And the second, sir?"

"Raise *Enterprise* on the radio and get me Admiral Halsey."

There was much planning left to do before the morning.

Battleship Kongo, 18 miles southwest of Oahu, Hawaii
19:58 Hours, 7 December 1941

Admiral Gunichi Mikawa lowered his binoculars and shook his head in wonder. When the *Ameko* destroyer appeared out of the deep black of the moonless night, the rear admiral fretted he lost the element of surprise. Instead, the enemy ship lay there silently as the battleship Kongo sailed past. If his aging eyes were not playing tricks on him, an *Ameko* sentry on the vessel actually waved at them! Incredible.

So far, the carriers and their insufferably arrogant pilots seized all of the glory, seriously damaging the *Ameko* fleet in a surprise attack, while it sat peacefully docked in their port. Tonight, the real Navy of battleships, torpedoes and cannon would destroy the enemy out on the open sea during a proper battle.

For years, through trial and error, the Imperial Japanese Navy trained hard to perfect the art of night combat in preparation for a decisive battle against their *Ameko* rivals. Tonight, his sailors were putting their training into practice like clockwork.

Flying at low altitude above the black waters, a spread formation of scout planes swept ahead, searching out the enemy fleet. When the pilots found their quarry, they radioed their approximate positions and started dropping parachute flares over the enemy ships.

After Mikawa ordered the fleet to move at full speed toward the flares in the distance, spotters chosen for their excellent night vision employed special scopes to precisely direct their ships straight towards the illuminated *Ameko*.

Once on proper course, one Japanese ship after another launched their full loads of Type 93 torpedoes. This new generation of torpedoes enjoyed a long range of nearly 40 kilometers and were designed to run fast and unseen, without the tell-tale bubble trail of earlier models.

As these deadly fish raced off towards the unsuspecting enemy, Mikawa gave a second order for the fleet to split into two lines, moving along both sides of the *Ameko* formation.

The admiral looked down at his watch. Two minutes left. Two more minutes for something to go wrong. Yet, the *Ameko* did nothing. No anti-aircraft fire against the floatplanes dropping flares. No gunnery against Mikawa's closing ships.

Most likely, the enemy was simply confused. The Japanese admiral was certain his counterpart had never seen these tactics. In one more minute, the enemy admiral would receive a very pointed education.

The float planes started reporting geysers of water rising beside the enemy ships as the torpedoes arrived at their destinations.

"Captain, you may begin firing your main guns," Mikawa calmly requested.

In perfect synchronization, all eight of the *Kongo's* fourteen inch guns fired, the recoil pushing the ship back to the starboard. Following the lead of their flagship, the rest of the Japanese fleet unleashed their big guns at the *Ameko*, catching them in a deadly crossfire.

Mikawa's vessels initially used the flickering illumination of the flares above the enemy ships to adjust their fire. Soon, the ships themselves were ablaze and easy to spot through the pre-moon pitch.

In contrast, the enemy was essentially firing blind. They could only see the flashes of the Japanese guns in the darkness, without any means of accurately gauging their locations.

The one-sided battle lasted less than an hour before the surviving *Ameko* ships fled to the east, leaving behind nearly twenty burning wrecks.

Mikawa nodded in satisfaction. With this success, the proper order of things was restored between his battleships and the damnable carriers.

U.S.S. Enterprise, 83 miles west of Oahu, Hawaii
03:40 Hours, 8 December 1941

For the first time in his life, Bull Halsey felt trapped, his only options ranging from bad to worse.

The news from fleet was horrific. During the darkness between sunset and moonrise yesterday, the enemy fleet somehow finished off the Pearl Harbor survivors in a surface engagement. How in hell the Japs could see to engage at night was beyond him. The bottom line was most of the Pacific Fleet which started the day at Pearl Harbor was now lost or withdrawing back to the States, leaving the Jap fleet controlling all the approaches to Pearl Harbor.

One bright spot remained. With the return of his Scouting Squadron Six from Oahu and the arrival of the carrier *Lexington* and its Task Force 12, the admiral finally consolidated all the surviving American air power under his command. But what to do with it?

In order to maintain morale, Halsey withheld the information of tonight's disaster from everyone except for his senior officers. Nearly all of them were counseling withdrawal. The surviving carriers faced damned long odds. If the estimates of attacking enemy aircraft were correct, the Japs probably fielded five or six carriers in addition to their large surface force.

Still, the idea of shagging ass before the carriers even saw action stuck in Bull's craw like a large piece of gristle wedged between his molars. God knew how many thousands of sailors the Jap sons of bitches murdered over the past hours. His boys had to hit back.

Retreat might not be possible in any case. The Jap surface fleet now lay between Halsey's task force and resupply at Pearl Harbor. After the long runs to Wake and Midway, most of his ships were low on fuel and would likely run out of gas before making base at San Diego.

Bull did have one trump card left to play. The radar on Oahu finally got up and running late yesterday and tracked the movements of the last wave of Jap scout planes. After some elementary triangulation, the admiral had a very good idea where the enemy flat tops were located.

An hour before dawn, Halsey would launch every plane under his command in a spread formation to find the enemy, leaving nothing behind to defend the ships. His only hope against these odds was to land the first punch at first light and make it count. The strike bombers would need every fighter to protect them during their attack runs to deliver that blow.

Meanwhile, Bull made his way down to the *Enterprise* flight deck to be with his pilots. Each could use all encouragement the other could give.

Carrier Akagi, 73 miles northwest of Oahu, Hawaii
07:01 Hours, 8 December 1941

Mitsuo Fuchida looked up from the deck of *Akagi* at certain death and began to pray to his ancestors.

The flight commander was readying his scout planes to depart, when the *Ameko* aircraft arrived not long after dawn. Instead of dealing one unified blow, though, the enemy pilots flew in small sections, attacking from seemingly random directions.

The Japanese *Zero* fighters circling overhead swooped down like falcons to tear apart the piecemeal attacks before they could engage the precious carriers. A far smaller number of *Ameko* fighters rose up to protect their bombers, but the Japanese were too talented and too many for them. One after another, the enemy birds of prey fell into the sea. In their eagerness, though, Fuchida's falcons over-committed and were all down at sea level when the last of the enemy dive bombers appeared.

A loud crack running across the water announced the *Ameko* arrival. Plumes of fire rose from the carrier *Soryu* as enemy bombs found the aviation fuel and munitions stored below decks.

Then the scream of diving engines drew Fuchida's attention upward. The flight commander recognized the pair of bulky planes streaking downward towards *Akagi* as enemy Douglas SBD-2s. They were about midway into their dives and seconds away from releasing their bombs on top of him.

Mitsuo made no attempt to flee. Instead, the naval officer silently asked the spirits of his ancestors to provide him with strength in this, his moment of death. Soon he would join them in honor. The *kami* refused to accept him, though.

A stream of rounds from one of *Akagi's* anti-aircraft cannon lashed off the wing of the lead dive bomber. Then, one of Fuchida's falcons roared up from behind and shredded the cockpit of the trailing plane before the pilot could release his bomb onto the carrier.

Like a short and violent storm at sea, the *Ameko* attack suddenly ceased and their surviving planes turned for home.

Fuchida stared in wonder at the now empty sky. This was the second time in as many days he escaped near death. During the Pearl Harbor attack, his plane sustained far more damage than he realized at the time. An entire section of the fuselage was shredded by enemy ground fire, but every underlying cable necessary to keep the bird flying remained unscathed. Now, this miracle.

Returning to the world again, the flight commander jumped up onto the lead scout plane and pointed at the withdrawing enemy aircraft. "Lieutenant, follow the *Ameko* back to their carriers," Fuchida yelled over the idling engine into the pilot's ear. "Radio your locations as you proceed. I will be leading the counterattack myself."

With a sharp bow of his head, the scout acknowledged the order, pulled his goggles down over his eyes and accelerated the engine for takeoff. As the plane leapt off the deck, *Akagi's* elevators brought the combat aircraft up onto the deck, with torpedoes and bombs affixed in equal measure.

Fuchida's engineer fetched his flight suit and gear from the hold. As he stepped into the pant legs of his overalls, the flight commander looked over at the flaming wreck which used to be *Soryu*.

Brothers, the gods spared me to avenge you. I will not fail.

U.S.S. Enterprise, 88 miles west of Oahu, Hawaii
08:19 Hours, 8 December 1941

Watching the celebrations around the *Enterprise* bridge, Admiral Bull Halsey bitterly concluded he failed his men and the Navy.

The smiling bridge officers recounted the radio chatter reporting hits on one or two Jap carriers. These were the navy's first victories of the new war and Halsey's men were grasping them tightly like a man overboard holding onto a rescue line.

What the admiral took instead from the reports was the Japs had four to five fully operational carriers left over after the air strike. Only a fraction of his pilots who left before the dawn were returning with the day and many of their birds were shot to pieces. *We can't stop them.*

Immediately after the last plane touched down, Halsey ordered the task forces to move south, southeast at top speed. If they withdrew and San Diego could send out some oilers to refuel the ships, maybe he could save what's left of the Pacific Fleet. Bull knew this wishful thinking, though. He gave up any real chance of making it home by throwing the dice on a counter attack and them bones came up craps.

The Japs came faster than the admiral expected. Just twenty minutes after the fleet turned, the skies started filling with a couple hundred enemy aircraft. More planes than Halsey had ever seen in the air at one time.

The celebrations on the bridge quickly turned into panicked argument. When the Enterprise captain denied permission for the returned fighters to take off again, the commander of the air group demanded to know why. The skipper got in the CAG's face and shouted the planes were nearly out of fuel after the morning air strike and he wasn't about to watch his pilots ditch into the ocean.

Turning to his officers, Halsey interjected, "Let 'em go. If we don't get some air cover up right now, there won't be any ships left to cover."

While the fighters took off again, the ship anti-aircraft batteries provided the task force's first line of defense. A battleship and several cruisers and destroyers surrounded the two carriers, their guns throwing up a cone of tracers and lead over the flat tops.

The combined defenses initially held. Here and there, streams of anti-aircraft rounds tore a Jap plane to pieces, the flaming remnants falling into the water below. A pair of F4F *Wildcat* fighters jumped a section of Jap dive bombers approaching Enterprise from the port side, splashing all three of them.

Then something strange drew Halsey's attention away from the battle above. A *Wildcat* with a stationary propeller was slowly approaching the carrier deck. The pilot must be out of gas and trying to glide in for a landing.

C'mon, son. C'mon. You can do it.

The *Wildcat* made it within 200 yards of the deck when all hell broke loose. Two groups of Jap torpedo bombers were coming in hard and low on each side of the *Enterprise*.

"Helm, hard to port! Full speed ahead!" yelled the carrier skipper.

The captain's effort to minimize the target the carrier presented by showing his bow and stern to the incoming Jap torpedoes took away the gliding *Wildcat's* landing strip. Bull saw the pilot close his eyes just before crashing into the superstructure below the bridge.

God help him. God help us all.

Immediately following the shudder from the plane crash, Halsey felt three other WHUMPS vibrate through the *Enterprise*. While the carrier's evasive action caused most of the incoming torpedoes to miss, three found their marks – two astern and one somewhere around the bow.

The Big E's end came rapidly. First, her propulsion and power failed as water poured into the engine room. Then, she leaned starboard as the ocean claimed the rest of the ship.

The remainder of Halsey's task force wasn't in much better shape. Maybe five knots to the east, *Lexington* was a raging inferno and another eight ships were slipping under the waves around the stricken carriers.

Like so many angels of mercy, the destroyers gathered around the doomed ships to rescue the surviving sailors. The wounded were hoisted aboard first, followed by grim-faced sailors in smoke and oil soiled uniforms.

The admiral was the last off the *Enterprise*. From the deck of the destroyer *USS Sims*, Bull struggled to hold back the tears as he watched his flag ship slide under the waves, leaving behind a glistening blue oil slick as the only remaining evidence of her existence.

How in hell could this happen?

CHAPTER 8

Haleiwa Air Field, Oahu, Hawaii
01:49 Hours, 9 December 1941

Billy Deal snuggled beneath a quilt on his feather bed. When the explosions first intruded on his sleep, he groggily turned over, wondering why in hell the Cripple Creek gold mine was using dynamite during the middle of the night. The next round of blasts painfully obliterated his rest altogether, turning his pleasant dream of home into a surreal nightmare. Instead of his bed, Deal found himself bouncing in a hole on the Oahu coast, choking on the sand showering down all around him. Billy's first thought was of being trapped in a giant saltshaker. His next was a recollection of spending the past two days actually looking forward to this.

After the initial air raids on Pearl Harbor and Hickam Airfield, the Twenty-fourth Division moved lickety split to its defensive line on the north shore. By noon on the seventh, the troops were dug in, ready to repel Jap landings which never arrived.

The rumor mill started working overtime. Morning meals trucked in from Schofield Barracks included healthy portion of scuttlebutt about Jap marines landing on other parts of the island. By lunch, the story changed to Jap paratroopers roaming the mountains to their rear.

Reality arrived with the sunset. The company commander went from foxhole to foxhole, personally relaying the bad news to the men. The Jap carriers wiped out what was left of the Pacific Fleet that morning. The Army was on its own.

Certain the Jap invasion would come just before dawn, Deal was determined to get as much shut-eye as he could between guard shifts. The enemy fleet interrupted his sleep plans.

 Billy couldn't say for sure how much time passed while the big naval shells pulverized the shoreline around him. Or exactly how long after the bombardment halted that he lay curled up at the bottom of his hole, covered in sand, with his hands jammed against his ears. At some point, though, he regained his wits and his feet.

Surprisingly, everything appeared to be OK in his little piece of paradise. The airfield between the foxhole and the beach was clear. No sign of a Jap landing yet. The corporal should have some time.

"Mike, keep a sharp eye out," Billy croaked. "I'm going to check on the rest of the guys." Morgan nodded from the other end of the foxhole, as he brushed the sand off of his face.

Bernier and Murray were dug in about fifty yards to the west. After trotting about halfway over, Deal took a knee and hissed out the password. No response.

Maybe the boys couldn't hear him after the Jap bombardment. Billy could barely hear himself over the ringing in his ears.

The corporal crept forward again, repeating the password in an increasingly loud voice, until he tumbled down into the darkness. The company perimeter was as a flat as a pool table. What the hell was this?

A parachute flare igniting overhead answered the unspoken question. The sputtering light revealed an enormous crater almost thirty feet across. One of the big battleship guns must have made this thing. Then, Deal saw the aiming stakes he placed in front of Bernier and Murray's foxhole yesterday. Except now they were at the edge of the crater.

Billy laid back and closed his eyes. The corporal's four-man section was now halved down to Mike and himself. Was half of the company also blown to hell?

No time for that now. The big artillery up in the Oahu hills was barking now, launching salvos back at the Jap fleet. The enemy landing force must be arriving.

Deal clambered up and out of the crater, looked back for moment, then out to sea. He had something for the Jap bastards when they came ashore.

The Ocean off Haleiwa Airfield, Oahu, Hawaii
01:58 Hours, 9 December 1941

Captain Otozo Hayashi hated the sea.

The voyage from Japan to Hawaii was unrelenting misery. The invasion fleet followed a storm across the Pacific to hide its approach from *Ameko* scout planes and ships. For days, the high seas buffeted the infantry transport *Sakura Maru* and the suffering *hentai* trapped within the ship's stifling hold. No measure of the company commander's considerable self-discipline could stave off the sea sickness which afflicted him and many of his men. The choking reek of vomit filling the hold only compounded the affliction.

When the fleet finally emerged onto the calm waters north of the Hawaiian Islands, Hayashi moved from illness to ill temper.

As the carriers launched their war birds against *Ameko* fleet, the captain whipped himself and his men into a frenzy in preparation to land on the northern shore of Oahu. Deeply honored to be part of the first wave landing on the beach, nothing less than total victory would this satisfy this officer of an ancient *samurai* clan.

The damned Navy would not allow the commander and his troops to escape their grasp, however. For reasons the admirals did not deign to disclose, the fleet cancelled the landings. Well-known for his furious tirades, it was all Hayashi could do to maintain his composure in front of the men.

The landings finally went forward the following night. By the light of the rising moon, the Japanese infantry boarded the open-topped *Daihatsu* landing craft and luxuriated in the fresh sea breeze. The relief was short lived.

Dozens of the *Daihatsu* lined up and slowly made their way to shore, well below their top speed, in order to maintain precise formations. Their cargo of soldiers stood helplessly as the *Ameko* shore guns on Oahu opened fire, launching massive shells towards them, screaming overhead like freight trains. One landed just short of Hayashi's transport, the concussion tossing the boat back and drenching its passengers with seawater.

On the sacred land, the *hentai* could close the distance with the enemy at a run, moving from one cover to the next to avoid enemy fire. Here on the damnable ocean, a soldier's fate was out of his hands and left to chance.

After a half hour of serving as slow moving targets, the first wave of landing craft finally approached the shore. The clatter of an *Ameko* machine gun reaching out for the landing craft from a pill box off to the left barely registered with the captain. This threat was a known quantity. Instead, with growing horror, Hayashi's attention was drawn to the breakers crashing on the beach. The waves were nearly as tall as the boat!

The Navy pilot idled the *Daihatsu* near the shore for a moment and then gunned the engine in an attempt to ride one of the waves onto the beach. Instead, the boat ran ahead of swell, which broke underneath, tossing the front of craft onto the sand and rocks. Thirty cursing men were thrown violently forward on top of one another and then back again as the rear of the boat joined the front on the shore.

The boat's crash landing destroyed the mechanism to lower the bow to allow his *hentai* to charge forward onto the shore. Instead, the company commander and his sergeants yelled and pointed for the men to climb over the sides of the stricken craft.

Some of his troops were too injured to make the climb. One of the China veterans looked helplessly as his broken right arm flopped down uselessly every time he attempted to raise it up. Three others lay on the deck, twisted in unnatural positions and unable to even stand.

Cursing the fates and the Navy in equal measures, Hayashi pulled himself up and over the twisted front of the landing craft, landing hard on his back. Before he could regain the wind knocked out by the fall, water from yet another wave surged past the boat and covered him up. Choking on the brine, Otozo thrashed about to find a foothold on the land, but found none in the tumbling water. The spent wave then retreated back to the sea, dragging him with it.

No, he would not die this way!

When the water brushed him against the landing craft, Hayashi shot out his arm and grabbed a twisted piece of metal, holding on with all of his remaining strength. Finally, the sea released him and left him lying on the sand, coughing out the cursed seawater.

Regaining his feet before another wave could take him, the *samurai* staggered up onto the blessed land, profusely thanking his ancestors for saving his life so he could restore his family's honor.

Haleiwa Air Field, Oahu, Hawaii
02:14 Hours, 9 December 1941

Billy Deal tuned out the clatter of the battlefield, focusing all of his attention on the far end of the Haleiwa Airfield and patiently waiting for the next flare.

The Japs were offloading on the beach along the opposite end of the field, mostly out of sight under the edge of the airstrip, and definitely out of range for most GIs and their rifles. That didn't prevent excited troops up and down the line from firing like idiots at every shadow they saw in the distance.

Deal intended on making every round he put down range count. When he returned from the National Trophy Match with a finely calibrated rifle as a prize for putting up the best individual score, the corporal convinced the Hotel Company commander to allow him to mount a hunting scope on the *Springfield* and serve as the unofficial company sniper.

With this rig, Deal could hardly miss. All he needed was enough light to make out the targets. Someone down the line fulfilled Billy's wish. A parachute flare arced up from the American lines, then gently floated down over the shore.

The corporal gently panned his rifle from left to right until he came upon a pair of Japs hauling a tripod and a big machine gun up onto the airfield. That bad boy could definitely reach the American lines and cause some damage.

Deal waited until the men plopped the tripod onto the sand and then mounted the machine gun on top. Once the gun crew stopped moving around and settled in behind their weapon, the sniper went to work.

Nudging his riflescope crosshairs to a position below the gunner's helmet, Billy gently squeezed the trigger. The bullet plowed a hole through the man's cheek, snapping his head back, before his lifeless body collapsed back onto the machine gun.

One.

The Jap loading a belt of ammunition into the weapon shook the gunner on the shoulder, then got to his knees to push the body off the machine gun. A chest shot punched the man back into the darkness.

Two.

Deal kept his scope on the big gun. The Japs would send more men to reclaim the valuable weapon and put it into action.

Three more men appeared. One of the Japs kicked the other in the ass toward the machine gun. This one wore a soft cap instead of a helmet and carried a frigging *samurai* sword. An officer.

As Deal moved the crosshairs over to the ass kicker, the flare sputtered out and the scope went dark. He finished moving the *Springfield* to where the Jap last stood and pulled the trigger. Billy thought he hit the enemy officer, but couldn't count him as an official kill without seeing the Jap fall.

The sniper slowly exhaled and waited for the next flare.

Haleiwa Airfield, Oahu, Hawaii
02:23 Hours, 9 December 1941

With a crack and a white-hot tug on his shoulder, Hayashi fell back into the darkness. The fall was less from force of the *Ameko* bullet biting into his skin than a survival instinct to seek cover. When his back hit the sand, the captain crawled backwards like a crab towards the beach below.

Once sure he was out of sight, Hayashi reached under his uniform to check the burning spot beneath. His hand came back sticky, but not wet. The bullet merely creased him.

Looking back at his men lying around the machine gun, each killed with a perfect shot, the captain concluded the fiendishly talented *Ameko* sniper could not have missed him by mere chance. Again, the *samurai's* ancestors intervened to save his life. There could only be one reason for this divine assistance – to allow the son to redeem the family's honor from the sins of the father.

Three years passed since Hayashi last saw his father. A beautiful April day greeted the lieutenant when he returned on leave from China to the family residence in Oki. The red lacquered wood of the house gleamed in the midst of a pink and white cherry blossom trees in full bloom. It was so very good to be back home.

The son unsurprisingly found his father in the study. Arriving only an hour before by train from the Imperial General Headquarters, Colonel Hikaru Hayashi already had his desk covered with the work in which he was engrossed. Posted in the China department of the Army intelligence section, the staff officer was constantly struggling to decipher the enigma which was the Middle Kingdom.

When the colonel looked up from his papers, the captain saluted his superior officer, then the son bowed to his father.

"Ah, I am so pleased to see you back home – fit and well," Hikaru nodded. "Come, let us have some tea in the garden."

A gray crane stretched and lazily flew off as the men entered, causing a handful of cherry blossom petals to twirl on the surface of the pond at the center of the garden. A gentle breeze rustled through the perfectly manicured shrubbery.

When a servant left the tea, the father held up his cup to his only son. "You are making quite a name for yourself in China."

"Thank you, sir. I have worked very hard to do so," Otozo replied before sipping the hot liquid.

The men sat in silence for a time, drinking tea and looking out at the garden. His father appeared at peace in this, his favorite sanctuary from the cares of the world. When there was so much yet to accomplish, Otozo never understood the older generation's fascination with wasting time looking at shrubbery. Still, out of respect, he waited for the older man to finish his meditation.

Turning back towards the captain, the colonel finally broke the silence. "Otozo, I need your counsel."

The son sat up straighter, flattered his father sought his opinion.

"When the Europeans arrived in China with far smaller military forces, the corrupt Chinese mandarins routinely surrendered. In this war, our far larger forces have won great victories, but the Chinese persevere," the staff officer observed with a frown, as he placed the empty teacup back on the tray. "The reports we receive at headquarters are self-serving garbage. As a field officer, what is your opinion of the Chinese?"

The boredom of the garden left Otozo, as his mind returned to the overseas killing fields. "The Chinese are subhuman *chancorro*, who have to be convinced they are defeated. For the most part, our generals are insufficiently ruthless in this regard."

"Some of our generals have shown themselves all too ruthless," the colonel grumbled. "The incident at Nanjing was an abomination, bringing shame upon the Army and the nation."

Otozo bristled, but held his tongue.

"Your unit was in the Nanjing sector. What did you observe?"

"The Chinese refused to surrender, so they were disciplined."

"Disciplined? Mass murder and rape is not discipline!" the colonel exploded. "My son, I taught you better than this. Our family are true *samurai*, not like the common rabble in today's Army. *Samurai* honor the bravery of their opponents and protect the innocent."

Then realization ran across the father's face like a shadow. "Otozo, please tell me you were not part of this."

"My unit had the honor of participating in this discipline," the son snapped back.

"No…"

His patience exhausted by this cross-examination of his honor, the captain stood up and looked down upon the colonel in a cold fury. "Sir, I caution you against expressing these treasonous thoughts outside of these walls. Out of respect for you as my father, I will not report what you have said. However, others will…and traitors are dealt with."

Hikaru looked back up in appalled disbelief, then slowly stood and pointed to the door with a trembling hand. "You will say goodbye to your mother and leave this house immediately. Think upon your shame and do not return until you are prepared to act again like a true *samurai*."

Otozo stalked out of the home without another word. Times have changed, father. You may be too weak to be a modern *samurai*, but your son is strong enough.

A week before returning to his unit in China, Hayashi read of his father's death in a newspaper. Unidentified men cut the colonel down with swords in a street not far from the headquarters. No one admitted to seeing the attack.

The son looked up from the paper and wiped away the single tear on his cheek. I warned him. Why wouldn't the old man listen? Then, gray grief gave way to an even darker thought. If the Army punished the treason of the father, how would they view the son and his family?

Rising from the sand of the enemy beach, the young *samurai* shrugged off the memory and the hot burn of his shoulder. Victory on the battlefield was the surest way of restoring family honor and his first opportunity had arrived.

As the last round of *Ameko* flares sunk into the sea, Japanese bugles along the beach sounded the call to charge. Hayashi drew his father's sword and bellowed for his men to follow him towards glory.

Haleiwa Air Field, Oahu, Hawaii
02:27 Hours, 9 December 1941

A series of flares launched up from the American lines toward the sudden human roar rolling in from the shore. The sputtering lights floating down from above revealed hundreds of hollering Japs charging with fixed bayonets towards him.

For a couple seconds, Bill Deal could only stare. The approaching mob reminded him of a story Pop told him when he was a boy about a battle his great grandpop fought during the Indian wars.

Towards the end of the Civil War, Pete Deal was making his living in the Colorado territory as a civilian Army scout, when the Cheyenne, Arapaho and Sioux all went on the warpath. As a cold January morning gripped the fort outside of Julesberg, the scout led a couple dozen cavalry out after a handful of Indians, who had spent the past night taking potshots at the sentries.

The detachment galloped straight into an ambush. As soon as the cavalry moved out of sight of the fort, a couple hundred Indians came boiling out of a draw. The Sioux war party split the detachment, cutting off Pete and a handful of other troopers. By Pop's account, their ancestor shot every round he carried and then some more he took off of a dead trooper, killing over a dozen of the redskins.

There were just too many Sioux, though. Pete crawled under the dead trooper and played possum. Luck was with him that day. The Indians didn't take any scalps and instead took off after the rest of the detachment hightailing it back to the fort. Great grandpop snuck off in the opposite direction and lived to tell the story.

Billy grinned at the memory and took aim. There was no need to run from this mob. If the Japs were stupid enough to expose themselves in the open to get killed, he would oblige them. While his buddies along the company line shot randomly into the approaching mass of men, the sniper was more discriminating, searching out enemy officers. Cut the head off the snake, then all the body can do is flop around for a while before dying.

When his first bullet found its target, the Jap seemed to halt in his tracks in surprise, flinging his sword backwards, before falling onto his face.

The next shot was slightly off the mark. The enemy soldier fell to his knees and grabbed his shoulder, then actually got to his feet again and continued forward. Tough sonuvabitch, the sniper thought, as he adjusted his aim to finish the man off.

The last shot flew wildly off into the darkness as Mike Morgan shook Deal's firing shoulder.

"God damn it, Mike!" Billy turned and yelled. "What in hell did ya do that for?"

"Sweet baby Jesus, you can shut out the world when you're shooting. The First Sergeant just came by. The company is pulling out to the west end of the airfield."

"Why?" Deal demanded, pointing down range at the approaching Japs. "This is a goddamned turkey shoot."

"Because some other Japs got behind us and are fixin to cut us off," Mike yelled back, pointing in the opposite direction.

The sniper spit. Which dumb ass company down the line let the frigging Japs get through? Then, Billy's anger turned to resignation. Nothing dogfaces like them could do about it anyway.

"Sorry for blowing up at you like that."

"Apology accepted. Now, what do ya say we shag ass out of here before that bunch arrives?" Morgan urged.

Looking longingly back at the Japs for a second, Billy scrambled out of his hole and trotted off for the rear. This frigging war was definitely starting off in the wrong direction.

CHAPTER 9

White House, Washington D.C.
09:10 Hours, 12 December 1940

The anger and shock around the Oval Office were palpable. Although the men in the room discussed the possibility, even probability, of war with Japan for several months now, they were furious the Empire of the Rising Sun actually had the temerity to attack and even more appalled at their success.

As a military professional, General George Marshall couldn't help but be impressed with the enemy strategy. Although it was a mighty gamble, the invasion of Hawaii made perfect sense. While the United States held Pearl Harbor, we could project force into the rest of the Pacific. If the Japanese took it, the rest of the Pacific fell to them by default and the enemy could launch an invasion of the American mainland from the islands.

Georgie Patton predicted this back in March, the Chief of Staff recalled. I need to keep a closer eye on him.

The President was hardly in the mood to admire enemy strategy, though. Roosevelt was looking for heads to roll. Marshall had not seen this side of the Boss before. The normally gregarious politician turned sarcastic and vindictive, his voice thready and high.

"Gentlemen, the Japs caught us sleeping in Hawaii and I want to know why," Roosevelt demanded. "How could Kimmel and his Pacific Fleet not spot the Japs sailing across half the

Pacific? How could Short allow the Japs to bomb Hawaii's aircraft on the runways?" The President was already fully briefed on the situation in the Pacific and not really looking for answers, nor did any of the men around him offer any.

Glaring at the Secretary of War seated on the couch, Roosevelt ordered, "Henry, I want Kimmel and Short fired immediately and shipped back to Washington to answer for their incompetence."

"Of course, Mr. President," replied Stimson.

"Mr. President," Admiral "Betty" Stark interjected, "I'm sorry, but the Japanese fleet controls the waters off of the Hawaiian Islands. General Short and Admiral Kimmel will not be leaving for the time being. Until they can be replaced, I strongly recommend against relieving commanders in the middle of a fight."

"Remind me again, Admiral, what exactly does Kimmel command?" Roosevelt sneered.

Marshall uncomfortably looked down at the Oval Office rug, feeling for his fellow chief of staff. The Army general suspected the heads the Boss demanded were not all located on Oahu.

"Gentlemen, we can deal with the past in good time. Now onto the present," the President relented. "I will not allow the Japs to conquer Hawaii and treat American citizens like they do the Chinese. Such an outcome would be intolerable. How do we rescue Hawaii?"

Stark remained standing and again took the lead. "Time is not on our side, Mr. President. Without reinforcement, Oahu will likely fall in a matter of weeks." the admiral observed. "I propose to immediately move as much of the Atlantic Fleet as necessary to San Diego to accomplish this mission."

"George, what can the Army contribute?" queried the President.

"Sir, the Army's only combat ready division on the west coast is Seventh Infantry. This division is also only real defense against a Japanese invasion of the mainland."

Marshall shifted uncomfortably as Roosevelt's frown deepened at the unwelcome news.

"With respect, Mr. President," interrupted Stark, "We don't need the Army's help for this operation. The Navy can rail in all the Marines to San Diego and be ready to go by the time our ships arrive from the Atlantic."

Cracking a wan smile at the apparent flare up of inter-service rivalry, Roosevelt needled Marshall: "What do you think of Betty's suggestion, George?"

In fact, Marshal was secretly relieved by the Navy's offer. The general suspected any relief force would have to hit the beaches to get onshore at Oahu. Amphibious landings were the Marines' bread and butter, while Seventh Infantry would need weeks to train up. Weeks they didn't have.

"Mr. President, I agree with Admiral Stark. Send the Marines to Hawaii and let Seventh Infantry defend California."

"There it is, then," concluded the President. "Gentlemen, now is the time to be bold. Next week, Congress will double military funding, so there is no longer any reason to hold back and husband your resources. Prosecute this war with complete confidence in the unconditional support of your government."

Sōri Kōtei, Tokyo, Japan
13:51 Hours, 13 December 1941

As his staff car proceeded up the drive, Admiral Yamamoto contemplated how the modest Prime Minister's office and home, the Sōri Kōtei, did not properly reflect the growing power of its resident. Upon entering, the short and plump naval officer removed the cap from his shaved head and handed it to one of the soldiers staffing the residence. Another reminder the Army controlled the government.

Yamamoto found General of the Army and now Prime Minister Hideki Tojo bent over paperwork on his desk, pretending not to notice the arrival of his naval counterpart. The admiral rolled his eyes at the petty slight and strolled over to the Oahu operations map mounted on an easel in a corner. The well-established Army landing zones dominating the north and east coasts of the island were drawn in fire red, as were the arrows showing the planned attack meant to finally end enemy resistance on the island. Mounting Army casualties belied the prewar caricature of the *Ameko* as soft and weak.

Looking up, Tojo offered a smile which did not extend to his cold eyes. "Ah Admiral-san, you have arrived. So very good to see you."

"Mr. Prime Minister."

"Yes, yes, I am still getting used to that title. I much prefer general."

"Then General-san, shall we get started?"

"Of course. Please commence your briefing."

"Reconnaissance patrols have verified we enjoy complete naval control over the area around the Hawaiian Islands. The *Ameko* carriers *Enterprise* and *Lexington*, along with most of their Pacific fleet, are sunk or crippled at dock in Pearl Harbor. The surviving enemy vessels withdrew to the United States."

"Excellent, excellent…" Tojo replied, as he stubbed out one cigarette and lit another. "Admiral-san, Operation Orient will commence on January 13. You are to redeploy a carrier group from the Hawaiian operation to eliminate the remainder of the Royal Navy operating out of India, then to support the Army's advance through Southeast Asia."

"Sir, you promised the fleet would be fully committed to the Hawaii operation until the Army finished its conquest of Oahu," Yamamoto reminded.

"Plans adapt to changing circumstances."

"And when the Americans counterattack?"

"Do you really think this is possible?" the general scowled. "The United States will need months to redeploy their Atlantic Fleet to the Pacific. By that time, Oahu and the other Hawaiian Islands will be ours."

"General-san, this enemy is very good at one thing above all others – logistics," the admiral warned. "They move from one place to another much faster than you would believe possible."

"You worry too much, Admiral-san. We may have our disagreements, but I have total faith in your ability to protect our forces on Oahu. Please carry out my orders."

U.S. Navy Headquarters, Washington D.C.
10:18 Hours, 14 December 1941

Commander PJ Tigert's mentor was wrong. Just flat out wrong.

When Admiral Earnest King took command of the Navy, Tigert was delighted by the orders to join his staff, rather than being invalided out of the service for the loss of an eye. A few years back, PJ served under King at Naval Air Station North Island in California, developing the navy's budding aviation wing. Although a taskmaster with a volcanic temper, the brilliant admiral taught the commander much of what he knew about fleet operations.

On this Sunday morning, Tigert was participating in staff meeting to rebalance the defense of the U.S. mainland by moving ships from the Atlantic to reinforce the decimated Pacific Fleet. The lowly commander's role was to provide the assembled brass with the status and current mission of each ship, then note their deployment recommendations.

The staff rose as one when Admiral King made a surprise entrance into the meeting room. Taking a seat at the head of the table, King abruptly asked if anyone had a reason why every carrier and modern ship in the Atlantic Fleet shouldn't immediately sail to San Diego. While the room lay in stunned silence, PJ shot his boss an alarmed look that did not go unnoticed.

"Mr. Tigert, do you have something to say?" demanded King. "Don't be shy, son. Speak up."

"Admiral, I think we need to consider the threat posed by the *Kriegsmarine* and *Regia Marina* before making this decision."

"What threat, Commander? What on Earth are you talking about?" King boomed, in what looked like the start of a Category Four blowback.

"Sir, the Japanese wouldn't have committed to invading Hawaii without some promise of support from their allies. Over the past year, the German and Italian fleets have executed two successful joint operations against the English. Now, the Germans are moving towards the United States by establishing major forward bases in the Azores and the Canary Islands."

The admiral frowned, but PJ kept plowing ahead.

"Intelligence believes the *Kriegsmarine* just put six or seven modern battleships to sea. Based on my personal observations during the Battle of the English Channel, I strongly suspect the Germans also possess two or three carriers."

Stark shot him an incredulous look. "What observations Commander?

"Admiral, I submitted a detailed report from England through State Department's diplomatic courier describing what I observed on the battleship *Nelson* during that operation."

"Those idiots at Foggy Bottom probably deep-sixed your report in some embassy trash can in London. Gimme the nickel version."

Tigert described the gray German torpedo and dive bombers which employed Japanese-style carrier tactics to decimate the

Royal Navy task force. He estimated these aircraft numbered over 100, enough to outfit three U.S Navy carriers.

The other admirals seated around the table started peppering the commander with questions until King called a halt to the proceedings. "We're not accomplishing anything spit balling like this. Commander Tigert, did you keep a personal copy of your report?"

"Yes sir."

"OK, by tomorrow morning, I want copies of that report on the desks of every officer on the staff. Meanwhile, this meeting is suspended." As the commander gathered his binders, the admiral added, "PJ, I would like to speak with you in my office."

Tigert trailed King, preparing for a royal ass chewing. A lowly staff office does not contradict the top admiral in front of his peers. With King towering over the five foot six Tigert, PJ felt like a child at school being marched to the principal's office. The commander finished the short walk to the office at the position of attention in front of the admiral's desk.

"PJ, sit down and relax."

King pulled a pack of Lucky Strikes out of his shirt pocket and offered Tigert one. The men lit their cigarettes and PJ took a deep drag in relief.

"You showed some guts just now at the staffing," King noted, "but you don't know the full picture. Our mission has changed from a defense of the mainland to taking back Hawaii." Talking a healthy swallow of coffee from an oversized mug, the admiral continued, "I'll probably need the entire damned Atlantic Fleet to pull off this party and you go lay a turd in the middle of my punchbowl."

"Sorry boss, I thought you needed to know," Tigert replied.

"I did," King admitted. "PJ, over the next three weeks, I want you to put on your intelligence officer cap and provide me with your best guess of the *Kriegsmarine* and *Regia Marina* orders of battle and their potential moves against the United States."

"Next three weeks, sir?"

"Yes," King nodded, "you have precisely twenty-two days left before you take command of the new destroyer *Forrest*. Congratulations PJ, it's time you went back to sea."

The Empress Catherine, 23 miles northeast of Charleston, South Carolina
13:07 Hours, 18 December 1941

Kat Kolotsiev gently turned her yacht starboard to get a closer look at the mass of ships rapidly filling the horizon. Was this the *Kriegsmarine* invasion fleet she expected for months now?

After Kolotsiev participated in the July Marblehead to Halifax Ocean Race, finishing a very respectable fourth, "*Herr Doktor*" asked if she would return to winter in Charleston and report anything unusual. The city was a pleasant enough place, so she readily agreed. Weeks passed without note in the sleepy southern port until today.

Heinrich fetched the Zeiss binoculars stowed under her captain's chair, slowly scanned the horizon, then turned back to the rest of the crew. "*Amerikaner*," he reported, reverting to his native tongue.

When ashore in Charleston, Kolotsiev's *Kriegsmarine* crew were admirably disciplined, speaking only the Queen's English, even when they believed themselves alone. Only at sea would the crew relax and converse in German. Kat didn't mind. It gave her a chance to practice the language of new *Reich*.

Heinrich started calling out ship types and numbers, while Dieter jotted down the information in the log book.

An anomaly in the Yank naval formation gradually caught Kat's attention. Standing up and shading her eyes from the ocean glare, she could just begin to make out…

"Gentlemen, we have a visitor," she announced, pointing over the bow at an oncoming American destroyer. "'Harry' put the binoculars back under my seat. 'David,' tear that page out of the log book and prepare to throw it overboard."

As the men nodded their understanding and hopped to, Kolotsiev scoured her mind for ideas to keep their unwelcome guests from boarding the boat. Although the shortwave radios and code books were well-hidden behind the mahogany paneling of the main cabin and the antennas sewn into canvas of the sails, a really thorough search could find them and the jig would really be up. Then, the obvious solution came to her – when in America, act like Americans.

Kat found the Yank reaction to the Japanese attack on Pearl Harbor fascinating. Unlike the fatalism with which Europeans greeted the prospect of another Great War, the Americans seemed to look forward to the bloodletting. However, Yank patriotism was fueled by a completely undeserved arrogance. After the Japanese sank their Pacific fleet and laid siege to the Hawaiian Islands, the young men lined up to enlist, bragging how they were going to kill dozens of the slant-eyes to the cheers of the town folk. When all the male chest-beating became tedious, she fled to sea on her yacht.

"'Harry,' hoist the Yank flag, then I want everyone to wave and cheer the destroyer when it comes along side."

No one moved. Good heavens, the Germans could be obtuse when confronted with the unexpected.

"Gentlemen, listen to me closely," Kolotsiev ordered. "We are an American ship supporting our heroic navy. Unless you want to learn what the snug end of a noose feels like hanging from the yard arm of that destroyer, you will cheer the Yanks as if they were your home football team!"

When the destroyer swung around next to the slower sail boat, the crew switched back to English and shouted out all the derogatory things about the Japs they heard the Yanks use around Charleston. Meanwhile, Kat put on her prettiest smile and waved overhead like she was welcoming family returning home from a long trip.

The Yanks' initial response was less than cordial. An officer on the destroyer surveyed them through a very large pair of binoculars, while a group of sailors clustered around a nearby machine gun she could swear was pointed straight at her.

Kat tamped down her fear and broadened her smile. Steady, my girl.

Finally, the Yank officer ended the standoff by giving them a thumbs up and retiring to the bridge. With hostilities officially ended, the sailors secured their machine gun and returned her crew's waves and cheers. The destroyer quickly returned to swung back into formation and her *Kriegsmarine* crew inconspicuously returned to cataloguing the Yank ships all around them.

Kat rewarded herself with a cigar and the nicotine rush joined the adrenaline wave she was riding. While the dutiful daughter could hear her Papa lecture about avoiding unnecessary risks, the *Reich's* top spy was beginning to enjoy tempting fate and outsmarting her opponents. What good was life, unless you could really enjoy it?

Berlin, Germany
17:18 Hours, 22 December 1941

Popping into stores along the Friedrichstrasse for last minute Christmas gifts, then snuggling into a cafe for cups of steaming spiced wine, a wonderful day set into a magical evening.

Helmut made his surprise arrival that morning. Certain she was going to be alone without her new husband for the holidays, Louisa was working on her costume at the opera, when Helmut snuck up and literally swept her into his arms for a long-missed kiss.

The couple left the cafe arm-in-arm, Louisa steering Helmut right towards a watch maker's shop. Her plan was to ask him to look at a gold wrist watch she was considering for her father, but in reality had chosen for her husband.

A man bent over a crutch and a wooden leg came clattering out of the evening twilight towards them.

"Oh the poor man," Louisa whispered. "We should give him something, darling."

When Helmut stopped and reached into his uniform pocket, the stranger paused as well and studied the paratroop officer. Suddenly, the man pushed himself upright and swung his right arm up to his cap in a military salute. The arm ended in a stump just past the elbow and fell far short of its destination. The sudden movement caused him to totter and fall, though, like a toy soldier unbalanced by too many missing parts.

Brushing Louisa aside, Helmut surged forward, grabbed his fellow soldier's coat and pulled him upright.

"Thank you, sir," the soldier grunted, as he struggled to stand again. "I am still getting used to this new leg." Once he regained his feet, the man cocked his head strangely and asked, "Pardon me, sir, but aren't you the Lieutenant Arpke who captured the *Englander* king?"

"Yes, I am Arpke." Helmut frowned. "Ah, comrade… The truth is I found the king through dumb luck. You have given far more to the Fatherland than I ever have."

Louisa walked up to the men and gasped. A nearby streetlight revealed the hollows in the stranger's ravaged face, puckered flesh barely covering scull and tendons. She knew she should show compassion to the poor man, but all she felt was horror and revulsion. Louisa had seen badly injured veterans of the Great War on the streets of Berlin, but they were old men. This soldier was Helmut's age.

The stranger looked over at Louisa, lowered his head and covered his face with his remaining hand. "I'm sorry if I frightened you, ma'am. I am afraid beautiful women like you will never get used to this new face."

"I didn't mean…," Louisa protested, before relenting. "Oh, I'm so sorry for the way I acted. So very sorry."

Helmut walked over to pick up a partial porcelain mask which fell to the sidewalk when the veteran lost his balance, then helped his comrade replace his dignity. As the soldier hobbled off, the officer returned his salute.

Their perfect evening was ruined. Helmut's delight at her chosen watch did nothing to raise her spirits. When they sat down at the restaurant table the wife specially reserved for her returned husband, she had no appetite.

After a perfunctory look at the menu, Louisa took one of Helmut's hands in both of hers and started to tear up. "Oh darling, promise me you will never go back to war."

"What war?" Helmut asked, with a nonchalance belied by a darkening expression. "We won the war last summer and I am back home with you, safe and sound, in this beautiful restaurant."

"What about *Amerika*?"

Her soldier's face went rigid as he took a long swallow from his water glass. Louisa didn't know why she said that. A rumor Hitler was preparing an invasion of *Amerika* was making the rounds of the capital, but no one really believed it. *Amerika* was so far away.

"Honey, please believe me," Helmut asked, "we are not at war and I never want to leave you for another battlefield."

"Then resign from the *Luftwaffe*," Louisa pushed.

"You are not being fair, Louisa. We discussed this before we married. None of the services are releasing officers until England and France are incorporated into the *Reich*."

Louisa lowered her head and closed her eyes against the tears. The singer knew she was not being fair to her soldier. Her love had no choice but to follow orders. The *Führer* and his generals would decide whether he went to war again. But she also knew her soldier was not being completely honest with her. Helmut loved what he did and would go running if Hitler called.

Damn him. Damn them all.

Louisa finally raised her head with what she hoped was a smile. She could not waste what little time they had together arguing about things out of their control. Helmut eagerly returned her smile and wiped her cheeks with a finger, clearly hoping he was brushing away her fears with the tears.

Louisa's fears were not gone, though, but rather burrowed into the shadows of her imagination. While the wife changed the subject and chatted about her family's plans for Christmas, that skeletal face still lurked in the background, except that face now belonged to her husband.

Berlin, Germany
15:01 Hours, 23 December 1941

Grand Admiral Raeder frowned as he studied the war game table portraying the Charleston landing zone, then tentatively pushed the figurine representing the paratroopers onto the painted mock-up of the port facility.

It was a daring idea - a company of the *Luftwaffe's* paratroopers stowed aboard a merchant ship like the Greeks inside the Trojan Horse, taking the Port of Charleston by surprise. If any unreported enemy units lurked in the area, the paratroopers would suffer heavy casualties, but the chance to take the enemy city in a single day was worth any losses.

Raeder glanced up at the clock on the wall. He needed to wrap this up. Erich's wife Augusta made it crystal clear he would come home in time to entertain her parents this evening. Duty called.

The admiral longingly examined the table one last time. So many possibilities…

Since the Empress's report four days ago, Raeder felt positively giddy. The incredibly fortunate *Abwehr* spy took a pleasure cruise in her yacht and managed to blunder into an enormous *Amerikaner* task force, made up of at least three carriers surrounded by their most modern surface ships, all moving at high speed towards the Pacific.

When he learned of the planned Japanese attack on the Hawaiian Islands, Raeder thanked God he would no longer have to deal with the enemy Pacific fleet. Now, with most of their Atlantic Fleet moving off to relieve the besieged Hawaiian Islands, his combined *Kriegsmarine* and *Regia Marina* fleets would enjoy clear naval superiority off the *Amerikaner* east coast.

The normally conservative planner felt safe rolling the dice a couple times during the crossing, beginning with a commando raid on the Port of Charleston.

CHAPTER 10

Ko'olau Range, Oahu, Hawaii
08:09 Hours, 24 December 1941

Nestled behind a short bushy tree with a great line of sight along the trail over which he just withdrew, Corporal Billy Deal wondered whether he was the hunter or the hunted.

A *Springfield* rifle cracked nearby, followed by the snaps of a handful of Japanese rifle shots. Deal took aim down the path and waited. When Mike Morgan popped up over the next rise and trotted down the path, Billy gave a short, sharp whistle to disclose his location. Mike grinned and nodded his acknowledgment, before moving past to his next position.

The next face to arrive was not smiling. A skinny Jap with a helmet full of branches and leaves popped his head up, looked quickly around, then ducked down again. A few seconds later he rose up from his cover and cautiously walked down the trail.

Deal waited until the enemy point man was joined by one of his buddies on the path before firing. The point man collapsed with a scream, clutching his ruined belly. The trailing soldier grabbed his wounded comrade under the arms and dragged him into the bushes down the trail.

Deal and Morgan couldn't afford the mercy of quick kills today. The heavily outnumbered soldiers were playing a deadly game of shoot and scoot with a Jap patrol coming up from the south. The way Billy figured it, every Jap he wounded would take a second Jap out of the chase to care for him. Two birds with one shot.

The playing field for this game was the Ko'olau mountain range dominating the eastern shore of Oahu. The Ko'olau was not a range of separate mountains, but rather one long ridge, the remaining rim of the ancient volcano which created the island. There was no room for maneuver. The top of the knife's edge ridge was crowned with a footpath, while both sides to the east and west dropped steeply down. You could traverse the narrow path above or plunge into the jungle below.

Deal regained his feet and trotted down the ridge. At the first bend of the trail, Billy almost fell over Mike crouching down low. Morgan put his finger to his lips and pointed over to the next rise to the south. The corporal studied the foliage for a moment before making out the movement of figures wearing Jap helmets between the trees. Another frigging patrol was coming down from the north. Christ, we're surrounded again!

This was the third day of an unexpected patrol.

Their Twenty-fourth Infantry Division was entrenched north of Schofield Barracks, across the sugar and pineapple plantations dominating the island's central valley. The division commander considered the jungle on both sides of those plantations to be impassable and left these areas essentially unguarded. Having hunted the jungle for months before the war, Deal and Morgan knew this was dangerous horse hockey. While a couple dogfaces had no chance of seeing the general to straighten him out, the pair did manage to convince their company commander to allow them three days to scout the jungle to the east to see if the Japs were up to any monkey business on that unguarded flank.

Before dawn of the first day, Deal and Morgan left their company positions on the edge of the Dole pineapple plantation and quickly found one of the footpaths leading through their old hunting grounds in the dense Ewa Forest. After failing to find any Japs while creeping through the woods, the pair spent the next few hours working their way up the towering Ko'olau mountain range to get a better look around.

From those heights, Oahu looked peaceful and green. If you didn't know the ships parked off the north and east shores were Japanese, you wouldn't know there was a war going on at all.

For their purposes, the Ko'olau provided no special vantage to scout the Ewa Forest. Even with his spotter's binoculars, Morgan couldn't penetrate the thick green canopy below to determine if the Jap infantry were moving around the division's flank. However, the other side of the ridge provided a great view of Jap trucks running along the Kamehameha Highway along the east coast of the island.

The patrol was supposed to be a sneak and peek recon without any drama, but Billy and Mike couldn't resist getting in some action. Not due back for another two days, the men decided over supper to spend one of those days having some fun hunting Jap supply trucks down by the Waiahole shore.

Just after dawn the next morning, the sniper and his spotter crept down a draw in the Ko'olau, identified multiple locations with good cover overlooking the highway, and went to work.

Deal's first shot took out the driver of the lead truck of a morning convoy, causing the vehicle to flip and block the road. Mike used his binoculars to rapidly identify and guide his sniper to interesting targets down the stalled convoy, then Billy methodically picked off each in turn.

After five shots, the team displaced to the next sniping point, only to find several dozen Jap soldiers took advantage of the lull in fire to leave the cover of the trucks and swarm into the jungle looking for them. The sniper got in two more kills along the convoy before the team decided to get the hell out of Dodge and back up the draw.

The delay almost cost them their asses. The Japs moved through the jungle much faster than the American hunters expected and filled up the draw behind them. Deal and Morgan spent a couple hairy hours hiding up a mango tree while the Japs poked around. Finally, the slant eyes pulled out and the pair made their way back up the Ko'olau to camp for the night.

Now, here they were surrounded again on the Puu Kaaumakula peak with no prospect of the Japs backing off.

Deal swallowed hard. There was no alternative but to go off the side. While he was a Colorado mountain boy, Billy was scared as hell of heights. He said a small prayer before parting the bushes at the side of the trail to survey the western slope. Steep as hell, but thankfully plenty of vegetation to grab on the way down.

For a moment the sniper considered staying put and shooting it out with the Japs, then dismissed the thought and followed his spotter off the side. Billy went down feet first, facing the slope, careful not to look down. Grabbing one bush after another for dear life, his arms were soon burning and cramped from overexertion.

Suddenly, the rustle and crunch of the descent were replaced with shots and yells coming from above. Deal and Morgan froze and hugged the slope, certain the Japs had spotted them and were using their exposed backsides for target practice. However, there were no telltale cracks of passing bullets.

Then it all became clear. "Mike, the Jap patrols are shooting at one another, Deal hissed down.

"You're frigging kidding me," Morgan chuckled softly. "Let's get off this damned cliff before the sons of bitches realize where we've gone."

Resuming his descent, Billy profusely thanked the good Lord for looking after them and promised he would definitely be at Christmas services tomorrow.

*Kaukonahua Stream, Ko'olau Range, Oahu, Hawaii
11:24 Hours, 24 December 1941*

These *Ameko* were an unworthy enemy, Captain Hayashi concluded. After surrendering the northern coast of Oahu with little resistance, the *Ameko* fell back to the pineapple and sugar plantations across the island's central valley, where they hid in trenches, protected by what even the Japanese captain admitted was superb artillery. Now, the cowards appeared to have surrendered the jungle.

Hayashi's company was again honored to lead the regiment's attack, this time around the east flank of the enemy defenses. The area of operations was dense jungle broken by a series of streams flowing off what the natives called the Ko'olau mountains. Not too much different from the Formosa training grounds of the summer.

The company commander's *hentai* filed silently along the path cut through the greenery by the scout detachment. A series of pages torn from captured *Ameko* magazines and tacked on tree trunks marked the route. As he passed a page featuring a smiling woman with golden hair smoking a cigarette, the company commander idly wondered how American women differed from the women he used in China. Before this campaign was finished, Otozo promised himself he would find out.

The men wove branches and leaves into their helmets and uniforms to make them almost indistinguishable from surrounding jungle. Despite the concealment, the lead sergeants proceeded cautiously, halting frequently to peek into ravines and between the Koa trees reaching up into the sky. The jungle offered many opportunities for ambush to a skillful foe.

The *Ameko* were not such a foe. When the scouts first reported the jungle was free of enemy positions, Hayashi did not believe them. Yet, after hours moving unhindered down the scout trails, the incredulous company commander could no longer argue the point.

During the training for war with the United States, the Imperial Army officer corps was sharply divided over what to expect from the new enemy. Hayashi and the other junior officers were nearly unanimous in their belief the *Ameko* were soft and unwilling to endure the rigors of war.

Opinions were mixed among the senior staff, though. Those who served in the United States before the war told stories of a nation where millions worked in factories, producing enough automobiles and other household machines for everyone. In turn, enemy military schools trained their officers like factory managers, who viewed battles as efficient allocations of weapons and supplies. Contrasting the sparse material situation in Japan, where nearly everything was always in short supply, these officers concluded a war with the *Ameko* was hopeless.

Hayashi rejected these qualms. The enemy described by these fearful old men lacked an Emperor and a spiritual base. The captain recalled one western general who understood this weakness. Among his maxims of war, France's Napoleon Bonaparte noted the moral is to the physical as three is to one. The army with the superior moral strength would always prevail over a better equipped enemy.

Today was the *Ameko's* crowning disgrace. Hayashi could not believe any enemy would leave their flanks unguarded. Were these round eyes like young children afraid to enter the jungle? Or were they simply lazy? If a Japanese general demonstrated this level of incompetence, the Emperor would invite him to slit his belly! The company commander cracked a toothy smile. If the gods are with me, maybe I can slit the enemy general's belly for him.

Waikakalaua Stream, Ko'olau Range, Oahu, Hawaii
18:41 Hours, 24 December 1941

As twilight deepened, the sniper forced himself to slow down and mentally rehearse how they would re-enter friendly lines. Because they came off the Ko'olau further south than planned, he figured they would make first contact with the boys guarding Wheeler Air Field. Billy was badly mistaken.

Deal walked point along an animal path paralleling a stream coming down off the Ko'olau, with Morgan trailing about ten yards behind. Billy figured they were only about a half mile away from home. The soldiers wanted to make that hot Christmas Eve meal, but not enough to get their asses shot off by some overeager sentry.

Deal stopped and raised his left hand in a fist, causing Morgan to fade into the jungle and take a knee just off the path. Some other noise up ahead was joining the constant gurgle of the stream. It sounded like…splashing.

The sniper silently crept ahead at a low crouch and peeked around the next turn in the path. About a dozen yards ahead, a single file column of Japs was crossing the stream, carefully looking both ways for the enemy. Deal melted back into the foliage as quietly as possible to avoid their gaze. As he slowly turned back towards Mike, a second column of Japs emerged from the jungle and entered the stream, cutting him off from his partner. Boxed in.

Billy lowered himself to the ground and rolled on his back under a low-hanging tree. A short, squat soldier brushed the tree and snagged a branch with the mortar tripod he was carrying. With what sure sounded like curse under his breath, the Jap yanked his tripod free with two hard tugs. The last tug pulled the branch to the side, exposing the American lying beneath.

For a very long moment, the enemy soldier seemed to look him straight in the eye. Damn! Billy's entire body stiffened and he pissed a little into his skivvies, before placing his finger on the trigger. No avoiding a fight now.

Instead, the Jap obliviously released the branch, slapping Deal in the face, and rejoined his comrades crossing the stream. No warning shouts, no killing shots.

The sniper slowly unclenched and plopped his head onto the ground. *Billy boy, you definitely used up your ninth life.*

Another five minutes crawled by before the Jap columns passed and Deal was free to make his way back to Morgan. The men pulled back another quarter mile upstream and hashed out the situation.

"What do ya think we're looking at?" Mike wondered as he scratched at his three-day growth of beard.

"Something big," Billy replied. "At least a company passed us just now, carrying machine guns and mortars. And they're headed for the airfield."

The sniper took an angry swallow of water from his canteen and screwed the cap on tight. "We shouldn't have gone up the Ko'olau. If we stayed down here, we could have spotted this bunch and reported back."

"Billy, don't beat yourself up. We did spot them. The problem is they are between us and the rest of the division."

"Well, without a phone or a radio, there's only one way to warn the division."

"Neither one of us is about ready to sprout wings, good buddy, so what do ya have in mind?" Mike inquired.

"What we do best," Billy grinned back. "Pick a fight."

Wheeler Field, Oahu, Hawaii
19:01 Hours, 24 December 1941

Captain Hayashi refused to allow the firefight erupting behind his company to distract him from the prize to his front - Wheeler Airfield. Despite the nearby pops of rifles and the replying the clatter of a machine gun and blasts of knee mortars, the airfield remained dark and quiet in the moonless night. Given the *Ameko* proclivity for firing at shadows and giving away their positions at night, the company commander could only conclude the division objective was undefended. A plum ripe for his picking.

The captain rose and waved his men out of the jungle. The company slowly advanced down the cement landing strip in tight skirmish lines. The bomb-damaged hangers loomed to the right and the wreckage of gutted aircraft cluttered the left, with a sandbagged emplacement of some sort at the other end of the runway. Still no sign of life in the gloom.

Suddenly, the world filled with blinding incandescence, as every exterior light up and down the field turned on one after another. Rifle and a machine gun bullets from the hangers clattered like hail, while anti-aircraft gun at the end of the field barked in a deeper voice.

Hayashi raised his sword and pointed it at the hangers, yelling the command to charge. Trained to unquestioning obedience, the company surged forward with a roar.

The *Ameko* fire took a terrible toll on the *hentai* as they advanced. The heavy rounds from the anti-aircraft guns were the worst, dismembering the men they hit and hurling shredded flesh onto those nearby. The rifles into which the Japanese charged took their own bloody harvest. The enemy could hardly miss at a range of 100 meters and closing.

For their part, the *hentai* were armed with unloaded rifles, affixed with bayonets smeared with mud to conceal them in the night. The bayonet was the common soldier's *samurai* sword. Once the *hentai* closed, no enemy could stand up to a determined bayonet charge. Once his men closed.

A handful of *hentai* collapsed to the ground in front of their commander, felled by terror, rather than any genuine wounds. Hayashi sprinted towards his paralyzed men, stumbled when a bullet tore at his hip, then forced himself forward again at a hitched trot. Stumbling to a halt and looming over his men like a wrathful god, the company commander shrieked at them to continue the advance, raising his sword high for emphasis,

When a sobbing soldier rolled on his back and defensively folded his arms over his face, Hayashi lost all control and swung his sword down in a rage. The tempered steel blade sliced through the man's arms like twigs, then drove deeply into his skull. What remained of the disgraced man's arms flopped to the side, spraying blood over his comrades lying nearby.

As the captain stepped on the man's chest and pulled his blade out of the corpse, the other *hentai* sprang to their feet, running with a scream from their commander towards the *Ameko* soldiers. Better to risk enemy bullets than certain death under his sword.

Hayashi resumed a pained jog behind his newly motivated men to ensure they reached their objective and performed their duty. There would be no cowardice or surrender under his command.

Dole Pineapple Plantation, Oahu, Hawaii
03:33 Hours, 25 December 1941

Major General D.S. Wilson's hand shook as he put the handset back onto the field telephone. Communications with Schofield Barracks were completely down.

Somehow the Japs got behind the Twenty-fourth Infantry Division's trenches, overran Wheeler and then the reserve battalion at Schofield. With the enemy simultaneously attacking from the north and pinning down the frontline units, Wilson had nothing left to send south to retake the base. Nothing left to rescue his family.

Olive was volunteering at the hospital tonight. She would have left the kids alone at home under the care of the oldest. Ah Christ, alone at home…

Wilson cradled his forehead on the palms of his hands and struggled not descend into unreasoning panic. His entire life was ruined. Not only was his command surrounded and threatened with destruction, his family could be in Japanese hands…or worse.

It's all my fault and there's no way I can ever make this right. No way.

The general sat up at the field desk, unholstered his pistol and put the muzzle into his mouth.

Schofield Barracks Hospital, Oahu, Hawaii
14:14 Hours, 25 December 1941

Captain Hayashi strode through the hospital doors in a particularly foul mood. The company commander was bone tired after four days of jungle movement followed by street fighting. Now that victory was theirs, his men deserved a good meal and a well-earned rest. Instead, the morning brought new orders to take the *Ameko* soldiers at the hospital prisoner and march them back to a new detention center at the airfield.

Prisoners? The *hentai* would never choose surrender over death. The resulting disgrace would be more than any Japanese could bear. On the other hand, these loathsome round eyes seemed to strive for dishonor. Now, his superiors were ordering the *samurai* officer and his company to participate in that disgrace!

Hayashi entered a large bay. The *Ameko* wounded overflowed from the beds lining both sides of the room onto mats between the beds and along the walkway. A man in a white coat broke away from the haggard-looking staff tending to the wounded and approached with his arms outstretched towards the Japanese captain, as if to push him out of the ward. The insolent *Ameko* jabbered away, without even rendering the basic courtesy of a bow.

Hayashi impatiently waved over his third platoon leader, the only soldier in his platoon who understood the enemy gibberish. "Lieutenant Tada, please translate our orders to this American."

"Yes, Captain-san."

After a short exchange, the *Ameko* in the white coat became quite animated and started arguing with his platoon leader.

"Enough, Tada!" Hayashi interrupted. "Why aren't the prisoners moving as ordered?"

"Please excuse me, Captain-san," Tada half-bowed. "This man is the chief *Ameko* physician for this facility. He claims all of the wounded soldiers who could walk left yesterday to defend this base. Those who are left cannot be moved and…"

"Nonsense!" the company commander thundered. "If these *Ameko* had any honor, they would have ended their lives. Order these men to move out and gather at the front of the hospital in five minutes."

When Tada turned and delivered the order, the *Ameko* doctor pointed at a nearby bed and yelled something at his platoon leader. The lieutenant stood there in silence, as if unsure what to do.

"What did the *Ameko* say?"

"Uh…I am unsure how to translate this, Captain-san."

"Tell me what this dog said, word for word."

Tada swallowed hard and relayed what was said: "The American doctor refused the order. He pointed at the man on the bed there with the amputated legs and asked: 'How is this man supposed to move? Walking on his hands?'"

Hayashi moved without hesitation, drawing his father's sword from its scabbard and neatly separating the insolent *Ameko's* head from his neck in one smooth movement. The head bounced down the bay walkway, thumping off the floor like an overripe melon, spraying crimson across the white tile as it spun.

Rather than learning their lesson and proceeding as ordered, the *Ameko* started yelling and two even approached menacingly. Hayashi considered the enemy dogs coolly for a moment and then looked back at his *hentai*.

"Sergeants, you are to conduct bayonet practice on any *Ameko* soldier who fails to leave this bay in the next sixty seconds."

"Captain-san, what about our orders?" Tada exclaimed, as the non-commissioned officers gave the order to fix bayonets."

"Sixty seconds, Lieutenant."

The platoon leader turned toward the *Ameko*, repeating the order again and again in a pleading tone of which his company commander did not approve. The enemy only continued arguing. This was useless.

"Men, commence with the bayonet drill," Hayashi ordered. Pointing at the *Ameko* nurses, he grinned. "After your bayonets taste blood, you may do as you please with these cows. Reassemble in front of the building in one hour."

As his *hentai* roared their approval and surged forward, their company commander squatted down and casually wiped the blood off of his sword on the white coat of the beheaded doctor.

Rising again to survey the progress of the bayonet drill, Hayashi spotted a blonde *Ameko* nurse cowering in a corner. Otozo walked over, swatted her ample behind with the flat of his sword and pointed with his free hand towards a supply room off the bay. The woman shrieked and ran into the room as directed. He followed and closed the door behind them.

I promised myself I would sample these *Ameko* women before this campaign was through. Now was as good a time as any.

Central Valley, Oahu, Hawaii
06:10 Hours, 26 December 1941

Mike shook Billy from a deep sleep back into a nightmare. Deal sat up as best he could in the make shift sugar cane shelter they lashed together the night before, his mind and body throbbing. Despite a couple hours of rest, the sniper and his spotter were still dog-tired and nearly out on their feet.

After three days on patrol, the soldiers spent yesterday unsuccessfully struggling to sneak through Jap lines and back to their division. Used to engaging the enemy at long distance at his leisure, the sniper considered the close quarters and occasional hand-to-hand fighting of the past couple days as the toughest time of his life. Deal was about to discover he had no idea what tough really meant.

Washing down a small package of crackers making up the last of their rations with metallic canteen water, Deal and Morgan discussed their predicament in whispers. Almost out of ammo, the pair didn't have the firepower to break directly through to their unit. Their only apparent hope was to swing south and try to come back up along Highway 1. Surely, the Japs hadn't surrounded the entire division.

Mike took point, as they crept southward through the morning twilight. Chewing and sucking on chunk of sugar cane in a vain attempt to quiet his grumbling stomach, Deal pulled up the rear.

After a few minutes, Morgan froze in place and took a knee. Deal crept up to see what drew his friend's attention. Mike looked back and motioned to the left with the muzzle of his rifle. An erratic rustling, interspersed with groans, emanated from the adjacent row of sugar cane.

What the hell? If this was a Jap infiltrator, the idiot definitely didn't know his business.

Billy nodded to Mike and parted the green stalks to take a peek. A dark figure was slowly crawling forward through the shadows. As the sniper raised his rifle to take aim, he spied a tech sergeant's patch on the man's sleeve.

"Hold where you are," Deal hissed at the figure, "We're Americans."

The sergeant turned onto his side and croaked, "Water… please…water."

After the prone man took a couple large swallows from Deal's canteen and came up for air, the sniper asked, "Can you walk? This place is filled with Japs and we need to move out."

The man whipped his head back and forth, grimacing in pain.

"Let us take a look at you."

Deal and Morgan carefully moved the man onto his back and their hands came back covered with mud and blood. The sergeant groaned and passed out as Billy opened his uniform and knocked off clods of blood and mud looking for wounds. He counted no less than five bayonet holes seeping blood. Christ! How was this man still alive?

The sniper and the spotter did their best to patch the sergeant up, using their two field dressings on the worst wounds, then strips of cloth ripped from their own uniforms for the rest. Afterward, they lashed Mike's poncho onto a couple wooden poles they found marking the ends of sugar cane rows to build a makeshift stretcher.

Sometime during this process, the man's eyes fluttered back open, regaining consciousness and the ability to speak. "Thanks, felluhs. Don't think I could have gone much further."

"Where'd you come from, sarge?" Morgan asked as he tied off the last end of the poncho onto the pole.

"Schofield…Schofield Hospital."

"Christ, that's a couple miles away. Did you crawl all that way?"

"I was able to limp along for a while, until my leg gave out."

The one with the two stab wounds, Deal figured. "What happened?"

The man remained silent for a minute, tears streaming down his cheeks, then turned away as if trying to escape the memory. When he finally replied, the words came out in sobs. "The Japs came on Christmas afternoon. When they entered the ward, one of them stuck me in the side with his bayonet. I hit the deck, but the bastards kept sticking me and sticking me…sticking me."

The man coughed, then clenched in pain. "When they thought I was dead, the Japs started in on the patients lying on the beds."

The man grabbed Deal's arm and stared crazily into his eyes. "Then, they took Nurse Roberts…over and over again. When they were done, one of them shoved his bayonet up her privates. The son of a bitch actually laughed as she screamed."

Billy and Mike looked at one another in disbelief.

"It'll be OK, sarge," Billy grunted as he picked up the stretcher with Mike. "We'll get you to the medics, then get the Jap bastards who did this. We'll pay them back in spades."

Carefully picking their way through the plantation, the little group didn't make Highway 1 until midmorning. All the traffic was heading south, soldiers trudging along the side of the road and the occasional vehicle driving down the middle.

Morgan tried to flag down an ambulance truck, but the driver only slowed to yell they were full up. Two more vehicles passed by obliviously. Finally, Mike stepped out in front of an officer's car, banging on the hood as the driver almost hit him during a screeching halt. A full bird colonel stuck his head out of the rear window and bellowed for him to get the hell out of the road.

"Sir, we have a badly wounded man here who will die unless he gets to the hospital," Deal explained.

"Find a damned ambulance, corporal. I'm late getting back to Honolulu to report to the general."

Billy just stared at the incredible asshole and unshouldered his rifle. "With all due respect, sir, if you don't step out of that car right now, so we can put this man in the back seat, I will blow your fucking head clean off."

The colonel glared in fury at the corporal, then looked around at the soldiers gathering around the staff car and relented.

"Thank you, sir," Billy offered as he and Mike moved the sergeant into the back seat of the sedan and closed the door.

"Corporal, what's your name and unit?" the bird colonel demanded.

"William Deal, Hotel Company, 19th Regiment." the corporal replied from the position of attention. "Sir, do you have any idea how I get back to my unit? By the look of things here, I'm sure they need my help."

The bird colonel studied Billy for a moment, before his glare softened into weary resignation. "Son, your division is surrounded." Gesturing at the soldiers around them, the staff officer explained, "These boys are part of the 35th Infantry Regiment counterattack which went in on Christmas morning to open up a supply line to Schofield. They ran into an entire Jap division and now they're pulling back to Pearl."

The bird colonel walked back to the car and informed the driver they would be stopping at the naval hospital on the way back to Honolulu. Turning back to Deal and Morgan, he concluded, "You men can still pitch in, but it won't be with your old division."

CHAPTER 11

U.S.S. Saratoga, 118 miles south of Oahu, Hawaii
13:11 Hours, 6 January 1942

The minutes dragged by like days for Admiral Bull Halsey. A carrier battle at sea is a giant game of hide and seek. The winner is the first to find the enemy carriers and land a punch. The loser is sunk.

The scout planes were in the middle of their second runs of the day. So far, Blueberry Four found the Jap blockade of Pearl Harbor, but no sign of the enemy flattops.

The admiral glanced out of the carrier *Saratoga's* bridge window at the mostly cloudy skies, punctuated by a squall in the distance. Hardly ideal weather for aircraft reconnaissance. Were the Japs hiding beneath the clouds?

Bull sighed and fired up his first stogie of the afternoon. Nothing to do but wait.

Halsey still couldn't believe he was back in Hawaii at the helm of the largest combat operation in U.S. naval history. After losing *Enterprise* and *Lexington*, he figured the brass would hang him from the nearest yardarm when he returned home. Bull felt so ashamed that he was ready to provide them with the rope. Instead, newly minted Pacific Fleet commander Chester Nimitz, the Secretary of the Navy and a brass band greeted Halsey at the San Diego dock as a returning hero and whisked him away on a train to Washington D.C.

During the cross-country trip, the admiral caught up on current events. Hawaii was such an unmitigated disaster, the press desperately grasped for any good news to offer a shocked public and latched onto Halsey. The papers transformed him into some sort of modern-day John Paul Jones, bellowing in defiance "I have not yet begun to fight," while standing on the deck of a sinking ship. All Bull could do is shake his head in disbelief.

More astonishingly, Washington held a similarly high estimation of Halsey. The initial meeting with Admiral King was a pep talk rather than a dressing down. Ernie commiserated with the tough spot Bull found himself in Hawaii, but promised next time would be different. Next time?

King and Halsey then hopped into a staff car for a quick trip over to the White House. Roosevelt aged badly since the men became friends years ago, when Franklin was Assistant Secretary of the Navy hopping a ride on Bull's destroyer *Flusser* off Campabello Island before World War I. Polio relegated the vigorous man he remembered to a wheel chair and every year of the Depression and the disastrous opening to this second world war carved deep care lines into Roosevelt's handsome face.

"Bull, it's damned good to see you," FDR exclaimed, his old familiar smile and twinkle of the eye returning. "How are Frances and the kids?"

"Well, I hope," Halsey replied. "I haven't had a chance to see them since I got back to the states."

"Right, right. I'm sorry you haven't had time for a leave since this business started," the President commiserated. "You are a man who gets things done and I have a big job for you which cannot wait."

Roosevelt and King proceeded to hand him the keys to the kingdom. Halsey would command the Hawaii relief force, including four of the five remaining fleet carriers and nearly every other modern ship in the fleet. His mission was to break through the Jap fleet blockade and land the Marines to rescue the Army garrison on Oahu. Shaking his friend's hand, Bull promised the President he would not let him down.

Saratoga's captain interrupted the admiral's reverie with the first good news of the day. "Sir, the destroyer *Maury* radioed they have radar contact with multiple ships about 41 knots west southwest of Pearl Harbor. They're closing and will report when the radar picks up more detail."

The *U.S.S. Maury* was one of the radar-equipped destroyers Halsey deployed well forward of the fleet. A second set of eyes never hurt and this one appeared to be paying off.

"Admiral, the *Maury* now reports they have radar signals for 29 ships. The enemy formation appears to be consistent with a carrier task force."

The location made sense. If he were defending Oahu and the most direct approach from the States was from the northwest, Bull would tuck his carriers behind the island in reserve.

There was something else about the *Maury*… Oh yeah, their radar operator, George Jones, found the Enterprise during maneuvers last summer. Good man.

"OK, Captain, I think *Maury* probably found the Jap flat tops. However, let's be sure," Halsey directed. "Send Blueberry One to the coordinates of the radar signals to visually confirm the sighting.

"Yes, sir…uh wait, we have another report. Oh great…"

"What is it Captain?"

"Admiral, one of the CAP fighters reports shooting down a Jap flying boat…maybe two or three knots to the north."

"Well, it looks like they found us," Halsey sighed. "Get the coordinates from the *Maury* sighting to the CAGs on all the carriers, with orders for the planes on deck to fire up their engines and prepare to launch at my command."

Bull sat down and took a couple puffs from what was left of his stogie. *If Blueberry One does not report back soon, I'll have no choice but to roll the dice and launch without confirmation. We have to land the first punch.*

Blueberry One came through, though. The cloud cover was heavy and the scout plane could only make out about a dozen ships, but the pilot gave positive conformation of three enemy carriers.

Halsey smiled broadly. *I've got you sons of bitches.* "Captain, transmit the launch orders."

Carrier Akagi, 42 miles southwest of Oahu, Hawaii
13:21 Hours, 6 January 1942

The tedium was grinding on Mitsuo Fuchida. Because the *Ameko* Navy made no significant appearance in weeks, the high command diverted his pilots to bombing enemy trenches in the Oahu central valley and their flight commander was relegated to following their departures and returns on the radio.

Admiral Nagumo and Fuchida finally agreed on something – this was a singular waste of already scarce fleet resources. However, Yamamoto himself gave the order in no uncertain terms. Apparently, Army casualties on Oahu were reaching crisis levels and the Navy needed to rescue their sister service. Although he followed the spirit of the order, Nagumo maintained *Akagi* and its full complement of aircraft in reserve in case the enemy fleet returned.

After noting in careful script when the latest sortie of bombers completed their mission in Oahu, the flight commander received a radio teletype message from the communications officer. One of the *Kawanishi* H6K flying boat scouts out from Kaneohe airfield radioed it was ditching into the ocean approximately 160 kilometers south of Oahu, before the signal was lost.

South?

Fuchida walked over the bridge operations map. The current location of each submarine patrolling northeast of Oahu was marked in bright red. This was the fleet's outermost early warning screen of any enemy movement from the United States.

The routes of the flying boat patrols radiating 360 degrees out from Oahu were marked in dark blue. These were the Navy's primary eyes out into the vast Pacific.

The fleet itself was split in two – Admiral Mikawa's battleship group blockading Pearl Harbor on the southern end of Oahu and Nagumo's carrier group behind the island to the southwest.

Only four of the original six carriers remained. The fleet lost the unfortunate *Soryu* during initial battle and Yamamoto dispatched *Zuikaku* to keep the remnants of the English Navy from interfering with the Operation Orient offensive in Southeast Asia.

The missing *Kawanishi* was well off the anticipated avenues of approach from the United States, but it was possible for the *Ameko* to approach from the south if they refueled at sea, as did the Japanese fleet after the long voyage from its home ports to Oahu. And if the enemy, rather than mechanical failure, downed the scout plane, it meant *Ameko* carriers and their fighters were in the area.

"Admiral-san, would you please come to the map."

Nagumo glanced over from across the bridge and asked, "Did something go wrong with the bomber sortie?"

"No sir. Something new has arisen. So sorry, please come to the map, Admiral-san."

Fuchida quickly relayed the news of the lost scout to his commanding officer and recounted why he believed enemy carriers were approaching from the south.

Nagumo frowned and studied the map. "Your evidence is very thin, Fuchida. Very thin."

"I know it, sir. However, we cannot ignore the possibility of enemy carriers within range to launch an air strike."

"I suppose not." Pointing at the map, the admiral ordered, "Redirect the nearest scout from here to the last known position of the missing plane. Instruct them to report back any enemy sightings and to rescue the downed air crew."

"Immediately, sir. May I also deploy the combat air patrol fighters over the fleet?"

Nagumo previously ordered the fighter patrols suspended in order to conserve aviation fuel for the bombing sorties on Oahu. The admiral considered the request for a moment, then asked a question for which he already knew the answer. "Has any ship spotted an enemy scout plane or any unaccounted for aircraft?"

"No sir," Fuchida conceded.

"Then alert the pilots, but do not deploy the fighters until we confirm there is an enemy fleet."

"Yes, Admiral-san."

The flight commander dispatched the admiral's orders and then returned to his station to review the day's flight plans. How long would it take to land, refuel and rearm the returning bombers in case the *Ameko* Navy was actually in the area?

Fuchida glanced over as rain began pelting the bridge windows. Another one of the squalls they experienced over the past two days engulfed *Akagi*. The commander hoped the other carriers still enjoyed clear skies. The bombers would be returning soon and landing in a thunderstorm was extremely dangerous.

U.S.S. Saratoga, 110 miles south of Oahu, Hawaii
14:13 Hours, 6 January 1942

Admiral Halsey placed the aircraft primary radio frequency on the *Saratoga's* bridge intercom and furiously puffed away at his cigar waiting for the first pilot reports.

The admiral enjoyed a reputation as a hard ass, who brushed off adversity like dandruff. In reality, Bull had not slept more than two hours over the past couple days and struggled to maintain his never say die demeanor. After the catastrophic losses of last month, he was terrified of failing again and getting hundreds more of his sailors killed. Now, here he was again, helplessly waiting to see the results of his latest roll of the dice.

"Mongoose Leader, this is Mongoose Seven," the speakers squawked. "I have twenty-plus enemy ships at two o'clock. One…two… Jumping Jesus! Three flattops in the middle of that mob."

Mongoose was the code name for the *Hornet's* dive bomber squadron, Halsey recalled.

"Settle down, Mongoose Seven. I confirm your sighting. I count twenty-eight total ships, three carriers."

Halsey tapped the ash off his cigar, straining to hear the next transmission through the background static.

"All squadrons, this is Eagle Leader. I see no *Zeros* on patrol above that Jap task force. I repeat, no *Zeros*."

Eagle was Saratoga's fighter squadron.

"Eagle Leader, this is Cobra leader. Keep your eyes peeled. The bastards have to be somewhere. There's no way we got that lucky."

"Roger, Cobra Leader. We'll keep any bandits off of you. Time for you boys to go to work."

Halsey and *Saratoga's* CAG looked incredulously at one another. No *Zeros* providing air cover? How the hell was that even possible?

Radio traffic spiked as the squadron leaders coordinated their attack. Each carrier's aircraft chose an enemy flat top to target, while *Saratoga's* pilots held back to destroy anything left over.

The radios went silent for a few moments as the attacks went in, then the reports started rolling in fast and furious.

All semblance of radio discipline was lost. The pilots sounded off like a bunch of Firsties in the stands of a Academy football game, cheering on Navy against Army.

"Raven Leader to flock, follow me in and release your fish when I give the order."

"Eagle Leader to all squadrons, still no sign of bandits."

"Raven Leader to base, multiple torpedo hits. The Jap flattop is leaning hard to starboard. The dive bombers are beginning their run."

"Cobra Leader, this is Cobra Six. Two of three bombs hit. Look at that big bastard buuurn!"

"Mongoose leader to base, scratch three flattops. Sweet mother of God, how did we get so lucky?"

"This is a Goddamned turkey shoot. Lay into 'em boys!"

Unable to restrain himself any longer, Bull Halsey pumped his fist in the air and unleashed a thunderous "Hell yeah!" to the applause of the rest of the bridge crew.

We finally got the Jap bastards and we got 'em good.

Nakajima B5N bomber, 90 miles south of Oahu, Hawaii
15:39 Hours, 6 January 1942

Mitsuo Fuchida led the *Akagi* air group over the peaceful blue waters of the Pacific in a state of shock. The flight commander could not believe the evil karma which ravaged his beloved carriers. An *Ameko* task force somehow evaded all of their scouts and struck the carrier group before it could raise an effective defense.

By what black magic did they find us? No *Ameko* scout planes were sighted overhead. The lost flying boat provided the only warning something was astray and their last radio transmission failed to report an enemy presence.

Fuchida seethed at the absence of a fighter combat air patrol over the carriers.

If only Yamamoto had not diverted their air group and its precious fuel to Oahu.

If only Nagumo heeded his recommendation to deploy the combat air patrol when the scout plane ditched.

If only.

Blame would not bring back the lost carriers, however.

Mitsuo vividly recalled the carnage arrayed before him as *Akagi* emerged from the squall after the enemy air strike. Through his binoculars, the air commander could see *Kaga* slipping beneath the waves, while *Hiryu* and *Shokaku* burned in place like funeral bonfires.

Moments later, the Japanese bomber sortie returned from Oahu, finding no place to land. As uncharacteristically panicked requests for orders filled the airwaves, Fuchida furiously worked to find his orphaned birds a home. *Akagi's* deck was filling with its own planes and had no room for the circling bombers. The only alternative was to send the bombers to Kauai Island and then transmit a flash message to the airfield there to make room for their surprise visitors.

With that fire put out, Fuchida returned to the bridge and was finally rewarded with some good news. The diverted flying boat found a very large *Ameko* fleet protecting four carriers. Hiding from enemy fighter patrols in the clouds, the scout pilot stayed on location to guide *Akagi's* air group in for a counterattack.

The task at hand was to destroy as many *Ameko* carriers as possible. Currently, the enemy carriers massively outnumbered *Akagi*. Unless the air commander could even up those odds, the entire Hawaii campaign would fail.

To accomplish this mission, Fuchida maximized his remaining firepower. During the preflight briefing, the air commander hurriedly assigned each section of three torpedo or dive bombers a specific task against the standard *Ameko* carrier formation. His pilots were not to waste any time assessing the situation. Instead, once the enemy carriers were sighted, each section would accelerate to full speed and carry out the attack before enemy fighters could stop them. When they strode off to their aircraft, the pilots displayed none of their usual humor and bravado, just somber determination.

Unfortunately, the air battle played out as Fuchida expected, not as he had hoped. His pilots executed their orders flawlessly, but the enemy admiral protected his carriers as the Japanese air group commander would have done, layering ships and their antiaircraft guns around them like circled wagons in an *Ameko* western film. Those guns threw a cone of steel rounds up over the flat-topped ships, taking a terrible harvest from the low and slow flying torpedo bombers, and somewhat fewer of the higher-flying dive bombers.

Fuchida's falcons enjoyed better fortune. The *Zero* fighter escort out-maneuvered and clawed into the slower, blocky *Ameko* birds, dropping them into the ocean or at least keeping them fighting for their lives, while the surviving bombers completed their tasks.

After the Japanese commander's trio of B5N dive bombers emerged from the cone of death. Fuchida carefully set his bombsight on the *Ameko* carrier in the center and ordered his pilot to begin began his descent. The planes on each side precisely matched their leader's dive, while their bombardiers fixed their eyes on Fuchida's plane to release their bombs when he did. When the B5N section pulled up again, their trio of bombs continued onto the carrier deck, one igniting a tank of aviation fuel and another detonating a cache of bombs. The resulting blast shook the commander's departing bomber and put a wan smile on his face.

The satisfaction of revenge well-taken did not last, though. As his bomber regained altitude and gave Fuchida perspective, the commander confirmed only a pair of the Ameko carriers were burning. *Akagi* would still be outnumbered two-to-one in the morning.

U.S.S. Saratoga, 89 miles south of Oahu, Hawaii
15:34 Hours, 6 January 1942

As the last Jap bombers banked away for home, Halsey closed his eyes and kneaded his forehead in a vain attempt to push back an emerging headache. The American first strike was not the knockout blow they assumed and the Japs counterpunched all too well.

Task Force One lost half its carriers in less than a half hour. *Hornet* exploded and sank, while *Wasp* lay motionless on the horizon, belching dark black smoke. Unless the latter ship's crew pulled off a minor miracle to restore the engines and power, the admiral would have to scuttle the stricken vessel.

Despite their effectiveness, the enemy planes were relatively few in number. The enemy couldn't have more than a one carrier left and Bull was determined to sink the bitch before the day was through. The question was how to find her?

Halsey's last sighting of the enemy fleet was hours old. *Maury* lost track of the enemy when a Jap cruiser forced the smaller destroyer to withdraw. If the Jap admiral was competent, he would change direction and displace to a different location at full speed as soon as his last plane landed.

Glancing up to the bridge clock, the admiral knew he had to throw away the manual. There wasn't enough time before dark to launch the scout planes, find the enemy flat top, and then launch another air strike.

Bull took another puff from his cigar and racked his tired brain for a viable alternative. Wait a minute. Why not let the air strike perform its own reconnaissance? We could send each squadron on a different path into the area where the Jap fleet should be operating. The first squadron to find the bastards will call in the rest to join the party. That's the ticket!

"Captain, call the CAG up to the bridge. We have work to do."

*Carrier Akagi, 36 miles west/southwest of Oahu, Hawaii
17:30 Hours, 6 January 1942*

The air commander was pouring over damage and casualty reports, calculating how to assemble a first air strike in the morning, when the alert sounded. Snatching up his binoculars and running to the bridge window, Fuchida quickly located the Douglas TBD-1 torpedo bomber squadron approaching from the port side of *Akagi*.

Damn! How did the *Ameko* find us again so quickly?

The section of *Zero* fighters assigned to carrier defense dove into the enemy formation, splashing half of the unprotected torpedo bombers and scattering the rest, but not before the *Ameko* launched a spread of four torpedoes.

Akagi's captain ordered the helm to execute an evasive maneuver with limited success. Two of the enemy fish detonated amidships, but within the same watertight compartment. The carrier was slowed considerably as the single compartment flooded, but the ship would not sink.

For all of their prowess in reconnaissance, the remainder of the *Ameko* attack was curiously inept. In contrast to their coordinated first strike in the morning, the enemy squadrons arrived individually with the setting sun, allowing the nine surviving *Zeros* to jump them one by one.

The handful of *Ameko* bombers which managed to break through found *Akagi* shrouded in smoke. No longer able to maneuver, the captain decided to play dead, ordering the engine room to issue smoke out of the exhaust ports to simulate a ship on fire. The ruse appeared to fool the *Ameko* as the enemy pilots turned away without engaging the wounded vessel.

The Hawaii Group's remaining carrier and its birds survived to fight another day, but would that day be tomorrow?

As soon as the *Zeros* confirmed the last enemy bird had departed, Admiral Nagumo assembled his commanders and sent Fuchida into a rage.

"*Akagi* can no longer defend herself and the fleet cannot afford to lose another carrier. Captain, you will sail Akagi back to Japan with a destroyer escort," Nagumo ordered. "I will unite the remainder of the group below Oahu for the final battle with the *Ameko*."

Fuchida could not believe what he was hearing. "Sir, to retreat now in the face of the enemy with the battle in the balance would be disgrace!" the flight commander nearly screamed. "Allow me to recall our aircraft from Kauai before the sun sets and a full strength *Akagi* will stand with the combined fleet in the morning."

"Mind your tongue, Commander," the admiral growled. "The fleet battleships will be more than sufficient to protect Oahu."

"Admiral-san, how well did the *Ameko* battleships protect Oahu against our carriers?"

As Nagumo's face flushed a deep red and his hands balled into fists, Fuchida executed a quick tactical retreat. "If *Akagi* is returning to Japan, sir, may I at least fly my birds to join the rest of the air group on Kauai, so we may continue the battle from there?"

Taking the offered opportunity to save face, the admiral rasped, "Commander, get your insubordinate carcass and aircraft off my ship in the next half hour."

Fuchida suppressed a triumphant smile and rendered a smart hand salute to his commanding officer. The battle goes on.

*U.S.S. Saratoga, 67 miles south/southwest of Oahu, Hawaii
18:48 Hours, 6 January 1942*

Bull Halsey watched the sun sink under the horizon like a slamming window, leaving the inky darkness you only find on the open sea. Every electric light in the fleet was turned off or safely hidden behind steel walls. The Japs were not likely to find his ships, nor were his missing pilots.

"What are the plane counts?"

"The bombers are all accounted for, Admiral, but *Yorktown* and *Saratoga's* fighters are still missing," the CAG reported. "They were likely covering the withdrawal when they lost the sun."

"How much more fuel do they have?"

"Sir, it's hard to tell because both squadrons had to redirect to the Jap carrier and I'm not sure how long they spent over the target."

"Guess."

After a pause, the CAG replied, "Twenty minutes or so, if they're lucky."

Moonrise was not for hours. The only way the admiral's missing pilots would find their home carriers in this pitch-dark is if they managed to fly directly overhead. Good luck with that.

Bull took a couple puffs from his stogie. The choices were bleak. Turn on the lights and risk the Japs hunting down the fleet or maintain light discipline and lose two dozen pilots and the fleet's fighter cover. The air battle had drawn his task force north, within striking range of Jap fleet blockading Pearl Harbor. On the other hand, the lights would only be on for a half hour tops. Screwed if you do, screwed if you don't.

"Captain, transmit instructions to turn on every light on the *Saratoga* and *Yorktown*," the admiral commanded. "I want both carriers lit up like Christmas trees so our boys can find their way home. Radio the pilots and the escort ships to let them know what's happening and to keep a sharp eye out for the Japs."

Battleship Kongo, 45 miles south of Oahu, Hawaii
18:51 Hours, 6 January 1942

Admiral Mikawa knitted his brow as he read the alert teletype from the Hawaii fleet commander. Nagumo tersely announced the carrier group's support ships would unite with the blockade group at approximately midnight, at which time he would take over command of the combined force.

No mention of the carriers. Were they all lost today?

While Mikawa did not worship the carrier as did many in the Imperial Japanese Navy, the admiral did recognize the benefits of air support for his battleships and cruisers. This alert suggested his air cover was at the bottom of the ocean and the surface fleet would be on its own against *Ameko* air strikes in the morning.

Lost in thought, Mikawa did not immediately recognize the approach of the *Kongo's* captain, until a discrete clearing of the skipper's throat penetrated his superior's distraction.

"Admiral, the destroyer *Akizuki* radioed a pair of *Ameko* ships turned on their lights for some unknown reason." After Mikawa shot him an incredulous look, the captain replied, "I know, sir, I did not believe the report either until the destroyer retransmitted the message."

"Where is *Akizuki* located?"

The captain pointed south and handed the admiral a pair of binoculars. Sure enough, Mikawa could make out a faint electric glow in the distance. Incredible. Then, the lights went on in admiral's head. The *Ameko* were offering him an opportunity to turn the tables!

Within minutes of Mikawa issuing a rapid-fire series of orders, the blockade fleet leapt to life in a series of well-practiced movements. The blockade line of ships first pivoted into two columns, then surged forward toward the flanks of the *Ameko* fleet. Sea planes catapulted off the decks of the battleships and buzzed off for the southern glow.

To command the first night battle finishing off the enemy Pacific fleet was an honor. This opening to finish off the *Ameko* Atlantic fleet as well was the wildest stroke of fortune.

Before his ships could leave their assigned sector around Pearl Harbor and Honolulu, however, Mikawa needed Nagumo's permission. No Japanese officer would consider leaving his post without orders, no matter the opportunities an opponent offered. The admiral was confident his superior's permission would be shortly forthcoming. Only a great fool would forgo this opportunity.

U.S.S. Saratoga, 60 miles south/southwest of Oahu, Hawaii
19:00 Hours, 6 January 1942

"Hot damn! This is Eagle Leader to Eagle Nest, we see the way home."

"Good news, Eagle Leader," *Saratoga's* CAG nearly shouted into the radio mike back to the carrier's fighter squadron leader. "What's your fuel situation?"

"Ummm… not so good. Landing at the nest will be a close thing. Really close."

"Let's shorten the distance for the boys," the Admiral Halsey interjected. "Captain, please make your best speed northwest towards our prodigal children and tell the rest of the task force to follow." We may just pull this off.

Minutes crawled by, then the radios came alive again with unexpected messages.

"Admiral, *Massachusetts* is reporting a Jap aircraft is dropping flares overhead. They're engaging with anti-aircraft guns."

Halsey looked out the starboard windows, but couldn't see anything past the glare of the *Saratoga's* lights.

"Now, I am getting similar reports across the fleet, sir," the communications officer added. "I have issued a force wide radio requesting clarification."

Flares? What the hell were the Japs up to? You only use flares to illuminate…

"Lieutenant, request an immediate radar report from the destroyer screen. Do we have any party crashers?"

Looking up from a new message, the comms officer asked, "How'd you know, sir? *Dale* just reported two groups of Jap vessels coming in hot from Oahu."

The enemy blockade force was coming out to play much quicker than Bull expected. Unless the anti-aircraft batteries were able to knock out the enemy planes hiding in the darkness above, the closing Japs would easily engage his illuminated ships. Clever sons of bitches.

The admiral quickly gathered the bridge officers and asked one simple question: Could the fighters land before the Jap ships came within firing range? After some quick radio chatter and calculations, the grim-faced answers were unanimously no.

Bull drew deeply on his stogie and launched an angry stream of smoke at the nautical chart, searching for some way out of this trap. The marked-up paper offered no answers.

"Order the fleet to go dark and move south at full speed, then give the pilots the news." The bridge officers nodded back and quietly carried out the admiral's order.

The radios broadcasting over the bridge loudspeaker turned into a funeral dirge of pilots reporting their last known locations in hopes of morning rescue, before parachuting into the long night. When Eagle Leader added a request for the CAG to mail his wife the letter on top of his locker, a crying commo officer reached over to turn off the intercom.

"Leave it on, Lieutenant," Bull countermanded. "The least we can do is hear the boys out."

The pilots were largely through talking and the bridge speakers were reduced to static. Minutes after the last one signed off, the *Dale* sent a second alert, reporting the Jap ships stopped for some unknown reason.

"Ask them where," the admiral ordered.

After a quick exchange of radios, *Saratoga's* executive officer updated the enemy location on the chart. The Japs stopped well short of the task force's last location before the jog south. Well out of firing range.

Oh God in Heaven! We could have stayed put and landed the pilots.

Battleship Kongo, 22 miles south of Oahu, Hawaii
07:38 Hours, 7 January 1942

Three *Ameko* torpedo bombers buzzed in low towards *Kongo*, flying just above the morning mist. One fragmented and cartwheeled into the ocean when an anti-aircraft round sheared off a wing. The other two dropped their deadly fish into the water and flew past the bow of the battleship, wagging their wings to taunt the helpless battleship.

The Japanese admiral ground his teeth. No reason for this. No good reason at all.

The *Ameko* were almost within his grasp when Nagumo bluntly denied him permission to leave the blockade line and attack the inexplicably illuminated enemy ships. The report was mistaken, the admiral insisted. No enemy commander would illuminate his fleet at night. Maintain your positions.

Mikawa ordered his advancing ships to halt within the blockade zone and briefly considered renewing his request. However, the enemy fleet caught wind of their approach, went dark again and fled south. Even if the admiral could convince his superior to release the blockade force, the *Ameko* would be long gone by the time permission arrived.

His superior should know he would never report anything without verifying it first, Mikawa seethed. Damned fool!

The next morning, Nagumo took commander and fixed the blockade force in place, like a tiger tied to a stake surrounded by a pack of hyenas. To their rear were the enemy shore guns protecting the Pearl Harbor base. To the front, the *Ameko* relief fleet's battleships and cruisers approached in three groups. The Japanese vessels waited in a line formed during the night, like so many metal ducks in an *Ameko* carnival shooting gallery – just out of range of the shore guns, but easy targets for the approaching enemy fleet and their bombers.

The bombers arrived first, covering the advance of the three *Ameko* task forces, in a coordinated attack. Nagumo ordered the blockade line to stand fast and concentrate their fire on the more numerous enemy ships, while absorbing whatever damage the bombs and torpedoes inflicted.

Kongo unleashed a volley from her fourteen inch main guns, while Mikawa watched the bubble trails of the incoming *Ameko* torpedoes streak towards the stationary battleship. Seconds after the impudent enemy pilots drove their machines between *Kongo* and the next ship on the line, the pair of torpedoes they dropped slammed into the stern of the battleship.

Fortune graced the beleaguered admiral with wan smile. The flooding of a single watertight compartment would list, but not sink the admiral's flag ship. Similarly, radios from across the fleet reported the first enemy air strike bloodied, but did not remove any other defending ships from the blockade line.

Unfortunately, the cannon salvoes the Japanese ships launched against the approaching *Ameko* were only marginally more effective. Only a handful vessels fell out of the enemy formations, before the remaining *Ameko* pivoted into line and returned fire.

In a surface battle, the reinforced Japanese blockade force could probably hold their line against the enemy attack at a high cost. However, *Ameko* air superiority shifted the odds decisively in their favor.

As Mikawa sourly contemplated this final stand, cheering erupted from the far side of the bridge. "Silence!" the admiral barked. "Get back to your stations immediately."

The captain of the *Kongo* bowed deeply and immediately bounced back up to point towards the starboard windows. "So sorry, Admiral, but please direct your attention to the skies off the bow."

A quick pivot of Mikawa's binoculars revealed dozens of bombers flying south over the blockade force, every one displaying the rising sun of the Imperial Japanese Navy.

Nakajima B5N bomber, 55 miles south of Oahu, Hawaii
08:09 Hours, 7 January 1942

Fuchida raised his hand to block the glare of the morning sun laying low in the southern sky and was rewarded with a stunning view of the *Ameko* carrier task force spread out below – just where the submarine I-168 reported they would be. The exhausted commander swore he would seize this one last chance at redemption or die in the attempt.

Mitsuo was ashamed at how his pig-headed arrogance almost cost him this opportunity. After shepherding the last of his flock from *Akagi* to the Kauai airfield, he strode into the largest hanger and started firing off orders at the airfield mechanics to repair, refuel and rearm his bombers for a morning attack.

When the 701st Air Group's commander walked up, Fuchida crossed the line from insolence to insult. "Ah, it's you. Please call your officers together in a half hour, so I can brief them on the morning's attack."

Lieutenant Commander Joji Higai fixed him with a level gaze and replied, "Sir, you may be the ranking officer, but you have no authority over my unit. Your pilots and planes are guests on my airfield. I suggest you act accordingly."

Fuchida felt his face flush as if struck. After a moment's reconsideration, he realized the slap down was well deserved. "You are correct, Commander," Fuchida replied in a half bow. "I am very sorry for my rudeness. It has been a long and very bad day."

"I accept your apology. Now, let us begin this conversation anew."

"Commander Higai, will your unit attack tomorrow?"

"Yes sir. Less than an hour ago, Admiral Nagumo withdrew us from Army command and ordered us to begin preparations."

"Excellent. May my carrier pilots join your attack?"

"Let us inspect your planes."

The officers walked the ragged line of Fuchida's aircraft parked just off the airstrip. The surviving planes were a pitiful flock. No munitions and very little fuel. The only items in plentiful supply were holes and gashes torn out of the birds' hide by enemy machine gun and cannon rounds. His pilots and bombardiers were in no better shape. Nearly two dozen of them lay wounded around the airfield hanger waiting for care from the airfield's only doctor.

After returning to the hanger, Higai took Fuchida into his small office. "So sorry, but I cannot use your unit tomorrow. Your pilots obviously fought bravely today, but these men and their planes are combat ineffective."

"My fleet pilots must be given the opportunity for their vengeance, Commander!"

"I understand how you feel, but my answer is still no."

Mitsuo blinked away tears of frustration. "Please, Commander-san, at least allow my section and I to represent the fleet. I am begging you. Do not ground me during this final battle."

Higai leaned back in his chair and considered Fuchida. "Very well, you and your wingmen may fly with me during our attack tomorrow."

Fuchida banished these awkward memories and refocused on the vessels below. With nearly the entire *Ameko* surface fleet trading cannon salvoes with the Japanese blockade force, only a handful of destroyers remained behind to defend the pair of carriers below. The enemy anti-aircraft fire should be minimal.

The Japanese pilot was more concerned with his *Ameko* counterparts. Because his own surviving falcons were grounded and the 701st was a bomber unit, the air strike did not enjoy a fighter escort and expected to suffer heavy losses to the enemy combat air patrols. However, the brilliant blue sky above was empty apart from some wispy cirrus clouds. The carrier decks below were covered with bombers in various stages of rearming and refueling, but no fighters.

No time to lose.

Instead of waiting for the enemy falcons or Higai's attack orders to arrive, Fuchida and his section bolted ahead and began their dive onto the nearest carrier. Their immediate threat seemed to attract every anti-aircraft cannon of the *Ameko* task force. The sky around the trio of descending dive bombers filled with streams of bright tracers and exploding projectiles. The commander ignored the fireworks and bent over his bomb scope, giving his pilot course adjustments to align the dive bomber with the looming carrier deck.

A loud crack like a truck backfire caused Fuchida to glance up and over to the left. Lieutenant Ginza's adjacent bomber shuddered as smoke belched out of its engine compartment, only shards remained of the glass cowling around his cockpit.

The commander snatched up his radio microphone. "Tiger Two, this is Tiger Leader, what is your status?"

Only static responded for a few moments before a reply arrived. "Tiger Leader, not good. :::cough::: My bombardier joined his ancestors, I am not far behind. One duty left. Out." Ginza's bird then plunged into a sheer dive, one far too steep from which to recover.

Fuchida tore himself away from his friend's demise and returned to the bomb scope. Target acquired. Bomb released.

As his pilot pulled the dive bomber up and away, Mitsuo watched as two bombs and Ginza's plane plowed into the *Ameko* carrier, the latter taking out the ship's bridge.

As the commander continued to gain height, he gained perspective. Both enemy carriers convulsed with explosions and belched smoke, while the surviving destroyers spitefully spit fire at his withdrawing bird.

With their primary targets destroyed, Higai ordered a ceasefire. Any aircraft left with bombs and torpedoes were commanded to use them during the return flight on the *Ameko* battleships and cruisers engaging the Japanese blockade force.

Fuchida leaned his head back and closed his eyes, the resulting darkness matching his mood. Victory was finally theirs, but the taste was so very bitter. So many friends, birds and ships lost. How would his beloved carrier air fleet ever recover?

U.S.S. Saratoga, 80 miles south/southwest of Oahu, Hawaii 08:53 Hours, 7 January 1942

Bull Halsey regained consciousness sprawled on the deck, surrounded by a angry swirl of black and gray. The admiral blinked rapidly, clearing his vision after a moment or two. The bridge around him was a smoky ruin. A breeze flowing in from a car size gash in the exterior wall mostly kept the roiling blackness issuing from the rest of the bridge at bay. Mostly.

Bull coughed out the acrid air and a blinding pain exploded from his gut. When he instinctively curled into a ball and his belly, the agony redoubled.

The stricken man lay very still, panting shallowly, for what seemed like an eternity until his suffering subsided. Then, he very slowly pulled his right hand away from his gut. Blood dripped from the fingers onto his face. Well son, looks like you really bought it this time.

Halsey never really contemplated his own death. Life was always a big beer glass from which he drank deeply. Now, he just hoped it all ended quickly without too much more pain.

A few minutes later, yells from a search party below calling out for survivors broke through his gloom like a brief ray of hope. Bull shut that thought down fast. I'm too far gone, he concluded. Better to go down with his ship than to bleed out in some life raft in front of his men.

Unable to enter the wrecked bridge, the sailors moved on, their voices fading into the distance and then vanishing altogether. That's the ticket, boys. Get off the ship and save yourselves. The Navy will need you alive and kicking to win this war.

As the minutes painfully lagged, the admiral started to fall in and out of consciousness. Faces of friends and comrades who died over the past weeks haunted this twilight of his mind. Most prominent among them were the fighter pilots he left behind.

Bull awakened to find himself sliding down a tilted deck into rising sea water. He was too weak to take a last breath before the oily salt water swallowed him up, scoring his wound and filling his nose and mouth. The last thing the admiral heard was the scream of the *Saratoga's* rending steel as the old lady broke apart on the way to the bottom.

CHAPTER 12

Schofield Barracks, Oahu, Hawaii
15:59 Hours, 12 January 1942

Lieutenant General Walter Short slowly stewed. The Army commander for Hawaii and his two aides were about to begin their fourth hour waiting in a conference room for the Japanese commander to arrive and begin negotiations. Rank disrespect was what this was. If he had his druthers, the general would have left hours ago, but he checked his anger. Too many lives were on the line for this mission to fail.

Short knew the building well. Until a few days ago, this was the U. S. Pacific Fleet headquarters. However, when the Navy failed to break through the Jap blockade, the Army pulled its troops back to Honolulu to shorten its defensive lines for a final stand. All aboard for the God-damned Alamo!

Just before the clock on the wall reached the next hour, the Japanese delegation walked in, led by a short officer with a shaved head and general's insignia. Instead of working through a translator, though, the officer opened the discussions in flawless, British-accented English.

"I am Lieutenant General Masaharu Homma, commander of the Hawaii Expeditionary Army Group. What would you like to discuss, General Short?"

"General Homma, thank you for meeting today. Please excuse me for dispensing with the formalities, but let me get right to the point."

The Japanese general nodded and motioned for his counterpart to continue.

"I would like to negotiate safe passage for the civilians of Honolulu and all wounded to sail out of the battle zone to the other Hawaiian Islands."

Homma paused to allow Short to complete his comments, but the *Ameko* general sat there in silence, apparently waiting for a reply. After the Japanese victory at sea, the Army commander expected the Americans to negotiate the terms of their surrender. Was this some sort of opening gambit?

"And what do you propose for your soldiers?" Homma prodded.

"Our mission to defend this island remains unchanged."

The Japanese general slowly poured water from a captured *Ameko* pitcher into a captured glass, then took a long sip to allow himself time to consider this turn of events. The Americans apparently wished to die in combat as would any honorable *samurai*, but again disclosed the peculiar Western concern with the fate of the wounded and civilians. Homma decided to use this concern as leverage.

"General Short, your request is quite impossible without the simultaneous surrender of your forces. In the case of surrender, there is no battle and the safety of your civilians and wounded is secured."

Walter Short seethed. "So you guarantee the security of our wounded and civilians if we surrender?"

"But, of course."

"Like your forces did at the Schofield Hospital?"

When the Jap general stared back uncomprehendingly, Short exploded. "Your men butchered our wounded in their hospital beds as well as the medical personnel treating them, then raped our nurses. God knows what happened to the civilians in their homes on the base." The general growled, "There will be no more surrenders."

Initially taken aback by the rude outburst of his *Ameko* counterpart, Homma maintained his temper. Short's fury appeared to be genuine and the man plainly believed what he was saying. Did his soldiers kill the enemy wounded? Many of his men were veterans of the China campaign, where little mercy was shown on either side. Yes, it was very plausible.

Regardless, the Americans must be forced to surrender. The Hawaii campaign was far bloodier and dragged on longer than anyone anticipated. With every new dispatch, Tokyo was making its impatience clear. Perhaps a threat against Honolulu's civilian population might make the American general relent?

"General Short, I will look into your claims. However, your surrender is not a matter for negotiation. Your forces have until 12:00 hours tomorrow to lay down their arms or I will unleash the full power of my Army and Navy to level Honolulu. If you do not care about your own men, consider the residents of the city."

The *Ameko* general's face reddened and he stalked out of the conference room without another word.

Perhaps not.

Aloha Tower, Honolulu, Oahu Hawaii
07:41 Hours, 14 January 1942

Folded into the Twenty-fifth Infantry Division defending Honolulu, Billy Deal and Mike Morgan looked down on the world from observation deck of the Aloha Tower, a ten-story lighthouse with a dominating view of Honolulu and the ocean off the coast. A sniper's dream.

At first, the view sort of reminded Billy of the time he climbed Pikes Peak back home in Colorado. On that glorious

August day, he could see over 50 miles in all directions. It was like looking down on Earth from heaven above. Looking down from the Aloha Tower over the past days was more like a view into hell.

The fire and brimstone first arrived by sea. On Wednesday morning, the Navy finally got their asses back in town. Billy and Mike took turns chowing down on breakfast and watching the sea battle through a pair of spotter binoculars. Tiny ships on the horizon spit fire at one another, while mighty cracks and crashes rolled in across the emerald ocean to the shore. Every time the Navy boys would hit a home run and blow a Jap ship to kingdom come, the soldiers would jump up and down and cheer. It was so much better watching war as a spectator, Billy concluded, than crouching in the middle of the shit.

Just as their hopes were getting up, bad news arrived by airmail. As they had for weeks now, the Jap bombers droned in from Kauai. Instead of plastering the poor sons of bitches in the Oahu's central valley, though, this time the formations took a hard right turn into the naval battle. The bombers returned a half hour later with big gaps torn in their ranks. However, the Navy boys vanished altogether, leaving the Jap blockade in place. Billy had a sinking feeling they would not be back.

Two days later, the official word came down confirming Billy's intuition. There would be no reinforcements. No resupply. No evac for the wounded. No real hope of making it through this mess.

This morning, the Japs started their final assault on Honolulu with a thundering artillery barrage from land and sea. The enemy was not targeting the lighthouse, the port facilities or anything else they could use in the future. Instead, the evil sons of bitches were blowing the hell out of entire neighborhoods.

The sniper panned his rifle scope across the nearby homes. There was no sign of life on the streets. The civilians must be huddled in the homes which the Japs were methodically reducing to kindling.

When a movement caught his eye, Deal slowly panned back and saw a little figure limping down the street. He couldn't tell if the child was a boy or a girl. The hairless head was a charred mess and the arm… Oh, God in heaven. Hanging only by a cord of flesh, the arm dangled down, bouncing off of the child's side with every step. Billy reached up to wipe away a blur from his eyes. When he looked back, the child was gone.

Billy slid his back along the wall of the observation deck wall, plopped on his rump and prayed for God to have mercy on them all. Then, something flared and hardened within him.

Lord, in the Bible, You said vengeance is Yours. Please, God, use me as the instrument of that vengeance. I won't let you down.

Moiliili Japanese School, Honolulu, Oahu, Hawaii
13:22 Hours, 28 January 1942

Captain Hayashi was certain an *Ameko* scurried into the school house, but the enemy had gone silent. The *hentai* tread softly down the hallway of the school, straining to hear any cough or creak disclosing the enemy's location, but the only sounds were the clatter and rumble of war seeping in from outside the building.

Two *hentai* stopped on each side of the first classroom door, while a third kicked it. The men swung their rifles, bayonet first, through the entrance ready to fire. The survivors of Hayashi's company learned this dance through bloody battlefield trial and error. The Army trained the *hentai* to fight in the open, not to clear city buildings. The Japanese soldier's preferred weapon – the rifle affixed with a long bayonet – was extremely awkward to use indoors. Far too many of his men died in doorways after their rifles snagged on a surrounding wall or fixture.

No shots. The first classroom was clear. This dance repeated itself peacefully down the hallway until the *hentai* reached a bathroom on the left. Corporal Sato swung into the doorway and an enemy bullet, before collapsing back onto the wooden floor, coughing up blood.

Sergeant Major Tanaka pulled the safety pin from a Type 99 grenade, struck the head fuse on the top against his helmet and side-armed the explosive through the doorway.

Immediately after the crump of the grenade explosion, Private Nakamura charged into the bathroom and a second shot rang out. An *Ameko* rifle shot. Tanaka's call to Nakamura went unanswered.

Turning to his commander and raising his palms in the air, the sergeant major sourly reported, "Captain-san, that was the last of the grenades."

Hayashi had lost too many good *hentai* to these honor-less *Ameko*, only to lose more charging a damned urinal. Standing tall and pointing at the men stationed at the hallway entrance, he commanded, "Bring up the machine gun!"

The gunner trotted up with the automatic weapon, placed it opposite the bathroom wall where the company commander pointed and went to work. The rapid-fire shots were unnaturally loud in the confines of the hallway, ripping through the thin wall into the bathroom, first to the left and then the right.

Tanaka pointed at the next *hentai* in line, who leapt up with a scream and plunged into the bathroom. No shots this time. Just a call from the soldier that the room was clear.

Hayashi glanced inside to see his man driving his bayonet into the sprawled *Ameko* to ensure they were actually dead this time. The enemy made his final stand in the wrong room. The only exit apart from the hallway door was a tiny window high on the exterior wall.

With the last of the rooms cleared, the company commander reformed his men in the hallway to move out again and clear the next building, when a series of thumps echoed along the corridor behind them. A green pineapple shaped *Ameko* grenade slid to a rest on the floor in the midst of the hentai, nearly at Hayashi's feet. Before the captain could react, his sergeant major leapt onto the bomb with a yell, which was savagely cut off by the explosion shredding his chest.

As the rear squad sprinted down the hallway looking for the enemy rat who tossed the grenade, Hayashi looked on his dead comrade lying face down in an expanding pool of blood. Tanaka was the oldest of his China veterans. More of an uncle than a subordinate. After so many victorious battles together, for his uncle to die in such a cowardly ambush.

Ripping his sword out of its scabbard, Hayashi ran to join his rear squad in their counterattack on the *Ameko*, but the company commander was too late. Pointing at the opened window of a previously cleared classroom, the squad leader reported the enemy soldier crept into the building behind them to lob the grenade, then fled out the same way.

Hayashi slammed his fist against the chalkboard on the wall, causing it to crash onto the floor. Seeing his men gawking back at him in fear and uncertainty, the commander screamed at them to resume their positions in the hallway and wait for his return.

As his men fled the room, the captain struggled suppress his rage and regain the control expected of a *samurai*. The damned *Ameko* were rats. As soon as the *hentai* cleared one room and left for another, the vermin returned.

While glaring at the walls, he noticed the classroom was covered with Japanese calligraphy. Army briefings before the invasion reported a substantial population of Japanese emigrated to the Hawaiian Islands over the years. This must be one of the schools where the emigres educated their *nisei* children in proper Japanese language and culture. Once the Army was through exterminating the rats, these brethren would run the islands for the Emperor.

Fish Market, Honolulu, Oahu Hawaii
07:19 Hours, 4 February 1942

Corporal Billy Deal's fellow soldiers emerged from the ruins of a warehouse like a parade of scarecrows, their ragged uniforms hanging off of them like window drapes. The battalion commander led the way carrying a dirty strip of white cloth tied off on a stick. The rest followed with their hands raised.

A handful of Japanese soldiers emerged from their cover, screaming at the Americans and motioning with their rifles for the surrendering soldiers to form up along the road. One of them appeared to be an officer, pointing a *samurai* sword to direct his men. From his vantage point on the second floor of a nearby ruined house, Deal moved the cross hairs of his rifle scope onto the Jap officer's head.

Last night, Major Douglas gathered his battalion's survivors into the warehouse and confirmed the news everyone expected. "Let's get right to it. General Short has ordered everyone to surrender."

"Excuse me sir, but what the hell?" a first sergeant interrupted. "I'm not giving myself over to those Jap bastards so they can use me as a bayonet dummy. And God help Nurse Jenkins if she falls into their hands," he punctuated, jabbing his thumb towards a petite woman in the corner.

A handful of others added their grumbles in agreement, but far fewer than Deal expected. The majority of the men were starved, wounded and whipped.

Douglas nodded gravely. "I know, I know. Everyone remembers Schofield. You also need to know the division staff surrendered yesterday to test the Japs and they were taken prisoner without any problem."

Scratching at his lice ridden scalp, the battalion commander gave his final pitch, "Listen men, I'm not ordering anyone to surrender. You need to make your own decisions. But we have no more ammo, food, or meds. If you keep fighting, you'll have to make do with what you're carrying right now."

"What does everyone think?" Douglas asked. "Speak freely."

As the men softly began their discussion, the sniper leaned over to his spotter and whispered, "Mike, I'm heading back up to the mountains. We have the ammo and food we scrounged. And we can hunt up there."

"I'm with you brother."

Deal nodded and returned his attention to the unit discussion. A heavy majority of the men leaned toward surrender. The rest followed when the first sergeant, who raised the initial objection, agreed to give up.

Major Douglas asked for a show of hands of everyone who intended to surrender. Only the sniper and his spotter kept their arms down.

"What do you intend to do, Corporal Deal?"

"Sir, Morgan and I are heading to the hills to fight from there."

"Are you sure? You know what'll happen if the Japs catch you out there after the surrender."

I know damned well what will happen if I do surrender, Deal thought.

"Sir, we know the risks. Could I ask for something before we leave?"

"What's that, Corporal?"

"Can we have all the ammunition from the men who intend to surrender?"

The battalion commander looked around and then nodded. "Everyone, give up your ammo to Deal and Morgan."

While Morgan was collecting the ammo, Nurse Jenkins tapped Deal on the shoulder. "Corporal, I need to speak with you."

The couple walked over to a cluster of fish stalls on the far side of the warehouse before Jenkins spoke. "Can I come with you? I won't be a burden and you'll need someone to patch you up when you get wounded."

Deal had to think on that one. Billy and Mike were a tight team, who could almost read one another's minds in the field. The sniper really didn't want to mess with that chemistry. On the other hand, Jenkins was a damned good nurse. She dug some shrapnel out of his side last week and dealt with far worse since joining the unit several days ago. Those skills would be invaluable in the field.

"Corporal, please," the nurse pled. "You know I can't surrender to those animals and I can't make it on my own out there. We need each other."

"OK, you can come on one condition."

"What's that?"

"In the military, you're an officer and I have to follow your orders. Where we're going, I'm in charge. Can you live with that?"

"Makes sense," Jenkins responded, as she took the captain's bars off her collar and handed them to the sniper. "Do we have a deal?

"Yeah, we do. What's your first name?"

"Sally."

"OK, I'm Billy and that lug over there is Mike. Now, let's find you a rifle."

"No need. I scrounged a rifle when I arrived here and I know to use it. Let me get my gear."

Billy cocked his head as he watched the nurse walk away. This should be interesting.

A half hour later, the trio snuck out of the warehouse, winding through the surrounding rubble, until they found an intact second story building with a good view of the street in front of the warehouse.

Billy didn't trust those Jap bastards as far as he could spit. One false move and they would pay.

Fish Market, Honolulu, Oahu, Hawaii
07:23 Hours, 4 February 1942

The Japanese company commander emerged from a dreamless sleep curled in the corner of a shattered building wondering why his men were shouting. Last night, headquarters issued a warning the surviving enemy agreed to surrender today. Was this commotion a surrender or another *Ameko* sneak attack? The parade of enemy soldiers assembling along the road at bayonet point provided the answer. The rats had finally given up.

General Homma's strict orders before the Honolulu offensive were the only reason the *hentai* were taking prisoners. Most true Army *samurai* considered Homma a weak officer who preferred western values to Japanese, but he was the commanding general and his orders must be obeyed without question.

Captain Hayashi sighed in resignation and relief as he straightened his tunic. No matter how distasteful, the enemy surrender meant a long overdue victory. His company earned more than its share of glory, but the blood price was high. Perhaps now, his family honor would be restored.

Once the *Ameko* soldiers were fully assembled, Lieutenant Tada trotted up to his company commander and reported his platoon was ready to escort the enemy to the division assembly area north of the city. Hayashi nodded his assent and the *hentai* started screaming at their charges to move out.

The prisoners were a pathetic lot. Before they shuffled down a single block, the first fell out on the side of the road. The *Ameko* lying on the sidewalk showed no obvious injury and was waving away a comrade bending over to help him to his feet. When one of his sergeants ran up and ordered the prisoner to his feet, the stupid round eye looked back uncomprehendingly.

Hayashi strode up and kicked the man squarely in his ribs. Pathetic dog! If the enemy had any honor, he would have killed himself. At the very least, he can walk in shame. When the *Ameko* attempting to assist the dog turned and started yelling, the *samurai* officer grabbed the handle of his father's sword. Before his captain could act, though, the sergeant settled the matter with two bayonet thrusts. Hayashi started to nod his approval when a bullet ripped through his skull.

"Sniper!" Lieutenant Tada screamed as he dove for cover behind the corner of a building.

Peering past the rubble at the new threat, the new company commander concluded this was not a random sniping. Snipers were generally cowards, firing a shot or two then withdrawing. The *Ameko* were making no attempt to hide their position, firing round after round to deadly effect. This filth used their comrades' surrender to lure the *hentai* out into the open.

While studying the area for covered approaches on the building, Tada yelled for his old platoon to gather around him. When only a handful of *hentai* came to his side, the lieutenant looked around for the rest. The missing men were slaughtering the *Ameko* prisoners with the fury of the betrayed. So be it. This ambush crossed a line. Although he considered his former captain a harsh man, Hayashi was correct in the end. The round eyes were without any measure of honor.

Concluding this squad would be sufficient to exterminate this last nest of rats, Tada waved his men forward.

Fish Market, Honolulu, Oahu Hawaii
07:39 Hours, 4 February 1942

Corporal Deal was shooting as quickly as he could, rhythmically acquiring a target and firing, until he ran through the ammo in his rifle. Billy and Mike were hitting nearly everything they aimed at, but it wasn't enough. Two rifles were just not enough.

After the sniper took out that officer, the damned Japs went ape shit. Part took cover and returned fire, but the rest started killing the surrendering Americans. The sniper and his spotter concentrated their fire on latter. Every Jap they killed saved an American and gave them a chance to escape. But there were just too many Japs.

"Mike, stop shooting," the corporal ordered. "We don't have the ammo for this."

As he slapped in another magazine of ammo into his *Springfield*, Deal jumped as someone fired a shot right behind them. The sniper and spotter swung around to meet the new threat, only to find Nurse Jenkins standing there, chambering a new round into her rifle. Face down in the doorway was one very dead Jap soldier. Sally wasn't fooling about being able to handle that rifle.

"Gentlemen, we have company downstairs," Jenkins matter-of-factly reported.

Morgan jumped up, pulled the body out of the doorway and then ducked through. A moment later, rifles cracked, followed by hurried stomps up the stairs.

Mike appeared in the doorway, pivoted to face downstairs and cursed. In one smooth motion that would be the envy of any shortstop, he snagged a Jap grenade out of the air with one hand, chucked it back down the stairs and dove into the room. The downstairs explosion shook loose dust from the wrecked roof above and yells from the Japs below.

"Come on, I think it's time to leave," Jenkins observed, just before stepping out on and over the rear balcony.

Deal glared at the empty porch. Dammit, that woman can't go off any time she pleases!

Glancing over from his position covering the doorway, Mike said, "I think she's right, Billy. It's time to get the hell out of Dodge."

Billy walked onto the balcony and peeked over the side. It was two stories above a backyard littered with debris from the war-ravaged home. Not exactly a feather mattress. The nurse found cover in the next yard and was motioning furiously for the men to join her.

"You wanna jump first or should I?" Mike asked.

"I'll go," Billy grimaced, struggling to push back his fear of heights.

Clamping his eyes closed, Deal jumped into the void and landed feet, ass and head onto a pile of stucco blown off the adjacent wall. With a groan, the sniper forced himself to his feet and staggered over to the nurse. While his body complained bitterly about the less than graceful landing, everything still appeared to work.

Morgan accomplished the leap with more aplomb, but had to scramble to avoid the bullets cracking all around him. The Japs in the house were now wise to their escape.

Hunched low, the trio wound their way through the wreckage of the neighborhood, sprinting across open areas from one patch of cover to another.

After the past couple weeks of sniping, Deal and Morgan knew the area well, but the enemy positions around the city changed constantly. After the firefight near the grocery, every Jap within earshot would be on alert, if not actively looking for them. They had to find a place to hole up until nightfall.

Billy almost fell into that hole. After carefully scrutinizing the surrounding buildings for Japs, the sniper dashed onto Punchbowl Street and had to dance around a gaping sewer entrance before reaching the other side.

Hand-signaling the others to stay put, Deal studied the road. A bent manhole cover lay a few feet away from the sewer hole. A mortar must have landed on the cover and threw it off.

Then an idea took root. Looking around one more time, the sniper ran back across the road. Huddling with Mike and Sally, Billy laid out his plan in whispers. "I found a hidey hole. There's sewer entrance right on the other side of that curb. We could use the sewers to walk across town right under the Japs without them noticing a damned thing."

"Not bad, brother." Morgan nodded. "Not bad."

"OK, you two scoot down first and I'll give you cover."

Mike sprinted to the curb, quickly glanced into the hole and clambered down a ladder he found there.

Sally's entrance was more eventful. As she ran to the hole, two or three Jap rifles opened up from a building down the street. About halfway down the ladder, the nurse let out a squeal and fell out of sight. That didn't look good.

Billy popped the pin on his last grenade and tossed it onto the street between the Japs and the hole. As the grenade exploded, the sniper was already running. Yelling for Mike to catch his rifle as he dropped it into the hole, he slid down the sides of a ladder attached to the concrete tube.

The ladder ended before the ground and Billy ended up on his ass. Mike gave him a hand up, before handing him his rifle and vanishing into a dark tube of concrete.

His eyes adjusting to the gloom, Deal cautiously made his way forward with his arm extended, until his hand found a dark form standing there. It was Sally was pressing a field dressing down onto her left shoulder, trying her best not to let on she was in pain.

"Lemme see," Deal demanded as he reached for the wound.

"Keep your filthy hands off of it!" the nurse hissed.

Billy raised his hands in mock surrender. "Whoa. Ok, ok..."

"I'm sorry, Billy, I know you were just trying to help," Sally sighed. "The wound isn't bad, just a bullet graze. But we're in a sewer. If I get any of this filth in the wound, I won't survive the infection."

"OK, can I help you tie off the dressing?"

"I'd appreciate that."

Once the nurse was bandaged up, Deal pointed down the tunnel and issued his orders: "OK, follow me single file. Mike, you take the rear. Sally, you stay in the middle. It's dark as hell down here, so hold onto the person in front of you."

When the others whispered their understanding, the sniper started sloshing forward down the sewer tunnel. After a couple steps, his nose wrinkled at the stench and Billy suddenly realized what he was walking through.

Oh, perfect. They were now truly up shit's creek without a paddle.

Pele Street, Honolulu, Oahu, Hawaii
20:14 Hours, 4 February 1942

Bobby Logan was really scared. Since the sun went down, the gunshots and screams kept getting closer and closer. Over the past couple weeks, there were lots of scary war sounds, but nothing like this.

Bobby's bestest friend in the whole world was his next-door neighbor – Nate. Their daddies were both in the Navy and hadn't been home in a long time. Nate thought his dad was dead, but Bobby didn't want think about things like that.

A few minutes ago, the boy swore he heard is friend yell and then scream from the house next door. When he went to open the curtains to look, mommy grabbed his arm and yanked him into the kitchen. When his sister Peg came into the room, mommy kneeled down and put her arm around both of them.

"Do you remember what I told you to do when the bad people come to the house?"

The children both nodded.

Looking them each in the eye, mommy said, "Well, I want you to go there right now and be very, very quiet. No matter what you hear, no matter what happens, you need to stay quiet. Can you do that for me?"

They nodded again.

"OK, go hide now."

Peg went into mommy's bedroom and wriggled under the big bed. Bobby ducked into the coat closet.

The six year old peeked through the closet door slats into the living room. Mommy wasn't hiding. Instead, she was pacing around the room smoking a cigarette, occasionally stopping to glance back at the closet and bedroom. Once, mommy caught her son's eye and raised her finger to her mouth to remind him to shoosh.

The waiting finally ended when the front door was kicked open with a loud crack and five soldiers walked in and looked around.

Mommy bowed to the men like the boy saw the Japanese people do at the fish market. A smiling soldier in front pulled her head back up by the hair with one hand and ripped her shirt down with the other. One of her boobies fell out and the man grabbed it.

Holding one of her hands over her big belly and using the other to push away the man's hand, mommy pled, "Please no, honorable sir. Can't you see I'm pregnant?"

The soldier stopped smiling and punched mommy in her big belly. She collapsed to the floor with a loud groan.

Bobby put his hands over his mouth to stay quiet like mommy told him to, but he couldn't stop the tears from flowing.

The soldier ripped off mommy's other clothes and started bouncing on top of her. When he tried to kiss her, she kept moving her face away, but didn't say a word.

A crashing noise came from the bedroom and another soldier dragged Peg out of the room by a leg, kicking and screaming.

Mommy yelled really loud then. Louder than he had ever heard her yell before, even when he was being very bad. "You bastard! Let her go! Let her go!" Then she started sobbing and begging, "Please don't, she's only eleven. Take me, not her. Please, no. Please…"

The other soldier didn't listen. He picked up Peg from behind, bent her over the bar where daddy kept the grown-up drinks and pulled down her little skirt. His sister shrieked and squirmed as the bad man kept pushing her against the bar with his hips.

Bobby didn't know what to do. He was almost too scared to think. Then, the boy remembered what Daddy told him before he left. "Buddy, I'm going out to sea on a big battleship. While I'm gone, you're the man of the house. Can I depend on you to protect your mommy and sister?" The little boy was never prouder than when he saluted his dad with a loud "Yes sir!"

Now the good son knew what to do. Swinging open the closet door, Bobby charged out at the soldier hurting his sister, screaming: "Leave her alone!"

The bad man effortlessly swung his arm back and swatted the little boy across the living room floor.

The soldiers all laughed at him.

After he regained his feet, Bobby suddenly found himself swung up in the air, facing the ceiling, flailing his arms and legs trying to find the ground again.

His insides hurt so bad. Really, really bad. Too bad to scream. Almost too bad to breathe.

When he looked to see what was hurting him, Bobby saw the knife blade sticking out of his tummy toward the ceiling. It was a knife the soldiers put on their rifles.

Bobby grabbed the knife, pulling and pulling at the blade, cutting up his hands. But he just couldn't pull it out.

The soldiers only laughed harder.

Punchbowl Crater, Oahu Hawaii
22:02 Hours, 4 February 1942

Billy Deal and his companions emerged from the sewers into a horror show almost beyond comprehension.

After regaining the surface north of Queen's Hospital, the trio found they were only three blocks short of their objective – the Punchbowl – an old, overgrown volcanic crater which dominated the east side of Honolulu. From there, the Americans could escape into the mountains. First, though, they had to cross those three blocks.

Bodies littered the first block of Miller Street, some with uniforms, some with hospital gowns, many parted from their heads. When a Jap patrol appeared out of a side street, the trio dove to the ground and pretended to join the dead.

As the enemy soldiers sauntered by, Deal thought he would lose his mind. The stench of the rotting dead filled his nose, while flies from nearby corpses crawled all over his body. It was all he could do to keep from slapping at the insects and screaming.

After what seemed like forever, the Jap footfalls finally faded away and the three fled this road of the dead. Jogging sideways over to Pele Street, they turned again for the Punchbowl. Two more blocks to go.

Creeping from one house to the next, the trio managed to cross a second block before stopping behind a front porch. About a dozen enemy soldiers were hanging around in the front yard of the next house, with a couple rotating in and out of the house every so often.

When Deal looked back to the others, Morgan pointed at another Jap patrol coming up the road behind them. Need a place to hide.

As quietly as they could manage, the three crawled onto the porch, one after another, then through the broken front door of the house. The living room wasn't dark. A kerosene lantern hissed on top of a hutch on the far end of the room. What the flickering light revealed was even worse than the road of the dead. Far worse.

A naked woman sprawled out on the floor in a pool of own blood, her throat cut in a jagged tear. The mother's lifeless arms were draped over her dead unborn child, whose umbilical cord led back to a slashed open womb.

When Deal turned away, he only found more horrors. In the corner were two dead children. The boy's face was contorted in pain from a bayonet wound. The girl…oh my Good Lord…the girl was naked below the waist and bleeding from both sides down there. After they were through with her, those animals stomped her head into the floor.

The soldier fell to his knees and heaved. If there were any food in his belly, it would have gone all over the floor.

After he collected himself, Billy looked back at the others. Sally was bent over the woman, closing her dead eyes. "Please, get something to cover these poor people," the nurse begged in a husky voice.

After they laid blankets over the family, Mike said a soft prayer and then the three stood there in silence.

"People, I can't spend another minute in this this slaughterhouse," Deal said. "I say we run through the backyards and then up onto the crater. If any Jap son of a bitch gets in the way, we kill 'em."

The others quickly nodded their agreement and followed him outside. God had mercy on them for once. The Japs were nowhere to be seen behind the houses and the little band was able to crest the Punchbowl in just a few minutes.

Before the war, the Hawaiian National Guard used the wide flat space inside the crater as a shooting range. The trio crossed the entire range before finding the current occupants. An American soldier was standing sentry, watching out over the road leading up to the Punchbowl. About ten feet away, his buddy was curled up and sleeping on the ground.

When Deal softly gave the last password he could recall before everything went to hell, the sentry nearly jumped out of his shoes and hissed back, "Who goes there?"

Morgan took over. "Mac, we're Americans – two soldiers and a nurse. We're coming in. For God's sake, don't shoot."

The sentry and his partner were spotters for division artillery, stationed up on the Punchbowl for nearly a week. The phone link went dead a couple days back and they just stayed in place waiting for relief.

"What's happening down in Honolulu? It sure don't look good from up here."

Morgan shook his head. "Honolulu's gone." Then, he told the story of what happened over the past couple days, without holding anything back.

The plainly shaken sentry looked down at the ground and cursed softly. "Corporal, what're you going to do now?"

"We're headed into the mountains to hunt Japs," Deal responded. "You two can tag along, if you do exactly what I say. No bellyaching, no questions. Got that?"

The artillery spotters looked at one another and nodded. "Whatever you say, Corporal."

The sentry turned and pointed over to a boulder shrouded in shadows. "One thing, though. What should we do with him?"

Deal walked over and his stomach tightened. A Jap soldier sat against the boulder, bound and gagged.

"A Jap patrol came up the road this morning. We ambushed them pretty good. Killed three and shot this one in the leg. The son of a bitch kept fighting right to the end. When he ran out of ammo, we wrestled him to the ground and tied him up."

"We don't take prisoners anymore," Deal said tonelessly.

The sentry looked back at him for a long second, then released the safety on his rifle.

"No. Don't waste your ammunition on him. You'll need every round where we're going." The sniper's face turned as terrible as wrath. Tears from his icy cold blue eyes washed a path through the grime covering his cheeks, before disappearing into a week's growth of beard. "Use your knives instead…and take your time."

Sally went wide-eyed and shot him a shocked look. Billy just stared her down, until she retreated into the darkness. The two spotters just stood there confused.

"Have either of you ever dressed a deer," Morgan asked, while pulling out his hunting knife.

Both of the men quickly shook their heads back and forth.

"Well, let me show you how it's done."

The prisoner's gag only muffled his shrieks as Morgan went to work.

One day when he was twelve, Billy constantly bugged his pop to tell him stories of his great grandpop Pete's adventures as an Army scout during the Indian wars. His father kept putting him off, until finally relenting just before supper.

"After your mother goes to bed, I have something to show you. Until then, be quiet."

Later that night, Pop took a seat by the fireplace, carrying a glass of whisky and a leather satchel. He pulled three shanks of black hair out of the satchel and handed them to his son. In the low burning fire, they looked like cut up parts of mom's wig on the bedroom night stand.

"Son, those are scalps Pete took off the heads of Indians he killed."

Billy's stared back at hair in his hand. That wasn't fabric holding the hair together, it was dried skin. Feeling a little sick, the boy dropped the hair on the floor and looked back at his father. "I thought only the Indians scalped people?"

Pop took a long drink from the glass. "You need to understand something, Billy, and let this sink in real good. War isn't some God damned game. It's butchery, plain and simple."

Then, his Pop leaned forward. "The Indian wars were the worst. Both sides were killing everyone – women, kids and even little babies. The Indians took scalps to show how bad ass they were and so did we."

"But, Pop, we're not like the savages. You always taught us that Christians show mercy to their enemies."

His father sighed and leaned back in the seat again. "God is free to show mercy from Heaven. In a war down here on Earth, where it's kill or be killed, mercy is only for the merciful."

Billy Deal finally understood what his Pop was saying.

III. THE ATLANTIC

CHAPTER 13

Charleston Yacht Club, South Carolina
20:08 Hours, 11 March 1942

Oh my, this one does like to hear himself talk, Kolotsiev concluded, as she finished her desert sherbet. Captain Brent Marcus, United States Navy, was ship proud and enthusiastically educated his dinner partners over the past half hour about all the outstanding features of his new command – the destroyer *U.S.S. Leary*. And there were many such features in the good captain's opinion.

Kat dabbed her lips with her napkin, put on a polite smile and patiently waited for a pause in Marcus's monologue.

The *Leary* was a WWI-era destroyer that would be an afterthought in the open ocean, but was definitely a big fish in the small pond of Charleston Bay. If the Germans were planning on visiting the States through Charleston harbor as she suspected, then the presence of a destroyer in the bay could present a rather sticky wicket for the visitors.

When she discretely inquired around the yacht club about the new arrival, an excited club commodore informed Kolotsiev that he was hosting the captain of the *Leary* for dinner that very evening and asked if she would like to join them. Kat assured him she would be delighted to attend.

When Marcus interrupted his exposition on his destroyer long enough to light a cigarette, Kolotsiev changed the subject.

"Captain, is the *Leary* here to defend us against a German invasion?"

Giving her an incredulous look, the captain dismissed the idea. "The fleet's current mission is to keep the Atlantic an American lake and protect our shipping. The *Kriegsmarine* could not hope to carry off an invasion of the United States, even if they wanted to."

"I am sure our Royal Navy admirals thought the same thing last year before the German invasion of England," Kolotsiev dryly observed. "Yet, the Germans are occupying my country and here I am as your guest."

Marcus took a drag on his cigarette and blew an annoyed stream of smoke into the air. "My dear, the English Channel was a glorified river crossing. The Atlantic is an ocean and the *Kriegsmarine* is not a true blue water navy."

Kat felt the familiar icy anger return.

Family money allowed her to join a handful of women admitted to study at Oxford. University was a profound shock to Kolotsiev. Although Papa's personal tutoring and her own formidable intellect provided her with a greater mastery of the material than some of her professors, Oxford's male faculty and student body dismissed Kat as a girl worthy of little more than consideration as a future wife. The dutiful daughter concealed her fury and quietly demonstrated her competence in exams, graduating near the top of her class. Apparently, male condescension was no different here in the States.

"The war is in the Pacific with the Japanese," lectured Marcus. "Humanity generally expands westward – the barbarian tribes into Rome, the Mongols rampaging across Asia into Europe, and now America winning the west and moving into the Pacific. Conflict with Japan was inevitable."

Kolotsiev saw an opening to steer Marcus back to the subject of her interest, while simultaneously tweaking this pompous twit. "Let me see if I understand you correctly. Are you saying that America's westward expansion led to war with Japan?"

"Well, the Japs did attack us first, but you have the general idea."

"Then wouldn't Germany's expansion west into France and England make war with the United States inevitable?"

Marcus at first appeared nonplussed, but then ruefully smiled. "Excellent point, Miss Kolotsiev. You've hung me by my own petard."

Kat raised her glass of port to the officer. "Thankfully, we have the *Leary* and her brave captain to protect us from such a future."

"Hear, hear," joined the yacht club commodore.

Marcus's face colored slightly, but it was clear that he was enjoying the praise. Time to pry. "Captain, please tell us the *Leary* will be staying in Charleston."

"Do not concern yourself, my dear," Marcus reassured. "My destroyer will be based in Charleston for the foreseeable future. Of course, we'll be on sea duty from time to time, but our primary mission will be to see to the security of this port."

"I am so glad to hear that, my dear captain," smiled Kolotsiev.

"*Herr Doktor*" will not be happy to hear about this. Not happy at all.

Kriegsmarine Headquarters, Berlin, Germany
07:48 Hours, 12 March 1942

Erich Pfeiffer's head fell forward and bounced off his chest, sending his cap tumbling onto the floor of the Mercedes and his mind back into semi-consciousness. Unsure if he wanted to rejoin the world yet, Erich cautiously opened his eyes into slits to look out of the car window. That was a mistake. The brilliant sunrise stabbed and twisted like a knife into his hungover brain.

Squeezing his eyes shut again, Pfeiffer groaned, "Are we in Berlin yet, Fritz?"

"We are close, sir. We just passed Spandau."

Erich was an academic by training, with a doctorate in political economy. While he held the rank of a *Kriegsmarine* corvette captain, his subordinates knew him simply as "the Doctor."

The commander of the *Abwehr* naval intelligence section possessed two vices – a fondness for schnapps and pretty blonds. Erich was partaking liberally of both the night before at the Spitzen Gebel, when the section duty officer fetched him back to work to review an urgent message. The report awaiting him was the latest radio communication from the agent in Charleston code named "Empress" and was marked highest priority. That did not sound like good news, Pfeiffer thought. Two careful readings of the decoded report more than confirmed his initial fear.

The Empress was the code name for Germany's only active spy in the United States and without a doubt its most successful. After the damned *Amerikaner* FBI rounded up nearly every other *Abwehr* operative in the United States over the last year, Pfeiffer jealously guarded his remaining agent and allowed only two other men to be read-in on her reports – the *Abwehr* chief Admiral Canaris and *Kriegsmarine* Grand Admiral Reader. Erich had driven all night from Bremen to Berlin to personally deliver the Empress's disturbing message to the second man on the short list.

After making himself presentable in the headquarters restroom, Pfeiffer was led to the Grand Admiral's office. Raeder was reviewing a report with another officer Erich did not recognize.

Pfeiffer snapped to attention, clicking his boot heels together, and smartly saluted his commander. Raeder casually returned the salute and motioned to the other officer. "Captain, I would like to introduce, Admiral Theodor Krancke. Now please tell us the message that brings us here from the operations center."

Pfeiffer paused for a moment. "I mean no disrespect, but Admiral Krancke is not cleared to know about this source. This message is for your ears only."

"The Admiral is my chief planning officer for Case Black and is cleared to know everything that impacts that operation. Please brief us on the new intelligence without discussing the source."

"Very well. Gentlemen, may I direct your attention to the area around Charleston, South Carolina?"

The admirals gathered on both sides of the captain as he pointed generally with his pen at a map on the wall.

"Until yesterday, our intelligence suggested the *Amerikaner* Navy did not base any operational ships in Charleston harbor, just a handful of destroyers in various stages of construction at the ship yard." Shifting his pen to the Port of Charleston, Pfeiffer announced, "The situation has changed. The *Amerikaner* have based their destroyer *U.S.S. Leary* here on what appears to be an indefinite port protection mission."

Shaking his head, Reader responded, "I suppose it was just a matter of time. I did not believe the *Amerikaner* would leave a port this size undefended for long." Looking over to his planning officer, the admiral asked, "Theodor, how does this affect our current landing plans?"

Krancke tapped his index finger on his chin. "Admiral, the entire operation is predicated on the commando raid taking the port facility, so our transports can dock and directly offload the troops into the city before the *Amerikaner* army can respond. None of that can happen with a destroyer docked at the port."

"And how can the fleet neutralize the enemy ship?" prodded Raeder.

The chief planner remained silent for a moment, considering the possible options.

"Admiral, I suppose a handful of destroyers, maybe a light cruiser, could operate within the confines of Charleston Bay. Even then, it would take time to hunt down the *Amerikaner*. If the enemy ship decided to make a stand and sank in the main shipping lane, our landings could be delayed even longer.

"That will not work," Raeder muttered. "That definitely will not work."

The three men silently considered the map table for a time. While he was not a trained naval officer and had no tactical solution to offer, Pfeiffer seemed to recall a prior intelligence report which might help. After wracking his hungover mind, the solution jumped out like a rabbit from a thicket.

"That's it!"

The admirals looked crossly at the captain.

"I apologize for the outburst, Admiral, but I just recalled our comrades in the *Regia Marina* possess a highly classified solution to our problem. Allow me to explain."

White House, Washington D.C.
15:04 Hours, 15 March 1942

Clement Attlee and his chief code breaker, Alastair Denniston, stepped out of the sedan which picked them up at Union Station and strode into the American White House. Since being appointed by the Queen Elizabeth to head the British government-in-exile in Canada, this was the new Prime Minister's first meeting with President Roosevelt. The conference proved to be a delicate affair from the outset.

Ushered into the Oval Office by a colored butler, Attlee and Denniston were greeted by the President and his entire foreign policy team. Everyone rose for the Prime Minister apart from Roosevelt, who remained seated behind his desk. The MI6 reports that the American President was crippled by polio appeared to be true.

After some perfunctory chatter about the Prime Minister's trip and what brand of Scotch whisky he preferred, Attlee got down to business. There really wasn't a moment to spare.

"Mr. President, thank you for seeing us on such short notice. I do not mean to be impolite, but our message includes top state secrets of Her Majesty's government and is only for your consumption."

When Secretary of State Cordell Hull rose to protest, Roosevelt cut him off with a glance. "Gentlemen, would you give the Prime Minister and myself the room, please?"

After the other Americans left with more than a little grumbling, the Prime Minister leaned back and pulled a pipe out from his jacket. "May I smoke, Mr. President?"

"Of course," Roosevelt smiled, firing up a cigarette inserted in a holder.

"Please call me Franklin. May I call you Clement?"

Attlee detested American informality, but assented with a nod.

"Franklin, at the risk of being melodramatic, I need your promise our discussion today will remain strictly confidential and you will not relay its contents to anyone else in your government."

"Very well."

Attlee nodded to Denniston, who rose to tell the American President about Britain's most closely held secret – the ULTRA code-breaking system. ULTRA used a new machine called a computer to decipher the previously impenetrable German and Italian military codes in comparatively short order compared to previous code-breaking techniques.

Roosevelt listened raptly and interjected when Denniston paused his briefing. "Is there a reason why my cabinet and top military staff cannot be read into ULTRA?"

Attlee took two puffs from his pipe and then leaned forward on the couch. "Truthfully, Franklin, American security is very poor and we do not trust the secret outside of this room."

The American president grimaced, but did not dispute the point.

"For example, ULTRA has intercepted multiple messages from a German agent codenamed the Empress located in the United States providing Berlin with detailed reports detailing your defense dispositions along the Atlantic. Mr. President, you have a leak."

"How long have you known about this Empress?"

"Several months now."

"Why the hell didn't you tell us before!" Roosevelt exploded.

"Mr. President, Hitler is likely read in on anything of importance going on in your government. My inclination was not to disclose ULTRA to you even under these limited circumstances, but something new has arisen which forced our hand."

Roosevelt's demeanor cooled to caution. "You have my full attention, Mr. Prime Minister."

"Decoded intercepts indicate much of the German *Kriegsmarine* has put out into the Atlantic and the volume of the radio traffic suggests a major operation." After pausing for effect, Attlee concluded, "Our assessment is the Germans are executing an invasion, with Canada or the United States as its likely destination."

The American President leaned back in his seat and audibly exhaled. "I'm sorry for losing my temper just now and I'm profoundly grateful for this warning," Roosevelt began. "When do you believe the Germans will arrive?"

"Enemy radio traffic spiked about six days ago and then went silent. We assume the enemy fleet are sailing under radio silence and will complete the journey in days, if not hours." Attlee added apologetically, "I am sorry about the delay, but I hopped on a train to Washington DC as soon as the translations were completed and we were sure of what we had."

"May I share this information with our military without disclosing its source."

"Of course. I would not have provided it otherwise."

"Thank you, Mr. Prime Minister. Do you have anything else for me?"

Attlee shook his head no.

"In that case, if you will excuse me, I have work to do."

Charleston Police Station, South Carolina
16:53 Hours, 15 March 1942

FBI special agent Sam Denard studied the suspect sitting in the office of the chief of police. Katarina Kolotsiev was a tall woman at five foot eleven, with stylish sunglasses fixed in her wavy red hair flowing down over a bright yellow sundress. Definitely a high class broad. Self-assured as well.

Denard and his partner Dennis Smith responded to a suspicious person report from the naval yard and picked up Kolotsiev that morning. Instead of the German agent with binoculars and a camera they were led to expect, the woman was dabbing at a painting of Charleston Bay.

Kolotsiev did not appear to be concerned when Denard flashed his badge. In an unexpected English accent, the suspect freely admitted to painting the naval yard and the destroyer in its slip, asking innocently if she had done something wrong.

The visa she provided checked out with immigration. Kolotsiev was a British refugee permitted an indefinite stay in the United States.

The references she provided at the Charleston Yacht Club also checked out. The club commodore described how Kolotsiev arrived in Charleston on her yacht shortly after the fall of England and made the city her home. The club thought so highly of her they were considering electing her to its governing board.

Dennis walked up and handed him a cup of coffee. "The woman appears to be who she says and we really don't have anything on her. What do ya wanna do?"

Denard took a sip of the hot coffee. There was something about Kolotsiev that just did not fit the profile of a wealthy, pampered refugee. Something hard and slippery.

"Let's talk with her for a while and see is something shakes loose from her story."

The woman looked up and smiled when the FBI agents entered the room.

"Miss Kolotsiev, your papers and reference all checked out. We just have a few more questions before we wrap up our investigation," Denard opened.

"Very well."

The FBI agent went over the particulars of the suspect's story one more time to put her at ease and then asked, "Ma'am, our knowledge of the politics of England is very limited. Would you be willing to tell us what you know of them?"

"Of course, I'll help in any way I can."

"Is it true that some Englishmen supported Hitler before the war?"

"Not many, but yes, there were some."

"Why would they do that? Didn't they know that Germany was the enemy?"

The woman's eyes brightened and she appeared to warm to the subject. "Before the war, most of my countrymen could not conceive of a German invasion. However, some in England agreed with the way the *Führer* cleaned out the reds and the

Jews, then restored order to Germany. They thought England should follow suit."

"You say that almost admiringly, Ms. Kolotsiev." Smith interjected. "How do you feel personally about 'the *Führer*?'"

The woman's eyes started to tear up, but her expression remained hard. "Agent Smith, how do you think I feel? I've lost my country and the Nazis are probably living in the home I left behind. If it were not for America taking me in, I do not know where I'd be now."

This broad is a smart cookie, thought Denard. Her defenses are up and she's not going to give us anything.

"Ms. Kolotsiev, you've been very co-operative,' Denard concluded. "You're free to go, but we need you to stay in Charleston in case we have any further questions."

"But, of course," Kat replied with a twinkle in her eye. "Where else could I go?"

After the suspect left, Denard turned to Smith and shook his head. "I still don't trust that dame, Dennis. Send a cable to the English Special Branch in Canada and see if they know anything about her."

CHAPTER 14

*Submarine Scirè, 6 miles east of Charleston, South Carolina
00:38 Hours, 16 March 1942*

Captain Valerio Borghese slowly panned the periscope in a full circle search of the waters around the submarine *Scirè*. The air of the bridge was thick with anticipation and cigarette smoke. Wiping the moisture from his hands onto his trousers, the Italian submariner re-grasped the periscope handles to begin another circle. The *Americanos* were closing again, but where the hell were they?

The *Scirè* was at full stop, with its divers working furiously to release the 'pigs' from their pens on the still submerged deck of the submarine. Until that task was accomplished, his boat could not move and was utterly vulnerable.

On the third rotation of the periscope, Borghese located the object of his concern. The enemy Coast Guard cutter appeared slightly off starboard, on course to cross over the *Scirè* in a minute or two!

The captain received the emergency orders leading up to this whorehouse mess only hours before. Instead of a simple reconnaissance mission rooting around Charleston Bay, his top secret 'pigs' suddenly became hunters again for the first time since last year's operation against the *Inglese* naval base in Alexandria, Egypt.

The problem was the new target was considerably more distant - past the Port of Charleston and up the Cooper River. In order for his pair of 'pigs' to arrive and complete their mission under cover of darkness, the *Scirè* would need to slip through the shallow shipping lane into Charleston Bay and release its charges close to the enemy city.

Borghese's plan was simplicity itself. Instead of burning time and battery life creeping underwater into the bay powered by the boat's weak electric engines, the *Scirè* would charge down the surface of the shipping lane using the diesel engines and pray to the *Madonna* that speed, darkness and a lack of night time shipping would conceal their entry from the enemy. The *Americano* had other plans.

As the submarine began its approach on Charleston Bay, a low-slung ship steamed out of the darkness ahead to fill the captain's binoculars. The old ship did not match any *Americano* naval vessel of which he was aware. Borghese guessed the unwelcome guest was an enemy Coast Guard cutter, as he slid down the conning tower ladder into the submarine bridge to order an emergency dive.

With a year of combat experience against the Royal Navy, the *Scirè's* veteran crew executed the dive with efficient ease. The ocean shallowed considerably during the approach on the *Americano* coast and the submarine settled on the sandy bottom in less than a minute.

With his hands cupping headphones against his ears and his eyes clamped shut, the hydrophone operator hissed short reports to a silent bridge. "Enemy vessel continues to approach... Yes, the propeller noises are getting louder."

Soon, Borghese could hear the thrum of the enemy propellers through the hull. The *Americano* cutter was passing overhead only meters above the submarine. As the captain and his crew grabbed nearby bridge fixtures to brace themselves, the "Black Prince" hoped his face displayed the serene calm expected of an aristocrat. Enemy depth charges could hardly miss at this range.

The cutter left nothing behind, though, apart from the diminishing sounds of its churning propellers. No sonar pings disclosing the location of his boat. None of the teeth rattling depth charge explosions the captain vividly recalled when an *Inglese* destroyer worked over the *Scirè* near Spain.

Maybe the *Americano* simply misjudged their location and would drop their deadly cans over some nearby patch of ocean?

Minutes passed, but still nothing. The enemy cutter probably never sighted the *Scirè* at all.

Borghese lit a cigarette and considered whether to resurface and resume the surface approach. The original plan anticipated a clear shipping lane, but the hydrophone operator reported the enemy vessel was still cruising the area. The unwelcome company was not leaving. With the *Germano* invasion fleet still hours away, *Scirè* could not risk the cutter spotting the submarine and alerting the *Americano* navy.

Turning to Lieutenant Commander de la Penne standing off to the side of the bridge, the captain ordered, "Get your boys suited up, Luigi. We will launch the 'pigs' from here." The target was barely within the maximum range of these highly classified weapons, but there was no longer any other option.

When the frogmen were lined up by the submarine coning tower ladder, Borghese took his place by the periscope and commanded the helm to execute a slow surface. The compressed air gradually moved the ocean water out of the ballast tanks until the boat rose up out of the cradle of the sandy bottom with a shudder. When the captain called out as the top of the coning tower broke the surface, the executive officer stopped the rise of the submarine to keep the rest of the boat submerged.

De la Penne and his frogmen scrambled up the coning tower ladder, out the hatch and into the water covering the forward deck where the 'pigs' were penned. The captain then ordered a slight submersion to periscope deck to conceal the conning tower from any prying *Americano* eyes.

As he panned the periscope across the sea around them, Borghese listened to the metallic clangs and squeals of the divers removing the 'pig pens' as they had dozens of times over the past two years. Tonight, however, his men did not have the luxury of time.

The *Americano* cutter returned out of the same quadrant into which it disappeared, cruising back at a slow and steady speed. Borghese doubted the enemy knew of their presence. Likely, the *Americano* coastal vessel was on routine patrol of the shipping lane into Charleston Bay. The problem was cutter's course would take them directly over the *Scirè*!

The submarine captain could do nothing but stare helplessly at the approaching cutter as his men completed their work. 1,500 meters away. 1,000 meters. 500 meters.

Madonna, finish up already, Borghese raged silently. As if responding their captain's thoughts, the reserve divers slammed shut the conning tower hatch and slid down the metal ladder.

Without waiting for orders, the crew scurried forward towards the bow to weigh it down for the coming dive. The submarine tilted downward and slipped back into the safety of mother ocean, but at a painfully slow rate. Too damned slow.

As the sound of the enemy ship's churning propellers filled the bridge again, the helmsman wailed, "Come on, you bitch! Dive! Dive! DIVE!"

DD-461 U.S.S. Forrest, 73 miles northeast of Bermuda
06:29 Hours, 16 March 1942

Commander Tigert was finishing shaving in his quarters, when a call came from the bridge: the *U.S.S. Forrest* was surrounded by dozens of ships!

Wiping off the last of the shaving cream with a wash rag, PJ bounded up to the bridge to take a look for himself. It was unlike his executive officer, Frank Morris, to exaggerate or get very excited about much of anything, apart from his beloved New York Yankees. The XO handed off the binoculars to Tigert, who slowly scanned the horizon. Christ! Dozens of ships, grouped in what appeared to be at least three task forces, bracketed the *Forrest*. We must have blundered into them in the deep early morning dark.

"A *Kriegsmarine* force this large can only mean trouble," opined Morris.

Tigert handed the binoculars back to his first officer. "Mr. Morris, you need to brush up on your ship identification. Our unwelcome guests are Italian *Regia Marina*." Pointing to left, the commander added, "If you look three points to port, those big bastards are the new *Littorio* class battleships."

Both the *Forrest* and her crew were unprepared. The Navy rushed his destroyer out of the construction yards without her radar array to fill the void in left by the redeployment of much of the Atlantic Fleet to the Pacific. Without this early warning, they sailed smack dab into this mob in the dark.

While Tigert and his new crew made progress over the past two months, there simply wasn't nearly enough time for a full train-up on even basic skills. During the initial shakedown cruise after leaving the Boston shipyard, nearly all their time was occupied fixing the niggling mechanical problems a spanking new ship offers in abundance. Before they could complete the shakedown, *Forrest* was ordered down to Bermuda to join a destroyer screen across the central Atlantic.

The cruise did provide time for the crew the gel, however. Despite the heavy workload, the men took a liking to their new skipper, nicknaming him "Blackbeard" on account of his eye patch. In turn, they started calling themselves 'Tigert's pirates.'

Now that they were in the middle of the shit, his pirates would get some on the job training.

The current patrol was a last-minute affair. *Forrest* wasn't scheduled to rotate out of King's Wharf for another couple days. Just before midnight, however, the entire task force went on alert with orders to put out to sea by 02:00 to form a picket line across the area. The word was the German *Kriegsmarine* was on the move and their orders were to find it. No one said anything about the *Regia Marina*, though.

"Mr. Morris, you're correct that a force this large can only mean trouble. Go to general quarters. Turn the ship to a course of 220 degrees and increase speed to 25 knots," ordered Tigert. "I want to shadow this mob so we can keep sending reports back to base. But, if our big neighbors become hostile, we'll need to shag ass as quickly as possible."

Bracing himself as the ship began a hard turn to port, the skipper turned to the communications console. "Mr. Cork, please radio the fleet to report our position and our sighting of between 40-50 ships of the *Regia Marina*, including battleships and transports, on a course for Bermuda. Report we are shadowing sighted ships. Suspect this is an invasion fleet. No hostilities so far. More details to follow. Request instructions."

R.N. Littorio, 45 miles northeast of Bermuda
06:32 Hours, 16 March 1942

Carlo Bergamini stood on the bridge of *Littorio*, sipping on a small cup of espresso and contemplating the drizzly twilight outside.

After his English Channel victory, Bergamini became the most celebrated Italian admiral since Octavian defeated Antony. Confident he would protect them and bring them victory, the sailors of the Special Naval Force started calling him "Papa."

However, Papa often worried he could not possibly justify their faith and today was one of those days.

As Bergamini drained the dregs of the strong black liquid, the fleet radios came alive. "Admiral!" barked out the communications officer, rather more loudly than he intended. "*Carducci* reports sighting an *Americano* ship, a destroyer or light cruiser. Other ships are confirming the report."

Carlo did a quick calculation. The *Carducci* was assigned to…the transport escort. *Madre di Dios*! How did the enemy ship get past the security screen during the night?

"Where exactly is the *Americano* located?"

"A moment sir, they are transmitting the information now." That minute dragged into five. "Admiral, the *Americano* ship is a destroyer and is approximately 23 kilometers southwest of *Carducci*, in between Divisions 1 and 9. It is bearing north by northeast towards the transports."

The *Supermarina* fleet headquarters did not believe the U.S. Navy had any significant force in the Central Atlantic, but this desk-bound brass was located over 3,000 kilometers back in Italy and their "intelligence reports" concerning this operation were often nothing more than wishful thinking. In truth, Bergamini had very little idea what was in the waters around his ships.

Most likely, this single destroyer was alone on patrol rather than forming the vanguard of an enemy attack. Best to shoo this fly away and proceed with the original invasion plan.

"Order Division 1 to deploy the *Zara* cruiser squadron with orders to move the *Americano* ship out of the Force perimeter or sink it. All other Divisions are to go to the highest alert and report any other incursions. The landing schedule continues as before."

DD-461 U.S.S. Forrest, 43 miles northeast of Bermuda
06:44 Hours, 16 March 1942

"Sir, you may want to amend your radio report concerning hostilities," Morris urged. "Three…no four, Italian cruisers have broken off from the forward task force and are approaching at high speed."

"Increase speed to thirty-five knots." Tigert ordered.

The larger Italians unexpectedly matched the speed of the fleeing *Forrest* and opened fire at twenty kilometers, some three kilometers beyond the maximum range of the American destroyer's smaller five inch guns. The incoming Italian shells landed starboard of the destroyer, throwing up columns of water, but none came close enough to do any damage.

"I guess than means we are officially at war. Mr. Morris, change course to 230 degrees before these fast bastards adjust their aim."

The *Forrest* heaved up and down as the destroyer nearly sailed into a second volley of the big eight inch shells, the closest of which landed within yards of the bow. Christ, that was close! If changing course wasn't working, Tigert reasoned, let's see if we can pull out of range.

"Mr. Morris, increase speed as far as the engines will tolerate. Full speed ahead. Let's see if we can get some distance from these people."

The commander grinned as the next volleys of shells fell behind the destroyer. Maybe *Forrest* would get out of this in one piece.

PJ should have known better than to tempt fate, though, as the destroyer bridge suddenly filled with howl of a late incoming shell, followed by the crash and clatter of steel splinters gouging the bridge roof above.

R.N. Littorio, 44 miles northeast of Bermuda
06:51 Hours, 16 March 1942

Admiral Bergamini's frustration level was rising rapidly. Ever since the break in radio silence to identify and respond to the *Americano* destroyer, the radio room produced over a dozen further sightings of enemy ships, each followed a few minutes later by an admission of a false report.

Nearly twenty minutes had passed, though, without a report from the *Zara* squadron on their pursuit of the only confirmed sighting. Had the *Americano* escaped? His patience at an end, Bergamini told his communications officer to raise the squadron commander and request a situation report.

"Admiral, the *Zaras* say they hit the *Americano* destroyer and are returning to the defensive perimeter," the communications officer responded. "Also, our forward destroyers are now off the north coast of Bermuda and report no enemy ships in the area."

"Good, good," Bergamini replied, before sitting down, holding his hands together and touching his lips as if in prayer. It appeared the *Americano* destroyer really was alone. With that fly swatted, the landing of the San Marco marine regiment could go forward as scheduled. If Bermuda lacked a significant ground defense, the island's airfield should be available for *Luftwaffe* flights to the United States by tomorrow morning.

The United States. With his own small crisis resolved, the Italian admiral's thoughts shifted to his *Kriegsmarine* partners. Bergamini assumed the enemy destroyer was able to radio at least some information concerning the Force to the *Americano* Atlantic fleet. Combined with the *Force's* own radio chatter, the enemy must know something was up.

The *Germano* radio channels remained silent, though, so Bergamini assumed the enemy had not yet sighted *Kriegsmarine* invasion fleet. Still, over an hour remained before the planned landing on the *Americano* coast. Ample time for something to go wrong.

The Italian admiral said a silent prayer for his *Germano* counterpart, before returning his attention to deploying the Force's forward division into position to conduct a shore bombardment.

U.S. Navy Headquarters, Washington D.C.
06:14 Hours, 16 March 1942

What in tarnation was going on?

Yesterday afternoon, the President personally telephoned U.S. Navy Commander in Chief to relay a mysterious warning from the Brits that the German *Kriegsmarine* put to sea nearly a week ago for potential operations against the Eastern seaboard. Nothing about the source or credibility of this intelligence, just a vague suggestion to take appropriate action.

Admiral Ernest King immediately ordered additional air and sea patrols, then slept in his office last night to act on any reports. It was a restless night trying to get comfortable on a couch too short for his long frame, with nightmare invasion scenarios running around his head. Sometime after 04:00 hours, King finally gave up on sleep and returned to the operations center with its constantly refilled coffee pot.

The first radio sighting report came in just before dawn, but it found the wrong navy! One of his former staff officers, PJ Tigert on the *Forrest* off Bermuda, provided a flash message describing a large formation of Italian *Regia Marina* ships, followed by an excellent breakdown of the observed ships and their heading. PJ was always detail oriented. Good man to have delivering reports.

The *Regia Marina*? Where the hell was the *Kriegsmarine*? Were the Germans and Italians conducting a joint operation? If so, what were the enemy objectives?

Far more infuriating questions than answers. Then, King recalled Tigert's prediction before the Hawaii relief operation - the Japanese would not commit everything to invade Hawaii without the support of their Axis allies in Europe.

The admiral was not taking any chances this time around and issued a rapid-fire set of orders to get the Navy out to sea. Every ship in the Atlantic Fleet not on patrol was to deploy from their US ports and assemble off of Norfolk, Virginia. The Caribbean Fleet was to move east of Puerto Rico and the hopelessly outnumbered flotilla off of Bermuda would join them.

If any enemy force approaches our coast, we'll hit them fast and hard with everything we have.

CHAPTER 15

Port of Charleston, South Carolina
06:35 Hours, 16 March 1942

The *Amerikaner* customs inspector boarded the Greek freighter *S.S. Aneos* just after dawn, far earlier than expected and only meters away from blowing the entire operation.

Captain Yiannis Christidis and a pair of his seamen greeted the inspector on the freighter deck. 'Christidis' was actually *Kriegsmarine* Commodore Ernst Muller, who served as the assistant naval attaché to Greece before the war and possessed a good mastery of the English and Greek languages. The "seamen" were paratrooper company commander Wulf von Plessen and his platoon leader Helmut Arpke, both of whose English was weighted down with heavy German accents. The ship's captain would do all the talking.

"Welcome aboard the *Aneos*, sir. I am Captain Christidis."

"Captain, I'm Charlie Clark," the customs man replied, while shaking hands. "Sorry about coming aboard so early, but one of our inspectors is out sick and we weren't expecting y'all to arrive last night. We have a full plate today, so let's get right to work."

'Christidis handed over the manifest and the group descended into the hold.

"Captain, are you carrying any passengers apart from the crew?"

"No. Why do you ask?"

"A Portuguese ship tried to smuggle a group of German Jews into New York two days ago, so we are checking extra careful for any other stowaways."

Arpke glanced at Von Plessen, then reached into the pocket of his seaman's jacket and wrapped his fingers around the Lugar pistol within.

'Christidis' laughed and replied: "As you can see, all we are smuggling into the United States is the oil of olives for your salads."

"We'll see," remarked the customs man.

The *Amerikaner* proceeded to knock on a series of cargo crates with his fist and suddenly stopped. He hit the crate a second time and the echo returned.

"What's in this container? It sounds hollow."

"Olive oil, like the other crates. Some are not packed fully, depending on the order," "Christidis" deferred. In reality, this was a dummy container leading to the hidden quarters of the paratroop company.

Operation Trojan Horse called for the *Aneos* to dock at night, then land the paratroopers the following morning when the *Kriegsmarine* opened its attack on the Charleston's defenses. Arpke's company would hold the port until the invasion fleet broke through and reinforced them.

Last night's docking went without incident. The *Aneos* was a registered freighter of neutral Greece captured as a war prize in an English port. So far as the United States knew, the ship was still Greek flagged. Then, this inspector threw sand into the gears by arriving before the *Kriegsmarine*.

"Open up the crate," commanded the customs man.

"You have arrived early and my crew is still at breakfast. The ship is due to unload at 9:00 this morning. You could see the entire cargo then."

The inspector frowned and pointed at von Plessen and Arpke: "These men are not at breakfast. Open…" His eyes coming to rest on von Plessen, Clark stopped in mid-sentence and the color left his face. The inspector quickly turned back to 'Captain Christidis' and stammered, "You know, that would be a good idea. Uh… I see I haven't even brought the correct forms for this inspection. I'll head back to my office and return at nine when you are unloading."

Helmut looked over to his company commander, swore under his breath and pulled his pistol on the scurrying *Amerikaner*. "Halt and raise your hands!"

The terrified inspector dropped his clipboard and complied with the order.

"What the hell, Helmut!" von Plessen demanded.

Arpke turned to his commander and tapped on his own collar. "Sir, your rank is showing."

The paratrooper officers were wearing their field uniforms under the seaman's overalls and the collar of von Plessen's uniform was exposed. The customs man must have seen it.

Von Plessen looked down and grimaced. "So much for my career as a spy."

The telephone on the wall of the hold started ringing and 'Christidis' answered. Turning to the paratroopers, the ship's captain said: "We have another man from customs asking to board and speak with our guest here."

"We can't wait for the *Kriegsmarine* to arrive," sighed Von Plessen. "Captain, if you could assume custody of this gentleman, we will take off these sailor costumes and properly introduce our company to the city of Charleston."

Charleston Naval Shipyard, South Carolina
06:38 Hours, 16 March 1942

Lieutenant Commander Luigi de la Penne was shaking uncontrollably, cocooned in a sodden cold. During the hours long journey from the *Scirè*, the bay and then river water seeped into his wet suit, soaking the woolen clothing within meant to keep him warm. To make things worse, the water also made its way into his partially submerged, full-face dive mask; forcing him to sip the brackish stuff to keep from drowning, until he was sick to his rebelling stomach. With his target at last in sight, the miserable Italian frogman only wanted the one-way trip to end.

De la Penne shivered as he recalled how this cursed mission almost ended before it began. As the commander and his men moved their two 'pigs' off the deck of the *Scirè* at the painfully slow speed generated by their small electric engines, the surrounding water thrummed with the propeller sounds of the closing *Americano* vessel. The frogman looked over his shoulder to see the bow of the cutter slice through the water between the 'pigs' and the mother submarine, barely missing the *Scirè's* deck by less than a meter, before disappearing again into the night water.

Even after they were safely underway, the mission was still what the *Americano* would call a "long shot." Everything had to go just right.

His men were not the problem. De la Penne and his team were decorated frogmen of the Decima MAS - the *Regia Marina's* underwater commando unit - and veterans of multiple engagements with the *Inglese*.

The challenges were distance and time. The team rode into combat atop two SLC 200 'pigs' - submarine torpedoes modified so a pair of frogmen could sit on top of them and up to an enemy ship to blow her to hell. However, *Scirè* released her 'pigs' much further out in the Atlantic than planned. If the vehicles did not travel close to top speed to their distant target, the sunrise would lift the cloak of darkness before they arrived; but if they swam too fast, the batteries powering the 'pigs' would give out short of their target and leave frogmen stranded in the bay.

Pushing these concerns away, de la Penne's SLC 200's began their journey well underwater to avoid being sighted by the *Americano* cutter. Without any landmarks under the dark waters, each 'pig' driver used a compass with a radium dial mounted on an instrument panel to stay the course towards Charleston.

While entering the bay, an unexpected cross-current buffeted the 'pigs.' For a few minutes, de La Penne turned into the current and kept his eyes glued on the compass to maintain course. When the waters stilled again and the commander looked up, the second 'pig' was gone.

The waters were silent. No murmur from the enemy ship in over an hour. The commander decided it was time to surface and take a look around. With fortune, he would be able to sight his missing 'pig.'

De la Penne and his number two, Petty Officer Emelio Bianchi, popped their heads above water and refocused their eyes on the unexpectedly bright surroundings. The lights of Charleston washed across the bay, enabling the frogmen to see hundreds of meters in every direction, but their comrades were nowhere within that expanse.

Decima MAS frogmen knew from hard experience every mission was extremely dangerous. They all lost friends, not only to the enemy, but also to equipment failure and plain evil fortune. If God was merciful, these latest lost friends were alive and able to swim to shore to await the rescue of the coming invasion. Meanwhile, it was up to de la Penne and Biachi to complete the mission so the invasion would succeed.

Hours later, the last 'pig' and its miserable crew made the final turn of the Cooper River to sight their objective - the *Americano* destroyer *Leary*. Although their battery power and oxygen lasted the trip, the frogmen lost their race with the dawn. The low clouds behind them turned from gray to pink, as the twilight rolled up the river.

Even through his partially fogged dive mask, de la Penne could make out the sailors gathering on the warship's deck. Although only their black rubber covered heads broke the surface of the river, a pointing enemy sentry appeared to see them as well. Time for the 'pig' to make its final run on the destroyer.

With a small push on the steering handles, the SLC 200 slipped beneath the surface of the Cooper River. While the world above was brightening rapidly, the tea-colored river water remained opaque.

De la Penne could hardly see past the snout of the 'pig' and slowed the SLC 200's speed to a mere drift forward. After a long minute passed, the hull of the destroyer suddenly loomed out the gloom. The 'pig' was running too shallow and the nose of the converted torpedo glanced off the ship's keel with gong-like clang.

Damn! If the enemy sentry above was not sure what he saw above the water, the 'pig' unmistakably announced its presence below. No time left to spare.

De la Penne turned the SLC 200 down the keel of the destroyer and reversed the propeller for a moment to stop the 'pig' near the bow of the *Americano* ship. Bianchi slipped off, unwound a few feet of steel cable from a spool, then screwed down a clamp at the end of the cable onto the keel. The commander than reversed the 'pig' several meters to allow Bianchi to clamp the other end of the cable onto the bow keel.

Now for the final task. Bianchi pulled the middle of the cable down, attached it to a hook atop the torpedo's 330-kilogram explosive warhead, then disengaged the warhead from the SLC 200 so that it hung from the cable underneath the ship.

Once his Number Two set the timer to detonate the warhead and retook his seat on the 'pig,' de la Penne would drive the remainder of the SLC 200 at full speed to the far shore, where the frogmen would await the *Germano* invasion.

Suddenly the destroyer's engines came to life and pulled the ship away from the dock. The unexpected backwash yanked Bianchi off the warhead and pushed the 'pig' back toward the docks.

Madonna! Were the explosives set to detonate?

Charleston Yacht Club, South Carolina
06:39 Hours, 16 March 1942

FBI Special Agent Sam Denard and his partner Dennis Smith raced the bureau Packard across a largely empty parking lot, then came to a squealing halt in front of the Charleston Yacht Club. Maybe they could find the bitch on her boat.

A couple hours earlier, the agents came off shift conducting surveillance in an unrelated case and checked their messages at the office. The Brits responded to the cable Smith sent a few days back with a priority message - Katarina Kolotsiev was a likely German spy who was suspected in the murder of two Special Branch agents. The news sent the partners on a wild goose chase around the city.

Kolotsiev's rental home was dark when the agents arrived. When no one answered his banging, Denard kicked in the front door. The only thing they found for their trouble was a key lying on a letter from the spy to her landlady thanking her for her hospitality.

The Charleston Yacht Club was similarly locked up hours before opening. Running around the stately old structure, the agents found a handful of boats sitting silent and unoccupied in the slips of the marina, with only a single crew performing maintenance on a large mahogany yacht near the end.

Flashing his badge, a breathless Smith asked, "Do you fellas know a tall redhead with a yacht docked here?"

"Kat Kolotsiev?" asked a burly man working the lines. Smith nodded.

"Everyone knows Kat. Hard to miss a high-class English lady sporting that red mane and smoking Cubans on her boat."

"OK, do ya know where she's at?" Denard pressed.

"Y'all just missed her. That's Kat and the *Empress Catherine* out on the Ashley River over there."

Knowing it was useless, Denard ran to the end of the dock anyway and yelled for the Nazi bitch to stop.

Kat took another pull on her cigar and exhaled into the light breeze, allowing the smoke to wash over her face. Going back to sea always relaxed her, but something she couldn't quite make out was disturbing her peace like the whine of a fly in a quiet room.

Kolotsiev looked back over her shoulder, then grinned. *Why it was Special Agent Denard shouting from the dock and looking extremely cross. I wonder what he could possibly want?* Mischievously, Kat cupped her hand by her ear and shook her head back and forth. Denard furiously snatched off his fedora and threw it down onto the dock, where it promptly blew into the brown river. Everyone on the yacht broke out in laughter at the expense of the hapless FBI agent.

The levity was short-lived, though. As the *Empress Catherine* slowly approached the Coast Guard station just down the road from the yacht club, Kat wondered how long would it be before the FBI agent gathered his wits and dispatched the cutter docked there after Kat's pleasure boat.

Tossing her cigar overboard, Kolotsiev ordered the crew to hoist the full set of sails on the yacht. Even with every foot of canvas deployed, the yacht could not long evade a motorized pursuer, but every mile she could put between her and the cutter would buy her time to find a way out of this mess.

When the additional sail and a freshening wind launched the *Empress Catherine* past the Coast Guard docks, a wave of relief swept over Kat. The slip was empty! By some stroke of luck, the cutter was out to sea and the route across Charleston Bay was clear.

The yacht skipper had no idea her exciting morning was only beginning.

A massive explosion cracked across the bay from the other side of Charleston, causing Kat to jump in her captain's seat and swivel towards the noise. A column of oily smoke rose to the northwest…in the direction of the naval yard…where the *USS Leary* was the only docked ship.

The German spy nodded in self-satisfaction. "*Herr Doktor*" somehow managed to act on her report and removed the only Navy ship defending Charleston Bay. The long-suspected invasion could not be far behind. As the Yanks were fond of saying, they needed to get the hell out of Dodge.

As if on cue, when the *Empress Catherine* prepared to depart Charleston Bay, groups of gray warplanes arrived from the Atlantic. German Messerschmidt fighters and *Stuka* dive bombers she recalled from innumerable newsreels back in England during the Blitz. Hopefully, none of them would mistake the *Empress Catherine* for a Yank target of opportunity.

Instead, the fighters flew a large, lazy circle around Sullivan Island off the port-side of the yacht, while the *Stukas* slowed somewhat, then plunged into screaming dives onto the shore batteries guarding the bay entrance. One after another, they dropped their bombs, until fire and smoke boiled out of the island.

Turning back to steering the *Empress Catherine* into the Atlantic, Kolotsiev found her absent Coast Guard cutter. The Yank vessel was cruising down the center of the shipping lane straight towards the yacht!

Kat's enjoyment of the pre-invasion fireworks immediately gave way to calculation. The sudden appearance of the cutter could be innocent happenstance, but she did not believe in coincidence. She had to assume the FBI managed to radio the cutter to intercept her yacht.

If Kolotsiev turned the *Empress Catherine* for shore, the pause to change course would give the motorized enemy ample time to close on her sailing yacht.

Fighting their way out into the open ocean was not a realistic option. The pistols she and the crew carried were hardly a match for the cutter's main cannon.

Then, the Coast Guard vessel forced the issue, entering into a wide turn Kolotsiev could only assume was meant to block the Empress Catherine's escape into the Atlantic. Nothing to do for it but to sell their lives dearly when the Yanks boarded. Kat and her *Kriegsmarine* crew were sure to face the gallows as spies if they surrendered.

With a shout and an arm pointed off the bow, one of the crew broke through their captain's melancholy. Two white bubble trails cut across the bay entrance towards the enemy cutter. After Kolotsiev shot her crewman a questioning look, Heinrich shouted back. "Torpedoes, Captain. Torpedoes!"

Kat marveled as one of the deadly fish broadsided the cutter with a crash and a shudder. The small vessel rapidly filled with water and rolled on its side, its sailors shouting at the *Empress Catherine* in puzzlement and anger as the yacht sailed past into the Atlantic without rendering aid.

Kat fired up another cigar and took a couple puffs, before tacking south for Cuba. As the boom of the main sail swung over the deck, she recalled one of her Papa's more frequent lessons - luck was as important as talent in navigating this dangerous world. "The Empress" certainly enjoyed more than her share of both.

The Citadel, Charleston, South Carolina
08:46 Hours, 16 March 1942

Cadets William Boone and Doug Sherman reported as ordered to the president's office. The Citadel was abuzz with rumors of a Germans commando raid on Charleston, which the faculty declined to confirm or deny as they ordered the student body back to their billets to await further orders. Maybe now they would get the straight scoop.

The Citadel's president was a legend. Retired Army Chief of Staff, General Charles P. Summerall, took command of the military academy a decade ago and recently reached the ripe old age of seventy-five years without showing any signs of slowing down.

After a sharp knock on the office door, a voice from within bade them to enter. The cadets smartly marched in front of the president's desk, assumed the position of attention and saluted.

Dressed in a WWI field uniform, the general was reassembling an equally old Colt .45 pistol. After casually returning the salute and telling the cadets to stand at ease, Summerall got straight to business.

"Gentlemen, I just spoke with the chief of police and he confirms the rumors are true – a group of German commandos has captured the Port of Charleston. Those explosions we heard were bombs falling on Fort Moultrie. I believe these moves are a prelude to invasion."

A chill ran down Boone's spine. "Any word from the Army, General?"

"Mr. Boone, the nearest Army base of any size is Fort Jackson, too far away to do anything, at least for a couple days." The general rose from his desk and locked onto the eyes of his cadets. "Gentlemen, Charleston is on its own and we are its only defense. It is up to the men of the Citadel to retake the port before the Hun invader arrives. Specifically, you and your units."

Boone was the cadet commander of the Richardson Rifles, which gained national renown during the Great Depression as the best precision marching platoon of the military academies. However, this team carried unloaded *Springfield* rifles and many of its members had never fired a weapon before.

Sherman's team of rifle marksman were different. The Citadel issued them live ammunition and they were some of the finest shots in the country. However, there were only a dozen of them and they had no more infantry training than did the Richardson Rifles.

Was the general actually contemplating throwing them into combat against German commandos?

"General, what are your orders?" Boone asked.

"Muster your units at the armory and draw your rifles and all of the ammunition. Load your rifles and then each man will carry an ammo can on the march. Be ready to depart at 09:20 hours."

Boone's unease descended into fear. The cadet desperately wanted to reason with the commandant. They were students, not trained soldiers. But the cadet was even more afraid the great man would think him a coward. All he could do is fidget in place.

Summerall obliviously plowed on. "We will march across the city, make our approach on the west side of the port. From there, we can hit the Hun in the flank."

Boone suddenly remembered he was the senior cadet present. Did the general expect him to lead this attack? How? His military history class only consisted of arrows on maps, representing general movements of troops sweeping across long ago battlefields. Nothing on how to command a real-life platoon during actual combat.

"Sir, who will command the cadets?"

Summerall cocked his head slightly in surprise. "I will, of course, Mr. Boone. You men just need to follow orders and we will emerge victorious today."

The tall blond-haired cadet swallowed hard and saluted.

Primrose House, Charleston, South Carolina
09:58 Hours, 16 March 1942

Lieutenant Arpke studied the burning police car burrowed into the home across the street. Helmut hoped the fire did not spread to the old wooden structure. Fire fighters were unlikely to deploy onto battlefields and an unchecked fire could burn down half the city!

The police arrived soon after the paratroopers evicted the occupants from the row of homes and shops behind Bay Street and set up a defensive perimeter around the Port of Charleston. The firefight was short and sweet. A single machine pistol burst from next door stitched the side of the wailing vehicle, forcing the driver to swerve into the porch. No one emerged from the crash.

Tasked with securing the right flank of the large port until the invasion fleet arrived, Arpke was forced to spread out his platoon far more than he preferred. Only sections of three to four paratroops guarded each structure. The platoon leader positioned himself and a pair of machine guns in a stately two-story home on the far right of the line with wonderful lines of sight down the surrounding roads.

While the thin defenses were more than adequate to deal with the local police, the platoon leader knew they could not stand up long to a determined enemy infantry attack. Thankfully, *Amerikaner* army had yet to make an appearance. In a pleasing turnabout, the intelligence reports appeared to be correct for once. The *Amis* left the entire city undefended.

A strange sound drew Arpke's attention to the south. Was that boots marching in unison? The lieutenant slowly scanned the approaching streets with his binoculars until the source of the rhythmic thumping came into view.

Helmut could not quite credit what he was seeing. A column of young soldiers, four abreast, were marching in perfect precision towards his position. They were dressed in grey tunics with two rows of gold buttons descending toward bright white pants. On their heads were perched tall black leather hats, topped with black ostrich plumes. Each carried a *Springfield* bolt-action rifle with a shining bayonet affixed on top of the muzzle. Leading them was a very old man wearing an *Amerikaner* officer's uniform, which Helmut swore dated back to the Great War.

Arpke exchanged incredulous glances with his platoon sergeant and asked: "Are you seeing this, Erich? Have we wandered onto the battlefield at Waterloo?"

"Apparently, Lieutenant," replied Schuster. "What would you like us to do about these splendidly dressed young men coming to pay us a visit?"

Arpke thought for a moment and ordered: "I will take Martin out front to get the drop on our guests. Let's see if they will piss their pants and surrender. If they give us any trouble, lay into them with the machine gun."

Through the gaps in the latticed brick surrounding the garden next the home, Arpke watched the formation approach down George Street in impeccable order and then execute a perfect right turn onto Bay.

When Helmut bellowed for the *Amerikaner* boys to stop and drop their weapons in his best broken English, the old man in the Great War uniform nearly jumped out of his shoes. Quickly regaining his wits, the officer ordered the column to halt…and then to execute a right face toward the Germans.

Arpke's men in the two adjacent homes joined the platoon leader, shouting in a mixture of German and English for the *Amis* to drop their weapons. Instead, a scattered handful of the panicked young men unslung their rifles and pulled back the bolts to chamber rounds.

Schuster's machine gun quickly ended the standoff, cutting down the neatly arranged *Amis* like a scythe slicing through young corn. The one-sided fight was over in seconds.

Surveying the *Amis* sprawled across the road, Helmut walked up to a blonde-haired young man writhing in the street. The boy stared back at him with eyes wild from pain, holding a badly bleeding belly wound with his left hand and reaching for a rifle with his right. Arpke kicked the rifle away and called his medic over.

This is madness. What kind of people send boys dressed like toy soldiers into battle?

Berlin, Germany
17:12 Hours, 16 March 1942

After closing her empty post box and walking up the Oberwahlstrasse toward the opera for her afternoon rehearsal, Louisa was in a cross mood. Helmut had not telephoned or written her in over a month now. Didn't he care about her big news?

Their ongoing separation was unavoidable. Louisa was the lead soprano of the Linder Opera, while her darling Helmut served as a paratroop officer based a hundred kilometers west in Stendhal.

Her husband was always a devoted correspondent, though, posting a letter to her every two or three days describing his military life and comrades. While her soldier was not a particularly good writer, she cherished every word and reread them often. Even this limited avenue of communication abruptly ended on the first of February, when a short and cryptic note from Helmut arrived, saying he was entering special training and would not be able to write as often.

As she entered the back of the opera house, Louisa was greeted by military music. This was not the orchestra practicing, but rather issued from a radio behind the stage surrounded by a handful of the staff.

Grafenberg sighed. "Could someone please turn the radio to something less somber?"

"All the stations are playing the same music," the secretary reported. "The *Führer* is scheduled to speak to the nation in a moment from the Sportpalatz."

Louisa stopped and stared at the radio. The last time the stations played this music was before the war with France and England.

After an introduction followed by the Sportpalatz crowd's repeated refrain of "*Sieg Heil*," Adolph Hitler's voice filled the opera stage. The Führer began calmly, listing the offenses and provocations of the *Amerikaner* gangster president Roosevelt against the *Reich*, from supplying weapons to England to degrading the *volksdeutsche* living in the United States. "These crimes can no longer be tolerated," the *Führer* shouted to thunderous applause.

Louisa shut her eyes. No, it can't be. No, no, no…

"Yesterday, brave sailors and soldiers of the *Reich* landed in *Amerika*. I call on the millions of *volksdeutsche* there to join with your liberators to overthrow the gangster Roosevelt and the Wall Street Jews who control him."

Louisa audibly groaned. Helmut must be over there. That is why he has not written me for so long, she concluded, feeling ashamed for her earlier anger with him.

The Grafenbergs were not a devout family. They were social Christians, who made the minimal religious observations required of the German middle class. Still, Louisa found herself praying urgently to a God she hardly knew to protect her husband from dangers of a war she could hardly imagine.

After the silent prayer, a realization came to Louisa. If her soldier was unable to write, he probably has not received the singer's letters. He does not know about her news.

CHAPTER 16

U.S. Navy Headquarters, Washington D.C.
00:19 Hours, 17 March 1942

Damn it, we're almost completely blind, General George Marshall fretted.

The colonel from Army intelligence finished up his all too brief briefing in less than five minutes. There were only two points of interest.

Just after dawn, the 61st Pursuit Squadron at Charleston Airport radioed that a couple dozen German fighters appeared overhead and shot down nearly all of their *Air Cobras* as they were taking off. Their last radio transmission at 11:45 reported German ground troops were on the runways.

The survivors of the Fort Moultrie shore guns guarding Charleston Bay called in on a civilian telephone to report German dive bombers flying in from the sea wiped out their battery. Afterward, a parade of freighters sailed into the harbor to unload a cargo of soldiers in camouflage uniforms. Instead of staying put and sending in regular reports, though, the soldiers took off for what the colonel hoped was the nearest Army post.

Naval intelligence wasn't much more informative. The handful of Navy and Coast Guard ships keeping watch on the South Carolina coast were either sunk or swept away without reporting anything significant about the composition of the

Kriegsmarine main force. Bermuda fell this evening, with the last radio transmission reporting being under attack by Italian marines. The last sighting of the *Regia Marina* fleet was eighteen hours old.

After the briefings, the service commanders just looked at one another across a large conference table.

Marshall broke the silence with a question for his Navy counterpart, "The news on the radio is filled with reports of German invasions all along the east coast. Ernie, do you think Charleston is the Kraut landing zone or just a diversion? It seems so far from DC and our major cities."

"Most of the news is bullshit," Admiral Earnest King replied, shaking his head. "Apart from two credible U-boat sightings off Virginia, everything is quiet outside of Bermuda and Charleston."

"Why Charleston, though?"

King tapped his fingers on the table a couple times before answering. "My best guess is the bastards don't have any landing craft. Remember how the Krauts used trawlers and barges to cross the Channel to invade England? Without landing craft, the only way they could take a port is by docking their transports to unload just like they are doing at Charleston."

George felt himself losing his temper. "And why the hell didn't the Navy have ships guarding Charleston harbor?"

"We did!" King snapped back. The admiral took a breath, leaned back in his chair and began again in a lower key. "The destroyer *Leary* was stationed in Charleston Bay, but somehow the bastards sunk her at dock without warning. Without access to the wreck, my boys are stumped on how they pulled it off."

"Let's leave that for the intel boys to figure out later," Marshall commiserated. "How do we respond now?"

"I see a divided enemy fleet I intend to destroy piecemeal," King replied. "The main Atlantic Fleet is concentrated off the Virginia coast, while the remaining ships from the Caribbean fleet are gathering off Florida. The two task forces will meet at Charleston and sink the *Kriegsmarine* before the *Regia Marina* can arrive to reinforce them from Bermuda."

Marshall turned to the general standing on the opposite side of the table, "And what can the Air Corps get into the fight?"

"Most of my planes are on the west coast waiting on a Jap invasion," responded General "Hap" Arnold. "However, 20th Heavy Bomber Squadron with the new B-17s just set up shop in New York for coastal patrol duty. Tomorrow morning, they will be over Charleston. If the Kraut Navy is there, my flying fortresses will sink it."

Marshall and King looked dubiously back at Arnold, but said nothing. A dozen bombers were not going to sink a fleet. However, the B-17 raid should give them a good idea of what air cover the *Kriegsmarine* had over Charleston. Any damage they managed to inflict would be gravy.

"The Army only has one division in the Charleston area - the Thirtieth Infantry at Fort Jackson, near Columbia, South Carolina" Marshall reported. I've ordered them to send a recon in force into Charleston and recapture the port if they can. These are Carolina National Guard, so they'll know the area."

"Gentlemen, this is the first foreign invasion of the United States since the War of 1812," Marshall concluded. "I don't have to tell you what's at stake. We will get this right."

KMS Bismarck, 163 miles east of Charleston, South Carolina 06:10 Hours, 17 March 1942

Seated in the captain's chair of his flagship *Bismarck*, Admiral Gunther Lutjens sipped from a cup of tea, impatiently waiting for the first glow of dawn to paint the horizon. It was nearly time to spring his trap.

The first *Kriegsmarine* vessels to reach the United States were the U-boats. Wolf packs of the underwater craft arrived off of every major *Amerikaner* naval base along their Atlantic coast before the invasion fleets even left Europe. Their mission was not to engage the enemy, but rather to lay low and keep watch. If a major enemy force left port, a pair of U-boats would trail and radio the enemy's location to the invasion fleet.

In this way, Lutjens knew the whereabouts of every major enemy formation during the Atlantic crossing and avoided them. When, as anticipated, the *Amerikaner* ships boiled out of their northeast ports like a hive of angry bees after the Charleston landing, he sidestepped them again by moving back into the Atlantic off their state of North Carolina, leaving behind a small flotilla to protect the transports and Charleston.

The *Kriegsmarine* admiral had no intention of standing in place to exchange blows with a still dangerous United States Navy, especially under the handicaps from which his own fleet suffered. The German Navy itself existed for less than a century, only fighting a literal handful of battles during that time, leaving behind a relatively brief institutional memory. The recent expansion of the fleet scattered the experienced personnel possessing that memory. Consequently, the powerful new ships under his command were manned by largely green crews.

Making things worse, his three carriers were primarily equipped with fighters to protect the landing zone from *Amerikaner* air attacks. Lutjens only possessed a single squadron of torpedo bombers and another of dive bombers with which to attack the enemy carriers.

Thus, the cautious admiral considered it absolutely critical his fleet land the first blow and cripple the enemy before they could exploit the German shortcomings. In this, the *Kriegsmarine* enjoyed an advantage over the *Amerikaner*. While enemy scout planes were grounded during the night, Lutjens' U-boats stalked the approaching *Amerikaner* force, regularly reporting its location. The last radio transmissions had the enemy moving within the range of his bombers.

The predawn liftoff proceeded almost flawlessly. First, the heavily-laden Heinkel torpedo and *Stuka* dive bombers took off, one after another, and assembled into their formations. The far faster Messerschmidt fighters would depart last, then catch up to take their places above the bombers. The only flaw was a malfunctioning fighter having to ditch into the ocean because the carrier decks were filled with departing aircraft.

By the time dawn arrived, the *Kriegsmarine's* war birds should be on top of the enemy fleet. Lutjens wished his pilots good hunting.

Port of Charleston, South Carolina
10:03 Hours, 17 March 1942

Dearest Lu,

I am very well. The landing has been a blazing success. Incredibly, the Amerikaner army has left Charleston undefended and has yet to send a single aircraft or patrol to the landing zone. The Navy ships are unloading our soldiers onto the docks at a smart pace. Even without the Amerikaner, there is still a frightful lot to do.

I do not know when this letter will cross the Atlantic and get to you, so my very best early wishes for your birthday.

General Erwin Rommel chewed on the nub of his pen in case anything else came to mind. The dutiful husband wrote frequent, but short letters to his wife. Satisfied he reported all he needed to, Erwin signed the letter and tucked it into an envelope.

Squinting against the morning sun from his requisitioned *Amerikaner* staff car parked on the Charleston docks, the Army commander watched as a crane hoisted a *panzer* out of the hold of a freighter before carefully lowering it onto the deck to drive off to the motor pool at the end of the facility.

The SS *Libenstandarte* regiment was first off the ships. As soon as each company of men married up with their vehicles, they immediately pushed out to establish a defensive perimeter around the landing zone. Rommel had his doubts about the combat worthiness of the *Führer's* former bodyguards turned *panzer* troops, but at least they proved themselves quick off the mark.

Washing down a bite of black bread and jam with a swallow of cold coffee, the general turned his attention to the port commander's offloading status report. Breakfast and every other meal were squeezed in or foregone completely while performing the commander's never-ending march of duties.

Rommel's head snapped up from the report when the staccato cracks of a single anti-aircraft gun brewed up from the Charleston airport. Had the *Amerikaner* finally arrived? There were no sounds of attack, though. No cannon or bombs. Nothing but the clatter of the gun.

Suddenly, a handful of brown fighter aircraft, displaying white stars on their wings, howled over the tree line and dropped down towards the docks.

Where the hell was his own air cover? The high command promised Rommel the *Kriegsmarine* carriers would provide his air support until the *Luftwaffe* arrived in strength. The Navy had other plans, though. Just one day after the landing, the fleet sailed north without notice, taking every single aircraft carrier. The sky overhead was empty of the *Kriegsmarine's* sleek gray ME-109 fighters.

Without waiting for an order, Rommel's driver slammed the car into gear and stomped on the gas pedal to move his general out of danger. The fighters split apart and took off in pursuit of the German vehicles fleeing helter skelter from the docks. Turning sharply away from the oncoming aircraft machine gun fire tearing into the docks, the driver flipped the open-topped car and threw his commander into the air.

Rommel landed hard on top of a pile of folded tents. Lying on his back gasping for air, the general stared uncomprehending at a dozen *Ami* bombers slowly making their way across the blue sky above. The air filled with the whistling of falling bombs, followed by the thunder of explosions, repeatedly boxing his ears with roaring pain. The assault on the Erwin's senses was mercifully brief, as the air raid ended in a single pass. The last *Ami* fighter to fly over waggled his wings as if to taunt the helpless general.

Another moment or two passed before the general regained his wind and pushed himself up into a seated position to survey the damage. Most of the bombs landed harmlessly in the river, but smoke billowed from a troop ship docked in a nearby slip. The port facility itself was littered with torn and burning vehicles from the fighter attack.

Wilhelm! Rommel looked around and spotted the overturned staff car several meters away. Sliding off of the pile of tents, the general staggered over to the wreck and peered inside. His driver stared back lifelessly, crushed between the car and the ground like a rag doll at the bottom of a toy box.

Wilhelm Steiner faithfully served with him since the desert campaign and became something of a confidant for a general, who would not allow himself to become familiar with his subordinate officers. Erwin closed his eyes and pressed his head against the wrecked vehicle. Now, he would have to write Steiner's wife. And they were expecting their first child in the summer.

Rommel collected himself and stood back up. Death was part of war, but there was no reason for the lives lost today.

Summerville, South Carolina
12:23 Hours, 17 March 1942

The roar of approaching engines filled the house as the family finished grace and started lunch. Florrie excused herself from the table and strolled towards the living room window. Had the Army finally arrived?

The day before, news of the German landings in Charleston spread like wildfire, followed by a crawl of refugees from the city driving past the house down Main Street. Summerville was the first substantial town west of Charleston and a natural way stop for the panicked city folk.

Florrie spent the rest of the day struggling to call Jim at Fort Jackson, but the lines were jammed and, after a while, the local operators stopped answering at all. The folks at the phone company probably joined the exodus.

During supper that evening, the family discussed leaving. Florrie and Bonnie Sue wanted to drive to Wilmington up in North Carolina to stay with their mother, at least until the Army did its job and threw the Germans out of the country. They heard enough Great War stories over the years to know the family didn't want to be anywhere near a shooting war.

Bonnie Sue's husband, Henry, would have none of it. After years of Depression, his grocery store rang up record profits selling food to the refugees and he was going to milk that cow as long as she lasted. When Florrie pointed out all the dollars in the world would be worthless if the Germans took Summerville, Henry angrily replied the Army would be here by morning and he was not leaving. Because he was taking the family car to work, no one else was leaving either. And that was that.

In the morning, Henry dodged the jam of refugees on his way to the grocery by driving across the field behind the house onto a nearby side street. Meanwhile, the sisters brought sandwiches and sweet tea out to the poor souls stuck out front. After accepting the profuse thanks of a particularly pitiful looking family in an old truck, Florrie asked for the latest news out of Charleston.

"It's bad," the man driving the truck replied in between bites of a chicken salad sandwich. "There was no Army in the city, but the Germans were still shooting up the neighborhoods by the docks." Putting his truck back in gear when the traffic started moving again, he warned, "We were barely able skedaddle outta the city before the Germans arrived in our part of town. Darn near the last to get out. You folks need to leave too."

The man was right about being among last to leave. Not long after the old truck disappeared down the road, the flow of refugee traffic ebbed. By the time the sisters made lunch for the family, the street was deserted.

When Florrie hopefully looked out the living room window for the source of the new engine noises, what she saw was not the Army, at least not her Army. The vehicles slowly making their way down Main Street were unlike anything the American woman had ever seen before - big metal monsters with wheels in the front and tracks in the back, painted strangely with splotches of green and brown, manned by soldiers dressed in uniforms of similarly odd coloring.

As Florrie eased herself behind a window curtain to hide from the newcomers, Jeff Glendon burst out of the front door of his home across the street carrying a rifle. Her neighbor was a middle-aged veteran of the Great War, who expressed an easy hatred of "the Hun" whenever a discussion turned to Europe.

Glendon's new war ended quickly. After Jeff raised his rifle and fired a shot, a German soldier on one of the steel beasts swung his machine gun around and cut him down with a horrible ripping sound. Her neighbor collapsed on his porch, twitched and died in a spreading pool of blood.

Florrie glanced back and found Bonnie Sue and the kids gathered around her, wide eyed and horrified. "You children scoot up to your room and hide," the mother hissed. When they looked back at her uncomprehendingly, she raised her voice and pointed. "Git!"

As the kids fled upstairs, Florrie looked back outside. The German vehicles were stopped in the road and a tall soldier was directing others into the house across the street. A few short moments later, the soldiers reemerged, pulling Mary Glendon and her two small boys out with them.

When she saw the crumpled body of her husband, Mary let out a shriek and broke away to reach him. A cursing soldier grabbed her long hair and dragged the thrashing woman out into the yard with her children, then forced all of them onto their knees.

The tall German casually walked up to Mary, pulled out his pistol and shot the sobbing woman in the face, then both of her boys. When one of the boys started to crawl away, a soldier repeatedly smashed the child's head with the butt of his rifle until he stopped moving.

Standing over the bodies, the tall soldier surveyed the neighborhood and hollered in some guttural tongue. Although the language was incomprehensible, the meaning was brutally clear. If anyone dared fight back, the invaders would slaughter them and their families.

When the German's gaze fell on the living room window, Florrie could swear the murderer was looking straight into her eyes. Losing all composure, she ran sobbing into the dining room with Bonnie Sue and hugged her sister tight.

Oh Jimmy, where are you and the Army?

Führer Headquarters, The Berghof, Berchtesgaden, Germany
21:13 Hours, 17 March 1942

The Grand Admiral looked forward to briefing the *Führer* tonight. After a long, nerve-wracking crossing, the *Kriegsmarine* finally engaged the main enemy fleet. Raeder was certain Hitler would be very pleased with the results

Something was wrong on the Army side of the shop, though. An hour before, a loud murmur erupted from the other end of the headquarters facility Hitler constructed on the grounds of his alpine home. A colonel emerged from a group of grey uniformed officers to hand a radio message to Army chief of staff, General Alfred Jodl. After studying the document, Jodl shot Raeder a long cool look across the room, then sent his aide de camp over to inform the admiral that his general would be too busy to take part in their usual pre-briefing preparation.

Raeder and Jodl were polite rivals. While not cordial, the officers enjoyed a good working relationship. The sudden cold shoulder was damned peculiar.

Adolf Hitler interrupted Raeder's contemplation by striding into the operations center and immediately demanding the *Kriegsmarine* status report without his usual preamble monologue. The admiral immediately switched mental gears to the task at hand.

"My *Führer*, I have the pleasure to report that Admiral Lutjens prevailed in his initial engagement today with the *Amerikaner* fleet. Our carriers landed the first blow, sinking the enemy carrier *Long Island*. The enemy response damaged, but did not sink our carrier *Europa*. With a three-to-one advantage, Lutjens is confident one final air strike in the morning will sink the surviving enemy carrier *Ranger*."

Rather than being pleased, Hitler glared in disbelief at the *Kriegsmarine* commander, causing Raeder to fidget.

Deftly exploiting the opening, General Jodl interjected: "My *Führer*, the *Kriegsmarine's* 'victory' came at a high cost. While the carrier fighters were out at sea instead of providing air cover for the landing force, enemy bombers attacked Port Charleston and sank a transport with nearly a battalion of infantry on board. One of the docks will be out of commission for the foreseeable future, substantially slowing our buildup. Admiral Raeder, when can we expect our air cover to return?"

"Did I not order all *Kriegsmarine* carriers to provide air cover for Charleston?" Hitler snarled at Raeder.

"Yes, my *Führer*."

Waving his hands in front of him, Hitler shrieked: "Did you give that worm Lutjens permission to violate a *Führer* directive?!?"

"Uh, no my *Führer*, but…"

"BUT NOTHING!"

Raeder unconsciously snapped to the position of attention. No one had dressed him down like this since he was a naval cadet decades ago.

"The reason our crossing of the English Channel was a victory instead of a wretched defeat is because I ordered every single *Luftwaffe* and *Kriegsmarine* aircraft to defend the landing force," Hitler screamed. "I ordered you to perform the same mission at Charleston, but because of this Lutjens' treason, the entire enterprise is in danger!"

Treason? While he had heard stories of Hitler's volcanic temper, the admiral himself had never been the target of the *Führer's* fury. Raeder's mind raced to find the proper response.

Gunther Lutjens was a dour Jew, with few friends in the *Kriegsmarine*. While the service could conceal the admiral's ancestry from the Gestapo, the admiral did not help his cause by openly disdaining the Nazi Party. He deliberately antagonized Hitler during the *Führer's* final inspection of the fleet by rendering the traditional naval hand salute instead of the Nazi salute.

Still, Lutjens was the *Kriegsmarine's* best sea commander and his decision to use the carriers to defeat the enemy fleet was the correct one. Raeder forced down his own well-developed sense of self-preservation to defend his fleet commander.

"My *Führer*, may I speak?"

Hitler fell silent for a moment, then nodded in assent.

"Your orders to the Lutjens correctly required the Navy to both provide air cover for Charleston and to defeat the *Amerikaner* fleet when it arrived."

Hitler remained silent, so Raeder continued.

"Admiral Lutjens faced a quandary. If the fleet stayed in place to provide air cover for Charleston, the enemy carriers could move about freely and send air raids against our ships. If the fleet moved to defeat the enemy carriers, the *Amerikaner* Air Corps would be able to strike against Charleston. Lutjens knew that the enemy carriers were approaching, but had not seen any sign of the Air Corps, so the admiral tried to follow your orders to the best of his ability and moved to defeat the enemy he could see."

Raeder bowed his head. "Please forgive Admiral Lutjens, my *Führer*."

Hitler face softened and appeared mollified. "My Grand Admiral, your defense of the fleet commander is well-reasoned."

Raeder exhaled and felt a nearly unbearable urge to pee.

"However, there is a way to accomplish both of my directives Lutjens failed to consider," Hitler instructed. "You are to order the fleet commander to immediately return my carriers to guard Charleston and employ the rest of my fleet to destroy the enemy tomorrow."

Without the carriers, Raeder puzzled?

As if reading his admiral's mind, Hitler concluded his lesson. "During the Norwegian campaign, two small battleships chased down and sank the British carrier *Glorious*. Lutjens commands seven of the *Reich's* new super battleships. Surely, he can sink one *Amerikaner* carrier?"

"It will be done, my *Führer*."

"And my Grand Admiral," Hitler warned, "I will not tolerate any further treason."

KMS Bismarck, 211 miles northeast of Myrtle Beach, South Carolina
17:58 Hours, 18 March 1942

The crew on the bridge of the battleship *Bismarck* all stared at Gunther Lutjens, after the normally stoic admiral slammed his fist down on the arm of his chair, sending his cup of tea flying into the air. Feeling the eyes of his men, Lutjens looked up from the message with a glare and the crew's eyes immediately returned their work, while a steward scrambled to pick up the broken crockery.

Don't take it out on the men, Gunther. They are not responsible for the Austrian idiot's latest lunacy. The admiral ground audibly sighed and returned his attention to the message. Grand Admiral Raeder's radio was short, leaving most of the writing between the lines.

Fleet Commander:

Dispatch carriers and all necessary support vessels back to Charleston immediately to provide combat air patrols for landing zone. Führer directive. No discretion allowed.

Attack US Navy fleet and surviving carrier with battleships. Remember the Glorious. Full discretion permitted.

Raeder

Lutjens recalled the *Glorious* engagement during the Norwegian operation. The Royal Navy was stupid enough to leave a carrier unprotected in the North Sea and the *Kriegsmarine* stumbled onto it with a pair of battleships. Dumb luck was not a viable operational plan, though. This enemy would jealously protect their remaining carrier with the remainder of their fleet. Raeder would know this and was almost certainly relaying the grand naval strategy of their glorious leader.

The fleet commander forced himself to refocus. Hitler may be an idiot, but crossing him was a fatal proposition -

definitely to one's career and often for one's life. How do I win with what is left to me?

If given the choice, the *Amerikaner* fleet commander would keep his distance and hammer the *Kriegsmarine's* new battleships with long-range airstrikes until the odds of a surface battle moved in his favor.

The obvious solution to this problem was to eliminate the distance. According to the latest U-boat reports, the enemy fleet changed course during the evening to the northeast and unwittingly closed with the *Kriegsmarine* fleet. With a full speed movement to contact, Lutjens could cover the remaining distance before dawn, when the *Amerikaner* planes resumed operations. Forcing a full surface engagement would be damned expensive, but his new battleships enjoyed the advantage in a gunnery duel.

Lutjens issued the movement orders and gathered his staff to plan the execution of the coming battle. It would be a long night.

U.S.S. Ranger, 89 miles east of Morehead City, North Carolina 07:33 Hours, 18 March 1942

Task Force 39 was at full speed and still losing the race with the pursuing Kraut fleet. Rear Admiral John Wilcox concluded here was nothing to do for it but to turn and fight.

Just before dawn that morning, the destroyer screen reported a large formation of German vessels approaching from the flank at high speed, led by a half dozen large battleships of an unknown type.

The report puzzled Wilcox. How did the Krauts find them? After his aircraft landed back on *Ranger* yesterday afternoon, the admiral jogged his task force further out in the Atlantic under cover of darkness and there had been no sightings of the enemy until this morning.

More importantly, what the hell was his counterpart planning? During the previous days, the Wilcox believed both fleets lost a carrier. It made no sense for the Krauts to intentionally seek a surface engagement, when they outnumbered him two-to-one in the air.

Then again, maybe the enemy simply stumbled across them during the night in a case of bad luck?

In any case, Wilcox was not about to get into a surface battle of attrition with the *Kriegsmarine*. The Navy lost far too many ships and good men over the past few months in the Pacific.

The admiral ordered the task force to change course to the northwest and the coast to shake the Germans. More importantly, this movement would also draw the enemy further away from their Charleston landing zone and closer to American land-based air units.

Any hope Wilcox had of shaking the enemy was soon dashed, however. Most of his ships were older and slower WWI vintage vessels and his newer craft had to slow to maintain the formation. The Germans had no such problem. After WWI, the allies had forced Germany to scrap its old fleet and all of its current vessels were modern and fast. Very fast.

In a little over an hour, the *Kriegsmarine* closed the gap and left Wilcox without a choice. The carrier *Ranger* turned into the wind and launched its bombers and fighters, then the admiral ordered the battleships and cruisers to turn to engage the approaching enemy force. Although this was not his choice of battles, Task Force 39 would make its stand here.

KMS Bismarck, 10 miles southeast of Hatteras Island, North Carolina
07:43 Hours, 18 March 1942

The engagement began as badly as Admiral Lutjens feared, but not as he anticipated. Instead of the *Amerikaner* task force waiting for him arrayed for battle, the sun rose over an empty ocean. Radar reported the enemy was fleeing to the northwest and Lutjens ordered a full speed pursuit. Before his fleet could close on the *Amerikaner* ships, however, the enemy aircraft arrived.

Realizing their young fleet's lack of experience in modern combined arms warfare, the *Kriegsmarine* staff diligently studied their *Japaner* allies and *Englander* enemies to develop standard responses to anticipated situations. What they took away from the two Battles of Hawaii was torpedo and dive bombers could sink battleships and lesser surface ships at will. From the English Channel engagements, the staff noted the *Englander* success dodging *Luftwaffe* air strikes through evasive maneuvers. Thus, when not providing anti-aircraft defense for escorted carriers, doctrine called for *Kriegsmarine* vessels under air attack to imitate their Royal Navy rivals. With their carriers steaming back to Charleston, Lutjens' captains dutifully followed their manuals and ordered their ships to execute a choreographed sequence of twists and turns to evade the incoming torpedoes and bombs.

Holding onto the frame of a bridge window with one hand and a pair of binoculars in another, as the *Bismarck* turned hard starboard, the admiral tracked a section of four Douglas *Devastator* torpedo bombers closing from the north. The big battleship's evasive maneuvers did not appear to throw off the *Amerikaner* pilots, who easily adjusted the course of their aircraft like sharks closing on a lumbering whale.

The battleship's impressive array of weapons also did nothing to stop the progress of the enemy bombers. *Bismarck's* anti-aircraft guns were not designed to fire below the deck line and impotently shot dozens of rounds over the approaching war birds flying in just above the waves. The three *Devastators* were able to close within a mere two hundred meters of the flagship, before dropping their deadly fish into the waters below and banking away. Within seconds the torpedoes slammed into the side of the battleship, hurling columns of water into the air

Then, a trio of enemy Douglas *Dauntless* dive-bombers screaming in from above seized Lutjens' attention. *Bismarck's* massed anti-aircraft batteries enjoyed far more success against this exposed flock, exploding one as it began its dive, then ripping the tail off another after it released its bomb. The pair of bombs exploding around the second turret assaulted Lutjens' senses far more than did the torpedoes, launching a shock wave which cracked the bridge window and the admiral's ear drums.

The giant *Bismarck* shrugged off the enemy explosives, however. The torpedoes detonating against the battleship's thick steel anti-torpedo belt below the waterline only caused one minor leak in the third watertight compartment. After failing to report for a few long minutes, the second turret noted nothing more than a temporary power failure.

Radio reports from across the fleet confirmed the enemy ordinance was not nearly as effective against the heavily armored *Kriegsmarine* ships as they were lead to believe. However, the enemy warbirds did manage to royally tangle the German formation as the *Amerikaner* task force turned back on Lutjens' dispersed ships.

Naval tactics had not fundamentally changed since the advent of gunpowder. Opposing fleets would form lines so all their guns could bear on the enemy, then pound away at one another. Over time, the guns became more powerful and the distance between the ships ever greater, but the optimal formation for maximizing firepower was still the line.

As the *Kriegsmarine* ships ceased their evasive maneuvers, the *Amerikaner* line sent volleys of heavy shells screaming across the water, which increasingly found their slowed targets. In contrast, the Lutjens' ships were scattered and could not effectively respond.

Knowing his fleet would be ripped apart long before they could form their own line, Lutjens ordered every ship to immediately turn in place and fire freely at the nearest enemy vessel. Not the most efficient allocation of firepower, but the least-worst option.

From these disparate positions, the two fleets exchanged punches like two heavyweight boxers. Lutjens scanned the ocean, watching the big guns on each side jab at one another to a soundtrack of reports coming in over the wireless. Most shells would land harmlessly in the sea, tossing up giant plumes of water. Those which found their targets convulsed the unfortunate ships in flame and smoke.

Eventually, the firepower of the seven new *Bismarck*-class battleships won the day. When the *Amerikaner* sent over a volley of thirty centimeter shells, the German battleships would return a volley of thirty-eights. Where the incoming enemy rounds would damage the new *Kriegsmarine* battleships, the larger German outgoing rounds were sinking their *Amerikaner* counterparts.

The one exception was a large enemy battleship in the center, which was every bit as strong as the *Bismarck*. When one of this formidable enemy's rounds ripped through a cruiser off the flagship's port side, detonating its magazine of high explosive, Lutjens ordered all of his big battleships to concentrate their fire on the one *Amerikaner* ship to end this threat.

Volley after volley fell on the enemy vessel, silencing its guns one after another, until the ship burned helplessly in the distance. Even then, the magnificent *Amerikaner* dreadnaught refused to sink. Impressive.

Lutjens lowered his binoculars and ordered his battleships to seek other targets to allow the survivors on the stricken ship to evacuate in safety. Death would find far too many today without needlessly seeking out the evil one.

U.S.S. Ranger, 79 miles east of Nags Head, North Carolina
14:01 Hours, 18 March 1942

The bridge of the *Ranger* resembled a wake, the crew in various stages of shock and grief, with more than one openly crying. After valiantly exchanging blows with several of the new Kraut battleships, the *Washington* finally succumbed to its wounds and sank a half hour ago. Half of Task Force 39 preceded her to the bottom this morning.

Once it became clear the battle was lost, Admiral Wilcox ordered a general disengagement. First, *Ranger* and her escorts moved northwest and well away from the *Kriegsmarine* fleet. Once the carrier was safe, the surviving ships of Task Force 39 started producing smoke to cover their withdrawal. The remaining combat effective vessels joined the *Ranger*. The rest singly or in small groups limped back to their homeports at whatever speed they could still muster.

Although victorious, the *Kriegsmarine* fleet suffered heavy damage of its own and declined to pursue the retreating Americans. Instead, the Germans remained in place, lending aid to their stricken ships and rescuing sailors of both sides from the surrounding waters. These chivalric mercies were a welcome change from the Japs in the Pacific, who often used American sailors stranded on the ocean for target practice.

The rough handling of his ships was bitter to swallow, but Wilcox was feeling supremely confident. His task force drew the *Kriegsmarine* away from Charleston and bloodied her nose pretty well. Tomorrow, *Ranger* would find the missing enemy carriers and sink them, while the combined Caribbean and Central Atlantic Fleets destroyed what was left of the enemy off of Charleston.

Checkmate.

U-155, 63 miles east of Virginia Beach, North Carolina
03:03 Hours, 19 March 1942

"Keep coming, you bastard, keep coming," Captain Adolph Piening muttered under his breath as the *Amerikaner* ship grew in his periscope.

"Turn three degrees to port. All ahead slow."

The hum of the electric engines increased and the bridge lights dimmed slightly. In just another minute or two, the enemy should sail across the bow of the U-155.

"Ready torpedoes in all tubes"

"Torpedoes loaded and ready, Captain."

The enemy ship sailed within torpedo distance some minutes ago, but the U-boat skipper wanted her in close so his fish could not miss the big prize.

Suddenly, the *Amerikaner's* progress halted and its silhouette started to narrow. Damn! She's turning again, this time away from the U-boat. You will not get away so easily, my girl.

"All ahead full. Turn slowly to starboard."

The U-155 nudged ahead, maintaining the distance between it and the turning enemy prize.

As the bow of the U-boat turned from left to right, Piening ordered the torpedoes fired one at a time, in a spread aimed where the captain anticipated the *Amerikaner* ship would move next. Now, there was nothing to do but wait and see if his guesses were correct.

Yesterday evening, headquarters finally unleashed the wolf packs with orders to hunt down and sink the last *Amerikaner* carrier. Not an easy mission. The enemy carrier would be moving at high speed, while enjoying a protective escort of destroyers, along with a cruiser or two. While on the surface, a U-boat could use its diesel engines to match the carrier's speed, but the unarmored craft would be soon seen and sunk by the destroyers. While underwater and concealed from the enemy, the boat could only engage its underpowered electric engines and the enemy would quickly leave them behind.

By Piening's calculation, the only way to obtain reasonable torpedo shots at the carrier was to get in front of the *Amerikaner* formation, submerge and allow the carrier to come to U-155.

The wolfpacks last sighted the enemy ship yesterday afternoon and a half dozen boats converged on her expected area of operations. Piening won the jackpot when von Hymmen's U-408 radioed the carrier's position and a heading almost directly towards his boat.

The U-boat captain knew he should dive to safety, but could not resist watching his torpedoes close on the carrier, while his executive officer counted off the seconds until anticipated impact of the torpedoes.

The time lapsed on the first fish and nothing happened. Miss. Before the time lapsed on the second fish, though, the sound of an explosion cracked through the water surrounding the U-boat, followed a few seconds later by a second.

At first, Piening could not see anything though the periscope, then there was a bright flash on the port side of the stricken carrier followed by more explosive sounds in the water. The second fish must have hit the carrier's fuel or bombs.

"Dive to 100 meters."

U-155 slid further beneath the surface as the surrounding water echoed the metallic screeches and groans of *Ranger's* hull buckling.

Piening lowered the periscope. U-155 sank three cargo ships during the English campaign, but this was their first warship. Better yet, the grand prize of warships.

When he turned to shake his grinning executive officer's outstretched hand, the U-boat captain was thrown sideways into the ladder up to the coning tower, then down to the deck of the bridge, as the boat rocked between one explosion after another.

Depth charges Piening thought distantly, as he wiped away the blood running into his eyes from a gash above an eyebrow. The captain opened his mouth to order a hard turn to port, but no sound passed his lips as the ocean covered him up.

CHAPTER 17

DD-461 U.S.S. Forrest, 32 miles southeast of Charleston, South Carolina
03:53 Hours, 19 March 1942

As his destroyer sliced through the fog and darkness, Commander PJ Tigert found he much preferred charging toward, rather than fleeing from the enemy. Any time now, *Forrest* should break through the *Kriegsmarine* picket line on its way to liberate Charleston.

Escaping the Italians off of Bermuda was a damned close call. Just when Tigert thought the *Forrest* was breaking away from its far larger pursuers, an unlucky enemy shell snapped off the main mast and flipped it through the forward smokestack, knocking out the antenna lines and spewing smoke across the rear decks. *Forrest* kept plowing forward, but the Italian cruisers returned to their formation. The enemy must have thought they scored a kill shot and called it a day.

Despite that bit of luck, 'Tigert's pirates' still found themselves alone in the Atlantic, with what looked like the entire Italian fleet between the destroyer and its Bermuda port, and without any comms with their own Atlantic Fleet. Once the crew patched the smokestack, *Forrest* got underway for the fleet's main base in Norfolk. Tigert figured that's where the action would be. He was wrong.

Three hours into the cruise, Ensign Ray Cork managed to restore radio contact with the fleet. Assuming the *Forrest* was lost off Bermuda, headquarters was very pleased to hear from their prodigal destroyer and ordered Tigert to make best speed for Savannah, joining with ships steaming in from the Caribbean and South Atlantic to form the new Task Force 50. While the Atlantic Fleet engaged the main *Kriegsmarine* force off North Carolina, TF-50 would attack from the south and destroy all the enemy ships around Charleston – most especially the invading troop ships yet to unload their human cargos onto American soil.

When they arrived, Tigert found TF-50 was a creaking collection of old WWI cruisers and destroyers, fortified with a handful of faster modern ships like *Forrest*. While intelligence believed the joint force would outnumber the *Kriegsmarine* ships left behind to guard Charleston by two to one, the battleship *Scharnhorst* anchoring the Charleston defense heavily outgunned every American ship. Worse still, the Kraut carriers went missing over twenty-four hours ago and could be nearby.

The task force admiral decided to neutralize these German advantages with a night attack. The old WWI ships would close to point blank range under the cover of night and use their superior numbers to overwhelm the Krauts. Meanwhile, the fast ships like *Forrest* would slip through the resulting confusion and sink the transports anchored outside Charleston Bay.

After Tigert explained the plan to the men, his XO Frank Morris quipped: "Damn the torpedoes, full speed ahead, skipper?"

"That sums it up. Let's get this show on the road."

Lady Luck finally kissed the U.S. Navy. Not only did the moon set, leaving the expected inky darkness, a fog also rose to further obscure the early morning ocean. TF-50 blundered into the German defensive line and the opposing ships hurled death at one another as they appeared and disappeared again in the misty murk.

Hanging *Forrest* behind the main force, Tigert scanned the horizon for an opening like a football running back waiting for his offensive line to open a crease. A few degrees off starboard, a narrow sector stayed dark in between the flashes of gunnery and the burning of stricken ships. At its captain's order, *Forrest* sprinted into the void.

Once the destroyer passed the task force main line, Tigert couldn't see a damned thing. The foggy darkness obscured everything beyond the ship's bow. Ten minutes passed, then fifteen. Had *Forrest* managed to knife through the Kraut lines undetected?

As the commander checked his position on the area map for the umpteenth time, the bridge intercom came alive. "Large object, dead ahead!"

The outline of a larger ship cutting across the bow emerged from the fog. "Hard to starboard!" Tigert hollered. "Brace for impact!"

Forrest barely entered her turn when the two ships collided. Steel screamed as the smaller destroyer scraped the side of the larger ship, before breaking loose again with a shudder.

The captain turned and trained his binoculars on the receding ship. German light cruiser. Probably *Leipzig* class.

Before his boss could turn back again, Morris started issuing orders. "Helm, make for that fog bank, full speed ahead." Picking up the phone, the XO ordered all gun turrets to fire at will on the Kraut cruiser.

Irritated they never had the opportunity to return fire on the Italians, the ship's gunners were more than ready for this fight. The two stern guns fired simultaneously and both hit the superstructure of the enemy ship. Nice shooting, Tigert thought with no small amount of pride. *This crew is becoming a team.*

The Germans were also quick on the draw, though. The larger six inch guns of the cruiser's rear turret belched fire and one of the incoming rounds clipped off the tip of the Forrest's bow, pushing the front of the destroyer into the ocean before it bobbed back up again.

Tigert ended up on his ass and scrambled to regain his footing. By the time he regained his feet, *Forrest* slipped out of the battle and into the fog.

The captain changed the destroyer's heading twice to ensure the bigger German was not following her, before returning to the original course towards Charleston.

The damage reports were better than expected. While the bow and port side of the ship wouldn't win any beauty contests, the ship suffered no major structural damage.

Tigert was getting tired of tangling with bigger and better armed ships. Maybe the good Lord would see fit to give the *Forrest* a fairer fight the next time around.

R.N. Littorio, 18 miles east of Charleston, South Carolina 04:26 Hours, 19 March 1942

Admiral Carlo Bergamini closed his eyes and ran his fingers through his thinning hair. What the hell were they sailing into?

The concept was for the *Kriegsmarine* and *Regia Marina* invasion fleets to simultaneously invade Charleston and Bermuda, then his Force would escort the second half of *Germano* transports from the island to the South Carolina port.

The two fleets were to coordinate their operations by radio using the *Germano* ENIGMA code machine. However, Italy's comrades at arms did not trust the *Regia Marina* with one of their top secrets and instead provided an Italian-speaking *Kriegsmarine* liaison officer to operate the machine. The two fleets might as well still be at radio silence for all the information provided by this "liaison officer." All the taciturn Captain

Mayer would tell Bergamini during the morning briefings was *Kriegsmarine* operations were proceeding as planned.

As the Regia Marina fleet proceeded on its nighttime approach on Charleston, a visibly worried Mayer suddenly became very forthcoming, providing Bergamini with several pages of translated *Kriegsmarine* radio transcripts. Admiral Lutjens had taken the main *Kriegsmarine* fleet north, intercepting and defeating the expected counterattack of enemy Atlantic fleet. However, a very large *Americano* force was now attacking from the south. The badly outnumbered German squadron left behind to protect the Charleston landing zone was losing a pitched battle and pleading for reinforcements.

The arrogant bastards! If the *Germano* deigned to keep him informed of *Kriegsmarine* operations, the Force would already be off Charleston turning back the *Americano* attack. Now, the entire operation was at risk.

"Captain Mayer, inform your admiral I am immediately dispatching our lead warships at full speed to assist his ships defending Charleston. I will hold the remainder of the Force back to protect the transports until the area is secure."

As the *Germano* officer turned to leave, Bergamini added, "Do you have direct contact with your ships at Charleston?"

"The communications are sporadic, sir."

"Do your best and let me know when you have established contact. We cannot coordinate operations with your fleet without it."

Bergamini then ordered his new battleships *Littorio* and *Vittorio Veneto* to lead the new Zara heavy cruiser division in a full speed advance on the coast. This mission into the unknown would require speed and strength.

As the Italians approached, flashes of gunnery and the dull glow of burning ships came into view, but not much else. Although the long-range optics occasionally discerned the shadows of surviving combatants through an early morning fog, there was no real way to distinguish between the *Americano* and *Kriegsmarine* vessels.

At about 15 kilometers out, Bergamini turned his ships into a line parallel to the coast and waited for the radio or sunrise to clarify the situation. The admiral was not about to charge the cream of the Force into a blind melee.

"Capitan Mayer, have you obtained contact with the Charleston squadron?" the admiral inquired.

"Not directly, sir. I transmitted the message to the fleet and they forwarded it to the local force."

"Did the 'local force' confirm receipt of the message?"

The German officer paused, then admitted: "I do not know."

"Find out," pressed the admiral. "Then get the Charleston squadron on the radio. This is your only mission until we get contact."

Bergamini's shifted his attention back to the bridge, which was now buzzing with activity.

"Admiral, we are under fire from an unknown vessel in the battle zone," reported the *Littorio's* captain. "The rounds fell about two kilometers short, but the size of the splashes suggest large guns consistent with a battleship."

"Locate the ship."

"I have already given the order, sir. However, the enemy ship will have to fire again before we can find her."

Looking back over his shoulder, Bergamini demanded: "Mayer, do you have contact with the Charleston squadron yet?"

"Sir, I am receiving their transmissions, but they are not responding to mine."

"Do their transmissions acknowledge our arrival?"

"No, sir."

We are playing blind man's bluff where the other players are deaf, Bergamini fumed. The admiral's hearing and that of the men on the bridge worked perfectly, though. Everyone looked up and cringed slightly at the freight train sounds of large gun shells passing overhead. Definitely a battleship and their gunners were finding *Littorio's* range.

"Admiral, we have an approximate location for the enemy ship…12,400 meters at 203 degrees," *Littorio's* captain called out.

"I want every ship on the line to fire a spread volley, with each turret firing at a different range between 12,000 and 12,800 meters," Bergamini ordered. "Just like we practiced back in La Spezia. Hopefully, one of them finds the enemy battleship."

A minute later dozens of guns all along the Italian line belched fire towards their unknown assailant. *Littorio's* bridge went quiet waiting for observer reports, then erupted in cheering.

"Admiral, the target is burning. I'll wager one of *Littorio's* crews hit the mark," the captain bragged. "I suggest we fire another salvo to make sure we have destroyed the target."

Mayer jumped up from his radio and yelled, "Admiral Bergamini, cease fire! Cease fire now!"

Bergamini raised his hand at the ship's captain and then shot a hard look at the *Germano*. "Mayer, what are you talking about?"

"Admiral, you hit the *Scharnhorst*!"

The Italian admiral raised his hands in ignorance.

"The *Scharnhorst* is the flagship of the Charleston squadron." Mayer explained.

Madre di Dios! The bridge crew went deathly silent as Bergamini ordered the Force to ceasefire and Mayer to verify the status of the stricken battleship.

Several minutes passed before the shaken *Germano* officer could provide an answer. "I finally established communications with the local force. *Scharnhorst* is sinking and her survivors are abandoning ship." Almost as an afterthought, Mayer added, "In a few minutes I should have the locations of the *Kriegsmarine* ships, so we can engage the enemy vessels."

Too late for those poor souls on the *Scharnhorst*, though.

DD-461 U.S.S. Forrest, Outside Charleston Bay, South Carolina 04:42 Hours, 19 March 1942

PJ Tigert's frustration grew as the *Forrest* swam through the gray mist surrounding Charleston. The same fog which allowed the destroyer to cut through the *Kriegsmarine* defensive line, now protected the German troop ships from his destroyer. Normally, Charleston would be illuminating the area with electric light, but the Krauts blacked out the occupied city to make night attacks nearly impossible.

The commander looked down at his wristwatch and scowled. The night would shortly give way to dawn, exposing the American destroyer to German sea and air power. They were running out of time.

Tigert ordered the engines turned off and the bridge windows opened. If they couldn't see the enemy ships, maybe the crew could hear them. Except for the gentle lap of waves, though, the morning ocean was quiet. No fog horns or bells peacetime ships would use to signal their presence to other vessels.

After a few minutes, Ensign Mike Rogers softly walked over to his commander and whispered, "Sir, I think I hear metal on metal noises off the port side." Tigert moved over to the window and strained to hear. Sure enough, the faint sound of an anchor chain being raised clattered through the fog.

The commander quietly ordered the engines restarted and a change of course towards the noise. They didn't have far to go. The hidden freighter was only a quarter mile distant and preparing to get underway.

Oh no, you don't. "Mr. Morris, turn five points starboard and come to a full stop," Tigert ordered.

"Aye, sir."

When the *Forrest* was aligned with the middle of the German transport, Tigert ordered torpedo tubes one and two loaded.

"Torpedoes ready to fire, sir"

"Fire both tubes."

The torpedoes leapt out of destroyer and covered the 100 yards to the freighter in seconds. The underwater explosions of the torpedoes hitting home were quickly followed by secondary explosions and a plume of flame surging up from the center deck of the stricken vessel. Burning fuel spread over the water as the freighter started to sink.

The surviving crew emerged from below decks, ran to the deck railing and stopped. Their hellish choice was the fire on the sinking ship or the fire on the water. One crewman on deck caught fire and leaped shrieking into the water below. The spreading flames on the deck soon forced the rest to follow.

The *Forrest's* crew started cheering, one adding, "Watch those Kraut bastards buuurn!"

Frank Morris lowered his binoculars and muttered, "Fuck 'em."

Tigert opened his mouth to tell everyone to shut up, then closed it again. PJ recalled what the Germans did to England and would do to the U.S. of A if given the chance. Let the men blow of some steam.

"Mr. Morris, turn to port and let's find some new targets."

The sun was just below the horizon now and the twilight revealed dozens of targets. A neat row of German freighters were weighing anchor and moving off in all directions to avoid sharing the fate of their comrades. None of these lumbering merchantmen could hope to outrun a destroyer, though.

Tigert ran the *Forrest* up to the nearest transport, plugged it with a pair of torpedoes, and moved onto the next to repeat the process. Like shooting turkeys in a pen.

KMS Bismarck, 13 miles south of Hatteras Island, North Carolina
06:09 Hours, 19 March 1942

Admiral Gunther Lutjens felt utterly helpless.

The radio reports flowing in during the night from the squadron protecting Charleston went from bad to worse. The *Amerikaner* launched an unexpected nighttime attack from the south, not only sinking the flag ship *Scharnhorst*, but also penetrating the defensive perimeter to reach the transports anchored outside the bay.

The radios became disjointed after the loss of the *Scharnhorst* and its command staff. The last situation report for the flotilla was over an hour old and there were none at all for the transports.

Once the seriousness of the situation became clear, Lutjens ordered his main fleet to turn back for Charleston, but the return trip would take several hours. Meanwhile, the forward elements of the *Regia Marina* were engaging, but their effectiveness would be limited in the pre-dawn dark. His carriers were standing by outside of Charleston to counter attack with the dawn, but the sun was still hiding below the horizon and the bridge clock seemed to crawl.

Had he won a battle only to lose the war?

DD-461 U.S.S. Forrest, Off Seabrook Island, South Carolina
06:51 Hours, 19 March 1942

PJ Tigert raised his binoculars beyond the German freighter sinking a couple hundred yards off the bow and saw nothing but trouble. To the north, above the dissipating fog, *Kriegsmarine* fighters were swirling around U.S. Army Air Corps bombers approaching Charleston from the north. Where there were Kraut fighters, the enemy carriers and likely the main body of their fleet would not be far behind.

Then, things got worse. Much worse. The bridge speaker came alive, announcing the rapid approach of three enemy destroyers from the south.

Once the sun returned, it was inevitable the Krauts would crash their party. But not all of them at once!

Forrest's options were all rotten. If they fled north away from the closing Kraut destroyers, the *Kriegsmarine* big ships of the line would swat Tigert's 'tin can' like a bug. On the other hand, standing their ground against the three-to-one odds advancing from the south didn't sound like a winning formula. After mulling over the situation, the commander decided to create a third option.

"XO, turn the ship towards our approaching guests. Full speed ahead."

After raising an eyebrow, Frank Morris cracked a smile and relayed his commander's orders. Everyone else gaped at their skipper in disbelief.

Looking around the bridge, Tigert explained, "Gentlemen, we're going to charge right past the Kraut destroyers with guns blazing, break out to the south and rejoin the task force."

Turning back to his XO, the skipper ordered, "Mr. Morris, load all torpedo tubes and tell the gunners to stand by to fire at my command."

The tension on the bridge built as the charging destroyers engaged in a high-speed game of chicken. Tigert found himself twirling a pen back and forth along his fingers like he used to do before tough exams at the naval academy. The Germans blinked first, veering away from the South Carolina coast in a line to head *Forrest* off at the pass.

With all of their six turrets now able to train on the U.S. Navy destroyer, the enemy ships unleashed their opening salvos. The incoming rounds flew over the ship and splashed behind them. The Krauts didn't account for ship speed the first time around. Next time, they would.

"XO, have the forward guns open fire on the Kraut destroyer in the middle of that line. Tell them to take their time. I want accuracy, not volume," the captain ordered. "Then, tell the torpedo room to be prepared to launch immediately on order. We're going to fire a spread of torpedoes on that trail ship."

The guns on both sides fired simultaneously in a very uneven contest. The aim of the pair of rounds from *Forrest's* forward turrets was true, both tagging the hull of the targeted Kraut destroyer. Smoke started issuing from the wounded ship, but the vessel managed to stay in formation.

The enemy aim was less accurate, but very nearly killed *Forrest*. Distracted by the plumes of water erupting around the ship, Tigert was completely unprepared for the German round punching through the front starboard corner of the bridge and out again into the ocean.

PJ found himself hunched over in his captain's chair, the explosion of steel still echoing in his ears. When he raised his concussed head to look around, the bridge swam around him, the crew appearing unnaturally distant. Ensign Mike Rogers rocked back and forth on the floor by the helm, hollering and holding his face with both hands, blood oozing out from between his fingers. The XO staggered over to take over the unmanned wheel from the fallen officer, the pomade in his hair smoking from the near miss.

The captain hopped off his seat to lend a hand and a sudden jolt of pain launched up his right leg. Grabbing the edge of the control panel to keep from falling on his ass, Tigert looked uncomprehendingly down the splinter of steel protruding from his thigh before pulling at it. A second jolt of pain disabused him of that notion. Since the wound wasn't bleeding much, the captain resolved to leave it alone and get back to work. This certainly wasn't the time to take off for sickbay.

With his commanding officers otherwise occupied, Chief Doug Martin scooped up the writhing ensign and handed him off to two sailors to take to the sickbay, then directed a fire control team to put out the small fires around the bridge.

The fresh sea breeze pouring through the gash in the bridge wall clearing his head, Tigert yelled for everyone to get back to their stations and prepare to attack. Picking up the telephone, the skipper raised the torpedo room. "Chief Roberts, are you ready to fire?"

"Aye, sir."

"We will be launching four torpedoes sequentially with about two seconds between each fish."

Tigert cupped his hand over the telephone handset and looked to the helm. "Mr. Morris, after we fire the torpedoes, be prepared to turn to port and make a run along the coast."

A third German volley splashed around *Forrest*, thankfully without scoring any hits this time.

Time to launch the fish and get the hell out of here. At Tigert's command, the torpedoes launched toward the German line of destroyers crossing the bow, one at a time, then the XO turned hard to port to get behind the enemy ships.

The first fish passed harmlessly between the enemy ships and then the trailing Kraut destroyer sailed right into the second and third. The resulting explosions tore gaping holes in side of the enemy ship, which quickly turned on its side and slid under the surface.

The *Forrest's* sudden maneuver behind them and the loss of one of their ships threw the surviving enemy skippers for a loop. They continued heading out to sea for precious minutes before turning back in pursuit of the American destroyer driving down the coast.

Now, let's play hide and seek. Tigert ordered the engine room to make smoke. The added fuel oil burned below, then boiled out from the stacks above in black billows. The early morning calm offered little wind to clear away the smoke and a thick haze soon obscured the area.

A final volley of shells cracked out behind them, but none of the telltale splashes rose around the ship. Whatever they were firing at was thankfully not *Forrest*.

With the Krauts blinded, all that was left was to make a high-speed run down the coast and shake their pursuers. *Forrest's* engines sounded labored, though, and Tigert doubted they were making better than 15 knots.

A call to the engine room confirmed the commander's fears. "Sir, we were hit below the water line awhile back and some sea water got into the engines," reported the chief engineer. "The hull breach is patched, but we need to shut down for a while to clean out the engines."

"OK, give me what you can until I can find us a place to lay up."

The commander hobbled over to the map, ran his finger down the coastline and then pointed to the bridge window. "XO, on the other side of the two islands up ahead is the Edisto River estuary. I want you to go past the estuary and then double back through the smoke screen and up the river."

The maneuver worked like a charm. The entire estuary was blanketed with smoke and neither of the surviving *Kriegsmarine* destroyers followed them up the Edisto.

After *Forrest* anchored in a tree covered inlet off the river and shut down her engines, Tigert studied the map again to figure out how they could withdraw south under cover of darkness tonight.

The XO relinquished the helm and tapped the commander on the shoulder. "Skipper, I've got this. Get down to sickbay, so Doc can patch up your leg."

Tigert started to argue, but bit his tongue. Morris was right. He couldn't function much longer this way.

"OK, Frank, the conn is yours. Find us a way home."

Führer Headquarters, The Berghof, Berchtesgaden, Germany
09:31 Hours, 20 March 1942

Grand Admiral Raeder doubted he enjoyed more than a few hours of sleep since the landing and was nearly out on his feet when he rose to present the *Kriegsmarine's* morning situation report. In contrast, the *Führer* appeared to be bright and chipper. Admiral Canaris over at the *Abwehr* naval intelligence division suspected Hitler was using amphetamines.

In any case, Hitler appeared to be unusually attentive this morning and Raeder was relieved to have good news to deliver. "My *Führer*, I am very pleased to report the combined *Kriegsmarine* and *Regia Marina* fleets have established naval and air superiority around the Charleston area. Of note, we confirm both *Amerikaner* carriers were sunk and the enemy northern and southern Atlantic fleets are withdrawing after suffering heavy losses."

Raeder minimized the *Kriegsmarine's* own losses by reporting how few ships the enemy sank, rather than the far greater number of ships the *Amerikaner* heavily damaged during the battles off the Carolinas. The only significant sinking was the battleship *Scharnhorst*, which the admiral very studiously declined to report as friendly fire incident. No need having the *Führer* raging at their allies.

"Admiral, what is the current air situation over Charleston?" Hitler inquired.

"Carrier fighters intercepted an enemy bomber formation north of the city and turned it away."

"You see, my Grand Admiral, what comes from following *Führer* directives? Never disobey me again."

The man's arrogant self-certainty was maddening. There was no perfect plan. In reality, even the combined Axis fleets did not have enough resources to cover all contingencies like the enemy's multi-directional naval and air attacks since the landing.

Hitler enjoyed the luck of the devil. The combined fleet was very fortunate to survive the crisis without heavier losses, perhaps even losing the battle entirely. If any one of the encounters had gone against the Axis...

When the *Führer* rose to conclude the briefing, Raeder left the Berghof for his quarters. Enough second guessing. Enjoy the victory and get some sleep.

CHAPTER 18

Goose Creek, South Carolina
06:18 Hours, 20 March 1942

Lieutenant Fraser fidgeted as he lay in the woods, waiting for his platoon's turn to join the fight. No one could see a damned thing through the trees, but the battle sounds up ahead were clear enough – rifles and machine guns chattering back and forth, punctuated by the crumps and crashes of incoming mortar rounds.

Jim was going down his mental checklist for the umpteenth time. The young platoon leader's constant concern was forgetting something that would get his men killed. Worrying about the platoon also kept his mind off of how he would do personally during his first battle.

Far more experienced officers than the lieutenant screwed the pooch since the war began. The initial reaction to the invasion was a fricken circus. Orders followed by counter-orders. Hurry up and wait. Two days passed before the powers on high figured out there were only enough trucks and supplies to send one regiment to Charleston and chose Fraser's 118th for the mission because the men hailed from the area.

The regiment finally mounted up and got underway, only to stop again halfway to Charleston. The highway approaching the city was clogged with refugees in cars and on foot, escaping the invasion the regiment was struggling to reach. It was one thing to read about these things happening in Europe, but another thing entirely to see your own terrified and exhausted neighbors fleeing for their lives.

Were Florrie and the girls out there on the road somewhere? Soon after the Germans landed in Charleston, telephone service in the area became irregular, then stopped altogether. Jim had not heard a word from Florrie or her clan. If they weren't on the road, then his family were likely back in Summerville trapped behind enemy lines. He refused to consider the only other alternative.

Thankfully, the regiment's route to Charleston took them north of Summerville. Although he would dearly love to rescue his family, Jim did not want them anywhere near an actual battle. Retake Charleston and his family would be free soon enough.

A shout from just outside the idling truck interrupted Fraser's fretting. "Hey, boss! Is that you?"

Jim refocused on the crowd for a long moment before seeing the smudged and grinning face of one of his foremen.

"Damn Bob, I almost didn't recognize you. Are you OK?"

"Yeah, I'm alright," he nodded. "Yesterday, a buncha Krauts with machine guns took over the dredging yard and told the crew we were working for them. I figured it was time to get the hell out of there." After a pause and a grimace, the foreman added, "Sorry about your business, boss."

Yeah, Dad's business plans definitely didn't include a German invasion.

"Do you know how far west the Krauts have pushed?" Fraser asked.

"I didn't see this myself, but the word is they're in Goose Creek now."

Further than the brass expected. His platoon's first battle was just up the road aways.

"Goose Creek is right where we are headed if this convoy ever gets into gear again."

"Hot dog! You Army boys show them Krauts what for. I sure would like to get back home again."

"Will do," the lieutenant replied with a thumbs up.

A soft murmur of agreement rippled through the crowd, followed by cheers and whistles. As the convoy started moving forward again, the defeated throng transformed into something more like a pep rally before a homecoming football game.

Time to show them what for, Fraser thought, as he waved his platoon towards an unseen enemy.

The racket ahead was supposed to be third battalion pushing across the highway bridge over Goose Creek to fix the Kraut defenders, while his battalion would hit them from behind, hopefully crushing the enemy defenses like a pecan in a nut cracker.

The lieutenant's platoon cautiously rose and moved forward in a ragged skirmish line. The boys were following their training, Jim thought contentedly, zig zagging from one tree to the next, so they were always behind or near cover.

The grinding burp of a Kraut machine gun and the scream of the point man let everyone know they had reached the enemy line. Fraser bounded forward with his first squad and dove behind a big oak as German bullets tore away chunks of bark and wood. After bringing first squad up on the left, Wolf Fleischer and his squad leader pulled out grenades and softly tossed them in high arcs at the Kraut machine gun nest, like basketball players firing long shots at a distant hoop.

The lieutenant ducked and listened. Two explosions later, the machine gun went silent. Peeking out to ensure the Krauts were not playing possum, he saw the barrel of the machine gun pointed skyward and its gunner slumped motionless over his weapon.

"Let's go!" Fraser yelled, while pumping his arm up and down.

First squad slipped into a trench leading away from the machine gun nest. A short exchange of shots was followed by calls of "all clear."

Third platoon earned their first battle victory, only to have everything go to hell. Flush with triumph, the boys whooped, hollered and cracked jokes, while gathering souvenirs from dead Germans instead of being on guard against the live ones.

The German counterattack started quickly, with grenades catching a couple of unlucky souvenir hunters out in the open. Enemy machine guns opened up from the flanks, while their camouflaged infantry charged up the middle.

Third platoon tumbled back into the trench and returned fire, but they were out-gunned. Every time the Americans stuck their heads up to fire single shots from their bolt-action rifles, the Kraut machine guns would hose down the line with dozens of rounds.

Cursing the Army which failed to provide his men with the automatic weapons the Germans seemed to possess in abundance, Fraser suddenly remembered where he could borrow one. Grabbing the first man he saw, the platoon leader hunched low and trotted back down the trench to the cleared Kraut machine gun nest. Private Johnson pulled the dead German off of the weapon and his lieutenant swung the machine gun back towards its former owners.

Fraser squeezed off short bursts of lead and glowing tracers, slashing into the exposed flank of the enemy assault platoon, dropping nearly a dozen of the camouflaged soldiers in seconds. The lieutenant figured the Krauts would pull back under the unexpected fire. Instead, the bastards charged him when the machine gun ran out of ammo.

Struggling to keep his nerve as the enemy soldiers bounded closer from tree to tree, Jim found the unfamiliar German weapon easier to reload than the big Browning machine gun he fired during a summer drill. Just slap in the new belt of ammo Johnson was holding out and the thing was ready to go.

Looking down range again, the first thing Fraser saw was a big Kraut holding a hand grenade over his head less than ten yards away! He mashed down on the trigger and poured rounds into the bastard, punching him into a bloody death dance. When the man finally fell, the grenade bounced free and detonated near another pair of Krauts huddled behind a big pine.

At Wolf Fleischer's very loud and profane urging, the rest of the platoon popped up out of the trench and laid into the remaining Germans. Caught in a cross fire, the Kraut counterattack finally faltered and melted back into the woods.

Third platoon didn't celebrate this time, returning quickly to the cover of the Kraut trench. Fraser was panning the captured machine gun back and forth, when he jumped at a tapping on his helmet

"Jesus, Wolf, don't sneak up on me like that!"

Sorry, boss," Fleischer replied, holding up his offending hand. "I think the Krauts have taken off. Can I get the men ready to move out?"

"Ayuh, and have the flank squads check for the rest of the company," Fraser added. "I'll let you know when the Old Man has new orders for us."

The platoon sergeant nodded and circled his hand above his head, calling his sergeants over to get things moving.

Jim unscrewed his aluminum canteen and took a healthy swallow of the metallic tasting water. He hadn't had a drink since washing down some crackers before dawn and his mouth was dry as dirt. Combat was a thirsty business.

After the sergeants trotted off to their squads, Fleischer turned back and looked at him for a moment. "LT, that was one smooth move with the Kraut machine gun. Saved our asses."

Fraser just screwed the cap back on his canteen and looked down the trench line. In the midst of the dead crumpled on the pine needle forest floor, the platoon medic struggled to save Bobby Jones by tying off his obliterated leg with a tourniquet.

Jim didn't feel like he saved anyone's ass.

Summerville, South Carolina
06:42 Hours, 20 March 1942

Florrie Fraser woke to thunder. Brushing off the cobwebs of sleep, she stumbled out of bed and opened the curtains. Sunshine poured into the bedroom. Not a cloud in sight.

"Mommy, close the curtains," Donna moaned as she pulled the covers over her head. Although it was a Monday morning, the girls were sleeping in because the Germans closed the schools.

Mommy instead opened the window and strained to make out the rumbling noise coming from the north. It reminded her of the explosions she heard one day as a child driving past the Bula phosphate mines on a trip to Charleston.

Explosions? Oh my…those are cannon!

The chill Florrie felt wasn't entirely due to the early morning air flowing through the opened window. She quickly dressed and looked for her sister. They had to get the kids out of here while they still could.

Instead of curled up on her bed hugging a pillow, Florrie found Bonnie Sue in the kitchen frying up a batch of pancakes for breakfast. Baby sister smiled wanly and handed her a cup of coffee.

It was good to see Bonnie Sue rejoin the world. After her husband Henry disappeared on Friday, she spent the past weekend in her bedroom sobbing herself into an exhausted sleep, only to wake to tears once again.

The sisters' search for Henry just made things worse.

When he didn't come home for supper, Florrie and Bonnie Sue shooed the kids into the living room to listen to the radio and discussed what to do while washing dishes. The phones were down, so they couldn't call the grocery. With the Germans doing God knows what in town, Bonnie Sue refused to wait for Henry to return on his own. They had to fetch him safely home.

Leaving Bonnie Sue's son, Ricky, in charge of the girls, the women cautiously walked downtown. The grocery was dark, unoccupied and guarded by two German soldiers. Bonnie Sue started to shake and went weak at the knees.

Florrie wrapped an arm around her sister before she fell, then spoke softly to the guards. "Excuse me. What happened to the people in the store?"

The Germans looked uncomprehendingly back at the women.

"Can't you understand English?" shrieked Bonnie Sue. "Where's my Henry?"

The guards motioned their rifles at the women and barked something decidedly unfriendly in their harsh language.

Florrie pulled Bonnie Sue away from the store and they started knocking on nearby doors. Except for an occasional parting of front window curtains, most houses remained dark and silent. The handful of folks brave enough to came to the door had not seen Henry or his employees. However, they had seen soldiers taking men and boys off the street and loading them onto trucks. The word was they were being taken to work in Charleston. Those who resisted or tried to run were shot.

The sisters trudged home in silence. Florrie did not want to imagine what Bonnie Sue was thinking after losing her husband. Her own worry was more practical. If Henry was a German slave or worse, who would look after the family?

Now, their situation turned from difficult to dangerous.

Florrie sipped her coffee and studied her baby sister flipping pancakes on the griddle. Was Bonnie Sue able to travel? After this weekend's meltdown, she wasn't so sure.

"Sis, how're you feeling?"

"I'm all right, I guess. This war is the awfullest thing, but I have to keep it together for Ricky."

"Have you heard the cannon up north?"

"Oh, is that what that noise was?"

"We have to get the kids out of here before the fighting comes to town."

Bonnie Sue moved the pancakes from the griddle onto the plates and called the kids to breakfast. Everyone took a seat and said grace.

"Did you hear me?" Florrie asked, passing the butter. "We have to leave."

"Leave?" Bonnie Sue shook her head. "No, no… We can't leave until Henry comes home from working in Charleston."

"The Army is here now and can free Henry. We have to think of the kids." After slathering her cakes with syrup, Florrie pitched her plan. "What do ya say we pack after breakfast, then go down to the grocery and pick up the car. We can reach Wilmington by dinnertime."

Bonnie Sue looked up and started to tear up again. "Henry had the only set of car keys."

Florrie closed her eyes and kneaded her forehead with her fingers, trying to push back an emerging headache. While her girls were giggling obliviously over something or another, the explosions started up again, louder than before. Mommy had to figure this out and fast.

Charleston, South Carolina
10:34 Hours, 20 March 1942

What the hell was going on with the SS? At dawn, an *Amerikaner* regiment attacked a single SS battalion in the vicinity of Goose

Creek along the most direct route from their Fort Jackson to Charleston. A long-expected counterattack. Still, the enemy outnumbered his defenders by a substantial three-to-one margin and radio communication with the battalion was now down completely.

Looking up at the situation map tacked to the wall of his ad hoc headquarters laid out across the produce stands of the old Charleston Market, General Erwin Rommel shook his head. The landing zone defenses were still so damned thin. As the *Führer* insisted, the initial defense was the responsibility of Hitler's oversized SS regiment *Libenstandarte*. The Army commander deployed two battalions of Hitler's former body guards west along the two most likely avenues of approach, then a battalion each north and south to complete the perimeter.

By today, regular Army units were scheduled to double that defense into something credible before the *Amis* counterattacked, but the unloading of troops and vehicles crawled. The Army commander was well aware of the damage to the docks suffered during the first *Amerikaner* bomber attack, but the *Kriegsmarine* port commander only yesterday informed him many of the freighters carrying the reinforcing troops and equipment were manned by decidedly unenthusiastic English and French crews and experiencing "coordination problems." After Rommel wondered out loud what in the hell the high command staff were thinking, the naval officer sheepishly explained Germany did not have enough crews to man all the merchant ships and enemy sailors were pressed into duty.

Water under the bridge. Rommel needed to solve the immediate problem of the enemy counter attack. The general shrugged on his coat and readied to leave for Goose Creek to evaluate the situation for himself, when his chief of staff called out across the room, "Sir, you need to see this before you leave."

Rommel took the typed message, raced through it and looked up. "Have you verified this, Crüwell?"

"We are doing so now."

The morning "radio failure" was not due to mechanical problems or the marshy terrain to the west. The incompetent SS colonel was too damned proud to call for help. According to the belated message in his hands, the *Amis* nearly surrounded the SS battalion over an hour ago, forcing them to withdraw down Highway 52 toward Charleston. No mention of the Charleston Airport.

Crüwell walked back from the communications table. "Sir, I confirmed the contents of the message with SS commander. I also telephoned the airfield to determine its status."

Rommel nodded. His chief of staff was one step ahead as usual.

"The *Luftwaffe* forward detachment officer reports no sign of the enemy, but the SS only left a single platoon behind to provide security."

Wonderful. All the *Amis* need to do to bag his only airbase in the landing zone was to brush aside forty men!

Charleston Air Field, South Carolina
11:31 Hours, 20 March 1942

The new company commander pulled out his dead boss's binoculars and scanned the Charleston Airport one more time before ordering the advance.

Captain O'Hara bought it during the battle of Goose Creek. Jim first learned about Mike's death during a break in the morning march, when the company first sergeant brought him O'Hara's gear. Helluva way to get promoted.

After the regiment nearly surrounded the Krauts south of Goose Creek earlier that morning, the Germans conducted a fighting retreat along Highway 52 back toward Charleston. The main body of the regiment pushed down the highway in pursuit, while Fraser's Bravo Company marched unopposed down a back-country dirt road on the American right flank.

Although the Charleston Airport was not among the regiment's objectives, Bravo's avenue of advance went right through the place. Might as well liberate it on the way to the city.

After halting the company at the wood line, Lieutenant Jim Fraser's first look at the airport suggested the place was barely defended – just a handful a fox holes on the perimeter of the landing strip, with the Krauts smoking and joking in the open instead of keeping an eye out for the Americans. Then, his binoculars fell on an anti-aircraft emplacement sitting at the end of the runway, sporting an automatic twenty millimeter gun surrounded by sandbags. That bad boy could cause some serious damage, especially over this open terrain. The airport was one big kill zone - flat and without any cover for hundreds of yards.

After this morning's blood-letting, the new company commander had no appetite for more casualties. Fraser sent a runner back to battalion with a long shot request for mortar support and a couple more men out to gather his platoon leaders for a planning pow wow. No more mistakes. Bravo would hit the Krauts hard and fast with a coordinated attack.

As his leaders returned to their platoons, Fraser was surprised to see the runner trotting back from battalion, with a couple guys spooling out wire providing a telephone line back to the mortar battery. The wire dogs explained the mortars hadn't fired a single round so far and were thrilled to get into the fight.

Now that he had his unexpected artillery support, the young lieutenant struggled to recall his classroom forward observer training. Fraser royally screwed up his first fire mission to the mortars, landing a spotting round three football fields to the left of the target and nearly out of sight. All he managed to do was wake up the Krauts.

Realizing someone was trying to drop a world of hurt on them, the German antiaircraft gun started barking, rhythmically launching its rounds into the woods across which Bravo Company was spread. As the enemy rounds splintered oaks and pines down the tree line towards his position, the lieutenant struggled to keep his voice steady, shouting fire adjustments into the telephone handset. Just before he finished the order, an incoming round ripped a large branch off the oak behind which he was laying, spinning the big chunk of wood to the ground with a thunderous crash.

Fraser cautiously reopened his eyes and raised his head to see the shattered branch lying just inches from nose. Damn, that was too frigging close!

The lieutenant pushed himself up on his knees to look past the wood and leaves, wondering whether the mortar boys received all of the last call. A sharp crack and a plume of dirt rising within yards of the big Kraut gun answered the unspoken question.

We're in business! Fraser ordered the battery to fire for effect and explosions erupted all around the anti-aircraft emplacement and nearby foxholes. Finally, smoke rounds arrived to blind any surviving Krauts.

The advance onto the airfield was far easier than the new company commander feared. The mortars knocked out the AA gun and his men overran the surviving Krauts in the foxholes in short, sharp firefights.

Walking behind the company skirmish line, Fraser stopped by a foxhole next to a mortar crater and studied the two dead Germans inside. One was an officer wearing a soft cap with a skull and bones insignia and a camouflage blouse with twin lightning bolts on the collar. This was not the enemy uniform in the Army pamphlets.

Suddenly, the other "dead" Kraut sat up and opened his eyes, which bulged blue and white out of the bloody mess of his shredded face. Jim jumped back in shock and pointed his *Springfield* at the grievously wounded man. His first instinct was to call a medic, rather than pull a trigger. However, the enemy soldier had no intention of surrendering for medical treatment. Furiously blinking the blood out of his eyes, the soldier felt around and grasped his rifle.

"Drop it now!" Fraser hollered.

The German instead raised the weapon and the horrified American shot him in what was left of his face. Jumping Jesus! Who are these crazy Krauts wearing pirate insignia?

A shout from the left drew his attention from this latest horror show. "Sir, I think we have more company," his runner noted, pointing east down the main landing strip.

Fraser raised his binoculars for a closer look. Whoever the crazy Krauts were, another couple companies of the camouflaged troopers were pouring out of trucks in the distance.

"Everyone get down," the lieutenant motioned with his arms and yelled down the company skirmish line. "When the bastards get within range, lay into them with everything you have!"

Bravo Company responded with rebel yells and hoots, then found positions with good, long lines of sight. Let the Krauts run into our guns for once.

Charleston Airport, South Carolina
11:46 Hours, 20 March 1942

If the stakes were not so high, General Rommel would have cracked a smile at the ludicrous scene playing out around him. Every manner of civilian vehicle, including a city bus, a newspaper van and even an ice cream truck, were unloading SS troopers along the edge of the airport landing strip.

While the SS reserve battalion safely landed two days before, its vehicles sank on a pair of freighters lost during the

Amerikaner naval attack. The SS battalion commander spread his men across Charleston to "requisition" every civilian vehicle they could find to motorize his unit, then presented a Packard convertible to his Army commander to serve as his new staff car. The man was an ass licker, but an enterprising one.

From the Packard, Rommel swept the airport with his binoculars. The squadron of transports which flew the Atlantic yesterday remained undamaged under camouflage netting by the tree line to the north. Their cargo of aircraft mechanics was nowhere to be seen, most likely hiding in the nearby aircraft hangar.

The *Luftwaffe's* plan was to fly its transports and then long-range bombers from Europe to the Charleston Airport, with refueling stops in the Azores and Bermuda. The shorter ranged dive bombers and fighters were partially disassembled and loaded onto the invasion fleet, to be reassembled at the airport by the missing mechanics. Unless the *Luftwaffe* got its planes in the air soon, the enemy Air Corps would eventually overwhelm the unreliable *Kriegsmarine* air cover.

Rommel swept the field with binoculars to find his *Ami* counterpart on his knees and looking back at him. All around the brown uniformed officer, Tommy-style saucer helmets popped up and down. Probably less than a hundred of them. Rommel's reserve arrived in the nick of time, forcing the enemy to go to ground just short of the precious aircraft and hanger.

Realizing the urgency of the situation, the SS commander waved his dismounted troopers forward to evict the unwelcome arrivals. His camouflaged infantry advanced in silence. Even though this enemy had not been to war in a generation, their fire discipline was impressive. No nervous wasted shots. The oppressive quiet was finally broken by a sudden cascade of enemy rifles, taking far too many SS troopers down before their officers ordered the survivors to seek cover and return fire.

The *Amis* were unfortunately living up to their reputation as fine marksmen. While Rommel had never faced this enemy as a Great War lieutenant fighting in the Alps, brother officers told him stories after the war of incredible shots made by these gangsters and cowboys.

Soon after landing in Charleston, local civilians started sniping at the German infantry spreading across the city. After shooting or hanging these miscreants, Rommel ordered a city-wide search for firearms. The general was appalled to find most homes were armed, many with multiple rifles and pistols. Facing these experienced marksmen serving in the enemy army was bad enough. What if the general population rose against his men?

Rommel filed away that unpleasant thought for future consideration and found another in the empty blue sky above. No sign of the naval air support he requested before leaving Charleston. The general realized nearly all of the *Kriegsmarine* fighters were either on combat air patrol or staged on the carrier decks to turn away *Amerikaner* bombers, but the admiral promised him a dive bomber squadron on call to deal with land threats like this one.

Without the air support card, Rommel played trump. The general sent a runner to the SS major, ordering him to deploy the *panzer* section. The transports managed to land a handful of STG-III assault guns and a pair accompanied his airport battle group. These low-slung vehicles featured a short seventy-five millimeter gun firing high explosive rounds. The HE rounds were not very effective against the armor of other *panzers*, but they could pound enemy infantry.

The pair of STGs rolled past Rommel's car, belching black diesel smoke from the rear and slowly worked their way up to the enemy lines. Groups of SS infantry fell behind the armored beasts, using them as cover against the potent enemy rifles.

In unison, the STGs halted. As *Ami* bullets careened off their metal hides, the *panzers* returned fire with their main cannon. The outcome of the uneven contest was never in doubt. The concussion and shrapnel of the high explosive rounds tore into the enemy line. After only two cannon volleys, the *Amis* broke and ran. A few at first, then the entire company started sprinting for the cover of the forest behind them. Sensing a rout, the entire SS battle group resumed its advance at a trot.

As if to pile on the hapless *Amis*, the long-delayed *Kriegsmarine* dive bombers finally appeared in the skies overhead and immediately dove for Earth. Rommel leaned back in his leather seat and grinned broadly. The damned Navy finally did something right.

Following the warbirds down, the general's smile transformed into open-mouthed horror. The naval air strike was falling well short of the fleeing *Amerikaner* company.

Midland Park, South Carolina
12:33 Hours, 20 March 1942

Lieutenant Jim Fraser looked at the sky over the Charleston Airport in slack-jawed amazement. Just as the enemy threatened to overrun his men, the fricken German Air Force arrives like manna from heaven and lays into their own people with bombs and machine guns. Forgetting about the Americans, the surviving German troopers fired back at the sky in uncomprehending rage.

"Thank Gawd, the Krauts are as screwed up as we are," Jim muttered to himself.

Fraser's boys were hardly out of danger, however. Even though the Kraut air strike scattered their infantry, the enemy tanks pressed home the attack. Like steel dragons, the low-slung German vehicles crawled forward, their machine guns spitting fire and diesel engines sorting black smoke. In the open, these dragons were damned near invincible, but they pushed their luck by entering Bravo Company's wooded lair.

The lieutenant sprinted into the pine forest looking for men to head off the enemy tanks. Up and down the tree line, his sergeants were yelling at their panicked troopers, ordering the men to stop and fight, but one familiar voice stood out from the rest.

"If you sorry sonsabitches don't fall in on me right now, I will kick your asses from here to Charleston!" bellowed one Wolf Fleischer.

Fleischer took over third platoon when Fraser was given Bravo Company, but there didn't appear to be many familiar faces around the platoon sergeant.

"How many of the men have you rounded up, Wolf?"

Looking back at his company commander, Fleischer growled, "Just this handful here and they're all from different platoons. The rest of the company shagged ass deeper into the woods."

"They'll be enough," the company commander replied. "Gather round people. We have a job to do."

Six minutes later, the half-dozen troopers were hidden behind trees paralleling the only passable route through these woods. Fraser and Fleischer took positions at each end of the ad hoc squad.

As the lieutenant expected, the pair of Kraut tanks came along shortly, carefully picking their way through the trees and down a narrow dirt track. The problem was stopping the beasts. They didn't have the axes or the time to drop trees in front of them like during the Carolina Maneuvers. Then, the Krauts kindly offered a solution. The driver of the lead tank popped his head out of a hatch to navigate the next turn. The last thing the startled German saw before the back of his head exploded was Fraser carefully aiming his *Springfield*.

The tank's progress came to a literal crashing halt. Without a driver's guidance, the lead tank idled in place. The rear tank broke too late and clanged into the stalled vehicle, then frantically backed over and high centered itself on top of a small boulder.

Like a pair of turtles retreating into their shells after spotting a dog looking for an easy meal, the Kraut commanders dropped into their tanks and slammed the hatches closed. And just as the turtles would be content to wait in their shells until the dog wandered off, the enemy tank crews appeared ready to stay put in their steel boxes until their infantry caught up.

Jim looked over to Wolf and raised his hands in frustration. The company commander didn't have time for this nonsense. With the tanks neutralized, he had to reorganize Bravo before the Krauts got their shit together and resumed their attack.

"Oh, for crying out loud!" Fleischer snapped. "LT, have the boys give me covering fire if the Krauts stick their heads out again."

The sergeant disappeared into the woods, then popped out again behind the rear tank. Hopping onto the engine compartment, he emptied one of the Krauts' spare fuel cans all over the vehicle. With a flick of a match, a roaring fire turned the impregnable steel box into an uninhabitable oven. Coughing and gasping, the German crew dropped out of an escape hatch on the bottom of their tank, only to find a grinning American sergeant pointing his rifle at them. After repeating the process on the lead tank, Wolf gave his company commander a thumbs up.

Time to get this show back on the road. Bravo Company was tired, but game. Most of the boys rallied and returned to their original positions before the airport attack, but everyone was short or completely out of ammo. They couldn't get back into the fight without bullets.

Returning from a supply run, the company top sergeant brought very little ammo, but a truckload of bad news. "Lieutenant, battalion supply is nearly empty and regiment isn't much better," First Sergeant Baxter reported. "Apparently, the brass back in Fort Jackson only provided us with enough ammunition for a recon of the area, not for an extended battle."

"Dammit, Top, can you scrounge some bullets from another unit?"

"Already tried. Everyone is about as tapped out as we are."

"OK, have all the sergeants take inventory and level out what ammo we have before we make the next push."

"What push?" The senior sergeant asked, becoming visibly frustrated with his younger commander. "With respect, Lieutenant, you're not listening. The regiment is tapped out. The scuttlebutt is we'll be bugging out to Goose Creek and maybe further. This operation is over."

Summerville, South Carolina
22:11 Hours, 21 March 1942

Florrie Fraser put her finger up to her lips and shooshed her girls, then looked down both streets. Although the electricity came back on yesterday, the neighborhood was almost completely dark. The Germans shut off the streetlights to conceal the town from advancing American troops, while the locals drew their curtains against invader snooping, allowing only slivers of incandescent light to seep into the street. Hopefully, the resulting darkness would hide them from the Germans.

Nothing could conceal the sounds they were making, though. The battle noise gradually vanished in the afternoon and the nighttime streets were dead silent. Even the crickets had gone quiet. Every footstep they took seemed unnaturally loud, as if the sound could travel miles. Probably just her imagination, but worrying all the same.

The streets appeared to be empty, but something just wasn't right. There was a… creaking noise behind them. When the mother glanced back, her daughters were being as quiet as little church mice, patiently waiting for her next instructions in this game of going to find daddy. Then, Florrie looked up and almost fell down. The Henderson boy was hanging by a rope tied off on the street lamp, his hands tied behind him and head cocked grotesquely to one side. Around his neck was a sign handwritten in blocked capital letters condemning the teen as a "PARTISAN."

Florrie snapped her head back to Earth, so her girls would not look up to see what drew mommy's attention and tears from her eyes.

Goddamned Germans! Tommy wasn't some partisan. He was just a child. Is there anything these animals will not punish with death?

Anything?

When she decided to escape Summerville this morning, Florrie barely thought about the curfew forbidding towns people from leaving their homes after dark. After all, this was America. You were free to come and go whenever you pleased. But, if the Germans would hang Tommy for nothing, what would they do to her and the girls for violating their curfew?

Florrie pushed back against the troubling thought. The bastards could just as easily catch them returning home as they could leaving town. Might as well keep going.

The mother looked around one last time, took her girls' hands and slowly walked towards the houses sitting catty-corner across the intersection. From the middle of the crossroads, she spotted a handful of soldiers walking slowly down the street, but the Germans didn't appear to see them. Without thinking, the mother tightly squeezed the little hands within hers and launched into a brisk trot. They had to get out of the road and find a place to hide.

"Mommy, you're hurting me," squealed Lisa.

Florrie released her girls, but it was too late. German shouts and stomping boots hurtled down the empty street towards them.

The second house on the left offered the quick cover of a high fence, so she scooted the girls through a gate and closed it behind them as quietly as possible. The Germans may not have heard their entry into the back yard, but a hound dog inside the darkened house did and began howling for all he was worth.

Florrie frantically looked around for another gate in the fence through which to escape and found none. Running onto a porch, she tried the door to the house, but found it securely locked and guarded by a now growling dog. Their sanctuary turned into a trap.

With German shouts coming closer, the frightened woman stared down at her feet, forcing herself to concentrate. There had to be a place to hide. Then, her focus shifted from her feet to the porch. Why not underneath?

The small girls crawled easily through the gap between the wooden deck and the yard, but it was a tighter fit for their plump mother. Mommy slithered underneath on her back as best she could.

Florrie whispered to Donna and Lisa that the soldiers were looking for them like their friends did during hide and seek. They had to be quiet no matter what happened outside. Could they do that? Both girls nodded back confidently.

Thank heaven, it was all still a game to the kids. Their mother was petrified.

No sooner had Florrie finished her instructions than the side gate crashed open. There were no more shouting, just boot steps crossing the porch and the sound of the doorknob being tried again. Mommy raised her index finger to her mouth and the girls nodded again.

Suddenly there was a cry of triumph and hands grabbing Florrie's feet, roughly dragging her out from under the porch. On the way out, the edge of the deck banged her on the forehead and the ground pulled her skirt almost up to her chest. The soldier standing over the bleeding woman considered her for a moment, then flung her legs apart with a crooked-tooth grin and started to undo his belt.

"No!" Florrie shrieked in horror. She frantically tried to push her skirt back down to cover herself, when two other soldiers grabbed her arms and pushed them down into the grass. Her legs were still free to kick out at the German above. Based on the bastard's curses, she landed one or two good ones where it counted.

Florrie's one-sided struggle didn't last long, though. The German angrily wrenched her legs apart again and fell on top of her.

This was too much for Donna and Lisa. Crawling out from under the porch, the girl's added their screams to those of their mother. Oh God no, not in front of the girls.

Suddenly, above all the caterwauling, boomed an order in German. Almost instantly, the soldiers released her and backed away. The mother scrambled to her feet without bothering to fix her clothing, scooped up her crying children and retreated to the fence.

Any relief Florrie felt from being spared the rape vanished when she recognized the man who provided the reprieve. It was the tall German who shot down poor Mary Glendon and her children the day the Germans came to Summerville.

As the officer walked up to inspect her, the mother protectively moved her children behind her and prepared to lunge forward. If he draws that pistol, I have to take it from him somehow. I can't let him murder my girls.

The man looming above her didn't reach for his pistol, though. Instead, he scowled and pointed to the gate. "*Mutter*, go home *mit die kinder*."

Florrie just stared back. She could understand the mixture of English and German, but couldn't make herself believe this second mercy.

"*Verstehen sie? Aus!* Go home!"

Florrie's defenses finally crumbled and she started to sob. "Oh God, thank you, thank you, thank you…"

Giving the soldiers who attacked her a wide birth, the mother took her daughters by the hand and scurried through the gate. Despite the girls' protests, Florrie did not ease her grip or slow her pace until she reached home.

Trying to make sense of the night's madness, Florrie wondered what she would tell Bonnie Sue about tonight. Heck, what do I tell Jim, whenever it is I see him again?

IV. Charleston

CHAPTER 19

Fort Jackson, South Carolina
13:31 Hours, 1 April 1942

Major General Patton strode into the new Third Army headquarters, with his staff struggling to keep up with their boss while toting an easel and several map boards. It was time to kick Rommel's ass back into the Atlantic Ocean and he had just the plan to do it.

George considered the German invasion a stroke of personal good fortune. War on American soil accelerated the Chief of Staff's long rumored schedule of promotions.

Marshall gave Patton a third star and the new First Armored Corps, the top Army tank command and the hammer for the upcoming counteroffensive to retake Charleston.

Patton's commander for the operation was Lieutenant General Walter Krueger.

During the 1941 maneuvers, Krueger set objectives and allowed his tank officers free reign in taking them. George could not have hoped for a better boss.

Now to make the Charleston operation his own. When Krueger summoned his corps commanders to begin planning for the new offensive, Patton immediately decided to deliver his own completed operational plan as a *fait accompli*. After all, since the armored corps was the key to the counteroffensive, the corps commander ought to determine where to employ his tanks.

After studying the area maps for a few minutes, George quickly concluded the location of the armored attack was really a choice between least worst alternatives. The area around Charleston was a snarl of rivers, forest and swamp with limited road access for vehicles. Then it dawned on him how this disadvantage could be turned against his opponent Rommel. His corps staff spent the next two days and most of the nights turning their general's insight into a viable plan.

The meeting at Third Army headquarters was a small affair – General Krueger, his two corps commanders, Patton and Bob Eichelberger, and the Army chief of staff, Al Gruenther.

Newly minted Brigadier General Gruenther's nickname was "the Brain" and was widely considered the brightest young staff officer in the Army after Dwight Eisenhower. The chief of staff briefed the three commanders about the area of operations and the two primary objectives of the operation – the Charleston port providing enemy reinforcement and supply from Europe and the city airport basing the *Luftwaffe*.

After Gruenther wrapped up his presentation, Krueger took charge of the meeting. "Gentlemen, I planned to brain storm ideas with you on how to best obtain our objectives using the map on the wall, but it appears the armored corps commander has come with his own visual aids. What are you up to George?"

"Sir, could I have ten minutes of your time?" Patton replied.

Krueger leaned back in his chair and crossed his arms. "OK, George, show me what you have."

Flipping charts on his easel and using his swagger stick as a pointer, Patton succinctly laid out his plan. "An attack from the west towards Charleston enjoys the most roads and the fewest terrain obstacles. However, those roads funnel into two crossings at Goose Creek. This is undoubtedly where Rommel has positioned his tanks."

Glancing at his chief of staff, who shrugged in return, the Army commander demanded, "George, how the hell did you know that? Air recon only found the Kraut *panzer* positions yesterday."

"Sir, that is where I would put my tanks if I were Rommel," George grinned. "We need to send my tanks where he'll least expect them and have the least freedom of maneuver."

Patton then put a board with this battle plan on the easel and explained his two-stage plan to fix the enemy in the west where he expected the attack and then swing around and kick him ass with his armored corps.

The response was silence. The generals rose from their chairs and clustered around the easel to more closely study the avenues of advance and the projected phase lines of the battle plan.

"Your proposed armored corps area of operations is hardly tank country," the Army commander objected. "The place is a forest with only one highway of note."

"I am counting on that, General."

"Explain yourself," Krueger ordered, again crossing his arms.

"Sir, I propose to use the bad terrain against the Huns. Rommel's tanks are in position to respond in every direction but this one. I doubt his men have been able to scout this area in any detail. However, I propose we use locals who know the area to flesh out our maps with every goat trail capable of bearing a tank."

Sweeping his arm in front of his with a flourish, Patton concluded, "The point is, we will have freedom of maneuver, while the enemy will be feeling his way around half blind."

Gruenther was the first to grasp the tank commander's point. "General Patton's plan can work, sir. With information on the trail network, my staff could refine his plan with specific avenues of advance for each of his armored combat commands. Optimally, First Armored Corps could capture our objectives in two or three days."

Looking at his other corps commander, Krueger asked, "Bob, do you have any alternative suggestions?"

"Not any longer, sir." Eichelberger responded. "George's operational concept is unorthodox, but it makes the most sense for his tanks. I have different dispositions in mind for my infantry, though."

Krueger nodded. "Very well, gentlemen. Let's use George's plan as a template. Have your staffs send any refinements you desire to Al, then I will kick the final plan up to General Marshall."

Summerville, South Carolina
18:52 Hours, 2 April 1942

Drying the last of the supper dishes, Florrie glanced into the living room to make sure everything was all right. As usual, the kids and the German soldiers were seated around the family radio, listening raptly to the Lone Ranger radio show.

These were different soldiers in every way than the bastards who first arrived a month ago. This bunch wore round helmets and green uniforms, claimed they jumped out of planes and parachuted into battle. More importantly, they displayed far better manners. Unfortunately, they also moved into the house.

The week before, several thousand of these German paratroopers marched into Summerville and announced every family would take about a dozen of their number into their home. Generally, they treated the family with respect, cleaned up after themselves and kept out of the way.

Although Florrie was reluctant to admit this to herself, the paratroopers came with benefits. Communicating in broken

English and hand gestures, the paratroopers agreed to share their rations with family, if the women cooked a communal meal for everyone. This was a Godsend because food had become increasingly scarce since the occupation. Before these Germans took up residence, the women were considering cutting back to two meals a day.

A soldier named Fritz joined Florrie and Bonnie Sue in the kitchen to prepare the meals. A chef and saucier before the war, the soldier brought a sour and savory flavor to the traditionally southern cuisine and did wonders transforming the German canned meat into something more than merely edible.

German occupation decrees barred civilians from owning radios in order to prevent them from coordinating with the American military, However, the paratroopers were delighted to discover the family's hidden wireless and eagerly listened to American broadcasts with the family when they were off duty. The Germans peppered the family with questions about American words and phrases they did not understand and quickly added them to the vocabulary they used around the house.

The paratroopers were particularly fascinated by American westerns like the Lone Ranger. A tall blonde officer explained the idea of a Wild West was something novel to Germans, whose lives were generally orderly and law abiding. To the amusement of the family, a couple of the soldiers actually believed most Americans were cowboys and asked why they had not seen any in South Carolina.

When the Lone Ranger signed off with a "Hi ho Silver," the sisters left the kitchen to hear the program for which they waited all day – the news at the top of the hour. Since the invasion, the war news was unrelentingly bad and the paratroopers took an obvious pride in hearing their enemy report on their triumphs.

This evening was different. The news announcer played a special message to the American people from President Roosevelt. The president began by reassuring everyone their government had things well in hand. Then he spoke directly to the people of "occupied America," asking them to remain steadfast and pledging help would arrive soon.

One of the young soldiers named Erich scowled, put down the machine gun he just finished cleaning, and turned the tuning knob across the dial to find something more pleasant. A smile returned to his face and a snap to his fingers, when he found the Glen Miller Band playing *In the Mood*.

Erich turned to Florrie, swept her into his arms and started to dance the swing. Recalling vividly the last time German soldiers laid hands on her, she wrenched herself away and shrieked at the young soldier. "Don't you ever touch me! If you do, I swear you'll regret it. You are guests in this house. Act like it!"

Erich looked truly sorry, but Florrie could care less. None of these German bastards would ever touch her again.

The blonde officer turned off the radio and quietly gave some orders in German. Two of the paratroopers went outside to guard the house and the rest started retiring for the night. Having adopted the soldiers' early to bed, early to rise schedule, the family followed suit.

Surprisingly, the paratroopers allowed the family to keep their bedrooms and slept downstairs in the basement. Based on Jim's descriptions of the Army, Florrie suspected this arrangement was less a matter of courtesy than of safety. The basement is where you want to be when the artillery falls.

After everyone finished up in the bathroom, the mother and daughters said their prayers and jumped into bed.

Florrie's thoughts returned to the events of the evening. After thinking on it, part of the reason she went off on Erich was probably because she used to dance with Jim to that very same song on the radio. Her husband was a bit of a klutz in general and very self-conscious about his shortcomings as dancer, but when the mood was right, she could convince him to give her a twirl or two in the privacy of their living room.

The wife clasped her hands again in prayer. Oh Jim, I wish I could talk to you and let you know the girls and I are all right. I pray to you're well. God willing, we'll be together again soon.

Before turning out the light, she kissed her finger and pressed it on the picture on the nightstand. In the photograph, Florrie was holding hands with Jim on the Myrtle Beach seashore during the far happier times of their honeymoon.

I love you, darling.

Great Cypress Swamp, South Carolina
17:24 Hours, 7 April 1942

His seemingly endless duties performed for the moment, Lieutenant Helmut Arpke sat down on his helmet and retrieved his wife's letters from his rucksack. A dozen letters she sent over the past several weeks arrived yesterday. It was all he could do to keep from tearing them open and reading them on the spot. Duty was duty.

Arpke thoughtlessly slapped at the latest mosquito to bite the back of his neck. General Rommel pushed the front lines well out from Charleston to protect its vital port and airfield from enemy artillery. In doing so, the Sturm regiment was moved from its comfortable accommodations in the homes of Summerville and spread out across this insect and vermin infested marsh.

Arpke's platoon was ordered to set up observation points across a kilometer wide stretch of the Great Cypress Swamp to provide early warning of any *Ami* attack. The map he received indicated a road crossed the marsh through the middle of his sector. If the road ever existed, the heavy rains of the past month submerged it and forced the OPs up onto a series of unsubmerged islands of relatively high ground. The lieutenant and his men spent nearly all their time struggling to make these patches of semi-dry earth somewhat habitable and defensible.

Helmut raced through Louisa's first chatty letters, reporting on rehearsals for her upcoming spring opera, then he stopped to re-read one in the middle of the stack.

My Darling Helmut,

I hope this finds you well. I have not heard from you for some time. I know you are probably on some military mission and are just fine, but please forgive me, I worry about you. I pray you are receiving my letters.

I have not been feeling well over the past week, so I took some time to see my doctor. He told me I am expecting our first child! I am so happy. I only wish you were here to share this with me.

Arpke looked up at the light blue afternoon sky, his mind a jumble of emotions. He always wanted a family, but did not think it would happen so soon and while he was overseas at war.

Platoon sergeant Erich Schuster sloshed up to his platoon leader's island to report on the day's work.

"Erich, Louisa is expecting," Helmut grinned, waving the letter. "I am going to be a papa."

"Well congratulations, Lieutenant," Erich replied, shaking his friend's hand. "Wait. I have just the thing for the occasion."

Digging into his ruck sack, the platoon sergeant produced a bottle of Jack Daniel's whisky he liberated from a Charleston store before the platoon was plunged into this muddy purgatory.

"To your new son. *Prosit!*"

Erich took a healthy swallow from the bottle, then handed it to Helmut, who did the same.

"Erich, do you think I will make a good father?"

"Well, if you can run herd on this platoon of miscreants, I think you can raise a son."

"Or a little girl," Helmut added hopefully.

The men took one more swallow from the bottle and Erich stowed it safely away for future use. The warmth of the whisky added little to the glow the father-to-be already felt.

White House, Washington D.C.
09:00 Hours, 18 April 1942

After his aide pulled the cover sheet up over the easel, General George C. Marshall tapped his pointer on the operations map below. "Mr. President, this is Operation Hammerfall - the offensive to retake Charleston."

Roosevelt and his civilian foreign policy team stared raptly at the bright graphic, where blue arrows representing planned Army advances raced around and through the red concentrations of German troops. Marshall smiled inwardly. There would be no problem maintaining their attention this morning.

"Gentlemen, we have assembled every combat ready Army division for this operation - four infantry and two armored. The Army Air Corps rebased all of their aircraft not committed to coastal patrols to the airfields and airports in the area. Finally, we committed all of our equipment and supply reserves to this effort. In short, all of our chips are on the table."

FDR leaned back in his wheelchair and took a puff on his cigarette. "General Marshall, what odds are our boys facing?"

"The Germans are very good at camouflaging their dispositions, but our best estimate is our tanks, artillery and aircraft outnumber theirs by about two-to-one, with both sides fielding four infantry divisions.

"Hardly overwhelming odds."

"No sir, but these are the best odds we can manage for some months. If Hammerfall fails and the Germans reinforce Charleston, then it will be a race to see whether we can train or they can transport more divisions into the United States." Marshall paused for effect. "Gentlemen, such a race does not favor the United States. It takes a year for us to properly train a division, while the enemy currently has dozens of battle-hardened divisions ready to go."

The civilians started murmuring to one another at this cold splash of reality.

"Then, we better win this battle, General," Roosevelt replied.

"Yes sir, my men are well aware of the stakes in this fight."

"Who will command Hammerfall?"

"General Walter Krueger, the commander of Third Army in last year's Louisiana maneuvers."

A shadow crossed the War Secretary's face. "Mr. President, do you think it's a good idea to appoint a general with a German name to head up this operation?" Henry Stimson asked. "After all, Hitler is openly calling for all Americans of German descent to take up arms on behalf of the invaders."

Walter Krueger had more than a German sounding name, Marshall reminded himself. The man was born in Prussia.

"Well, George, why did you appoint General Krueger to command Hammerfall?" the President inquired.

"Mr. President, General Krueger has the demonstrated best grasp on how to use the new armored forces. Our boys will need every edge they can get in their first outing against the Kraut *panzers*." Then, Marshall shot Stimpson a hard look. "I have no doubts whatsoever concerning General Krueger's loyalty."

Roosevelt stared at the ceiling of the Oval Office for a moment and then spoke. "We have something like 20 million Americans with German heritage. Far too many to lock up like the Japanese. They were loyal during WWI and I expect they'll be loyal again during this new war." The President leaned his elbows on top of his desk and clasped his hands together. "Indeed, I expect General Krueger's victory in Operation

Hammerfall will restore American confidence in their fellow citizens of German descent."

Marshall looked around the room and was relieved to see the President's support for Krueger quelled the doubts about his loyalties among his cabinet…at least for the moment.

Roosevelt turned to his Chief of Staff and gave him a thumbs up. "General Marshall, good luck and God speed."

Charleston, South Carolina
19:53 Hours, 20 April 1942

As the sun slipped beneath the horizon behind him, the German Army commander scoured the graying Atlantic sky for his surprise guest. Berlin's cryptic morning radio simply noted a very important person would arrive by seaplane in the evening and ordered the Army commander to clear a slip for the plane and greet the visitor on the docks with full military honors. With the *Amis* building up for an attack any day now, this mystery Nazi party big wig could not have picked a worse time to tour the front.

An increasing drone of aircraft engines over Charleston Bay announced the arrival of the largest aircraft the Army general had ever seen. The giant six engine seaplane escorted by a squadron of *Kriegsmarine* fighters looked like a flying whale surrounded by seagulls.

That beast could carry a company of infantry, Rommel calculated. How many guests will we be entertaining?

After the flying whale splashed down and sidled up to the dock, the honor guard snapped to attention and presented arms. Two black uniformed SS men popped out of the side hatch and lowered a gangway to the dock. Then a head with swept back black hair followed by a very familiar brown uniform emerged.

"My God, it's the *Führer*," Rommel muttered under his breath. Simultaneously, the general and his adjutant thrust out their arms and shouted, "*Heil* Hitler!"

Hitler casually swung back his arm to return the salute, strode up to his commander and vigorously shook his hand. "General, it is so very good to see you again. Shall we retire to your headquarters? We have a great deal to discuss."

Over the past month, Rommel cleaned the produce stands out of the old Charleston Market Hall by the harbor and converted it into his headquarters. Sections of the long hall were divided up to accommodate the forward staffs of all three services and the roof was festooned with radio antennas to relay messages between Berlin and the forward units. The commanding general turned the basement of the main building into his own map room to monitor developments on the front, on the rare occasion he was not there himself.

Once they arrived at the map room, Rommel wasted little time on pleasantries and oriented Hitler to the Charleston landing zone. "My *Führer*, we expanded the landing zone further than originally planned in order to keep the *Amerikaner* artillery well away from the Charleston port and the *Luftwaffe* at the city airport. Our defenses are now anchored in the forests to the north, behind the Edisto River to the south and behind the marshes along the Ashley River to the west."

"And the *Amerikaner*?"

Rommel jabbed his index finger down at the map. "Here and here are the two major highways running from the American interior, through our western flank, into Charleston. Three to four enemy infantry divisions have concentrated along these roads and we expect them to launch a major counter offensive in that sector any day now."

"Where are the enemy *panzers*?"

"So far, their *panzers* have not appeared," the general scowled. "However, I cannot imagine the *Amis* plan to launch a major offensive without them." Pointing at the blocks representing military units laying on the center of the map, Rommel continued: "My *Führer*, I am holding all our *panzer* forces in reserve here at the town of Goose Creek, the airport and in the city of Charleston. When the enemy *panzers* finally appear, I will release our reserves to destroy them."

"Very good, very good," Hitler muttered, while leaning over the map.

Hitler stood up and studied his commander. "Rommel, what is your honest opinion of these *Amerikaner*?"

The general considered the question for a moment before answering. "I cannot say I have their full measure yet, my Führer. We have only met them once in battle, a few days after the landing. A reinforced *Amerikaner* regiment made a reconnaissance in force against a battalion of the SS Libenstandarte defending the Charleston Airport. The enemy infantry fought hard, but withdrew after a few hours."

"My SS are superior soldiers," concluded Hitler.

Rommel was not about to tell Hitler that the *Amis* nearly threw his former bodyguards out of the *Luftwaffe's* only airbase. That near disaster never made it into the reports to Berlin.

Hitler motioned to an SS officer standing by the wall to approach, then turned toward his commander. "General, please come to the position of attention."

Rommel clicked his heels, wondering what Hitler was up to.

The SS officer opened a box from which Hitler retrieved a thick red and gold baton, studded along its length with Iron Crosses, and extended it to his Army commander. "You have been my finest general and now you are my newest field marshal. Congratulations."

"Thank you for this honor, my *Führer*," Rommel pledged, holding the baton up in his right hand. "I will not fail you."

"No you will not, my field marshal," Hitler intoned. "You will hold Charleston at all costs." The man's pale blue eyes bored into his own. "At all costs."

"Of course, my *Führer*," Rommel replied.

Hitler nodded and clapped his commander on the shoulder. "My pilot asks that I leave again before the dawn so my rather large seaplane does not attract unwanted attention from enemy fighter planes. I look forward to the day when the *Luftwaffe* rules the skies over this land, so the *Führer* no longer has to sneak in and out of *Amerika* at night like a thief!"

After escorting Hitler back to the harbor and watching the flying whale disappear into the night sky, the freshly minted field marshal considered the baton in his hand. While he was thrilled with the honor and relished the inevitable jealousy of his peers, Rommel was troubled by Hitler's demeanor and comments. Hold Charleston at all costs? Was this promotion meant as a reward or a warning? After all, no German field marshal ever surrendered his command. Well, Rommel did not intend to be the first.

Rudd Branch, South Carolina
06:56 Hours, 21 April 1942

Lieutenant Jim Fraser strode over to Bravo Company assembling for another day of training. Time to end Hitler's nonsense, right here and now.

The day after the invasion, Adolf Hitler called for all German-Americans to join his troops in overthrowing the United States. Instead of ignoring the evil son of a whore, the radio and papers gave credence to the propaganda by reporting rumors of German-Americans working as Nazi spies and saboteurs. Worse still, some commentators started calling for "real Americans" to turn into the police anyone with a German sounding name acting suspiciously.

The company commander never would have believed there were chowdaheads in the unit who actually believed this horse crap. On the other hand, this was a different company than just a month ago. Bravo took heavy losses during the fighting around Goose Creek and the Army sent a couple dozen replacements straight out of basic training to get the company back up to strength. Although the new guys were from outside the Carolinas and didn't know their asses from a hole in the ground, the sergeants were integrating them well enough… at least until last night.

Back during his days managing the Fraser & Sons Charleston operation, Jim found the best way to gauge his workers' mood was to walk around the worksite and simply listen. It was a practice he brought with him into the Army.

Before turning in last night, the company commander strolled into the bivouac of his old platoon and stood in the shadows. Wolf Fleischer was attending to his usual duties, delivering a guard roster to one of the old squad leaders, Staff Sergeant Sam Wilson, then discussing last-minute details concerning the next exercise in Rudd Branch swamp. When Wolf left, two of the new privates started a deeply disturbing conversation with their squad leader.

"Sarge, what do ya think about the platoon sergeant?"

"What're you talking about Kowalski?" snapped Wilson.

"Well, isn't Fleischer a Kraut name?"

"So what?"

"So, can we trust a Kraut running things when the fighting starts?" DelDuca chimed in.

Wilson shot the new guys a dirty look, before falling on them like a ton of bricks. "Y'all shut your holes! Wolf Fleischer is a good old boy and the best durn sergeant I know."

DelDuca retreated, but not much. "No offense, Sarge, but the way things are today, youse can't be too careful."

"Get your asses on guard duty now, before I get pissed," Wilson snarled.

Fraser shook his head. He'd have to get a handle on this and quick. There's a big push coming up soon. Can't have the men going into combat looking crosswise at one another.

The next morning after breakfast, the men assembled for another day of swamp maneuvers. Training would have to wait.

"Men, gather round and grab a piece of grass," Fraser ordered.

Bravo Company plopped down on the field around their company commander and looked back curiously. The officers didn't often conduct classes.

"Kowalski, what country did your family immigrate from?" Fraser asked.

"Poland, sir. Can't you tell from the name?"

The men laughed and Fraser grinned back at him.

"So, are you a Pole or an American?"

"One hundred percent red blooded American, sir."

"How about you DelDuca? Where are your people from?

"Mi Papa and Mama came from Sicilia," the Brooklyn private replied with a mock heavy Italian accent.

"So, are you and your family Italian spies?"

DelDuca turned red and jumped up with balled fists. "Take that back, Lieutenant. I'm as American as you are."

"So you think I'm being unfair by saying you aren't a real American because of your name?'

"Damned right! ...sir."

Fraser let that sink in with the men for a moment before replying. "You're exactly right, DelDuca. I take it back"

Slowly surveying his troops, the company commander raised his voice another notch. "Listen up, people. Hitler's trying to divide us by calling for Americans whose families came from Germany to join his troops. What little Adolf doesn't understand is that we're all Americans. Every single one of us.

This is our country he's invading. And we'll kick his ass back into the ocean together!"

The men started nodding and a couple of the Carolina boys added rebel yells.

"If I see anyone so much looking cross-eyed at another Bravo soldier, I will ship his ass out of here so fast his head will spin. Am I understood?"

"Yes sir!" Bravo Company yelled back, with Wolf Fleischer adding a knowing smile and a nod.

"OK, with that out of the way, what do you say we take a swamp?"

The men gave a good-natured groan, but quickly assembled into platoons for another day's work.

Berlin Germany
20:49 Hours, 21 April 1942

Tears streamed down Louisa Grafenberg's face as her crystalline soprano voice filled the auditorium. She was giving the performance of a lifetime, as the opera which she performed took on a new and ominous personal meaning.

Richard Wagner's *The Valkyrie* was the story of two doomed lovers – Siegmund and Sieglinde. When the opera's lead tenor playing Siegmund enters her home exhausted from battle, Louisa's Sieglinde revives and falls in love with the hero.

In the second act, Siegmund prepares to single-handedly defend his new love from the approaching warlord Hunding and his kinsmen. "Wait for our foe. Here he shall fall to my sword!" sang the tenor.

As Siegmund's words boomed out from the stage, Louisa recalled similar words her husband recently wrote her from an overseas battlefield. In his first letter in months, Helmut confirmed he was in *Amerika* and was thrilled to hear Louisa was expecting their first child. Then, her soldier spent the rest of the letter vainly attempting to convince the singer he was not in danger.

Please do not worry, darling. I am serving with the finest men I have ever met. With comrades like these, we can never lose. I swear I will return to you and our child.

When she gazed into the eyes of the tenor, Louisa saw her Helmut in mortal danger on a hellish battlefield of her imagination. Singing to the tenor, the soprano's heavenly voice conveyed genuine fear and anguish. "Hark! O hark! That is Hunding's horn! All his pack pursue in a mighty force, no sword can protect you against the hounds."

Madly thrashing in Siegmund's arms, Sieglinde stared wildly into a horrible future, tears streaming down her face. "There I see you, fearful sight!" the soprano sobbed. "The hounds take no heed of your hero's visage and fasten their fangs in your flesh. You fall and your sword shatters!"

When Hunding and his kinsmen surround Siegmund during the waning moments of the act, Sieglinde tries to sacrifice herself for her love: "Stop! Stop you men. Kill me instead!"

Heedless of her cries, the Norse god Wotan disarms Siegmund by shattering his sword, allowing Hunding to strike down her defenseless love. Staring vacantly across the stage, Louisa instead saw a faceless enemy shoot down her helpless husband on a foreign battlefield.

Later, as they waited for their curtain call at the end of the show, the members of the cast showered Grafenberg with compliments for the most emotionally wrought performances they ever heard. When the curtain parted, the audience rose as one to offer her a deafening ovation. Director von Karajan handed her the traditional bouquet of flowers, kissed her cheek and joined the other cast members in the applause. The exhausted singer curtsied mechanically in acknowledgement of the adulation and the applause rose even higher.

God protect Helmut, Louisa silently prayed, while nodding at an audience oblivious to her fear. Do not allow the enemy to strike down my husband so far away from home. Please send an angel to watch over him. Please.

349

CHAPTER 20

Colonel Koch liked to call his regimental outposts the tip of the spear, but Arpke's positions looked more like the ass end of the world. This was the worst terrain the paratroopers had ever seen. The platoon's thirty-two men were scattered in small penny packets across the tiny islands of land still left above the tea-colored swamp water after the rains. Arpke tried to set the outposts so they could see and support one another with small arms fire, but the terrain was so broken up with cypress trees and underbrush that every position was basically on its own. When the fog rolled in this morning, you could barely see twenty meters in any direction. The feeling of isolation was overpowering.

In order to travel between their islands, the paratroopers spent days laying logs as makeshift bridges. However, as the Helmut learned from personal experience, it sometimes took the skill of a circus high wire performer to navigate the slimy wood without tumbling into the muck.

This morning, after reviewing the day's plans, the lieutenant and his platoon sergeant sat down on a log for yet another "iron ration" breakfast of canned pork and crackers. Erich Schuster had a small fire going, cooking the food and brewing up some of the excellent *Amerikaner* coffee they liberated. Helmut knocked the mud off his boots against a pine tree and Erich handed him a steaming tin of the brew.

"Any word from regiment concerning the rumored *Ami* offensive?" the sergeant inquired.

"Not a damned thing."

Over the past week, the enemy started to probe their positions with increasing frequency. Yesterday, a section from second squad beat back a large patrol after a lengthy firefight. Something was definitely coming and soon.

"I have a hard time believing that the *Amis* would actually attack through this muck, when there is a nice highway leading to Charleston just north of us," Arpke observed hopefully, before blowing into the tin to cool the steaming liquid.

Schuster grunted, took off his helmet and futilely scratched at the lice setting up housekeeping on his scalp. "Maybe, maybe not. My Uncle Lutz fought the *Amis* in the Argonne Forest during the Great War and said they never did what you expected."

The lieutenant opened a package of crackers and stirred one into the coffee to soften it into something edible. He looked up quickly from the tin when the usual marsh sounds of songbirds and insects fell silent and were replaced by booming thunder rolling in from the distance.

"Incoming!" Schuster yelled, before grabbing Arpke's tunic and pulling his friend down into the nearest slit trench and on top of him.

Calling this shallow depression a trench was a joke. The water table was so high in the marsh that any sort of entrenchment on an island deeper than a half a meter oozed with water. The men were reduced to scraping away the thin top soil just deeply enough to mostly conceal a man lying on his belly. Mostly.

The *Amis* methodically walked their artillery across the islands where the paratroopers hugged the ground in their wholly inadequate burrows. The rounds falling into the surrounding marsh sent up plumes of water drenching the men, but did little other damage. Unluckier rounds splintered the stands of cypress trees around the islands, throwing spears of metal and wood into the defenseless soldiers below. The occasional round which fell directly on an island left little evidence of the previous residents.

When a salvo of artillery bracketed the lieutenant's island, bouncing him off the ground and into the air, Helmut started hysterically screaming for respite. "Holy Mary, Mother of God, please make it stop!" Neither the Holy Mother nor the *Amis* heeded his pleas, however. The artillery kept hammering away like the end of the world.

Great Cypress Swamp, South Carolina
06:18 Hours, 27 April 1942

The diminishing rumble of explosions in the distance made Bravo Company's situation frustratingly clear - Lieutenant Jim Fraser and his troops didn't have a prayer of keeping up with their artillery support. They were on their own.

The attack plan called for the infantry to closely follow an artillery barrage rolling through the Great Cypress Swamp, allowing the GIs could take out any surviving enemy positions before the Krauts had a chance to recover.

The staff brainiac who came up with this bright idea obviously never set foot in the Great Cypress. The heavy rains left behind nearly hip deep water through which to wade. The soft mud below sucked at their boots and unseen roots reached up to trip them, reducing Bravo's advance to a slow slog.

The racing artillery not only left Fraser and his men behind, but also an acrid blanket of white smoke and fog, concealing nests of trigger-ready Krauts. Under these conditions, crossing the swamp was like playing hide and seek, while blindfolded on a water-covered obstacle course, where the other players were trying to kill you. Wonderful.

Fraser jumped a little when a German rifle spoke somewhere to the right where third platoon ought to be. Squatting lower in the brackish water, he scanned the area to the front through his rifle sites. No Krauts. Nothing to shoot at. Just the gentle swirl of white mist.

Third platoon was not allowing the fact they couldn't see the enemy stop them, though. Punctuated with an occasional yell or curse, the men fired blindly into the fog. Finally, Sergeant Fleischer roared: "Cease fire, cease fire, goddammit! Only shoot when y'all can see a damned Kraut to shoot at."

After a moment or two, the shooting stopped and a nervous quiet returned.

Fraser allowed third platoon a chance to find their hidden German, before ordering Bravo to resume its advance. If individual platoons got snagged on Kraut positions and fell behind, the company could become hopelessly separated in this fog.

The company commander's patience was soon rewarded with the crack of a single shot from an American *Springfield* rifle. "Sarge, I got him," Corporal Stuart sang out. "All clear."

Bravo lurched forward again, sloshing through the black water, one laden step after another. If the company stopped every time they ran into a hidden German, Fraser sighed, this was going to be one long ass march.

Great Cypress Swamp, South Carolina
06:53 Hours, 27 April 1942

Helmut Arpke struggled to refocus while moving through a suddenly surreal world. The enemy artillery barrage left his ears ringing and eyes blinking against the stinging white fog floating over the marsh. The lieutenant could not hear or see much of anything else. For all he knew, he could be leading his men straight into an *Ami* ambush!

In case of enemy contact, Arpke's orders were for the platoon outposts to call in over the field phones with details of the advancing *Ami* units, then conduct an orderly withdrawal back to the regiment. After the enemy artillery blew his island's phone line to hell, the platoon leader's only alternative was to report back to regiment in person and hope the rest of his men did the same. Each surviving island of paratroopers was on its own.

The lieutenant's handful of paratroopers moved as carefully as possible back to the rear, but were forced to slosh through the marsh water as they struggled with each step to free their boots from the sucking mud below. Arpke's compromised ears could not hear the noise he and his men were making, but he was increasingly scared the enemy could and were closing in on his little band.

When two stands of cypress trees emerged through the mist to their front, the lieutenant raised his fist to halt the advance and studied the wooded clusters for an ambush. No sign of the *Amis*. Nothing looked out of place. *Need to keep moving.*

Waving his men forward, Arpke cautiously advanced between the trees to find the water shallowing and the ground below hardening, with the promise of an easier walk. Quickening his pace, Helmut suddenly pitched forward, with a splash and a yell. He blundered into a patch of what the locals called cypress knees - hard tree roots extending straight up out of the muck, but still hidden under the brown water. Nature's own perfect tanglefoot.

Arpke's curses attracted an unwelcome response from the cypress trees on the right. "Over there! The Krauts are over there!"

An *Ami* soldier walked out from the trees and took careful aim at the German lieutenant lying defenseless in the water.

Helmut held his breath and closed his eyes to await the unavoidable kill shot.

Instead, the rifle shot he heard was German. Snapping his eyes open, Arpke saw the *Ami* fall back and Erich bend over to grab his should straps. With a ferocious tug, the sergeant pulled his lieutenant off the wooden knobs and hurled them both back into deeper water.

The pair surfaced gasping for air in the middle of a furious firefight, Rifle rounds cracked all around them, one bullet glancing off Arpke's helmet, pushing it askew.

"Shit, Lieutenant, can you move?" Erich yelled.

"I cracked my ribs, not my legs. Let's go!" Helmut gasped, straightening out his helmet.

The pair furiously churned their legs into and out of the muck in a slow-motion jog and fell behind the first cover they saw – a big log on a small grassy knoll. Wiping the slime off his face, Arpke looked back to get a fix on his other men, but could not make out anything back in the fog. They needed to break this off.

Taking a painfully deep breath, the lieutenant bellowed: "Paratroopers, on me!"

The *Amis* responded first by firing unaimed shots in the general direction of his voice, one or two sprinkling them with clipped leaves and twigs from the tree above. Another long minute later, one of his two missing men limped out of the white.

"Hausmann?" Arpke softly asked.

The survivor shook his head and replied, "No. Dieter is gone, sir."

The paratroopers prided themselves on leaving no one behind, but the lieutenant could not justify recovering their fallen comrade with the swamp swarming with the enemy.

"How are *you* doing?"

"Some *Ami* bastard winged me, but I can keep up."

To demonstrate his ability to march, the surviving paratrooper took a big step forward, then promptly fell sideways into the water.

Arpke glanced back into the mist to ensure the splash did not attract any unwanted *Ami* attention, then asked Schuster to take an arm so they could stand and walk their wounded comrade. The paratroopers began a labored stagger through the cursed swamp. If navigating the mud and roots under the dark water was difficult alone, a trio of men attempting to walk through the muck in unison was at least three times as hard. To top it off, every misstep through the muck yanked on Helmut's battered ribs.

The crack of a rifle shot ricocheting off the water beside the lieutenant reminded him there were worse fates than a miserable march. The *Amis* had not yet given up their pursuit.

Arpke and Schuster swung around and plopped their wounded comrade down on a small grassy knoll, then prepared for action. The lieutenant looked over the other others and silently pointed at himself. The paratroopers nodded back. No one would fire before he did.

The pursuing enemy was not attempting to conceal his presence. After splashing through the swamp like a child learning to swim, a vague outline formed in the misty white.

Splashing? Aprke smiled with realization the ringing in his ears was gone and he could again hear the world around him. Thank God for small favors.

There was still this mess to survive, however. The platoon leader moved his finger from the trigger housing to the trigger and prepared to reward the advancing *Ami* with a short burst of lead to the gut, when a voice interrupted.

"God damn it, DelDuca, get your ass back in formation!" the voice hissed. "We have a deadline to keep."

"But, Sarge…"

"Right now!"

The figure slowly turned and disappeared into the mist, then a much louder sloshing sound drifted back. At least a platoon moving out with a purpose. No way his wounded band would beat the *Amis* back to dry land and friendly lines.

A glance to the east revealed the sun was peeking in through the trees and over the white. It also wouldn't be long before the morning warmth melted away the fog concealing them from the swarming enemy.

Paratroopers were used to being surrounded, but the young lieutenant had never faced a situation like this. How would he lead his men home?

New Hope Church and School, South Carolina
11:02 Hours, 27 April 1942

They really stepped into it this time, Lieutenant Fraser thought, as he ducked beneath the window to dodge another stream of Kraut machine gun fire chewing up the church. Bravo Company was hanging on by its fingernails as a couple hundred German paratroopers attacked from three sides.

The morning started out so promising. After a couple short firefights, the rest of the swamp crossing was uneventful. After emerging from the misty waters, Fraser's men easily pushed another mile north to the battalion objective – the New Hope Church and School.

The way this was supposed to work was the main body of the Thirtieth Division would attack along a creek to the west called Sandy Run and fix the German paratroop division there. Then, Fraser's regiment would cross the Great Cypress Swamp behind the Kraut defenses and cut off their retreat down the Jedburg Road.

The problem was Bravo was the only company to arrive at the objective on time. The rest were apparently still mucking around back in the swamp. For all Jim knew, his hundred-plus men were alone in the middle of several thousand German paratroopers!

Still, Fraser would be damned if he would give up the church without a fight. The company commander ordered his men to dig in around the structure and hold on until the rest of the regiment caught up.

The quick return of a scout down the Jedburg Road answered the question of whether the rest of the regiment or the enemy would arrive first. "There's a whole passel of Krauts comin down the road, LT," gasped the out of breath private.

"OK, Jackson, catch your breath and tell me how many Germans make up a passel," Fraser replied.

The private paused, then shamefacedly admitted, "I'm sorry, sir. I didn't exactly count 'em. They filled up the road for sure, so I thought I better get back here lickety split and let ya know."

"On observation post duty, your job is to observe. Next time, count first, then come back," the company commander instructed. "Now, go back to your platoon and get ready for a fight."

As the private scurried off, Fraser ordered the company top sergeant to get everyone into their holes and not to fire until he did.

The German paras with their baggy uniforms and round helmets emerged from the woods, marching in a dispersed formation down the Jedburg Road towards the church. Apparently unaware of the American swamp crossing, the Krauts didn't act as if they expected trouble. Well, they had trouble.

Fraser pointed at the gunner set up on a little rise, who nodded back and let her rip with his machine gun. Within seconds, every rifle of the two platoons spread out in slit trenches west of the church joined in like dogs in a yard furiously barking at approaching strangers.

After handful of German paras fell to the incoming bullets, the rest dropped as one and returned fire. No panic under ambush. They had obviously been through this before. While the Germans still enjoyed an advantage in automatic weapons, the Bravo boys were dug in behind cover. Standoff.

The company commander's slight smile of satisfaction disappeared when the church windows exploded inward. Finding himself sprawled across a fallen pew, Jim gently brushed the shards of glass from his face, then blinked slowly to ensue none of the jagged slivers made their way into his eyes. Thankfully, most of the glass flew over his head.

By the time Fraser peeked back over the window sill, the short German mortar barrage ended and a second company of Kraut paratroopers trotted in from the right, seeking to flank Bravo's defenses.

The lieutenant scrambled through the pews and out the back door of the church to the reserve platoon gathered outside. Discarding military formalities, Jim made a chopping motion with his arm towards a stand of trees on one side of the building and hollered, "Wolf, we have another company of visitors about two hundred yards that away. Stop em!"

"You heard the man," Sergeant Fleischer echoed. "Let's give the sons of whores a nice warm welcome."

As the platoon skirmish line disappeared into the greenery, Jim pulled back against the old familiar tug. He couldn't charge into battle with his old platoon. He was responsible for the entire company now and his place was back in the church issuing orders.

Returning to the shattered window, Fraser could hear, but not see the battle brewing up on the right. By the volume of small arms fire, third platoon seemed to be holding their own against the larger Kraut company.

Slowly panning his binoculars across the battlefield, the lieutenant's stomach fell. A third company of German paras were emerging from the woods on Bravo's left flank.

The Krauts now outnumbered Fraser's men three-to-one. Every one of his boys was fighting desperately to hold onto their assigned plot of dirt and there were no reserves left to counter the new threat.

As he fished around in his jacket pocket for a whistle to sound retreat, the darndest thing happened. The Krauts beat him to the punch and withdrew back into the woods surrounding the church, dragging their wounded with them, until they disappeared completely.

What? What the hell?

Jim bounded up the stairs two at a time into the steeple, his mind racing. The paratroopers had his boys on the ropes. What they were they up to?

The view from up top was excellent. He could see a mile or so in every direction. Far enough to answer all of his questions. A couple thousand Krauts were bugging out east to Summerville in long columns, covered by artillery landing along Sandy Run Creek in front of the main American force. One of the retreating enemy columns must have blundered into Bravo Company. When his boys refused to move out of the way, the Krauts simply pulled out and bypassed the church.

Down below, the men were cheering and jeering the retreating enemy. They had no idea how close they came to getting their asses kicked back into the swamp.

Let 'em celebrate. Bravo would need every ounce of bravado in the days ahead. These German paras knew their business better than those crazy bastards with the pirate insignia. Summerville would be a tough nut to crack.

Charleston, South Carolina
17:03 Hours, 27 April 1942

The air filling with the high whistle of falling bombs, Field Marshal Rommel dove onto the tarred roof of his headquarters and rolled on his back to look up at the sky. An awful day was about to became worse.

Before dawn that morning, *Amis* finally launched their offensive to toss his men back into the ocean. Four enemy infantry divisions attacked along all the anticipated routes, but only one was stopped. When the *Amerikaner* Fourth Division drove down the coast highway through the large forest to the north, threatening to overrun his outnumbered 71st Regiment, a massive *Kriegsmarine* naval bombardment broke up this enemy advance well short of Charleston.

That was the extent of the good news. The enemy Thirtieth Division flanked his paratroopers with an audacious attack through the swamps, then advanced with two other *Amerikaner* divisions behind an unexpectedly effective series of artillery barrages. The paras were forced to fall back toward the town of Summerville, enabling the *Amis* to make almost half the distance to Charleston in a single day!

What puzzled Rommel was the complete absence of enemy *panzers*. The German Army commander was sure the *Amis* fielded *panzer* divisions. He read the local newspapers reporting on the enemy training maneuvers over the past year. Yet, not a single enemy *panzer* made an appearance and the *Luftwaffe* reconnaissance flights had seen none behind their lines. Until the enemy showed his cards, the frustrated field marshal could not release his own *panzer* reserves to deal with the growing threat from the west.

The *Amerikaner* did not press their advantage, though. Enemy operations slowed to a halt late in the afternoon, allowing Rommel's men to complete their withdrawals largely unmolested to a new defensive line west of Summerville.

Without any further fires to put out, Rommel emerged from his headquarters onto roof of the old Charleston Market Hall to locate the source of the increasing drone from the north. The contrails of the final enemy bombing run of the day slowly made their way across the early evening sky straight towards Charleston.

The enemy air strategy was another puzzle to Rommel. While the *Amerikaner* Air Corps outnumbered his combined *Luftwaffe* and *Kriegsmarine* groups by nearly two-to-one, the *Amis* largely wasted their numerical advantage by dispersing their planes evenly across the front lines, instead of concentrating them at the point of greatest importance like the *Luftwaffe*.

The exception to this rule were the heavy bombing runs. The *Amis* did mass their B-17 bombers in morning raids against the German supply depots, but incomprehensibly sent them in without fighter protection. The big birds were covered with machine guns, but still remained slow, lumbering beasts. *Kriegsmarine* fighter pilots identified weaknesses in the B-17 defenses during the days following the invasion and used that knowledge to take a terrible toll on the enemy this morning. The *Amis* did not appear to learn their lesson. Far fewer B-17s arrived with the descending sun, again without fighter escort.

The field marshal watched as the aerial dance of death played out above him again. Braving the tracer lit streams of machine gun fire reaching out from the bombers, the gray ME-109s sliced through the enemy formation above. Three *Amerikaner* bombers quickly cartwheeled from the sky, taking one German fighter with them. This time, enemy discipline broke down completely. Panicked B-17 crews indiscriminately released their bomb loads overhead to gain speed and fled for home.

Rommel dove for the wholly inadequate cover of the market hall roof as columns of bombs obliterated neighboring homes, shaking the headquarters underneath him and tearing at his soul with jagged memories. Dying *panzers* from the cities of England to the deserts of Egypt. The lifeless eyes of his crushed driver. The screams and stench of his men burning alive. Oh God, the screams…

Erwin curled into a ball, clasped his hands over his ears and started sobbing uncontrollably.

After the last of the bombs detonated, the general lay there motionless as the memories faded into quiet oblivion, until the voice of one of his staff officers caused him to clench. "Sir, are you hurt?"

He continued to lay there, struggling to gather his wits, until his compromised position came into sharp focus. *I can't allow my men to see me this way!*

Rommel forced himself to his knees facing away from the concerned officer and quickly smudged the tears into his cheeks. Rising unsteadily to his feet, the field marshal struggled to resume the stoic demeanor of a German officer and walked back into the headquarters building without saying a word. The shaken man did not trust himself to speak.

Dawson Branch, South Carolina
23:19 Hours, 27 April 1942

Lieutenant Helmut Arpke was now convinced the old saying "it is always darkest before the dawn" was an undeniable fact. The moon set a half hour before and the platoon leader could barely see his surviving paratroopers crossing the stream right in front of him. The early morning quiet was broken with a yell and a splash as one of the men climbing the far bank slipped back into the stream. From that point, nothing was quiet.

Machine gun fire erupted from the left, hurling bright tracers and unseen lead into the unfortunate men crossing the stream. *German machine gun fire!* The paratroopers started yelling out the day's password and demands to cease fire, but the weapon pounded away. When the tracers worked their way over to Arpke on the near bank of the stream, he furiously dug his feet into the slick clay to retreat back into the woods, but only managed to slide closer to the stream and approaching death.

For a while, it seemed as if Helmut's luck had returned. This morning, the lieutenant's little band of paratroopers avoided capture or worse in the swamp by finding a dry island oasis in the brown water, sheltered by a stand of pine, to hide until the cover of nightfall returned.

Not long after sunset, Arpke's group emerged from the swamp without incident and quickly made their way to made their way to the old barn designated as the platoon rally point. However, the rickety structure stood empty and silent as a grave., with no sign of friends or foes. Did the *Amis* sweep the entire division apart from his handful of men?

The lieutenant stared into the deepening evening, contemplating his next move, when a soft bird song trilled out of the darkness. Wait. A song bird at night? Arpke squatted down by the door and hissed out the password of the day before. After a moment or two of silence, a paratrooper emerged from several stacks of hay bales laid across the center of an adjacent field and waved them over.

After his prodigal troopers entered this grass palace, squad leader Rudi Köhler and dozen other comrades swarmed them with broad smiles and claps on the back. The squad leader's group cleared the swamp in the morning, then ducked behind the hay bales short of the rally point as several hundred *Amis* followed them out of the brown water. The enemy did not clear the area until the early afternoon. By that time, they decided to wait to see if any friendly faces would emerge from the marsh before pushing on during the night.

Operating behind enemy lines was nothing new to the paratroopers. The trick was to find the path of least resistance to the objective. Arpke figured the division moved back to the Summerville area and the easiest route back to them would be through the tangled terrain on the edge of the swamp. After all, who else would go there if they could avoid it?

The lieutenant's intuition was correct. His men only came across two small groups of *Ami* infantry, both of whom were easy to bypass. These people were actually sleeping around roaring fires with only a couple men up providing security! However, tonight was not the night to make the enemy pay for their stupidity.

While exfiltrating around enemy positions was not difficult, re-entering friendly lines under these conditions was another matter entirely. When you went on patrol from fixed lines, the men you left behind knew when and where to expect your return. During an unplanned retreat through a pitch-black night, distinguishing friend from foe took experience and not a little luck.

Unfortunately, Arpke and his men enjoyed neither this night. The machine gun crew covering this stream were new replacements, who joined the division just days before it sailed for *Amerika*. Their first taste of combat was a precipitous retreat from a surprise attack. To these rattled men, every shadow looked like an enemy soldier moving in to kill them.

As he slid towards the bullets reaching out for him, Helmut felt someone grab his smock from above and yank him back up the slick stream bank as the machine gun finally ceased fire.

"Saving your life is becoming a bad habit," scowled Sergeant Schuster, looking down on his lieutenant sprawled out in the mud. "Excuse me, sir, but I have something for the stupid shits for brains behind that gun."

Schuster sprinted down the stream bed toward the machine gun crew like the wrath of God, smashing his fist into the face into the first one he reached. "You stupid ass holes! Why the hell didn't you give the challenge before firing?"

"But we..."

"You give me excuses!" screamed the platoon sergeant. "I should shoot you both." Then he cocked his machine pistol and pointed it at the sobbing men. "Hell, I am going to shoot you."

"Sergeant, stand down!" Arpke bellowed, before returning to a more measured tone. "There has been enough killing tonight, Erich. Go make sure the wounded are cared for. We are moving out in a half hour."

"Yes, sir," Schuster relented, with a less than respectful snarl. Turning back to the machine gun crew, the platoon sergeant kicked the kneeling men back onto the ground. "You two are the luckiest shits on Earth. Make sure I never see you again. Next time, there will not be an officer around to save your sorry asses."

A black mood rolled over Helmut as he watched Erich stomp off to carry out his orders. War is bad enough without losing comrades to their brothers' guns.

CHAPTER 21

Edisto River Bridge, Highway 17, South Carolina
06:43 Hours, 28 April 1942

Staff Sergeant Mike O'Malley lay as low as humanly possible behind the turret of the bouncing M3 *Stuart* tank, flinching at the cracks and clangs of incoming Kraut bullets. He was the sole survivor of a four-man section of engineers riding tanks straight through the Kraut trenches to the prize of this sector – the Highway 17 bridge over the Edisto River. Mike didn't much like his own chances of making it through this shit storm.

When the *Stuart* ground to a sudden halt, O'Malley made a practiced rolled off tank's deck and hit the ground on his feet, only to have a Kraut machine gun rip his rifle and a couple fingers out of his right hand. As the *Stuart* returned fire down the highway, Mike stumbled beneath the bridge clutching his torn hand, struggling not to scream.

At the edge of the river, the sergeant squatted and looked around for more trouble. He wished he still had his rifle, but the damned thing wouldn't be any use without a thumb and trigger finger. No sign of the Krauts, though. Better get to work before trouble did arrive.

Alternatively pulling himself up with his left hand and then hooking his right arm around the pilings, O'Malley awkwardly made his way up to the bottom of the bridge, where the engineer found what he expected – a bundle of detonation cords running under the bridge to unseen explosives. The Krauts had no intention of allowing the U.S. Army to take this bridge in one piece.

The engineer grabbed wire snips off of his belt and went to work. The sergeant won a place on this suicide mission because he was the fastest in the engineer company at slicing and splicing wire. But that was with a good right hand. Cutting the cords with a slippery, blood-covered left was fucked up beyond all recognition. After every squeeze, the snips would almost slip out of his hand. Mike had to carefully push them against cement bridge to reseat them in his palm to cut the next cord.

Still, he methodically attacked the diminishing bundle. Four left…three…two…

Then, his left knee exploded. O'Malley never heard the shot which took his leg out at the joint. Now, he couldn't think about anything else, shrieking and dropping the wire snips into the river so he could grab at the wound.

When his head cleared, Mike found himself hanging over the black river, with his right arm hooked around the two remaining detonation cords and his left hand holding the bloody mess which used to be his knee.

The shattering agony reduced the Mike's thoughts to broken shards.

Can't cut the last two cords without my snips.

If I keep hanging here, the Krauts blow the bridge and game over.

If I let go and drop into river, maybe I can swim far enough away to survive the explosion.

Mike began to release his right arm when one of detonation cords snapped, leaving him dangling from the remaining line. Wait. I can still do this!

The sergeant gently released his knee, reached up to grab the cord with both arms and then started bouncing up and down. The pain exploded from his hand and knee each time the cord snapped him back toward the bridge. Unbearable pain.

Come on, come on, COME ON!

Finally, the damned cord snapped, plunging O'Malley into the river below. Engulfed by inky cold, weighted down by exhaustion and agony, he sank in and out of consciousness. Moving hurts so bad, he dimly thought. So easy to fall asleep. So easy to let it all go…

But consciousness came flooding back again when O'Malley tried to take a breath and instead inhaled the foul river water. Thrashing to the surface with his remaining good limbs, Mike gagged and coughed out the tea-colored liquid, until he found the sweet air again.

Along with the air came voices. Familiar voices. The rest of the engineer company must have caught up.

"There he is! Hold on Sarge, we're coming to get you."

Splashes were followed arms on both sides lifting him up out of the water and onto the shore.

"Shit, he's bleeding. Medic! We need a medic over here!"

"Just lay still, Sarge, everything will be OK"

O'Malley just lay back and let his buddies tend to him. A prick on his thigh, followed by a warm morphine glow, gradually displaced the pain. Other hands sprinkled sulfa on his wounds and wrapped them in field bandages.

A few minutes later, strangers with red cross arm bands lifted him onto a stretcher and into the back of a truck. Before they closed the rear doors, the groggy sergeant sat up on his elbows and watched a parade of tanks crossing a very intact Highway 17 bridge.

Mike laid back and smiled. You did it, you son of a bitch. You did it.

Charleston, South Carolina
09:39 Hours, 28 April 1942

When the clatter of the headquarters communications section picked up sharply, the field marshal strolled over to his chief of staff. "We may have some activity south along the Edisto River, Sir," General Ludwig Crüwell reported without expression, handing his commander a sheaf of teletype messages.

Rommel flipped through the messages, then squeezed the bridge of his nose between his thumb and forefinger. Typical understatement by his taciturn chief of staff. The Seventeenth Infantry Division was reporting hundreds of *Amerikaner panzers* were crossing at multiple points along the river forming his southern flank!

The Army commander anticipated an enemy *panzer* attack for the past two days, but not from the south. The Edisto River only offered two minor bridges and the territory between the river and Charleston was a choked morass of forest and marsh he nicknamed the Warren. Hardly ideal *panzer* country.

Because of the inhospitable terrain, Rommel defended several kilometers of the Edisto with only two regiments of the Seventeenth Infantry concentrated at the two bridges. The remainder of the river was covered with company-size patrols moving along the Willtown Road. The field marshal took a calculated risk reducing his southern defenses in order to place all of his *panzer* forces in reserve rather than on the front lines.

The *Amis* called his bluff just as the Germans did the French in 1940 when they attacked through the "impassible" Ardennes Forest. Rommel's Seventh *Panzer* Division, along with the bulk of the German mechanized forces, stormed through those sparsely defended woods into the enemy rear. A month later, France had fallen. The field marshal was hardy about to allow history to repeat itself at his own expense.

Ordering his staff to gather around, the field marshal got right to the point with his characteristic bluntness. "Gentlemen, I believe the Edisto crossing is the main enemy attack. Here is my plan to destroy the *Amis*."

Rommel started firing off orders to deploy the *panzer* reserve with taps of his finger on the map spread across the table. "Gentlemen, by noon I want Seventh *Panzer* ready to cross the Blands and Bacon bridges over the Ashley River, and the Gross Deutschland Regiment to concentrate in the vicinity of the Warren and Capwell crossroads south of Charleston."

"When the *Ami panzer* general sticks his head out in the Warren, we will cut it off with a pincer movement between our forces," Rommel concluded, with a chop of his hand on the table.

The field marshal kept studying the map after his staff left to refine and distribute the commander's concept. Nice plan, he thought, but we still need time to execute it.

Rommel turned to his chief of staff. "Crüwell, get the Seventeenth on the radio. Tell General von Zangen help is on the way, but he must hold the Edisto line at all costs."

Giving his commander a knowing look, this chief of staff inquired, "Field Marshall, will you be taking the armored car or the scout plane to the front?"

"The ground visibility in the Warren is awful," Rommel observed. "Have the airfield fire up the *Storch* and be ready to fly in fifteen minutes."

Parker's Ferry, South Carolina
10:43 Hours, 28 April 1942

General George S. Patton fumed.

The corps started the morning off with a running start, his two armored divisions executing a picture-perfect series of river crossings along the Edisto. The First Armored Division pulled off a particularly spectacular raid to capture the Highway 17 bridge. Patton wrote himself a reminder to put the magnificent bastard who pulled off that feat in for the Congressional Medal of Honor.

Despite enjoying detailed knowledge of the backcountry, the armored division sprints for Charleston stumbled into long traffic jams just a mile or so north of the river. Now, the forward units were screaming for artillery and air support.

Patton jammed on his helmet and stormed out of the command tent to his armored car. The corps commander would see for himself what the hell was wrong and kick some butts to get things moving again.

As his driver sped up the highway, the general mulled the situation. The German Seventeenth Infantry Division only had two regiments of infantry standing in the way of Patton's two armored divisions. His boys enjoyed a three-to-one advantage. At best, the enemy commander could concentrate his limited forces on the two highways and a handful of lesser northbound roads. What about the surrounding woods?

When they stopped at the ass end of the Highway 17 traffic jam, Patton leaned over the side and ordered a bug-eyed second lieutenant to have his tank platoon fall in behind the armored car to provide fire support for a reconnaissance behind enemy lines. Then, the general took his swagger stick and pointed his own driver to take a left down a neglected dirt track.

Just as he figured, the only defenders of this backwoods road were the grasping tree branches his armored vehicle snapped off without pausing and the low hanging Spanish moss brushing his helmet and goggles. The corps commander's anger burned hotter with each turn. There wasn't a damned Hun in sight! Had his commanders forgotten everything he taught them about maneuver?

After a quick jog back to the right, Patton fell like an avalanche on the Highway 17 traffic jam. The first unfortunate officer the corps commander came across was one Colonel Raymond McQuillan, the Combat Command A commander for First Armored Division. Known to his men as "Old Mac," the colonel was a mild mannered and cautious man, who was completely unprepared for what was descending upon him.

McQuillan was bent over a map, nonchalantly discussing possible targets with his artillery battalion commander, when he looked up at a glowering Patton and offered a startled salute.

"Colonel, give me a situation report."

"Uh… yes sir." Pointing north up the highway, McQuillan recounted, "A company of Third Armored Battalion is engaged with a battalion of Kraut infantry just past that hill. We don't have enough of our own infantry to clear them out of the woods, so I am requesting division artillery clear the enemy position."

The colonel was right about the lack of infantry. After the maneuvers last year, Patton warned the brass they needed combine the two armored divisions into one big armored corps, then beef up the tanks with GIs for close quarters combat like this. He nagged Marshall into granting his first wish, but not the second. Consequently, all the Huns needed to do to deny his tanks a road was to drop trees or sprinkle anti-tank mines across it, then defend the obstacle with too many dug-in infantry for the handful of GIs riding the tanks to root out.

Thankfully, there were plenty of other roads.

"What's the rest of your unit doing, Colonel?"

"Umm…They're waiting on the highway to continue the advance."

"Why on God's green Earth are they not in the battle?" Patton nearly screamed.

"Sir," McQuillan whined, "the gap between the swamps up ahead is not wide enough to send the rest of vehicles forward."

George mentally kicked himself. *Why didn't I spot and fire this blockhead before the battle?* "Colonel, did it occur to you to scout the area for a way around the enemy flank?"

"Uh.. That was the next thing only my list after calling in the artillery."

"I've already been there. There are two good dirt roads just west of here that the Hun sons of bitches neglected to defend. Get around their flank and kick them in the ass!"

McQuillan just stood there like a trapped deer looking at an oncoming mountain lion.

"Colonel, if you don't get your men moving in the next five minutes, I will fire your ass and replace you with someone who knows his job. Do I make myself clear?" As the red-faced colonel started to scurry away, Patton added, "And put on your damned helmet!"

The corps commander waited until he was satisfied CCA was on the move again, then he took off to light a fire under the next combat command.

Summerville, South Carolina
13:13 Hours, 28 April 1942

The Lieutenant Jim Fraser was crouched low and peeking out of the window of a shot up living room, when the floor next to him began to rise. A throw rug slipped away, revealing a slowly opening trap door down to the cellar. Fraser jumped away and pointed his rifle down at the unexpected threat.

"Come out now with your hands up!"

"Don't shoot!" a woman's voice begged from the darkness. "It's just me and my kids."

A heavy-set blonde slowly emerged, followed by a plainly terrified boy and girl, all with their arms reaching high into the air. Jim slowly exhaled and lowered his rifle. He almost shot a mother and her kids.

Wait a minute. "Lizzy Bronson, is that you?"

The woman looked back doubtfully.

"I'm Jim Fraser, Florrie's husband. We met at church a couple years back during a visit with Bonnie Sue Morgan."

A dawn of recognition crossed the woman's face and she lunged forward and hugged the Army officer. "Lordy, it's so good to see a familiar face." Lizzie released him and smiled at the other GIs in the living room. "It's good to see all you Army boys."

"Lizzie, have you seen Florrie or Bonnie Sue since the invasion?"

"I think so… Yes, I'm sure of it. They were at the church a couple weeks ago trading for food."

Trading for food? It suddenly dawned on Jim that no food or anything else has been moving in and out of Charleston for weeks now.

Fraser shrugged off his rucksack, pulled out a C-ration can and extended it to the mother. "I know it isn't much, but hopefully it'll help."

"That's OK, Jimmy. We have food hidden away in the cellar."

Tucking the can back into his pack, Jim asked, "How did Florrie look? Was she OK?"

"Yeah, she's alright." Lizzie reassured. "I'm sorry I don't have more news for y'all, but moving around town was hard after the Germans arrived and darn near impossible since the fighting started."

"Ayuh, I'll bet. Speaking of which, you need to take your kids and get outta town and away from the fighting."

"No sir, we are staying put where we have food and a roof over our heads."

"I'm serious, Lizzie. You've gotta leave."

"Jimmy, bless your heart, but you don't know what it's like for people on the road. I could tell you stories about others who tried to escape and were forced to return." The smile ran away from her face. "It's bad out there, especially for women."

"Anyway, now that you boys are here, we're safe enough. I'm staying," the woman asserted, with her hands planted on her ample hips.

Jim thought about arguing some more, but decided against it. Lizzie was right. There was no safe place for miles.

"OK, I'm leaving Kowalski here with you until we finish clearing the block."

"That's very kind of you. I'll l whip up something to eat in the kitchen."

Whip something up in a kitchen in the middle of a battlefield? Crazy new world.

"Lizzie, who lives in the next house down."

"Herm and Dolly Parker used to live there, but they left when the Germans landed in Charleston."

Good, we won't have to worry about more civilians there. "Thanks. You and your kids stay safe."

"Sure thing. Say hi to Florrie when you find her."

Jim smiled back at the pleasant thought. "I sure will."

The lieutenant motioned for the rest of his men to follow him out of the house.

Summerville, South Carolina
14:11 Hours, 28 April 1942

Lieutenant Arpke waved his men into the house to clear the rooms of any *Ami* troops who might be at home. After creeping down the main hallway, Franz Zunkley peeked around the corner into the kitchen. The back of the corporal's head exploded into a red stream as an enemy bullet passed through.

Sergeant Schuster pulled the ignition cord on a potato masher and threw the grenade into the kitchen. Immediately after the explosion, he held his machine pistol out into the doorway and fired an extended burst blindly inside. Peeking around the corner, Erich paused and cursed.

Arpke walked over and looked inside the kitchen. After killing Zunkley, the *Ami* soldier fled, leaving behind a mother and her two children to face the consequences. The woman was dead, but her children were still clinging to life. The boy was wide-eyed with pain and struggling to breathe with blood bubbling in his mouth. The little girl was mercifully unconscious, a bullet wound furrowed across her skull and covering her face in blood.

After a quick examination, the platoon medic shook his head. "I'm sorry, sir, I cannot help these children. They are too badly wounded. Maybe the aid station?"

"Lieutenant," interrupted a voice behind him. "The company commander is outside and needs to speak with you immediately,"

Arpke looked over to Schuster, who was staring helplessly at the children. "Come on, Erich. I am sure the old man has new orders for us. Maybe he can help the little ones."

This new campaign was turning into a slaughter house, with death waiting in every room. After the friendly fire screw up this morning, Helmut's platoon was reinforced back to full strength with stragglers from other units, only to lose another half dozen shoving back an *Ami* push down this road to Summerville. Now the children. Mother Mary save us.

Leaning over a map spread over a picnic table, Senior Lieutenant Wulf von Plessen looked up and smiled at his approaching platoon leader. "It's good to have you back again, Helmut. Your attack here did the trick. Looks like the *Amis* have packed it in, at least for a couple hours."

Pointing at the map, Arpke reported: "Sir, I have my men reinforcing the houses here, here and here. In a couple hours, we will be dug in tight."

"Good thinking, but don't waste your time digging. We are moving again."

Von Plessen removed his helmet and lit an *Amerikaner* cigarette. "The engineers have finished fortifying the buildings along Ninth Avenue in Summerville and the regiment will be falling back into the new accommodations starting at 15:00."

Helmut felt something inside him snap. "Pull back? You cannot be serious sir! I just lost another six men taking these houses from the *Amis* and now division wants me to give them back?"

The smile left the company commander's face and his voice went cold. "Lieutenant, I am no happier than you about pulling back, but the Field Marshal himself gave these orders."

"Look at the map," ordered von Plessen. "We are facing an *Ami* division at our front and enemy *panzers* have broken across the Edisto River behind is. The division is forming a 360-degree defense of Summerville because we may be cut off at any time. Do you see now?"

"I apologize for losing my temper," sighed Helmut. "I understand the situation. I am just tired of losing good men and ground to the *Amis*."

"We all are," the company commander commiserated.

"Helmut, when you get to the new positions, keep reinforcing them the best you can. The *Amis* seem to have automatic artillery which can plaster any place they like with as many rounds as they like," von Plessen said, shaking his head slowly. "I have never seen anything like it in France or England. No matter the cost, we must hold this line until Rommel can throw the enemy tanks back across the Edisto."

As the company commander refolded his map, Arpke asked: "Sir, there are two badly wounded children in the house. Would it be possible to evacuate them to the aid station?"

"I'm sorry, no. We do not have enough medical supplies for our men."

As the company commander strode away, Arpke turned to ask Schuster to gather the squad leaders to receive orders, but the platoon sergeant was already walking into the house. *Erich probably read my mind again.*

Walking slowly back towards the house thinking about how to execute the latest retreat, Helmut jumped when he heard two shots go off inside. Sprinting through the back door, he found Erich walking out the kitchen with a pistol in his hand and tears running down his face.

"The children are no longer suffering. They are with God."

Helmut fought back his own tears and nodded back to his friend. *Better this way.*

Summerville, South Carolina
16:08 Hours, 28 April 1942

As she made her way down Main Street to the church, Florrie cringed at the sound of explosions a mile or so down the road. Every night she prayed for the Army to arrive before they ran out of food, but now that the Army finally arrived, would the family survive the coming battle?

Glancing at her watch, she picked up her pace. Only a little over an hour before the German nighttime curfew. The only remotely safe time to move around town to take care of necessities was after the fighting around town started to die off in the late afternoon. Even during this twilight, the Germans were getting increasingly trigger-happy the closer the Army got to Summerville.

Taking a turn off Main and around a row of overgrown shrubs, Florrie almost fell on her face. She looked down and found her foot wedged under the body of a dead woman sprawled out in a pool of drying blood. She gently withdrew her foot and wiped the tacky red goo off her shoe onto the green spring grass, before walking past without looking back.

Did the poor woman have family who would check up on her? Or were her children waiting alone at home with no one left to care for them?

Dismissing these grim thoughts, Florrie re-focused her mind on the needs of her own family. She didn't consider herself a callous woman, but it was amazing what horrible things a body could get used to.

The crowd at the church was larger than usual. Putting aside Jesus's admonitions against allowing money changers in the house of God, Minister McConaughey set up a market in the church to give his increasingly desperate flock a place to obtain food and other basics. The preacher assured his congregation their Savior would understand and forgive them this trespass.

As the parishioners ran out of things to trade, black marketeers made up the shortfall. Farming families brought whatever the Germans did not steal and hunters butchered game from the woods south of town. Occasionally, some daring men from outside the occupied areas would sneak through the lines with precious commodities like sugar and flour, which had all but vanished in town.

Florrie carried a big carpetbag, which was empty apart from the last of her jewelry she hoped to exchange for a couple day's worth of food and sundries. When the German paratroopers left for the front a month ago, they took their extra food with them. The family reduced their meals to two and now one…if they were lucky. Florrie lost all of the extra weight she used to jokingly call her "baby fat" and the girls were worryingly thin.

The tables set up around the church community room offered slim pickings. Worse still, the farmers and hunters refused Florrie's jewelry and demanded necessities their own families needed. After arguing, then begging for food without success, the mother was close to tears. How was she going to feed her kids tonight?

After sharing her plight, Minister McConaughey took pity on her. In exchange for allowing outsiders to sell their goods in the church, the preacher was taking a cut of the food to provide for the most destitute among his flock. McConaughey gave her three potatoes for supper and apologized that he couldn't do more.

After profusely thanking her benefactor, Florrie carefully placed the precious food in her bag and turned to face a large man loaded down with two oversized suitcases.

"Pardon me, ma'am."

"Why Ben Stockton, don't you recognize me?" she teased.

The man stood there and squinted at her for a moment, before dropping his bags and giving her a big hug.

"Oh good Lord, is that you, Florrie? I almost didn't recognize you."

"Don't fret none. I have lost some weight."

"Hasn't everyone," Ben agreed.

"So what are ya doing here so far from home?" she asked.

The Goose Creek Stocktons lived north of town along Lewis Creek. Publicly, they were hunters and fishers. In reality, they made most of their money selling moonshine. The clan went into bootlegging back during Prohibition and never stopped.

Ben nodded her over to an open table and unloaded his liquid wares on a table inside by way of explanation. "The war isn't all bad," he acknowledged. "Demand for the family blend skyrocketed in the occupied territory since the Krauts arrived and stole all the official booze."

Taking a seat, Ben turned the tables. "Now, I have a question for you, cousin. Why in tarnation didn't you get out before the Krauts arrived?"

"It's complicated," Florrie sighed. "We thought the Army would get to Summerville before the Germans. By the time we tried to leave, it was too late."

Ben looked around to ensure no one was eavesdropping. "Listen. After selling moonshine at places like this, I guide folks who want to escape the occupied territory back home with me, then boat them up Goose Creek to the American lines at Moncks Corner. I have one couple lined up already. Would you and yours like to come along."

"Oh God, yes!" Florrie exclaimed louder than she intended, before lowering her voice. "There are five of us. How much would it cost?"

"Well, I'll give you the family discount. Just enough to cover provisions."

Florrie pulled the jewelry out of her pocket and placed it on the table. "I don't have any cash left. Will this be enough?"

"For you, cousin, for you," Ben grinned, as he deftly swept the jewelry off the table and onto his lap. "Do ya know the old Jones place by Sawmill Branch?"

"Sure, it's just down the road a piece from where we're living."

"Be there tomorrow night, just before midnight."

Edisto River, South Carolina
17:04 Hours, 28 April 1942

Everything is taking too long, the field marshal agonized.

Rommel spent most of the day pacing one of the Charleston airfield hangers, waiting for the skies to clear so his scout plane could take off. The *Luftwaffe* and the *Ami* Air Corps engaged in a ferocious battle for air superiority above the only German air base. Fighters slashed at one another in looping dogfights. Anti-aircraft batteries hammered away at the enemy aircraft above, while struggling to avoid shooting down their own boys. Meanwhile, down below, exhausted ground crews doggedly worked to keep the runways open, dragging off wrecked aircraft and filling in bomb craters.

It was late afternoon before his pilot, Kurt Asendorf, seized a lull in the hostilities to get the *Storch* into the air, lifting off form a field of grass beside the main landing strip. The plane swung south for a quick run across the reserve staging areas, but Rommel's *panzers* were nowhere to be found. Working back north in a zig zag pattern, the field marshal found his missing vehicles miles snarled on backwoods trails well short of their objectives.

"Must be the damned maps!" Rommel growled to himself.

Germany did not possess any small-scale maps of the *Amerikaner* state of South Carolina. The operational commanders were using road maps requisitioned from local gasoline stations, which showed no detail of the Warren between the Edisto and Ashley rivers, apart from two blue highways cutting across white featureless paper. The tactical officers were only provided with hand sketches of the major roads.

The units spread across the Edisto and tasked with navigating the Warren complained bitterly about this shortfall, but his overworked staff always had more critical fires to put out. Now, that neglect raged into a crisis-level forest fire.

Rommel ordered Asendorf to fly south again until they found the enemy front lines. The trip took less than two minutes. While isolated pockets of the Seventeenth Infantry Division clogged up the few developed roads in the Warren, dozens of *Amerikaner panzers* were bypassing the roadblocks, snaking north along dirt trails towards Charleston.

As the field marshal contemplated his deteriorating position, machine gun bullets suddenly stitched the thin floor of the aircraft, ripping the binoculars from his hand and scattering shards of lens around the cabin.

Before Rommel could reach for the intercom switch, Asendorf's voice crackled into the field marshal's headset. "Sir, if we are going to fly over this many *Amis*, we need to gain some altitude and become less of a target."

"Very well, Kurt. Let's go home. I have a train to get back on its tracks."

As the *Storch* made a wide turn back north and rose to cruising altitude, the pilot started to radio the airfield and let out a shriek. Death lurked above as well as below. An *Ami* fighter dove unobserved out of the late afternoon sun and launched a burst of machine gun fire into *Storch's* engine and pilot. Smoke filled the cabin, as the plane lost altitude.

"Sir, I took one in the leg," the pilot groaned over the intercom. "I can still fly, but our bird can't. Brace for a hard landing!"

When intercom shut off, the engine followed suit. The only sound left was the the wind through the bullet holes puncturing the fuselage, a whistle which steadily increased as the descent accelerated.

Asendorf struggled to keep the *Storch's* nose up and on a glide path for a clearing, which looked far too small and was coming up far too fast. Just before reaching this destination, however, the pilot lost consciousness and control over the wounded bird.

Rommel braced himself for impact the best he could and screwed his eyes shut.

The *Storch* plowed into the forest, losing its wings to the treetops, then ricocheting off a tree trunk before slamming into the ground.

CHAPTER 22

Summerville, South Carolina
00:13 Hours, 29 April 1942

Lieutenant Fraser joined the other company commanders by a fire outside the battalion supply tent, tucked his helmet under an arm and scratched the stubble on his cheek. The fire was warm, but the conversation left him chilled.

"There's nothing these Kraut sons of bitches won't stoop to," Captain Bill Walters grumbled.

"What're you talking about, sir?" Fraser asked.

"Haven't you heard? After they pushed us back yesterday, the Krauts threw grenades on top of a woman and her kids in their own kitchen. When the grenades weren't enough to kill 'em, those damned animals shot the kids in the head."

"On the road we were clearing houses on yesterday?"

"Yeah."

Oh…God…no.

"Do you know their names?"

"Uhh, Bronson, I think. Yeah, that's it." Walters looked up from the fire and over at Fraser. "Why, did you know 'em?"

Before Jim could respond, Major Matt Moore raised the flap of the tent and waved his company commanders inside. The officers gathered around a map of Summersville lying on a crate next to a kerosene lantern. Firing up a cigar, the battalion commander began his briefing.

"Gentlemen, on our right, 119th Regiment moved from Jedburg and hit the outskirts of Summerville yesterday. They got their noses bloodied up pretty bad. The German paras have turned the place into a fortress. The houses are reinforced with sandbags and surrounded with barbed wire. Kraut machine guns have lines of fire down every street."

Moore took a couple puffs and spit out a bit of tobacco onto the dirt floor. Pointing his cigar had at the map, the major continued, "At 07:00, the division is going to attack in force here, here and here."

Looking back up at his tired officers, Moore concluded with some welcome news. "We won't be attending this party. Since first battalion been in the lead since this thing kicked off, regiment is going to move us back into reserve tomorrow. We need to be ready if called, but your boys can get some rest in the meantime."

The men won't be broken up hearing that news, Fraser thought.

"Meanwhile, the old man is tired of his boys fighting and dying for yards, so every piece of available artillery is going hit the Krauts for an hour before the division attack."

"Excuse me, Major," Fraser interrupted. "What about the civilians? My men have families in Summerville."

"Jim, the word from the division intelligence shop is that nearly all the civilians left when the Germans arrived."

"Pardon my language, but you know that's bullshit. We've been running into civilians since we crossed the Big Cypress. Some of them are dying alongside our troops."

The other company commanders nodded in agreement.

"Yeah, I hear what y'all are saying," Moore sighed. "My mom and dad are probably still in Charleston."

The battalion commander took another puff from his cigar. "Listen, there's nothing else the old man can do. Either we hit the Germans with everything we have and risk losing civilians or we lose our troops and the fight. I know every one of us would gladly give our lives to save our families, but the only sure way to save them is to win this damned war."

The major made sense. There was no choice. Yet, none of that relieved the growing terror Jim felt for his family. Not one little bit.

Walking back to the Bravo Company positions, Jim started to sob and then fell to his knees at the side of the road. He wasn't much of a religious man. On the rare occasion he went to church and prayed, it was to thank God for the blessings in his life. He never thought to ask for anything more. Tonight, he would.

"Gawd, please look after Florrie and my girls. Give them strength and protect them." Jim took a deep breath before making his final request. "If you have to take someone, take me and spare them. Please Lord, I'm begging You. Save my family."

Horse Savanna swamp, South Carolina
01:02 Hours, 29 April 1942

Rommel woke up feeling like a crumpled newspaper jammed into an overfull rubbish bin. He could hardly move. Everything was dark and everything hurt.

After two or three mighty tugs, he freed his right arm and delicately touched his eyes. They were glued shut under a crusty goo of dried blood. Erwin felt around his head until he found the source. The gash was painful, but no fresh flow of blood.

After scratching the drying blood off, Rommel pulled his eyelids open, blinked several times and looked around. Day had turned to night and he found himself cocooned in the crushed wreckage of the *Storch* scout plane.

Pulling on a low hanging tree branch with his free arm and kicking against the cockpit floorboard with his cramped legs, he popped free and ungracefully fell to the ground on his side.

Erwin's head throbbed and swam. He closed his eyes for a moment and waited for the dizziness to pass. His head must have taken a good knock during the crash. Better take care not to make it worse.

After a few moments, the field marshal gingerly rose to his feet and surveyed his surroundings. The *Storch* came to earth in a forest of tall pine clogged with brush. No visible roads or paths. The chorus of night insects continued unabated, so no one was moving around nearby. Their position should be secure for the moment.

Rommel approached the *Storch's* front cockpit and his pilot Kurt Asendorf looked back at him in obvious pain. The field marshal vaguely recalled the pilot saying he was wounded just before the plane went down.

He opened the glass cowling, reached under Kurt's arm pits and pulled him out as gently as possible. Asendorf had taken a bullet in the side of the thigh, but the wound was not bleeding much. After bandaging the leg, Rommel disappeared into the forest and returned with a long, fairly straight stick.

"Kurt, I need to reassume command, but I do not want to leave you behind. Can you lean on this pole and walk out?"

With his commander's assistance, the pilot got to his feet and gingerly tested his wounded leg, hobbling around the clearing. "Sir, my leg is not broken. I should be able to manage."

"Good man, follow me."

Using the north star as a guide, the commander crept and the pilot hobbled in the general direction of the Seventh *Panzer* Division staging area.

After a half hour, they finally came across a road. Ordering Kurt to stay hidden in the trees, Erwin cautiously approached for a closer look. The normally packed dirt surface was torn up by heavy vehicle tracks and tires. But whose vehicles?

The two men stayed under cover about ten meters into the forest and followed the road for a short time until they heard hushed voices ahead. Rommel crawled quietly forward. Before seeing the men ahead, he could smell the smoke of their cigarettes. *Amerikaner* cigarettes.

The field marshal very slowly pushed the tall grass aside and looked in on the *Amis*. There were a dozen of them on the road – half asleep around a truck and half on lax sentry duty. Probably the advance patrol of an enemy *panzer* division.

If this is the forward edge of the Ami lines, then we are getting close to our own. We need to work our way past this group first.

Gently releasing the grass, Rommel slowly backed away until he felt a fallen branch give way under his boot, with what sounded to him like a thunderous crack. To hide from any eyes drawn by the sound, he quickly fell to the ground and rolled against a patch of underbrush.

"Hey Mike, did you hear something out there?"

"Yeah, something's rustling around. Probably a wild pig. This place is full of 'em."

"I dunno. I think we should check it out."

The two enemy soldiers did not have far to go before they were literally on top of the field marshal. The tall one stepped on Rommel's hand and looked around. Clenching his teeth against the pain across his fingers, the German curled his free hand around his Lugar pistol, hoping the *Ami* did not think to look down. After what seemed to be an eternity, the enemy soldiers returned to their post on the road, satisfied there were no Germans around. They would never know how close they came.

Rommel lay there for a moment and flexed his throbbing hand, before working his way back to Kurt. The Army commander and pilot continued past the *Ami* position for another half hour before sighting the angular shadow of another vehicle in the road. Rommel instantly recognized this shadow as the rear of a one of his SdKfz 222 armored cars.

The field marshal gently called out the password of the day and asked to approach. The sound of the safeties being switched off on nearby rifles was followed by a hissed command to advance to be recognized. Rommel raised his hands and emerged onto the road. The outline of a German soldier walked up, closely examined his bloodied face and suddenly sprang to the position of attention.

"My God! Field Marshal, are you all right? We all thought you were dead."

"I need to clean up, but I am fine," the commander reassured the soldier. "However, I need a medic to tend to my pilot back there in the woods."

The soldier trotted back to his comrades, called for the medic to come up and passed on the news. "It's Rommel. The Field Marshal is back from the dead!"

Summerville, South Carolina
06:12 Hours, 29 April 1942

Like clockwork, the thunder of battle commenced with the morning twilight. The hungry family around the dining room table ignored the racket and instead concentrated on the last of the grits Bonnie Sue was ladling from the pan. Two tablespoons each and a big glass of water were just enough to keep the hunger pangs away, at least for a while.

Savoring her first bite, Florrie concluded she could get used to almost anything. While she wasn't quite used to the sounds of war, she wasn't afraid of them any longer. That would change in another second.

The first artillery shells exploded up and down Main Street, blowing in the house windows. Ignoring the ringing in her ears and glass covering her body, Florrie staggered over and helped the girls up from the floor. They were dazed, but appeared otherwise unhurt. The mother could barely hear herself yelling into their ears to run and hide in the basement. Her girls nodded their understanding and walked off, swaying as if they were drunk.

Picking herself up off the floor, Bonnie Sue shrieked. Florrie turned around to see Ricky still seated at the table, face down in his grits. The sisters shook the boy to wake him, without success.

A second round of explosions rocked the house, tossing the hutch with Bonnie Sue's china onto the floor with a crash.

"Sis, let's get Ricky down to the basement. I'll grab his arms, if you'll get his feet."

The women picked up the boy, crunched their way through the broken glass and dishes, then slowly made their way down into the stairs into the basement. As they laid him down on the dirt floor as gently as they could, the artillery crashed again and the lights went out.

Florrie stayed with Ricky while Bonnie Sue went to find candles and matches. She brushed the glass and grits off her nephew's face and gently called his name, but there was no response. Maybe the explosion knocked him unconscious?

As Bonnie Sue placed lit candles on the shelves above her son, the artillery mercifully stopped and Florrie could finally hear herself think again.

"Let's take his shirt off and see if he's hurt anywhere."

"Good idea."

Bonnie Sue sat Ricky up and Florrie undid the buttons and removed the shirt.

"Nothing on his chest or tummy," Florrie murmured. Then, she raised his left arm and saw the blood. There wasn't much. Just a little cut and a small trickle on the left side of the boy's chest. From the horrified look on Bonnie Sue's face, though, it might as well have been a river.

"Sis, let's lay him down again. I want to try something."

Once the boy was flat on the floor again, Florrie pressed her ear to her nephew's chest. No heartbeat. No breathing. She listened a few more moments straining to hear something, anything, but there was nothing but dead silence.

Florrie pushed herself back up on her knees, looked over at her sister through teary eyes and shook her head.

"No, no… You're just are not listening right," she insisted. "Let me do it."

Bonnie Sue stayed down there a long time, listening in the suddenly oppressive silence of the basement. Then, the mother hugged her boy tight and started to gently sob. "Don't leave me Ricky. Please, don't leave me. Don't leave MEEEE…"

Pulling on Florrie's sleeve, Donna softly asked, "Mommy, what's wrong with Ricky?"

Florrie looked back at her girls and replied in a husky voice: "Baby dolls, Ricky has passed away. God has taken him to heaven."

"Why mommy?" Donna asked. "Why would God do that?

"I dunno, darling. I just don't know."

Horse Savanna Swamp, South Carolina
10:45 Hours, 29 April 1942

After a morning of frustrating reverses, Patton finally found a gap in the Kraut lines. It was time for some open field running!

In a predawn attack to the east, First Armored Division threw everything against the German regiment which repeatedly stalled their advance the day before. This time, the tankers crashed through like a home run baseball through a house window. By first light, they were rolling across the last bridge before Charleston.

According to the reports, this was when everything went wrong. Instead of the fallen trees and anti-armor mines choking off Highway 17 yesterday, the Rantowles Creek bridge was defended by something far more deadly. Twenty-three tanks crossed before the last one exploded on the middle of the bridge, its turret hurled into the sky and its burning hulk blocking any escape. Two more tanks were lost before a company commander spotted the enemy preying on them.

A trio of eighty-eight millimeter heavy anti-aircraft guns were concealed in a grove of pines nearly a mile distant. The Kraut guns utterly outclassed the U.S. Army's top of the line tanks. The *Lee* seventy-five millimeter guns could not reach the bigger German guns from this range, while the incoming enemy rounds sliced through the heavy tank's armor as if it were cardboard. When the tankers charged the enemy guns to bring their own weapons into action, the forest around them erupted with German *panzer* fire. Seventeen minutes later, all radio contact was lost with the doomed battalion.

In the region of the Ashley River Road to the west, Second Armored Division's Combat Command B found themselves matched against an entire German *panzer* division. Choked off by the thickly forested terrain, neither side could maneuver or bring many of their tanks into battle against their opponents. Stalemate.

As best as Patton could tell, although his boys on the flanks could not land a knockout blow, they were doing a splendid job tying down Rommel's *panzers*. In a football game, when the blockers have the opposing defense in their grasp, the quarterback hands the ball off to the running back to barrel between the defenders for a touchdown. Second Armored's Combat Command B was the general's running back. As Patton's first tank command, CCB occupied a special place in his affections. Suffering only light casualties during the first day of operations, the regiment boasted a strength of nearly 100 tanks and was the perfect unit to make the final breakthrough to Charleston. George made sure he joined his old unit for their ride to glory.

The combat command led with its big *Lee* tanks, each with a handful of GIs piled on top to protect against Hun infantry, grinding single file among the dirt track traversing the Horse Savanna. Halfway through, the marshy forest gave way to a clearing about three hundred yards wide and a half mile long. In the middle of the field of scrub pine and grass was a handful of grey armored cars, clustered as if they were on bivouac, rather than expecting enemy contact.

We caught the Hun bastards with their pants down!

Patton ordered his driver to move off to the side of the clearing so he could observe the upcoming engagement through his binoculars. The lead company of *Lee* tanks deployed into a line, then paused for the GIs to jump off and fall behind the tall vehicles, before grinding forward again.

The general's one fear was the enemy scout vehicles might shag ass out of the clearing and down the dirt road on the far side. The narrow path cutting through the marshy wood was only wide enough for a one tank at a time. Disable that tank and this puny recon platoon could hold up his mighty CCB for hours until German reinforcements arrived.

Patton watched impatiently as the battle developed. As the *Lees* closed, the Hun armored cars started belching diesel smoke, but made no attempt to withdraw. Instead, when his tanks halted to fire, the Hun sons of bitches actually charged forward!

Arrogant bastards. This would be the kind of fight Patton loved – unfair and completely one-sided in favor of his boys.

The Huns threw the first punches to no effect. The small automatic twenty millimeter guns on the enemy SdKfz 222s were no match for the *Lee's* heavy armor. Dozens of German cannon rounds found their targets, with clangs and showers of sparks, only to careen off harmlessly.

The return fire of the *Lee* seventy-five millimeter main guns was far more effective, punching big holes in the thin armor of Kraut scout cars. After the first volley, two Hun vehicles burned in the field and another flipped over on its side.

The surviving armored car turned around and sprinted for the shelter of the woods. Initially, the *Lee* gunners could not get the range on the fast-moving vehicle, their armor piercing shells kicking up dirt behind the fleeing target. Finally, a lucky round tagged the armored car in the ass. The vehicle's engine started belching dark smoke, but kept pushing the vehicle forward into the dark wood and out of sight.

Damn! The thing would probably break down in there and plug up the road.

The lead *Lee* plunged into the wood after the wounded enemy vehicle. After several minutes passed and several dozen CCB tanks and trucks filled the clearing, the lead tank reversed back into sight, dragging the smoking Hun armored car out of the wood with a steel tow cable.

Hot dog! We're back in business, Patton exulted. Charleston was within his grasp.

Charleston, South Carolina
11:13 Hours, 29 April 1942

Walking slowly and deliberately into his headquarters after getting patched up at the field hospital, Erwin Rommel felt as bad as the situation map on the wall appeared.

The medical personnel washed the reddish crust off of his face, stitched up the gash on his temple, then wrapped the field marshal's head with bandages until he looked like a Persian mullah. Even though he was presentable, Erwin's head throbbed like a gifted drum pounded by a child on Christmas morning. The rest of his middle-aged body reminded him of the trauma it suffered with every step.

Rommel immediately asked his chief of staff for a status briefing. General Crüwell placed pen to map to point out the two enemy *panzer* divisions intelligence identified slicing into their southern flank. To the east, the Gross Deutschland Regiment and a couple batteries of eighty-eight millimeter anti-aircraft guns halted the first *Amerikaner* division at Rantowles Creek. To the west, the German Seventh *Panzer* Division was in a standoff with a single enemy regiment by the Ashley River. The balance of the second *Amerikaner* division went missing somewhere in the Warren.

"Do we know who is commanding the enemy *panzers?*"

"A general by the name of George Patton."

The name was familiar. Ah, yes, this was the man the enemy papers were calling the *Amerikaner* Rommel. Instead of feeling flattered, Erwin's head started throbbing harder.

"Crüwell, were any of my original orders carried out?"

"Yes, sir. This morning, I released the *Luftwaffe* bomber reserve."

Good. Victory was still theirs, if they could find and stop the missing *Amis*.

Rommel started flipping through the communications which flowed into the headquarters over the past several hours and stopped to reread one.

"Where is this reconnaissance company located?" the field marshal asked, handing the message to his chief of staff.

After studying the message and the map, Crüwell pointed at a large swamp drawn on the map, falling between Seventh *Panzer* and Gross Deutschland. The company of a few dozen men was too small to merit a unit marker on the situation map and the map itself showed no roads or paths through the marsh. Yet, the message said the reconnaissance unit was delaying a large number of *Amerikaner panzers* and urgently requested reinforcement.

Wait. Rommel knew this place. These were the recon boys who rescued him last night...guarding a dirt road straight through the center of the Warren. If the *panzers* belonged to the missing enemy regiment, they were only a couple dozen kilometers from Charleston!

"This Patton knows his business," Rommel muttered under his breath.

"Look here, Crüwell. I believe our missing *Amis* found a way across this marsh and will shortly emerge just south of the Ashley River. With Seventh *Panzer* tied down to the west, this Patton will almost certainly move east to hit Gross Deutschland in the flank. It is what I would do."

There was only one option left.

"General, order the last SS reserve from the airport to Gross Deutschland's right flank." The field marshal gave his chief of staff a hard look. "Tell the SS commander he must hold to the last man. Absolutely no retreat is authorized."

As Crüwell turned to issue the necessary orders, Rommel strode towards the exit to join the SS reserve. Erwin only made it halfway to the door, when his head swam and his legs failed him. Collapsing to his knees, he vomited up the breakfast he wolfed down an hour ago.

Arms reached down and helped him to a nearby couch. The rest of the staff watched from their stations with worried looks. All but one. The normally stoic Crüwell looked furious as he jogged over to the couch and ordered the others back to their stations, before kneeling next to his commander and friend.

"Erwin, you are wounded and no good to us if you finish the job and kill yourself. I am sending you back to the hospital to recover."

Rommel grabbed his chief of staff by the tunic and the words he struggled to form came out in a hiss. "You will do...

You will do no such thing! This battle will be decided over the next two hours and I am not giving up command."

Crüwell scowled and considered for a moment. "Very well. Then you need to sit down by the situation map before you fall down. Let your field commanders do their work."

The field marshal nodded at the compromise and allowed his chief of staff to help him over to the table.

Bula phosphate mines, South Carolina
15:13 Hours, 29 April 1942

Patton stood on top of his armored car parked on top of hillock searching for an opening in the German lines, but even with the assistance of his six foot two frame and a pair of powerful binoculars, he could find none. Glancing over his shoulder at the sun falling towards the horizon, the general frowned. Only a few hours of daylight left to reach Charleston.

Once through the Horse Savannah, CCB hooked a right up the Ashley River Road a couple hours ago for an easy jog into the port city, when his boys ran into a nasty surprise. The SS fanatics the local National Guard ran into just after the invasion were back, this time with *panzers*. That son of a bitch Rommel wasn't out of reserves just yet.

With the Ashley River to the north anchoring the SS road defense, the CCB commander sent half his force south through the Bula phosphate mines to flank the enemy position. Things went from bad to worse.

The mines were a maze of ditches and dirt piles, with no clear line of sight. Seemingly, around every corner waited a low-slung armored assault gun, supported by several infantry. While the German short seventy-five millimeter guns lacked armor piercing rounds, enemy high explosive rounds fired at point blank range took a considerable toll on Patton's men and machines. The SS troopers themselves fought to the death.

Still, CCB's sheer size relentlessly ground down the Huns. One more sustained push should clear the way to Charleston in the next hour or two. Patton hopped down off the car to study his maps yet again. There had to be a way around these people to save those precious hours.

A breathless captain the corps commander didn't recognize ran up and saluted.

"What do you want?" the general asked while returning the salute by touching his helmet with a swagger stick.

"Sir, I have a message from HQ."

"Give it to the major over there. I'm busy," George sapped, before turning back to his maps.

The captain paused for a moment, then persisted. "I'm sorry, General, but my orders are to ensure you receive this message personally."

Patton was about to rip into the junior officer, but thought better of it. His staff knew better than to bother him at the front unless it was important. "Very well. Deliver your message and make it quick."

The captain delivered his bad news fast and dirty. Rommel unleashed the entire *Luftwaffe* against the rear areas of Patton's corps and cut them off from the rest of Third Army. This morning, while Patton and CCB were moving through the Horse Savanna, *Stuka* dive bombers took out all four bridges across the Edisto River, then dropped the new bridges the engineers erected in the afternoon. When they were not destroying river crossings, the *Luftwaffe* was strafing the truck convoys supplying the armored divisions.

Christ. That's why CCB had not received resupply.

"Why the hell didn't headquarters get this message to me earlier?" Patton growled.

"We tried, sir. The swamp is playing hell with the radio signals and I couldn't get through to you personally until now. You're not an easy man to find, General."

Patton immediately swallowed his anger and disappointment to deal with the new situation. While his temper could sometimes get the better of him, George was above all a realist. The general's mind was already shifting gears from the thwarted advance on Charleston to coming up with a plan to save his command.

"Captain, get your vehicle fueled, then report back here in a half hour to receive my orders for the corps staff."

Summerville, South Carolina
21:13 Hours, 29 April 1942

It was now or never. Florrie Fraser was no longer willing to risk the lives of her girls, when her cousin Ben was waiting a down the road apiece to whisk them away.

The problem was Bonnie Sue refused to come along. Yesterday, when Florrie discussed Ben's offer, baby sister would have none of it, pointedly reminding her how the SS ended her last attempt.

But this morning tore out any renewed doubts about escape Bonnie Sue planted the evening before. The dawn artillery killed poor Ricky at the breakfast table and blew out sections of her sister's elegant antebellum house, leaving the place a drafty wreck. Next time, an unluckier round would finish off the house and everyone in it.

This latest taste of hell did nothing to move Bonnie Sue, though. Instead, just hours after they wrapped Ricky in a quilt and laid him to rest under the dirt floor of the basement, baby sister's mind took a scary turn for the worse.

This afternoon, Florrie put the girls to bed in the cellar for naps to rest up for the night's journey. After this morning, the mother could not hope to sleep. Every time an explosion went off, she flinched and ducked. Donna and Lisa seemed to shrug most of it off as background noise and were asleep after a few minutes of going down. Thank God for small favors.

When she softly walked up the cellar steps after the girls went down, Florrie overheard Bonnie Sue having a one-sided conversation with Ricky as if he were in the kitchen with her. An hour later, baby sister was cleaning Ricky's bedroom and making his bed. Giving her big sister a knowing look and a wink, she mock complained: "I am always cleaning up after that boy. A mom's work is never done."

Florrie couldn't stand the thought of leaving Bonnie Sue behind in such a delicate condition. As the women cut up the last of the shriveled carrots into a pot filled with water and a soup bone for what passed for supper, she raised the subject of escape one last time.

"Sis, after this morning, we can't hang around here any longer. It's too dangerous."

"I know. We should go."

Heartened by the unexpected response, Florrie pressed on. "I can help you pack your things and we can leave in a couple hours to meet Ben."

Bonnie Sue looked over at her sister with surprise and shook her head no. "I can't leave without Henry and Ricky. When they come back home, we can all leave together."

Oh God. She really does think they're still alive.

Florrie tried a different approach. "OK, what if you come with me and the girls tonight and we leave a note for the boys telling them to meet us at Goose Creek?"

"Oh, I couldn't do that. The house is a mess and I have to clean it up before they get home. Henry is always cross when he comes home to a cluttered house."

This was hopeless. "Sis, can you at least promise me you'll go to the basement and hide if the artillery starts up or they start shooting again?"

"Of course! Do you think I'm dense?"

While the soup was simmering, Florrie made her own preparations to leave, packing light bedrolls made up of a handful of food and other necessities wrapped and tied off in blankets for sleeping. She was careful not to overload Donna and Lisa, but they had to be prepared to live outside during the long cross-country trip.

Afterward, Florrie found Bonnie Sue in her bedroom and gave her an armful of clothes. "Can you take care of these for me?"

"I guess you've made up your mind to go then?"

"Yeah. I'm sorry, sis, but I've got to get the girls outta here. But I don't want to leave you behind."

"Don't you fret none. Ricky and I will be fine here."

An hour after sundown, Florrie and the girls were dressed for the trip and saying their goodbyes in the back room. Her eyes tearing-up, she hugged Bonnie Sue tightly, then quickly scooted her girls to the back door.

"Now remember what I told you earlier. We're playing hide and seek from the Germans again, so you need to be really, really quiet. When I tell you to go, we are going to run like bunnies to the woods right over there."

"Mommy, you don't have to tell me twice," complained Lisa.

Florrie smiled at her know-it-all daughter and put her hands on their backs.

"OK…ready…set…go!"

The girls were off like shots. Even though she had longer legs, mommy fell further and further behind. The lack of food and sleep over the past couple days weighed down her legs and lightened her head.

Breathing heavily, Florrie stopped about halfway across the field and turned to make sure no Germans were following. A single shot cracked out of the darkness.

CHAPTER 23

Summerville, South Carolina
02:37 Hours, 30 April 1942

The anticipation was almost unbearable. Jim Fraser raised his fist to halt the patrol and crept up to where the point man was kneeling. From there, they both crawled to the edge of the woods. Across a field was a row of houses along Main Street. Florrie and the girls should be in one of them.

This incredible opportunity presented itself at the regimental briefing just a few hours before. While Fraser's battalion spent the day resting in reserve, the rest of the regiment spent the time unsuccessfully banging their heads against the German fortifications surrounding Summerville. In one last attempt to find a weakness in the enemy line, the regimental commander, Colonel Tom Walker, began the briefing by proposing a night reconnaissance through the woods west of town.

Lieutenant Fraser immediately jumped to his feet before the old man could assign the mission to someone else. "Colonel, I'd like to volunteer Bravo Company for the recon. I know this area personally and my men are rested and ready."

"Lieutenant, you haven't even heard the mission plan yet."

"Sir, I know exactly how to move through this area undetected. Can I show you?"

Walker chuckled and handed his audacious junior officer the stick he was using as a pointer.

"Colonel, this map doesn't show it very well, but there's a creek which moves through the woods here and then into the middle of town. I propose to move my company down the creek bed and split up the platoons to recon Main Street and Ninth Avenue."

Turning from the map and handing the stick back to the old man, Fraser wrapped up his pitch. "Sir, so far, the German paras are fortifying the houses in the area to maximize their firepower, but have a bad habit of leaving wooded and swampy areas largely undefended. These woods may be our way into Summerville."

"Very well, lieutenant, you can have the mission. I want you to start by 23:00 hours and to return by no later than 03:00."

As Fraser anticipated, the woods were largely undefended. The lead squad flushed out a couple Krauts from an observation post and the lieutenant killed them with a burst of his tommy gun. A company commander had no business being this far up front on a patrol, but Jim could barely keep himself from sprinting through the woods to Bonnie Sue's house to rescue his family.

In the middle of the woods, Fraser split up his company as planned, sending first platoon east towards Ninth Avenue, taking third platoon north toward Main Street, and putting second between them to provide covering fire either way.

At the tree line, the lieutenant pulled out his binoculars and studied the rear of the homes along Main Street. Bonnie Sue's house should be second from the right. A passing cloud blocked the full moon and Jim couldn't make out much of anything in the shadows. However, when the cloud passed and the bright moonlight returned, he could see everything all too clearly.

In the field behind Bonnie Sue's house, Jim saw a white cloth flapping in the gentle early morning breeze. The lieutenant slowly adjusted the knob on top of his binoculars to bring the yard into better focus until he could make out...a woman's motionless leg and hip. The cloth was the skirt of a dress. A white dress with big red polka dots.

Jim knew that dress. It was his wife's favorite summer dress. The one she wore when they last went to Myrtle Beach to celebrate their anniversary.

"Florrie!" Jim shrieked as he dropped his rifle and binoculars and ran unthinkingly into the field. The Army officer's training, mission and all of his surroundings vanished. All that remained was a terrified husband desperately trying to reach his fallen wife.

The houses on the right along Ninth Avenue erupted with German small arms fire, but Jim was barely aware of the bullets cracking all around him. He had to get to her. Then, a red-hot pain lashed across Fraser's lower back and pushed him down into the dew-covered grass. An innate instinct for survival kicking in, he scrambled behind a big live oak and lay there for a few seconds, regaining his wits.

Jim sat up behind the tree, reached around and felt his back. The fingers didn't find any holes, but came back sticky with blood. A Kraut bullet must have winged him.

The husband ignored the pain and got on his knees. One more sprint would get him to his wife. Please, please, oh God, don't let her be... please.

As Jim leaned forward, screams from behind penetrated the panicked blackness of his mind. Glancing over his shoulder, the lieutenant found his point man, Bill DelDuca, in the middle of the field, rocking on his back, clutching and cursing his leg.

Oh no, what have I done? In Fraser's madness, DelDuca must have followed his commanding officer into the field. By some dumb luck, the lieutenant managed to make it to the tree in one piece. His point man wasn't so lucky.

Jim looked hard at Florrie one last time. Stop fricken lying to yourself. She's gone and there's no sign of the girls. Ah, honey, I'm sorry I didn't come sooner. I'm so damned sorry.

The lieutenant turned and ran back into the open field for the man he got wounded. "Hang on DelDuca, I am coming to get you!"

Summerville, South Carolina
02:40 Hours, 30 April 1942

Helmut Arpke opened the door to his Berlin flat and dropped his key onto the little table inside. "Honey, are you home?"

A delighted squeal pealed from the back bedroom, followed by his lovely wife carrying their child bundled up in a blanket. "Darling, come here and look," Louisa smiled.

Helmut walked up and kissed his wife, then reached down to pull away the blanket corner covering his child's face, when someone pulled back on his shoulder.

"Sir, wake up," Schuster repeated insistently, while shaking Arpke's shoulder.

The platoon leader fluttered his eyes and sat up as the world came back in focus.

"Lieutenant, you were really out. Must have been one hell of a dream you were having."

"None of your business, Erich," Helmut yawned. "What's happening?"

"We heard some machine pistol fire in the woods to the north. Sounded like an *Ami* tommy gun. Hans and Dieter up at the observation post are not answering their phone."

"And the men?"

"The platoon is up and at their positions."

"Good. Ensure everyone is keeping an eye out for the OP men. They could be coming in fast with the *Amis* on their tail."

Arpke scanned the unit sector of fire with his binoculars, but nothing was moving. His platoon was set up in two houses with connecting trenches, facing a grassy field just above Summerville's Main Street. The *Amis* apparently had a rule requiring every town to have a "main street," Helmut concluded, as he rubbed his bleary eyes.

The quiet was broken by a yell from the woods. Second squad fired up a parachute flare, illuminating two *Ami* soldiers sprinting from the wood line on the left towards a row of abandoned houses on the right along Main Street.

"What the hell are they doing?" Helmut muttered to himself.

Weapons all along the line erupted at the same time. The lead *Ami* slid behind a large oak about halfway to the houses along the road as if he were taking a base in the strange *Ami* game of baseball. The trailing man was not as lucky, catching two or three bullets before collapsing awkwardly into the grass. No sign of any other enemy troops. Strange.

The lead *Ami* sprinted back for his fallen comrade though the hail of bullets, slipped and fell, then returned to his feet and dragged the wounded man behind another tree. A few moments later, the *Ami* emerged again, staggering towards the woods with the other man thrown across one shoulder.

Arpke smiled in admiration. Anyone that brave or stupid should be allowed to live. "Cease Fire! Cease fire!" shouted the platoon leader. The order was echoed down the line.

Just as his men's weapons fell silent, though, *Ami* rifles and a machine gun opened up from the wood line to give their returning men covering fire. Suddenly, Helmut found himself on his back staring at the ceiling of the house. His chest hurt like hell as he struggled to take a breath.

Erich appeared over him and yelled for the medic. Helmut grabbed his friend's arm tightly as if he were a drowning man, desperately trying not to sink under the water one final time.

The medic ripped open his tunic and started yelling questions at his commanding officer. Helmut struggled to take a shallow breath and replied in a whisper.

"Louisa… mama…"

Charleston, South Carolina
07:23 Hours, 30 April 1942

Where the hell were the enemy *panzers*?

Although yesterday was a damned close thing, Rommel's plan finally fell together by the next morning. Before leaving on his ill-fated flight to scout the Warren for the *Amis*, the field marshal ordered his staff to unleash the *Luftwaffe* bomber reserve to destroy the bridges across the Edisto River, then start hunting *Amerikaner* supply trucks in the Warren. His own *panzers* would stay on the defense until the enemy ran out of supplies, then counterattack to crush the enemy against the Edisto River.

The enemy commander Patton almost split his defense in two and broke through to Charleston, but once again the *Amis* ended their operations during the late afternoon. Incredible. This enemy kept banker's hours!

Time to turn the tables. As the new morning dawned, Rommel ordered his *panzers* south. The reported advance was far too easy. Over the past hour, the forward units reported they reached one objective after another, but no contact with the enemy apart from of a regiment holding its position on Rosum Hill to the west. The rest simply vanished into the Warren once again.

Air reconnaissance was not much help today. The enemy massed all of their remaining fighter aircraft to achieve local superiority over the Warren. In many ways, the *Amis* were still amateurs, but they were learning fast. The enemy correctly identified the critical part of the battlefield and concentrated their air power there, just as any competent German commander would have done.

The Army commander stifled as yawn and gratefully took a cup of *Amerikaner* coffee from an aide. Erwin felt far better after a few hours sleep last night, but the monotony of sitting on his ass in the headquarters waiting for the next report was wearying. Rommel desperately wished to be at the front with his men, but the commander continued to mind his chief of staff's warning against leaving again until his head was right.

Looking up at the headquarters situation map, Rommel reminded himself things could be far worse than suffering from a little boredom. The remainder of the landing zone was holding fast. After grudgingly giving ground the day before, the paratroop and mountain divisions were holding the new defensive line to the west.

The northern forest and coastal road remained quiet. The *Kriegsmarine* shore bombardment must have rendered the enemy division above Charleston combat ineffective. Long past time the Navy carried its weight.

General Crüwell walked over with another handful of messages and what for him passed for a look of concern.

"What is wrong? Are the enemy *panzers* still missing?" Rommel inquired.

"No sir, we found them," the staff officer frowned. "These messages are from the surviving regiment of the 17th Infantry Division at the town of Givhans."

Givhans? The place was a small village to the southwest, well outside the enemy *panzer* corps avenue of advance.

The field marshal flipped through the radio messages, then crumpled them into a ball. This Patton foxed him again

Givhans, South Carolina
07:39 Hours, 30 April 1942

General Patton felt like the magician Houdini. One tired ass magician, but Houdini none the less.

George was proud of how his men set the stage for an historic vanishing act. During the night, the surrounded corps pulled out of the line, moved over 50 miles to the southwest, then set up for a dawn attack. The men even managed to tow out many of the disabled vehicles for repair and a return to action in the next drive on Charleston.

But could they execute the finale by breaking out to American lines? After fighting their hearts out for two days, then pulling this all-nighter to get the hell out of Dodge, Patton's boys were out on their feet. They were also nearly out of ammo because the damned Army Air Corps allowed the *Luftwaffe* to trash his supply lines. Less than a mile to the west, an unknown number of Germans were entrenched around the hamlet of Givhans between his men and resupply.

"Move out," the general instructed his radio operator.

Patton's armored car closely followed the lead battalion on an unnamed dirt track to Givhans. Within minutes, George heard the sounds of battle up ahead - a handful of machine gun fire bursts punctuated by the crash of a tank main gun. The column of following vehicles kept grinding forward, though, without a pause to deploy for combat.

The source of the commotion shortly passed on the left - the remains of a machine gun nest, reduced to handful of sandbags and dead Germans scattered by a high explosive round from a *Lee* tank. Must be an outpost. This one position couldn't be the enemy main defensive line.

Another quarter hour passed slowly and quietly before the sounds of battle roared back again. George scrunched down low as the armored car emerged into an open area and the general instructed his driver to stop along the tree line so he could study the field of battle. Instead of the entrenched Germans manning antitank and machine guns he was expecting, the meadow was filled with tents and piles of supplies under camouflage netting. Well, hot dog! The Hun commander left his ass unprotected and Patton's boys plowed straight into his headquarters.

One of the *Lee's* fired its seventy-five millimeter gun at crates of ammunition stacked at one end of the compound, starting the darndest fireworks display the general had ever seen. Hundreds of rounds of rifle and machine gun ammunition cooked off, firing in all directions, with tracers arcing here and there. Mortar rounds brewed up in a cascade of explosions, igniting nearby fuel barrels into plumes of orange flame reaching up into the beautiful Carolina blue sky.

Other tankers weren't wasting precious main gun rounds on the largely unarmed, rear-echelon types. Machine gun bursts here and there cut the running gray-clad soldiers down like a sling blade through weeds.

When the bullets ran out, the big metal elephants simply trampled their surroundings. One tank plowed into one end of the encampment's largest tent. When a staff officer emerged from the other end with his arms raised, a second tank swerved over towards the terrified man, crushing his legs under its tracks and leaving the rest shrieking in the mud.

The boys were taking every ounce of their fatigue and frustration out on the enemy. George knew he ought to stop this slaughter and take the survivors prisoner, but he was in no mood to give quarter to an enemy who had shown his nation damned little.

Welcome to America, you Hun sons of bitches.

Charleston, South Carolina
15:11 Hours, 30 April 1942

A morning of opportunity had given way to an afternoon of crisis.

Rommel's army was now stretched past the breaking point. After the *Amis* destroyed the last regiment of Seventeenth Infantry Division near the village of Givhans, the original defenders of his southern flank were all gone. In their place, Rommel was forced to send his entire *panzer* reserve just to hold the line. His single Seventh *Panzer* Division was now screening the two *Ami panzer* divisions reforming around Givhans.

The field marshal turned his attention from the tenuous situation map to a new intelligence report on the enemy *panzer* general, George Patton. The *Ami* proved to be a worthy adversary, aggressive like a German general, but rasher and more unpredictable. The man charged into the trap Rommel laid, then escaped again to land a hard counter-punch.

The man himself was a mess of contradictions. Patton ruthlessly enforced uniform regulations for his men, but designed his own uniforms and wore cowboy pistols. He believed himself reincarnated from a long line of high-born generals, but swore like a common soldier.

Rommel shook his head and closed the folder. He was fighting a madman, but would not underestimate this particular lunatic again. The field marshal's quandary was he had no obvious way of stopping Patton.

Rommel's first instinct was to pull his troops back to Charleston, allowing the infantry to man shortened lines and the *panzers* to go back into reserve to block any move Patton attempted. However, that would place his Charleston airfield on the front lines and the port within enemy artillery range.

The only other alternative was to hold the present line to the last tank. If Patton or any of the other *Amerikaner* generals broke through, though, there would be no reserve to stop the *Amis* from driving into Charleston.

Rommel started kneading his throbbing forehead, carefully avoiding the still tender row of stitches above his right brow. Erwin absently wondered what his wife, Lu, would think about the new scar.

Reopening his eyes to find his aide de camp holding three aspirin and a glass of water, the commander nodded and gratefully accepted the offered relief before turning back to the insoluble problem at hand.

His army's only real hope for survival was now at sea. The invasion's second and largest crossing was less than a week from landing and taking this intolerable pressure off of his troops. But would the second wave land its blow before the *Amis* could land theirs?

Berlin Germany
23:59 Hours, 30 April 1942

Louisa wiped away the rivulet of sweat running down her forehead and into her eyes, then studied her surroundings. Such a strange place. Instead of the familiar streets of Berlin, she found herself standing in front of an unusual oak, with thick and gnarled branches reaching out near the ground, draped with hanging green veils.

Helmut laid propped up against the base of the tree, dressed in a baggy field uniform she had only seen in newsreels. Her husband reached his hand out for his wife and mouthed words she could not make out in the shade cast by the giant tree.

Louisa leaned forward to run to her love, but instead her legs buckled and she fell to the ground in pain. Bent on her side and clutching her belly, the agonized wife could only stare at her silent husband. It was too soon. Too soon.

The brilliant blue sky darkened into a threatening gray, then an increasing shower of rain fell until Helmut disappeared entirely from view. She closed her eyes and flinched as the sky cracked and flashed.

When Louisa reopened her eyes, the rain splattered against and ran down the bedroom window of father's home. She lay in her childhood bed drenched in sweat and curled around a cramp surrounding her baby. When she reached down there, her fingers came back red.

"Papa!"

Doctor Grafenberg rushed into the room in just a few seconds. After false labor pains increasingly afflicted Louisa's pregnancy, he moved his precious daughter back home so he could keep close watch over her. When he wasn't visiting her room, reading her stories as if she were a little girl, her physician father was taking his meals or sleeping in the adjacent study.

"I'm bleeding, Papa."

The doctor yanked away the bed covers and grimaced. "I'm sorry, sugar plum, but I need to examine you."

Louisa turned her head away as he gently poked, prodded and listened with a stethoscope. After a few minutes, he replaced the covers over her.

"How is the baby? Am I going to lose him?"

"You suffered a near miscarriage, Louisa, but the child is alive."

"But, am I going to lose him?" the mother persisted, feeling tears running down her cheeks.

"I do not know, sugar plum," her Papa replied softly, taking her hand. "I just do not know. The next few days will tell."

CHAPTER 24

R.N. Littorio, 1753 miles east of New York City
04:19 Hours, 1 May 1942

After tossing in his cabin bunk for a couple hours in an unsuccessful search for sleep, Admiral Carlo Bergamini dressed and returned to the bridge. As he took a sip from a welcome cup of expresso, an ammunition ship exploded off the bow of *Littorio* - first in a flash of light, followed by a series of secondary explosions spinning into the sky like comets.

Was this the expected *Americano* counter attack?

The enemy fleet could hardly miss Bergamini's armada lumbering across the Atlantic. Where the first crossing was like a young porpoise, evading the *Americano* naval defenses by joining modern warships with the fastest new freighters to transport the invading *Germano* divisions, the second was a mother whale slowed down by her young.

After helping secure the waters off of Charleston, Bergamini's Special Naval Force escorted the emptied transports and damaged warships back to France, while the remainder of the *Kriegsmarine* fleet stayed on to support the landing force.

The final phase of the invasion plan called for the Force to land an entire *Germano* Army in the United States for a summer offensive. To accomplish this feat, the first wave of transports was joined by every freighter and tramp steamer the *Kriegsmarine* could commandeer. These new additions were generally slow and often barely seaworthy.

To make things worse, the resulting Whale was so large, the Force simply did not have the warships to adequately escort all the makeshift transports. Instead, Bergamini sent his destroyers out in a wide screen to the west to provide early warning if the remnants of the enemy Atlantic fleet sortied and kept his large ships in reserve to repel such an attack. This left very little behind to protect the Whale from *Americano* submarines below, like the one which torpedoed the ammunition ship.

The radios came alive with scattered freighters claiming submarine sightings. The reports reminded Carlo of the dogs of the small town of his birth. When one barked at something, they all joined in. The admiral refused to release his precious handful of remaining destroyers to investigate the reports until a freighter could provide positive identification.

Then, the enemy submarine disclosed its presence a second time. The next victim was an old freighter jammed with troops just a thousand meters starboard of *Littorio*. After suffering two torpedo hits, a terrible fire chased a handful of sailors onto the deck. The poor souls below had no chance at all.

Bergamini lowered his binoculars and softly gave an order to dispatch two destroyers to sink the enemy intruder. Too late. Much too late. Papa had failed his children again.

Carlo plopped onto the captain's chair and reached for his expresso cup, but his hand trembled uncontrollably as if palsied. He angrily clasped and squeezed the disobedient appendage until his arthritis howled. The admiral could not cannot allow his body to surrender to his personal failures. Several days and endless responsibilities remained before the Whale reached the *Americano* coast.

White House, Washington D.C.
15:35 Hours, 1 May 1942

It occurred to George Marshall that every time he accompanied Ernie King to the White House, they were always the bearers of bad news. Today was no exception.

From behind his desk, President Roosevelt hopefully inquired: "How is Operation Hammerfall progressing."

"Mr. President, there's a new development," King replied.

"Admiral King, since you are the one reporting," Roosevelt observed, "can I assume the new development is occurring at sea?"

"Yes sir," King nodded. "Mr. President, as you know, the Navy has a picket line of destroyers and submarines across the middle of the Atlantic Ocean keeping watch for enemy movements from Europe. Yesterday, one of our subs and then two destroyers observed a large force of Italian warships sailing east from the Azores Islands."

"What do you believe is its purpose?"

"Sir, the Italians are escorting a massive group of transports, larger than the first wave which landed at Charleston." Shaking his head in evident disbelief, the admiral concluded: "Hitler must have commandeered every damned merchantman in Europe to assemble this force. My people estimate it could lift another ten divisions."

Roosevelt seemed to age a decade during the pause before he spoke again. "What is the course of the Italian fleet?"

"Mr. President, on its current course, the enemy fleet could arrive off New York City in a week or maybe less."

"Christ almighty," the president croaked. "Can the Navy stop this new invasion?"

"No, sir," the admiral admitted. "The remaining combat effective ships of the Atlantic Fleet are deployed in an arc between Virginia and Maine, with a task force reserve off of New York. We can hurt them, but we just don't have the operational ships left to stop them."

Marshall took the baton from King. "Mr. President, most likely the Italian fleet is tacking back and forth to confuse us." Raising his voice to reinforce the point, the Army general urged: "I don't believe the Germans would risk dividing their ground forces by hundreds of miles. The second wave is reinforcing Charleston."

While the President processed this, Marshall plowed forward. "Sir, I am confident we can take Charleston before this new fleet can arrive. General Patton's tanks have destroyed one enemy division. If we make one more determined push, I believe Third Army can take Charleston in two or three days.'

"General, what if the enemy fleet does land near New York City? What does the Army have available to defend the area?"

"Two divisions…still in training."

"And do you expect them stop an invasion of, what was it, ten enemy divisions?"

"No, sir," Marshall conceded. "Our best divisions and nearly all of our supplies are committed to Hammerfall."

"Can you move any of the Hammerfall divisions from Charleston to New York by train?"

After calculating for a moment, the general responded, "Yes sir. Patton's armored corps is not currently engaged in combat. We could rail them to the north. We could also fly most of the Air Corps north as well."

"This may be a stupid question," the President asked hopefully, 'but could you take Charleston, then move north in time to stop a New York invasion?"

"I'm sorry, sir. We can do one or the other, but not both."

"Damn." Roosevelt cursed under his breath, closing his eyes and bowing his head. When the boss looked back up, he appeared defeated.

"George, you are probably correct that the enemy fleet will reinforce Charleston, but I cannot in good conscience take that gamble."

Marshall struggled to maintain his temper. Third Army was so damned close to throwing the Krauts into the ocean. He couldn't let the Boss screw this up.

"Sir, please consider the consequences of ending Hammerfall prematurely," the general pled. "When the Germans land their ten divisions at Charleston, they will only be the first of several waves of reinforcements. If this mob does not overwhelm the Army, it will take years and hundreds of thousands of dead to throw the Krauts out again. Mr. President, finishing Hammerfall is a gamble we must take!"

Roosevelt bristled. The Boss didn't like to be openly challenged.

"General Marshall, New York City is the nation's financial center and much of our industry is nearby..."

Not to mention your home, Marshall thought uncharitably.

"...If we lose New York to the Germans, we will definitely lose the war."

"But, sir..."

Slamming his open hand on the desk, Roosevelt barked. "The issue is settled. You will end Hammerfall immediately and send your tanks and planes north."

Marshall straightened as if slapped and quickly considered his options. None of them were good.

Resigning in protest wouldn't reverse the President's order and throwing a new chief of staff into the fire as a German second wave rampaged across the Carolinas certainly would hardly help the Army.

The general very briefly considered ignoring the Boss and finishing Hammerfall on his own authority, then letting the chips fall where they may. However, disobeying lawful orders was completely alien to his nature. For better or worse, Roosevelt was the commander-in-chief and his superior.

In the end, Marshall simply assumed the position of attention, saluted and offered a curt, "Yes sir."

As the general and the admiral turned for the Oval Office door, Roosevelt softly spoke again, "Gentlemen, please come back and take a seat on the sofa."

The Boss backed himself out from behind his desk and rolled his wheel chair up to the sofa. Marshall knew the polio-afflicted Roosevelt took pains to hide his disability from others.

Displaying it now to his top commanders could not have been easy.

"George, forgive me for snapping at you just now. It's not personal. I very much value your counsel and all of your hard work."

The President looked down at the carpet as if searching for just the right words. This an existential threat unlike anything our nation has faced before. Although it is frustrating and expensive in lives and treasure, I intend to play not to lose this war until we can face the enemy on more even terms. I just cannot… I will not risk the survival of this nation simply to win one battle."

Marshall sighed and nodded his understanding.

"Thank you, Gentlemen. Be assured your government will provide you with everything we can humanly deliver. Next month, I need your plans on how to defend this nation until we can go on the offensive again."

Givhans, South Carolina
09:02 Hours, 2 May 1942

General George Patton finalized his instructions to the corps staff for the upcoming offensive against Charleston. If stealth did not work, maybe brute force would prove to be the charm the next time around.

As he pulled back the flap of the headquarters tent to leave, Patton nearly collided with the Third Army commander walking in. Just the man he wanted to see.

"General Kruger, won't you please come in," Patton invited with a wave of his arm.

"No thanks, George. Would you walk with me instead?"

After a brief exchange of pleasantries, the corps commander pitched his new plan to Krueger. First and Second Armored Divisions would combine with Ninth Infantry to smash the

Hun *panzer* division, then drive along the Ashley River into Charleston. Of course, in order to make this work, Patton needed Krueger to transfer Ninth Infantry and most of the Air Corps over to his command.

"That won't be necessary, George?"

"Sir, I can't pull this off without the extra manpower."

"You don't understand. I'm shutting down Hammerfall."

George gaped at this commander with incredulity. "Are you shitting me, sir?"

Kruger's face tightened and his eyes went flinty. "General, I am not kidding you."

"Believe me, the bastards are at the end of their rope. If I hit them hard and fast, I can take the port by tomorrow night."

Krueger suddenly stopped and put his hands on his hips. "George, for God's sake, be quiet and listen!"

Patton straightened up and shut up.

"The order to cease operations comes directly from the President himself. Hitler put a second larger invasion fleet in the Atlantic on course for New York City. Your corps is the only reserve left on the entire Eastern seaboard to stop them."

Damned if he didn't step into it again. "General Kruger, I'm sorry. I didn't know."

"You are my best commander, George, but you keep opening your mouth when you should be engaging your ears."

"Yes, sir. What are my orders?"

"Get your corps back to Ridgeway ASAP and load your tanks on the trains we are staging there."

"Where am I going and what happens when I get there?"

"I honestly don't know, George," Kruger sighed. "You'll be under command of Second Army. They're still deciding where to unload your tanks."

"That's OK," Patton grinned, "I work best by the seat of my pants."

"That you do, George. That you do," the Army commander admitted with a wan smile.

"Damned shame about Charleston, though. We almost had the bastards."

"Yeah. We missed our chance. I'm afraid this war is about to get much worse."

George had no time to fret about the course of the war. His mind was already scrambling to recall the geography of the New York City area to figure out where he would invade if he were the Hun commander. This time, the Germans would not get a foothold. His tanks would hit the sons of bitches on the beaches and grind them into the sand.

Berlin Sportpalatz, Germany
20:12 Hours, 6 May 1942

Adolph Hitler triumphantly strode across the stage of the Berlin Sportpalatz to the podium, basking in the adoring refrain of thousands of roaring voices. "*SEIG HEIL! SEIG HEIL! SEIG HEIL!*"

Where the Grand Admiral sat with the rest of the high command, only feet behind the *Führer*, the air pulsated, painfully ringing Erich Raeder's ears. Hitler then raised his hands and silence returned, as the delirious crowd strained to hear the words of their leader. Amazing. The naval officer had never before witnessed such effortless mass control.

Raeder looked over to his Army counterpart to see if he shared the admiral's astonishment. General Jodl was oblivious to the spectacle around him, still seething over the *Führer's* proclamation at the afternoon meeting of the high command.

As the senior service, the Army began the staff briefings to the *Führer* punctually at 3 p.m. Jodl reported the *Amis* were in general retreat and the landing force was preparing for offensive operations. Raeder followed, confirming the second wave of transports arrived safely in Charleston the night before and the three Army corps they carried were disembarking on schedule.

"Then, is it your opinion the enemy armored forces are no match for our *panzers*?" Hitler asked the Army chief of staff.

"Yes, my *Führer*," Jodl answered, with what passed for a smile for the austere bureaucrat.

"I agree," Hitler nodded. "Therefore, I am ordering 50% of the steel currently dedicated to tank manufacture be shifted to the *Kriegsmarine* shipyards to complete the Plan Z expansion of the fleet."

"But, my *Führer*!" the Army general sputtered.

"Simple mathematics, my general. The fleet cannot transport our current *panzer* armies. Thus, expanding those armies at the expense of the fleet makes no sense."

Raeder struggled to conceal his delight. Hitler could be infuriatingly arrogant, but the secret sailor seemed determined to make the *Kriegsmarine* the preeminent navy in the world.

The admiral shifted his attention back to the *Führer* as Hitler began speaking to crowd with a quiet urgency. "Men and women of the new *Reich*, on March 16, the greatest battle in the history of the world began – the battle to free the German people of *Amerika*." Shaking his fist in the air, Hitler's voice rose with each sentence. "Here I say this: We have not been wrong in our plans. We have not been mistaken about the bravery of the German sailor and soldier. Nor have we been mistaken about the superiority of our ships and our *panzers*. Neither have we been mistaken about the dedication of the German homeland."

Turning back to his Grand Admiral with a knowing look, the *Führer* generously shared the glory. "In the greatest feat of naval arms in the history of any nation, the fleets of Germany, Italy and Japan joined together to smash the *Amerikaner* Navy and move our soldiers across the Atlantic Ocean."

The crowd clapped their approval and Raeder beamed back with pride. The *Kriegsmarine* was finally receiving its due.

"The soldiers of the *Reich* are now advancing to join the *volksdeutche* living across the United States. Germans of all nations will soon join to smash Roosevelt and his cabal of Wall Street Jews. Then, at last, all Germans will be united under one *Reich*!"

Without thinking, the admiral shrugged off his carefully cultivated reserve and was the first of the high command to raise his arm in the Nazi salute and join in the crowd's chants of adoration. Adolph Hitler had nothing left to prove. He was Erich Raeder's *Führer*.

Sōri Kōtei, Tokyo, Japan
12:19 Hours, 11 May 1942

Admiral Yamamoto assumed Prime Minister Tojo summoned him to the Sōri Kōtei for yet another status report on the recovery of the Imperial Japanese Navy from the costly battles around the Hawaiian Islands. The fleet commander was blindsided by what came next.

The working lunch Tojo served Yamamoto was simplicity itself. Thinly sliced stir-fired pork and bean sprouts was accompanied with *shio daifuku*, a heavy, glutinous patty of pounded rice containing salted bean paste.

After polite inquiries about his family, the Prime Minister asked for the expected status report on the remnants of the fleet. In between small bites of lunch, the admiral offered a succinct summary. In a series of one-sided engagements off of India, a Japanese task force eliminated what was left of the once formidable British Royal Navy. The Indian Ocean was now a Japanese lake. Yamamoto politely omitted the fact former General Tojo's Imperial Army was now as bogged down in India as it was in China.

Taking a sip from his small cup of green tea, the Admiral moved onto the future. After the heavy losses suffered during the two battles off Hawaii, only two of Japan's large carriers remained – *Zuikaku* and *Akagi* – the latter of which would not be repaired until later in the summer. Over the next month, the fleet's light carriers would double from two to four, as a pair of newly commissioned vessels finished their sea trials. Thankfully, many of the planes and invaluable pilots of the lost carriers escaped to a land base off Oahu and would soon return to sea on the surviving carriers.

"Excellent, excellent, Admiral-san, Tojo toasted with his tea cup. "What is your opinion of the German operations in the Atlantic?"

Yamamoto frowned deeply as a black mood returned. The Admiral was certain Hitler tricked Japan into sacrificing his beloved fleet in a battle of attrition with the *Ameko* to clear the way for his own Atlantic invasion, but he was not ready to admit as much to his rival across the table.

"After we destroyed the cream of the United States Navy, the Germans and Italians were able to cross the Atlantic against minimal resistance and landed several divisions on the *Ameko* east coast."

As the stewards cleared the plates, Tojo leaned back and lit a cigarette. "After the fleet's great sacrifices, do you believe Japan should share in this bounty or leave it all to the Europeans?"

"Excuse me. Prime Minister?"

"I propose we take the *Ameko* west coast for our own." Taking a small puff from his cigarette, Tojo gave his fleet commander a sly look. "Just as we attacked first at sea and bore the brunt of the *Ameko* naval strength, the Germans launched the first land attack and will draw the mass of the enemy land strength east to defend their capital."

"Do the *Ameko* have any carriers remaining in the Pacific, Admiral-san?" the Prime Minister inquired.

"No," Yamamoto admitted.

"The door is open then," Tojo smirked. "The *Ameko* Pacific coast lies undefended."

"Prime Minister, much of Japan's sea transport is currently committed to supplying our military and the civilians on Hawaii. These islands cannot provide for themselves."

Tojo's eyes narrowed and he stubbed out his cigarette. "Once reinforced and resupplied, our divisions in Hawaii can form the invasion force. As for the round eyes on the Hawaiian Islands," the Prime Minister dismissed, "let them go hungry. We are speaking of the future of the Japanese Empire."

Yamamoto was at a loss for words.

"Admiral-san, please begin planning for a second invasion.

Ridgeville, South Carolina
10:03 Hours, 13 May 1942

Jim Fraser stood at the position of attention in front of Bravo Company as the battalion commander pinned the twin silver captain's bars on the collar of his uniform and a bronze star medal above the pocket. While Major Matt Moore sang his company commander's praises to the cheers of his men, Jim stood there feeling like a complete fraud.

While Moore lauded Bravo for their recon of Summerville, paving the way for a successful attack the next day, Fraser knew he selfishly volunteered for that mission to fulfill his personal fantasy of rescuing his family.

When the major went on to retell the story of his new captain single-handedly saving PFC Anthony DelDuca under heavy enemy fire, Jim flinched. The only reason DelDuca caught a couple bullets was because the point man followed his idiot commanding officer out into that field.

Florrie was dead and Tony lost his leg, while he was being promoted and decorated. Life wasn't just unfair, it was plain nuts.

After the ceremony, Moore asked his new captain to walk back to the battalion HQ with him. They strolled in silence for a while as the major fired up a stogie and took a couple puffs.

"Jim, you don't appear to be none too happy with your promotion. In fact, you've been moping around for the past two weeks. What the hell is wrong with you?"

Fraser angrily turned to his commanding officer. "Sir, after the way I fricked up that last mission, I should be shot, not promoted. I never should have run into that field. I almost got one of my men killed."

Moore studied Fraser. "I spoke with DelDuca at the field hospital. He told me your orders to third platoon were to recon the houses along Main Street. Instead of endangering others, you personally performed that recon and told him to follow you. When he was hit, you pulled him to safety. In some colorful Brooklyn language, DelDuca opined that most officers were screw-ups, but he would follow you anywhere."

The major took another puff on his cigar and continued. "DelDuca will be going home with my letter of commendation and his own promotion. However, in the future, Captain, you will not take the point on a recon. Your job is to command Bravo and you can't do that job by getting your ass shot off."

Overwhelmed with guilt, Fraser almost blurted out the real reason he ran out onto that field, but instead clamped his mouth shut and stood silent. Crucifying himself would only make things worse. DelDuca was going home a hero, not some idiot stupid enough to follow a lunatic officer out into a kill zone. Jim couldn't take that away from him along with his leg.

"Listen Jim, you aren't the first officer to make mistakes in this war and you'll damned well not be the last. I've made bone-headed calls and my men paid the price."

Fraser audibly exhaled and shook his head. "How do you live with it, sir?"

"By doing the job," Moore shrugged. "We don't have the luxury of feeling sorry for ourselves. There is a war to fight and our families are relying on us to protect them."

Relying on us to protect them. I fricked that one up too.

The shorter major put his hand on his captain's shoulder and looked up at him. "Here's the bottom line. I need to know I can rely on you. Do you have your shit wired tight?"

Fraser paused to consider his response. Florrie was gone, but God willing, his girls were still alive out there somewhere. There really was no other choice but to keep on keeping on. Bravo was his family now.

The new captain straightened up and saluted. "Yes sir, you can count on me."

Moncks Corner, South Carolina
06:23 Hours, 15 May 1942

The dawn started filtering through the cypress trees behind them as Ben Stockton and Florrie Fraser gently paddled the canoe through the early morning mist covering the Cooper River. Her cousin bent forward and whispered that Monck's Corner and the American lines were around the next bend in the river. Their long escape was almost over.

Florrie knew she should be thrilled, but only felt a numb determination to save what was left of her family. The journey from Summerville was worse than any hell she ever imagined. While she was mostly able to block out the horrors of the night they left, more recent tribulations played over and over in her mind.

Even though cousin Ben carefully planned a route creeping along backwoods trails through swampy areas no sensible German would think of going, the war had different ideas. About halfway into the trip, the Army pushed the Germans right over them, plunging their little band smack into the middle of a battlefield.

In addition to his kin, Ben served as guide and provisioner for a young couple – Mike and Judy Preston. The Prestons were an impatient pair, constantly complaining about Ben's slow pace, carefully picking his way around Germans hiding in holes or waiting for enemy convoys to pass. For her part, Florrie vividly remembered falling into the clutches of the SS and murmured a little prayer of thanks every time her cousin avoided capture or worse.

Somewhere near Carnes Crossroads, the American lines to the west came into view. The Army boys looked so close you could almost touch 'em.

Ignoring Ben's constant warnings against moving in the open, the Prestons left the shelter of the trees and made a bee line for the American soldiers. Waddling across a newly plowed farm field, their progress was painfully slow, but by some miracle, no one took a shot at them.

Almost halfway across, an explosion tossed Mike into the air, flipping him in a grotesque cartwheel. In addition to corn, the farm field was seeded with a far more deadly crop of landmines. Florrie thought she saw the man's leg go in one direction and his body another, but she couldn't be sure and didn't really want to know.

Judy shrieked out her husband's name and bounded over. Cradling his bloodied head on her lap, the wife's screams turned into a continuous keen of uncomprehending loss. The crackle of rifle rounds erupted from both lines of soldiers to complete this symphony of the damned.

A weight left Florrie's side as her daughter sprinted out into the field.

"Lisa! Get back here now!"

The girl half turned and raised her hands in exasperation, "But we have to help them, Mommy."

A bullet cracked nearby. Too near. Lisa dropped holding her side, rocking on the ground.

"Mommee… it hurts!"

Florrie scrambled out without thinking, grabbed both of her little girl's feet and pulled her roughly back behind the tree. Ignoring the child's bawling, she pulled Lisa's hands away and ripped open her shirt.

The mother couldn't immediately credit what she saw. Instead of a bloody gunshot wound, her daughter's only injury was an angry red splotch along a rib about the size of a finger. Maybe a ricocheted bullet? The thing would bruise real good, but otherwise her girl should be fine.

Dear sweet Jesus, thank you!

Florrie cupped both of Lisa's little tear-streaked cheeks in her palms and shrieked, "Don't ever do that again! I can't lose you too. Not you too." As she hugged her child tightly, Judy Preston's distant cries went silent amidst the gunfire.

Florrie pushed away the awful memory and concentrated on rounding the last bend of the river. The past couple days were uneventful. Like a spring thunder storm giving way to the sun, the war seemed to stop. The Army pulled back west and the Germans followed, leaving the family in peace to finish their journey.

A weathered cypress house came into view through the mist. Florrie turned back and Ben nodded. This was where they get off.

The buzz saw noise of a German machine gun ripped through the early morning quiet. Ben and Florrie instinctively leaned away from the awful racket, tipping the canoe over. Donna and Lisa were asleep when they were unceremoniously tossed into the brown water. The girls came up sputtering, splashing and squealing.

Showered with the wooden splinters German bullets punched out of the flipped canoe, Florrie splashed over to grab both girls by their coats and started kicking furiously for the opposite river bank. By the grace of God and the river mist, the three managed to reach the cover of a little inlet, then lay low and out of sight in the shallow water.

After several seconds without an obvious target, the German machine gun across the river went silent. Putting a finger to her lips to shush her children, the mother turned and crawled out of the mud and into the woods with her kids following on each side.

Florrie looked back to the river and clenched. Ben floated by on the slow current, nearly submerged. One eye stared sightlessly into the sky. The rest of his face was gone.

She sat down grasping her knees and squeezing her eyes shut against the tears. Not again. Despite her best efforts to push them away, memories of that awful last night in Summerville came rushing back.

Florrie and the girls were dressed for the road and kissing their goodbyes to Bonnie Sue. What the artillery left of the back room of the house was softly lit by the stars peeking through a jagged hole torn through the roof.

"Sis, won't you please change your mind and come with us," Florrie pled.

"Stop that now,' Bonnie Sue chided. "You know I have to wait for Henry to come home. I'm sure he will be back by morning."

"Anyway, how do I look?" Her sister asked, twirling back and forth in a white and red polka dotted dress. "I hope you don't mind me wearing your dress for my boys."

Florrie struggled to keep her composure and offered what she hoped was a smile and a nod. Bonnie Sue always liked to wear her older sister's clothes.

"You look beautiful, baby sister. This one was Jimmy's favorite.

"I'll make sure to take good care of it for when you two come back for a visit."

Florrie quickly turned away to hide the tears flowing down her cheeks and scooted her girls out the back door. Donna and Lisa shot across the field to the far woods like a pair of bunnies. Momma rabbit was considerably slower.

Florrie glanced back to make sure no Germans were following and dropped her jaw. Bonnie Sue was strolling out into the field and waving them goodbye as if this were the end of any old family visit before the war. She stopped and turned, frantically waving her baby sister back to the house. Sis nodded and turned, strolling back to the house.

Oh, for Christ's sake… go, go, GO!

Before Bonnie Sue could reach the back door, a single rifle shot snapped out from the darkness. Baby sister paused as if she were looking for the source of a strange noise, before falling to her knees and then onto her face. She lay there still. Dead still.

Florrie almost shattered on the spot. All she wanted to do was to curl up on the grass, shut her eyes and escape this horrid new world that stole away everyone she loved. After a long minute, she drew all of her remaining strength to rejoin her girls in the woods.

Now with Ben gone too, Florrie felt that last bit of strength seep away. She was rooted to the ground, unable to move.

"Mommy, Ben is dead. Isn't he?" Lisa whispered.

Mommy could only nod.

"We're all going to die," Donna dully added.

Her daughter's words hit the mother like a punch in the tummy. Embarrassed and angered at her own inadequacy, mommy got up on her knees and grabbed the arms of her precious daughters.

"Listen to me," Florrie yelled. "You're not going to die. I won't let you." Glancing back through the trees to the river, she lowered her voice to a hiss. "Girls, we're gonna to get out of this mess and find your daddy. I don't care if we have to walk a thousand miles. We will find your daddy."

"Do you believe me?" mommy demanded.

Lisa and Donna were plainly scared, but nodded back with the implicit trust young children so readily give their parents. A trust no parent could hope to justify.

After wiping their tears away, the mother took her daughters by the hand and plunged into the forest.

Lord, please help me, Florrie prayed. I haven't got the vaguest idea what to do, but I can't let my girls down.

ABOUT THE AUTHOR

Bart Stark is a U.S. Army paratrooper and a combat veteran, who later entered a life of crime as a prosecutor and defense attorney. After leading a vagabond life which took them across America and Europe, Bart and his wife Brenda settled in the mountains of Panama.

When not hunched over his iPad writing, he hikes his dogs in the forest and daydreams dystopian futures for his characters.

Wolves at the Gate is Bart's first novel. The idea for *Wolves* came to him during the Persian Gulf War, when he surveyed the burning hellscape of war-ravaged Kuwait and wondered: What if this happened back home?

Warpath Press is dedicated to publishing the very best in military writing from around the globe.

We believe that writing that is rooted in the human experience of war and conflict, even when written by non-veterans, allows us as a society to examine how human nature responds under extreme pressure. It also gives us a means to ask the big questions about life.

"Military stories" aren't all action-adventure novels. We are committed to finding ways to push the boundaries of "military writing" in new directions, bending it into new shapes that serve society in better ways.

Many of the literary greats of the early to mid-20th century wrote about war and its effects. But Hemingway, Remarque, Dos Passos, Faulkner, Wouk, Greene and Waugh, only had the impact that they did because they were published.

Today, they would likely have been ignored by the major publishers.

And that is why we do what we do.

Made in United States
Cleveland, OH
21 April 2025